# *Humanity 2.0*

### *By Perry Doner*

*For Andy from Uncle Per*

*Names and persons in this book are entirely fictional. They bear no resemblance to anyone living or dead.*

*A big 'thank you' goes out to Suzanne Wilberg-Mills, Lynda Olson, and Miles Olsen for their assistance and sage advice.*

*"Humanity 2.0 was, quite simply, the most significant discovery in the history of mankind."*

*United Nations Report on Humanity 2.0 - April 2040*

# ***Chapter 1***

*"Concern for man & his fate must always form the chief objective of all technological endeavours.....in order that the creations of our minds shall be a blessing and not a curse to mankind".*

**Albert Einstein**

Song focused on her reflection in the window, melancholy for childhood. What she saw was a person she didn't know; a more mature woman now, weathered by tragedy. Gone was her childlike innocence. She was alone since the passing of her parents. An only child, Song now had no family at all. The world seemed so much more intimidating and she was unsure if she was up for the challenge.

Readjusting her focus, she looked out the window at the giant snowflakes laying a blanket of silence over the estate. Song reflected on the coming New Year. This one would truly be new. She needed it to be new. Goodbye childhood, hello adulthood.

Four years past, Song had come to Vancouver to attend a private school. When Song had first asked her mother about learning overseas, the deal had been made for Song to live with, and get to know, her maternal grandmother, a Canadian by birth. It was to be her final few years of school and her mother had been adamant that Song experience a life very different from her childhood existence in China. And what better place to blossom than Vancouver.

It proved to be a wonderful time for Song, allowing a freedom never experienced back home in Wuhan. Despite her age,'Granny McLellan' was a bright-eyed, affable person who guided her granddaughter through the customs and experiences offered in her new Canadian home. For Granny M, it was a late life opportunity to meet a granddaughter she barely knew, to be a mentor, a confidante. They formed a quick and deep bond, speaking to each other more like friends than a typical grandmother/granddaughter relationship. Things had changed a bit since Granny M went to school herself, but many of the teenage themes Song brought home from school hadn't.

At dinnertime, Granny M would always prod Song, asking, "So, my darling granddaughter, what did you learn today?" Song would wrack her brain, at first unable to come up with much. But within the first week, she raced home to the supper table bubbling over with some new tidbit she'd learned that day at her private school. Granny looked forward to learning about places like Egypt, or some new science discovery, but mostly she loved the energy of a child in her life again. Granny M spoke no Mandarin, so Song was happy her mother had only allowed English spoken at their home in Wuhan.

Surrounded by so many things to see and do in her adopted land, Song embraced it all. Granny M took her to the museums, art galleries and opera, educating her in Canada's cultural heritage. But for Song, it was the exploring alone that she liked best. The forests, trails and lakes were all so close. Stanley Park, Grouse Mountain, Kits Beach – she was in heaven. Back in China, Song's father was a military strongman from an elite family, so her childhood had been one of rules and restrictions. Seldom was she permitted to wander from the family compound, but now in Vancouver, she had the freedom of anonymity.

Her private school was at first unfamiliar to Song, who was grateful again for her mother's English only rule in the home. But, as teenagers do, Song quickly adapted to her new surroundings. Being quiet and withdrawn, she had difficulty making friends in her new land. So, each night, Song bubbled over, regaling Granny M., her green eyes sparkling with discovery. Granny recognized those green eyes, inherited from Song's mother, Melody, who'd inherited them from Granny M herself. But, Song's green was a bit brighter, almost as if she had lights shining from them. It was a distinctly exotic look; a girl with the face of a porcelain Chinese doll, but with sparkling, green eyes.

But alas, just when Granny M and Song had established a close bond, tragedy struck. Song awoke one morning to a kitchen lacking it's customary aroma of coffee and bacon. She gently knocked on Granny M's bedroom door without response, so slowly edged the door open, peering inside. Her grandmother was unresponsive, dead in her bed from a massive heart attack. Song tried to take solace in knowing there was no suffering, but there was no solace to be had. Song felt so alone again, and wept for her new friend and grandfather. She called 911, but knew it was too late. Before long, the funeral home collected the body, leaving Granny M's home eerily quiet. Heartbroken and unsure of what else to do, she called her Mom in China.

Melody Zhao (nee McLellan), caught the next flight from Wuhan and arrived the next day, in time to arrange her mother's funeral and file the associated paperwork. She was wracking herself with guilt for being gone so long from Granny M's life. Melody had taken her mother for granted, and now wished she hadn't spent so many years in China, away from her mother. So, Melody clung to Song, and she to her, and together they wept quietly for their last Canadian relative.

Despite the tragedy, Song was glad to see her mother again. In just a few short months, she'd lost her first and only real friend in Canada. Who would she tell what she'd learned that day? Her mind was in turmoil. After the service, Song leafed through Granny M's old photo album, shocked to see both her grandmother and mother as small children. Song felt it odd to see Granny M with flaming red hair, just like Melody's. And it was plain where Melody got her beauty from. Granny M had been gorgeous! There were photos of her wedding, allowing Song to study both Granny M's husband, Song's grandfather, and both sets of great-grandparents. Song had always looked at herself as Chinese, being from such a storied and historic Chinese family. But, here were photos of these white people that had contributed directly to her DNA. Song pored ever detail. These people were all born more than 10,000 kilometres from where she had been. Maybe she was exotic after all.

When Melody later asked what she thought about her time living with her grandmother, and Song answered simply, "Laughter". The house was now bereft of that.

Fortunately for Song, her mother dealt with the funeral home, the obituary, and the legal paperwork. But the time came all too soon for Melody to return to China, leaving Song alone again in a strange land. She'd tried to persuade Song to return home as well, but Song was adamant about experiencing more in Canada, with the new freedom she craved. So, since Granny had been renting her home, arrangements were made for Song to board in the dorms at her private girls' school. A student had recently dropped out, so Song took her place, rooming with a girl named Jacqueline Beausoleil, who became a godsend to Song's teenage life.

'Jackie' was one of those girls who seemed to have it all. She was seriously intelligent and tragically beautiful; the kind of girl boys would make fools of themselves over. But Song soon learned that Jackie had no ego, and seemed oblivious to the effect she had on men. After all, she was still in high school, a girls' school at that, so guys were still a bit foreign to her. Those she did meet were often tongue-tied or intimidated during conversations, where Jackie's intellect left them in the dust.

The two roomies became close. Jackie proved to have sympathetic ears and empathetic eyes, encouraging Song to offload her emotional baggage with an understanding few possess. In return, Song listened to Jackie's misgivings about growing up an orphan in the foster care system. For the next two years, they were each other's yin and yang, finishing each other's sentences and laughing at each other's jokes. Both were accomplished musicians who regularly filled the common room with the grace of their classical masterpieces. After graduation, the two young women moved into a new house Song's family built in Vancouver. Her parents planned to join their daughter when her father retired from the military,

After the death of Granny M., Song had retreated to her childhood habit of staying within the grounds. Her sense of adventure had paled, in favour of security. A year passed before it became Jackie's mission to get Song out for New Year's Eve.

The snow outside was now falling heavily, with flakes more than an inch across. In the window, she saw Jackie's reflection joining her own. "Song, aren't you ready yet? Hurry up! Bryce is impatient. He's already in the car, out front. New Years Eve at the club awaits! C'mon! C'mon!"

"Okay, I'm ready. I'm coming. Tell Bryce to chill." She braced herself for a night well outside her comfort zone as she followed Jackie, both tiptoeing through the snow in high heels. They were dressed to the nines and looked fabulous, if they did say so themselves. Song's dress was all-white, with one inch strips interwoven in diamond patterns, and Jackie had on a classic, black cocktail dress. Yin and Yang.

"Hey, Bryce," Song said in greeting as she wedged herself into the sports car's back seat. She wasn't the biggest fan of Jackie's boyfriend, but respected her friend enough to keep her thoughts to herself.

"It's about time, ladies! Chop, Chop! Whoa, you don't exactly look like you're dressed for the weather. We are in Canada, you know."

Jackie smiled at her beau, saying "You want us to look hot, don't you? Well, looking hot trumps mukluks when you want to party. And we oh, so want to party! Right Song? Yeah!" Jackie turned and high-fived her.

"Of course I want you to look hot. You're going out with me, aren't you? I don't want to be seen with a couple of skags."

Song rolled her eyes wondering again what a beauty like Jackie saw in a pompous fool like Bryce. But then, she knew the answer to that. Jackie was pretty, but hadn't had access to boys at the private girls school any more than Song had. Boys were a mystery to them both. Bryce had attended the private boys school down the road from their girls' school, and all it took was one joint Christmas Ball. Jackie was instantly worshipped by all of the nervous boys in attendance, but Bryce was just the most brash and got to her first.

"Your car isn't exactly built for Winter, either," Song chided.

"Appearances are everything." That pretty much summed up Bryce.

Song was not a party girl, but asked him to turn up the music as they headed for the Gastown club. She was glad Jackie talked her into going out. She was excited for the first time in a long time.

Bryce's car slipped and slid its way over the Lions Gate Bridge, with visibility near zero. Soon, the sports car pulled up to a flashing neon sign, and Bryce tossed the keys to the excited valet.

"Nice and close, ladies, so you don't have to trudge through the snow in heels." Indeed, the snow had built up several inches already. They held on to each other in lieu of traction. The door swung open to a huge room of pulsing electronic music and flashing, black strobe lights. The place was already rocking.

"I'll go get us drinks," yelled Bryce. Perhaps he was useful after all.

Song shone her green eyes around the club, sporting a wide, Cheshire smile. She had never been inside a Canadian nightclub and liked what she saw. Jackie was bouncing around excitedly beside her, capturing the eye of many. When Bryce returned, he barely had time to set the drinks down before Jackie pulled him onto the dance floor.

He knew many eyes followed Jackie, and his ego showed it. He did more preening and strutting than dancing. Bryce was the son of some Big Pharma king, and his attitude was one of entitlement. Song felt he always had his nose in the air.

So, while her friends danced, Song gazed around the club excitedly, taking everything in. She had never been to a place like this and her eyes positively sparkled! And the boys! She had never seen so many good looking boys! She may not have had much experience with them, but was willing to learn! This was to be a new year, with new experiences and a new life, starting tonight. Her hormones were active and on high alert, and she busied herself with people watching. Across the room, she noticed a boy looking directly at her. She quickly looked down at her drink, and blushed before looking up again, but he was still watching.

With the black lights of the club throbbing, her white, woven dress shone like there was a spotlight on her. That boy stuck out as well in his white t-shirt, tall with his above the crowd. He looked vaguely familiar, but she couldn't place him, even though he was so tall and very good looking. She'd normally remember a boy like that.

Drinking her cocktail nervously, she realized the glass was already just ice so headed to the bar for a refresher. Drinking is something she had very little experience with, but everyone else always seemed to have fun with it, so why not her? *"This is going to be a new year, with a new me"*, she told herself. At the bar, she had no idea what cocktail she drank, so she ordered a Mohito after the girl in front of her got one.

*'Mmmmm,we could become friends,'* she whispered to her drink.

When she returned, Jackie and Bryce were already at the table. "Whoa, you're on your second drink already? Where's shy Song gone?" Jackie teased.

"Shy Song isn't here. I'm her evil twin, party Song!"

"Well, alright then. Let's get this party started!" Jackie flagged down a waitress and ordered some shooters with funny names. They were the first of many.

"This is so fun!" Song raved to her friends. "We should do this every night!"

"Something tells me Song is going to have a quick lesson in hang-overs tomorrow," Bryce said. "Here. Try these. They're little fun pills I got from my Dad's stash." In his hand were a few tablets he offered the girls. Song was reluctant until Jackie snatched one up and downed it with her drink. "To party Song!"

"Bring it on!" Song cried, and downed her own. "Jackie! More drinks!"

While the waitress set down their shooters, Song noticed that the boy across the room was still watching her, even though his friend was animatedly talking to him. Cute and tall, how did she not recognize this boy? She did notice that he had no date, though. Just a wing man laughing alongside.

Another cocktail and one more shooter soon had her beginning to feel woozy. After prodding, Bryce asked her to dance, but she knew it was only because Jackie made him. After a single turn around the floor, they headed back to the table, which now had a three guys hovering around Jacks. Her long, blonde hair was curled into thick waves, highlighting her bright, blue eyes, and they didn't go unnoticed. Bryce quickly put his arm around his date, and kissed her, clearly demonstrating his claim. One person who didn't notice the attention was Jackie herself. She was still unaware of the hold she had on men.

This was the most fun she had ever had, Song decided. And while the shooters and Mohitos were so great, they were clearly having their effect. Dragging Jackie to the ladies room, they laughed and giggled at nothing at all. And, by the time they returned, the extra guys were gone and there was just Bryce, checking out the girls at the next table. "If only I was here alone." he said, quiet enough for Jackie not to hear. Song did. She gave him a disgusted look but neither he, nor his date, noticed.

But Song was having way too much fun for Bryce to ruin it. Heading to the bar , she ordered 3 more mohitos and 3 tequila shooters. As she wobbled away from the bar, she again saw that tall boy looking her way, so this time flashed him a big, drunken smile, spilling a drink onto her dress. She didn't even notice.

As time approached midnight, the crowd began to count down the clock. Bryce and Jackie held each other, ready for the big New Years kiss, but Song was alone.

She sheepishly glanced across the bar but that good-looking, tall, bad-boy must have gone to the bathroom. Or left. Muttering to herself, she grabbed her beverage for a toast, at least. She dropped her head, but as soon as the countdown began, her admirer was right in front of her! *'Oh God'*, she thought, mesmerized. *'He's so tall and good-looking'......*

Her eyes climbed his body as the crowd cheered "Three, two...." and suddenly the boy moved in closer. "One, Happy New Year!" He didn't speak, but lifted way up her to his level as the clock struck midnight, before kissing her deeply and thoroughly. Initial confusion gave way to her returning the kiss in kind, and what a kiss it was. For about ten seconds, watching in quiet disbelief was Jackie. When the kiss finally broke, Song looked into the eyes of her suitor, then at Jackie with bashful excitement.

"Whoa. There's party Song," Jackie cried.

For the rest of the night, he stayed by her side, attempting small talk over the cacophonous din. She learned that his name was Mage, but it was fruitless trying to have a real conversation, so they just smiled at each other like fools. It wasn't long before the alcohol had its full effect on Song. She slurred noticeably and began to lurch. Mage suggested they get some fresh air and Song nodded.

They stepped outside, bracing against the blizzard. Mage was able to have a better look, and was truly enchanted. She looked a bit Asian like him but there was something unique. It was her eyes. They were a luminous green, which was completely at odds with her Asian features. *'A man could get lost in those eyes',* he thought to himself.

When struck by the snowy wind, Song's eyes immediately became glazed and unfocused, before she promptly threw up on Mage and passed out in a snowbank. "Well, isn't that great?" he muttered aloud. "Now what do I do with you?" Both were now covered in vomit, and he couldn't go back into the club like this. Besides, he couldn't leave her out in the snowbank alone, while he went to her friend. She hadn't even brought her coat out with her, so he removed his own and wrapped it around Song. The flurries in the streets left them barren of taxis and buses, so he lifted her again, way up and over his shoulder, fireman style. He trudged off through the snowbanks, into the dark night.

The new year had begun.

# *Chapter 2*

*"Love is one grand sweet song, so start the music".*

### *Ronald Reagan*

Back at his apartment, Mage carried Song up the stairwell before brushing off the snow and gently lowered her into his bed. Shivering and blue, he removed his jacket from her shoulders but didn't think it right to remove the vomit-crusted garment while she was passed out, so he left it on and tucked in her blankets, throwing an old quilt over top. She was clearly out for the night. He rubbed his arms feverishly, coaxing warmth back into his skin. What had that girl been thinking, wearing shoes like that in a Canadian winter? He looked down at her, with her beautifully woven dress not looking so beautiful anymore. Vomit had frozen her hair in place, yet he thought she was the most beautiful creature he'd ever seen.

As he lay on the floor in his sleeping bag, Mage thought about Song – a lot. He remembered the moment he first saw her in the Intensive Care Unit of the hospital after his parents had been in their car accident. His mother had died at the scene, but his father put up a long struggle. Mage returned every day to visit, but his father's chances had been slim.

During those dark days at the hospital, Song had made quite an impression on him. Like sunbeams bursting through the clouds, the room became brighter when she walked in. Mage knew that the I.C.U. was not the time or place to approach her, but he'd been unable to get her delicate, sad face off of his mind. Her delicate face and the way she moved had Mage suddenly, and irreversibly, smitten with a girl he'd never met. So finally, one night as he'd laid in bed, Mage decided that the next day, he would approach her to share lunch in the hospital cafeteria.

Every day had been a struggle to visit his father when the prognosis was so dire, but on this day, he had a skip in his step and couldn't wait to talk to 'that girl', whoever she was. But alas, 'that girl' was not there that day, nor the next, and never returned. His opportunity had been lost.

Yet now, here she was, months later, sleeping on the same bed he'd dreamed about her in! His own bed! Granted, she didn't know she was in his bed, but *he* did.

Despite the uncomfortable floor on that fateful New Year's Eve, Mage had a smile on his face as he drifted off to sleep. *'The new year may be just what I need,'* he mused. *'Last year, not so much.'*

Morning arrived and Mage noticed that large snowflakes continued to float gently past the apartment's windows. He also became keenly aware of the effects of the hardwood on his back and his drinks from the night before. He forced himself upright, feeling his vertebrae creaking and cracking the whole way up, and at six and a half feet tall, it was a long way up. He yawned and stretched high enough to touch his ceiling, but his aches were soon mitigated by seeing the vomit encrusted porcelain doll sleeping peacefully in his bed. *'Wow! Just Wow!,'* he thought. Now, that certainly brought a spring to his step! After a quick trip to the little boys room, Mage began the job of uncluttering his bachelor apartment. Fortunately, Song had been passed out and had not seen what a slob he could be. Once satisfied that the disarray was now down to an acceptable level, he took out some bacon and began broiling it in the oven. Next was his trademark corn pancakes, and a fresh pot of java.

The bacon was sizzling nicely when he heard Song stir and groan. In a hungover daze, she could smell Granny M's bacon and coffee, but as her dreams drifted away, she came to the sad realization as to why people hate hangovers. *'I'll never drink again,"* she vowed to herself, as so many had before her. The cobwebs slowly began to clear, and she looked around the spartan apartment, knowing she definitely had never been there before. A strange man appeared, hovering over her, and when her eyes could finally focus on his face, she could see it was the boy from the club the night before. She sat up quickly, but her initial panic subsided when she realized she was still fully clothed. Her honour was intact......., sort of. But, sitting up quickly had definitely been a bad idea, so she laid back down. Her brain fog morphed slowly into mortification as she realized she was such a train wreck in front of that cute boy. *'Screwed that up,'* she muttered to herself. This was just not like her, and she was unnerved by her unfamiliar surroundings.

But the boy had a big, gentle smile for her which oddly relaxed her. Mage reintroduced himself, in case she didn't remember the night before, and Song told him her name, though he already seemed to know. Thinking back, she remembered him watching her from across the club and then the New Year's Eve kiss. What a kiss! She definitely was glad she remembered that part. But, she was too dim to recall anything that followed. Was it the alcohol that hit me so hard, or was it Bryce's mystery fun pills? Undoubtedly, both.

Looking down, she could see the vomit still on her dress and her mouth tasted like the Chinese Army had walked across her tongue in their sock feet. Song was mortified. Part of her hair was still stuck to the dress, and she felt as though the Skytrain was rumbling through her head. "Hi," was all she managed to get out, with a croak.

The look on her face was priceless to Mage, and he really, really wanted to always remember this moment. As for Song, she really, really wanted to forget this moment. Chuckling, Mage winked at her, handing her a towel, t-shirt and a pair of shorts.

"There's a shower just outside my door, so you can clean yourself up and rejoin the human race. Breakfast will be ready when you get back."

With her bladder about to burst, Song uttered a muted 'thanks.' She looked around but saw no bathroom. 'Why is the shower outside of his apartment?' she wondered. Undeterred, she closed his door to see two large, separate bathrooms for men and women in an otherwise empty hall. *'That's a bit strange.'*

She entered the one marked Ladies' find a large area with benches, lockers, stalls and showers. Wobbling over to the sink, Song looked in the mirror and was appalled at the cretin staring back. She couldn't recall a time that she had *ever* looked this bad. *'What must that Mage guy think?'* In her reflection, the beautifully woven, white dress which she'd been so proud of was now encrusted with smeared vomit. *'So classy'.* She shook her head ruefully and began removing her clothes with muscles that refused to function.

How had she ended up here? For that matter, where is here? And where was her purse? And her phone? Too many questions for her addled mind, so she stepped into the hot, indoor, heated waterfall and began her personal revival. *'Best invention ever'*, she thought as the warm waves cascaded over her. A few minutes later, she revised her rating to *'Second best invention ever,'* as she flushed the toilet. *'Plumbers just don't get their due,'* she decided.

After a good, hard scrub, Song began to slowly feel human again. These large washrooms had unlimited hot water and she took full advantage. Drying herself off, she made her way back to the sink to see if things looked better. Not much, she decided. Her hair was scattered, but when she went to brush it, she remembered she had no purse.

The dress she had worn the night before was definitely unusable, so she donned the shorts and superhero t-shirt Mage had given her. Not her best look, but at least she would be covered and clean. With one last look in the mirror, she headed back to Mage's, only to run into an old man in the big hall. He smiled and nodded a knowing grin before sliding into the men's. *'What's he thinking about this wild-woman with the witch hair?'* It felt like the Walk of Shame, but in fact her honour had remained intact. She turned the handle of the apartment and made her way inside, slightly chagrined.

"There she is," Mage boomed. "Ooh, nice hair! Hey, that t-shirt looks better on you than it ever did me."

When Song said nothing in return, he asked, "And so, fair maiden, how are you feeling this fine day?"

"Ssshhh..... Bad. Very bad. Do you know where my purse is?"

"You left it back in the club."

"Great. I hope Jackie's got it. And my phone." Mage handed Song a mug of coffee, which she held with two shaky hands. He could have sworn he heard her purr. She looked up, way up, and asked, "Okay, so how did I get here? Spill."

"I carried you."

"You carried me?" That was not the answer she expected. Looking outside, she could garner no hints as to her location. Snow covered windows blocked most of the view, but she could see that a blizzard was still

21

raging. She sneaked a glimpse at the boy tending his pancakes, seeing he was indeed 'hot'. Song even felt her pulse race a bit, but this was obviously not how she wanted to introduce herself.

"How far did you carry me? Where am I?" she continued.

"In my apartment."

"That part I guessed. And where is your apartment?"

"No more questions until you eat some breakfast."

"Ugh. I'm not hungry."

"Well, you better get hungry. I am Mage and I will be your server this morning." He put down a plate with the pancakes, bacon and a couple of pieces of toast to go with her coffee. "Eat what you can."

Song's stomach lurched at the thought of food, but was also keenly aware that she hadn't eaten since lunch yesterday. Thanking Mage, she took a few nibbles before settling in. Her tummy was rebelling slightly but she did manage to get some of it down."

"That's the first time I have ever had corn in my pancakes".

"House Special. Like it?"

"Yeah, actually. But that's about as much as my

stomach can take for now." She pushed aside a glass of orange juice and reached for her mug once more. "Mmmm, coffeeeeee."

Mage cleared the plates, while Song continued studying him. He clearly wasn't any threat, and seemed very nice. And handsome in a rough sort of way.

"So........., questions.........?" Song suggested.

"What do you want to know?"

"What happened, for starters? Why am I here? Where is my purse? Where is my phone? Where's Jackie?"

"Well, we stepped outside of the club when you needed some fresh air, but you began puking. On my boots, actually. And pants. And some on my shirt when I carried you." Song shrank back into her skin. "You got it all over your dress and were truly a mess, but then you passed out cold into a snowbank. I couldn't wake you, and I couldn't leave you in the snowbank. Nor could I take you back in the club, or even get you a taxi, since I wouldn't be able to tell the driver where you lived. Even going back to talk to Jackie would have left you passed out in the snow bank. So, I threw you over my shoulder and came here. I guess your purse is with her."

"And where is here, exactly?"

" We're above my grandfather's shop on Main Street, near Hastings."

"Was the old guy going into the bathroom your grandfather? He gave me the 'walk of shame' look."

"Yeah, that would be him alright," Mage said with a chuckle. "Don't worry. No shame involved."

"Then what's with the big, separate bathrooms? And the empty hall outside your door?"

"This apartment is above my grandfather's shop. My father used to have a Taekwondo school on this floor, but it's ends were turned into 2 apartments. My Grandfather lives in my parents' old apartment in the rear, and I took his old bachelor's pad here at the front."

"Which is why your bed is in your living room?" He nodded. "So, what happened to your parents?"

"They were killed last year in a car accident."

"Oh my God, I'm sorry."

"No need for you to be sorry. You didn't kill them. And, if it wasn't for the accident, I never would have met you. Fate is funny that way sometimes."

Confusion was plain on her face, and she raised one eyebrow in query.

"Well, you were at the same I.C.U. as my parents", Mage explained." I saw you there a few times before you stopped coming."

"I guess I stopped coming when my Mother

died."

"My Dad died there, too." Mage responded. "Now it's just me and Gramps." She blessed him with a sad, compassionate smile. Grief is the price we pay for love.

Changing the subject, Song decided, "I should call Jackie. "She's probably worried."

"You're not likely to get through, The power grid and cell phone towers are out all over town. It's been snowing like this since dinnertime yesterday, and the city is shut down. About three feet of fresh snow has fallen so far. No buses, no Skytrain, and no cars, actually. The mayor told everyone to stay inside while crews try to plow the roads. But there aren't many snowplows since it usually rains instead. When it gets cold like this, the heavy rain turn into this."

"Well, isn't that great! Now what am I supposed to do?"

"I guess you are stuck here with my scintillating company."

"Well, I guess that wouldn't be so bad," Song said with a slightly flirtatious look. At least she hoped it looked flirtatious. Judging by what he saw this morning, it's amazing he hadn't already run screaming into the streets.

Mage poured them each another cup. "Next question?"

"Do you mind if I hang out? Sounds like I'm going to be here awhile." This time she graced him with the full 100-watt smile and found it truly endearing when he actually got befuddled for a second. *'So cute.'*

"Yeah, you can hang out here for as long as you want to. Definitely."

"Okay. Then we have time to kill. How about you tell me a story. Tell me your story, starting with your grandfather."

"Wow. Okay." Mage looked up and ran both hands back through his hair. "Well, he was a teenager when North Korea closed the border to the south, way back in the '50's. After his parents died, all he had was a rubber dinghy and one oar. He set out one night, paddling south on the Yellow Sea, but got caught in a squall, and was forced to hunker down. He didn't know how long he'd been out there, but when he woke up, it was daytime and the dinghy had washed up on a beach on the South Korean side.

"Sometimes I wonder what my life would be like if he'd stayed in North Korea. Anyways, he offered his services on a Canadian merchant vessel in exchange for the passage to Vancouver. He was good with electronics, so he opened a TV & Radio repair shop, which is below us as we speak. He married and had one child, my Dad, but my grandmother died in childbirth and Gramps never remarried. He managed to raise my father alone while still running his shop.

"My dad, Woo Moon, married a French-Canadian

girl named Junette Bergeron. After they wed, Mom became June Moon. She used to say that every full moon in June belonged to her. Anyway, Dad helped my Grandfather in the shop and ran a Taekwondo school here on this floor. When he died last year, Grandfather was still trying to run the shop by himself but it wasn't going very well. Up until that time, I'd run a bit wild, getting involved with some people I shouldn't have. But, once my folks died, it was time for me to start taking care of Gramps instead of the other way around. So, now I work in the shop with him, helping make it profitable again. TV and radio repair isn't exactly big business nowadays, but I've added a new computer parts and repair department that's helping a lot."

Song smiled and asked, "So did you teach Taekwondo, like your father?"

"Only when he couldn't make it, I'd fill in."

"So, are you any good?"

"I guess."

"Yeah? Like how good? Do you have a belt?"

"Yeah, but Taekwondo has a couple of levels above my black belt, to be a teacher or a master."

"Okay. Any other talents?" Song nodded at several trophies lining the windowsill.

"A bit of motocross."

"Uh huh. I can see that."

"And I like to mess around with electronics and computers. Like grandfather, like father, like son, I suppose. Electronics is in our DNA."

Song stood up to get more coffee, but Mage jumped up, scooting past her. "Let me, let me." Standing there with nothing to do, she instead wrapped her arms around him from the back and thought to herself, *'I think I like this guy.'* He turned and hugged her back. It was briefly awkward, but not unbearably so.

"Thanks for rescuing me," she whispered.

The snow was still falling, and Song looked out the apartment windows, feeling nostalgic for home. She hadn't seen snow since she left China four years ago. Suddenly, she jumped up excitedly, her green eyes blazing. "Can we go play in the snow?" she cried. "Look, the wind has stopped."

"There are still huge flakes, though."

"That's when it's best! Can we?"

"In your high heels?"

"Oh, yeah. I guess this t-shirt and shorts wouldn't keep me very warm either. Awww. But I want to go play in the snow! It never snows in Vancouver! And look how deep it is!" Her fake pout face actually looked quite genuine.

"I'll tell you what. Let's go ask Gramps. Maybe he

stored some of my Mom's clothes. She was about your size."

"Yeah! Okay! Let's go check!" Her enthusiasm was infectious as she hopped about like a wee bunny.

"You might want to brush your hair before seeing Gramps again."

A horrified look came on Song's face as she exclaimed, "Oh my God. My hair has been like this since before breakfast? Why didn't you tell me?" she asked, punching him in the shoulder.

"Here," Mage responded. "Put on this touque. See? Problem solved. You're welcome."

"My hero," she joked, batting her eyelashes and clasping her hands beside her neck.

It turned out that Gramps did indeed have some old snow gear from Mage's mother's things, and soon, out into the elements they ventured. The snowflakes were as big as cotton balls, easily melted on the tongue. Song threw the first snowball, and from that point it was 'game on'. The snow was the perfect temperature for compacting and Song got off several rounds before Mage lifted her up so she couldn't reload. Instead, she tucked her snowballs down the back of his neck, leaping free when he recoiled. They both fell over and rolled over into the deeper snow, laughing like loons.

A truce was called, and a moment passed between them. This time, it didn't feel awkward at all. And unlike

New Year's, it was Song who closed in for the unexpected kiss. Mage was only too happy to oblige. She pushed him down onto the snow, climbed on top of him, and kissed him hard. She used the diversion to quickly grab more ammo, and stuffed it down his neck before breaking free again. The snow proved to be too deep to run in and Mage took her down easily with a quick Taekwondo take-down.

They called another truce, and this one held. Both tried to make snow angels, but it was getting crazy deep. The wind picked up again, whipping the falling snow into a horizontal blizzard, and right into their eyes. The snow in their suits had melted, and the wind was blustery and cold, so they headed back to the apartment for some well-earned hot chocolate. Removing the snow gear, they rubbed each other down to warm up. Hmmmm, that felt good. A little rub here. A little rub...oooh...there?

Mage's bachelor apartment was a different world for a rich girl, but she was loving it's cozy feel. Song put on a kettle while Mage got the hot chocolate, and they soon settled onto the couch, watching an old movie and making fun of the characters and plot. To Song, it felt like at Granny M's. A warm home full of warmth and laughter. Soon they had difficulty concentrating the movie, hugging and kissing and snuggling in.

Song stayed the night again, but this time Mage did not sleep on the floor.

# *Chapter 3*

*"If music be the food of love, play on. Give me excess of it, that surfeiting. The appetite may sicken, and so die".*

### *William Shakespeare*

When the lovers awoke for another round, the snow outside had finally stopped. Mage jumped out of bed, happy and energized. "C'mon, lazy lady. It's almost noon."

"Nooooo............" Song whined. "It's soooo warm and cozy in here." Eyebrows raised, she pulled back the covers displaying her naked body, teasing, "are you sure I can't entice you, good sir?"

"Well.........," Mage responded, "I can't do anything until I pee." Mage scooted out the apartment door and was gone. By the time he got back, Song was up and dressed, if you can call Mage's old t-shirt and shorts dressed. She had her serious face on, though.

"I should try to make it home today. People will be worried."

Deflated, Mage groaned. "Well, we can try, but transit is still shut down. You might just have to stay here forever."

"Lovely thought, but I do really have to get home

before Tang has a conniption fit. And........... wait a minute. When you say '*We* can try', does that mean you're coming home with me? Do it. Please. Come with me."

"Darlin', there may be a day when I can survive being apart from you, but today is not that day," He looked so cute, and a bit anxious. "Stay," he pleaded, wrapping his long arms around her in a cocoon.

She was a foot and a half shorter than Mage, and his hug could have wrapped around her twice. Tiny, wee Song moulded into him, her soft eyes shining with wonder. Wow, she really liked this guy. She'd missed being loved, even though it was parental love before. But, this was soooo much more. Song was a young woman falling in love for the first time. What could be better?

"Sorry, but I have to go," Song answered, eventually breaking Mage's embrace. "But I do want you to come with me. Yeah? How about we have some breakfast, shower together, and then I'll call for a car." And so it was. She felt so completely at ease with this hunk who, for reasons she couldn't understand, didn't scare off easily. Their shower proved to be urgent and erotic, with Song's feet seldom touching the ground. He pinned her to the stall's wall until they were both finally sated and satisfied. In the after-aura, they lazily shampooed and scrubbed every inch of each other.

Back in the apartment, she borrowed Mage's smartphone and managed to get a dial tone this time. Song spoke quietly with Jackie, occasionally glancing at

Mage and blushing.

Mage had been doubtful about her getting an Uber, but even through the snowdrifts, Song was confident that a car would come. They hugged in the cold while they waited, until Song finally announced, "Here it is." Mage's jaw dropped open. The "Uber" turned out to be a stretch Hummer, with a very angry Chinese man at the wheel. He leapt out, raging at Song in Mandarin, berating her conduct, and pointed at the pauper's clothes she was wearing. Initially, Song looked chastened, but soon her own fire kicked in, and she spoke just as sharply in return. Mage didn't know what either had said, but the driver quickly silenced himself, though with great difficulty. But, while it was clear he wasn't done yet, it was equally clear that Song was. The last word was hers. In silence, the irate man climbed into the driver's seat, steaming.

Mage followed her into the back seat of the Hummer limo, if you could call it a back seat. It was more like a room than a back seat. "This is awesome!" There was a pop-up, big screen TV and a full bar, and Song briefly switched on the light show's dry ice machine for him. It was like they were back in the club. Mage opened his window to clear the fog before his gaze fell on the rear-view mirror, where the irate driver's eyes were boring into him in. His glare at Mage was not without intimidation. The guy was just plain scary!

Song noticed, so she raised the privacy window. 'What's with that guy?" Mage asked. "I don't think he likes me. And I don't like the way he talked to you, even if I couldn't understand either of you."

33

"That's Tang. I'll explain later. Long story. But for now, kisses please." Mage was only too happy to oblige.

The Hummer cruised effortlessly through the snow and over the Lion's Gate Bridge before turning into a very elite section of West Vancouver. The homes looked palatial to a poor boy like Mage, but he was speechless when the driver pulled up at an entry gate and punched in a code. Inside that, there was a second gate that couldn't be opened until the first had firmly closed. Another pass code, and as they passed through, the estate opened up before them. The driveway wound through the grounds, which were very impressive, but the 'house' was unbelievable. Mage gawked up at an enormous pagoda style mansion at least 6 stories tall. Each floor was several times the size of Gramps's entire shop, and opulence wouldn't even begin to describe what he was seeing. Song peeked over at him and grinned. Mage was lost in Never-Never Land, with his head on a swivel, unsure what he'd see next. The Hummer drove down a slope, and entered one of the lower floors. The interior garage was larger than an arena, and was littered with collector cars, foreign sports cars, quads, a truck, and was now joined by the stretch limousine.

As they disembarked, the driver grabbed Song by her arm, dragging her away. He was yelling in Mandarin, but again, Song gave as good as she got, leaving Mage unsure as to whether to intervene or flee. She seemed to be holding her own, so he decided against either. Standing there alone, he felt awkward, and scared to touch anything for fear he could never pay it back.

34

Hearing a door open, he turned to see Jackie heading his way. Even though he'd already met her, he really didn't know her yet. Conversation at the club hadn't really been possible. But, damn, this girl was a supermodel! She'd sure looked good the other night, all dolled up for the nightclub, but somehow she was even more impressive in a plain blouse, jeans and no make-up.

"Hey there, Mage! Have you brought our lost duckling home?"

"If this is home, I guess I have. It looks more like a museum. Whose place is this, Jackie?"

"Why, it's Song's. Didn't she tell you?"

"No, I think there's a lot of things she hasn't told me," he replied, looking around.

"Well, she's kinda rich! Like, small country rich."

Mage didn't know what to say. He had no idea. Song? She hadn't seemed rich when she had vomit in her hair, or wearing his shorts and superhero t-shirt. And she was painfully shy, not at all indicative of a child of wealth and privilege.

"How is all of this Song's? She's like, twenty years old, isn't she?"

"Nineteen. She's an only child. She inherited it all when her mother died last year."

35

*'Ah, at I.C.U. time,'* Mage guessed. She hadn't looked like a rich girl back then, either. Just a shy, broken porcelain doll that he'd desperately wanted to put back together.

Jackie continued, "Song asked me to move in with her after we finished private school. We were dorm mates, did she tell you?"

"It's all new to me." And he was right. He'd given his entire family history to her, but she was still a mystery. A large and growing mystery.

"I'm surprised she was able to talk to you at all, she's so shy."

But to Mage, she hadn't seemed shy, just embarrassed. In fact, conversation between them had seemed effortless.

"After her mother got sick," Jackie continued, "I was able to help out with her care. Song didn't want strangers doing it, but it was very hard on her doing it alone. It's such a shame you won't get to meet her mother. She was a real firecracker, even as sick as she was. But truthfully, Song has been lost ever since her death. New Year's Eve was to be her rebirth. And, seeing as you are here, it looks like she's right on track!"

"My parents were in the same hospital as her mom. That's where I saw Song for the first time."

"So, you knew her before the club?" Jackie wondered.

"I knew her to see her. She didn't know me. It took me weeks to work up the courage to approach her in the I.C.U. waiting room, though it's not best best place to pick up chicks."

"Ha! I suppose not. You know, I think I remember you from the hospital when I visited Song's mom one time. You looked a bit familiar in the club, but I couldn't place you. Do you remember me?"

"No, sorry, just from the club."

For some reason, that pleased Jackie. In the past couple of years, when she and Song had been together, boys remembered her, but not Song. But, this boy was the opposite, and Jackie was happy for her friend. Song was amazing, and it was time more people knew it. Jackie turned and, sweeping her arm in invitation, asked, "So, good sir, would you like the 10-cent tour?"

"I doubt that there's anything worth 10-cents here, but yeah, absolutely."

"Okay, This level is mainly the garage, but if you go through that door, she said, pointing, there's the pistol and archery range. And over there, through that door, are the bowling lanes."

"They have a bowling alley in their house?"

"Yup. Well, two lanes, anyway. When her father was building this place, he envisioned Song being protected within it's walls, but cloistered, like back in China. He was a top military dude back in China, and his family was getting kickbacks and graft for generations. The affluence of this family is mind-boggling, and now it's all Song's. So much for Communism not being profitable, eh?"

"She comes from quite the family."

"The Zhao name dates back to the Song Dynasty and has been in the upper echelons of the Chinese nobility for generations. Richer, upon richer, upon richer."

"Zhao?"

"Yeah, that's Song's family name. Anyhow, Daddy didn't want Song to be bored. He wanted her staying in the compound, like in China, so he added lots of diversions here. Right now, we're on the third level. Below us is Tang's quarters, the guy who drove you here, and below that is the panic room. Well, it's actually more of a panic *floor* than a room, since it's the same size as the other floors. It's soundproof and bulletproof, so Tang uses part of it for a control room for the cameras and security stuff. It has a stocked kitchen and pantry, too."

Jackie led Mage down two of flights of stairs to a vault door that looked straight from a bank. She turned the hand wheel and pulled hard, swinging the 12-inch thick steel door open. Once she pulled it closed, all sound ceased. In Mage's neighbourhood, it was never quiet. Traffic and sirens never stopped. But this room offered a silence he'd never experienced before.

Jackie's voice infringed on the still air. "We actually practice playing down there, The acoustics are awesome."

"Playing?"

"Let me guess. Another thing Song hasn't told you yet? Yeah, sooo.... Song is a very accomplished cellist. She's good enough to make a living at it, but she really doesn't need the money. Every now and again, she'll sit in with the V.S.O., and has even been a premier, guest performer. But now, she mostly just plays duets and such with me."

"Cello? Like a big violin, right?"

Jackie's laughed. "Sure, a big violin." She led Mage further into the panic room which sported a grand piano, and the cello leaning against the wall.

"Duets? So you play the piano, I assume?"

"Yeah, mostly. Among other things."

"I've been dabbling in a little project myself of late. Musical algorithms, and such. I haven't made much headway on it yet, but it keeps me amused."

"Maybe I can help. Algorithms are my jam."

"Yeah...., maybe. It's pretty complicated, Jackie."

Jackie shrugged. "This is my gorgeous, white Steinway? Playing it is like having a gig in heaven!

39

Especially in this room. I'd never played such a high-end instrument before, and this isn't a baby grand, she's full-sized. Song and I jam down here now. I'm introducing her to a wider taste in music than classical, and she's loving it. We can make whatever noise we want, without disturbing anyone."

"Well, please disturb me! I'm looking forward to hearing you ladies play." He peered back toward the big steel, entry door before pivoting the subject back, asking, "So, what's with that rude Tang guy yelling at Song?"

"Yeah, well, Tang's not so bad. He's performed many roles for the family, not the least of which has been as Song's bodyguard. It's awkward, because he's kept her safe since she was a baby, and is having a tough time with her becoming an adult. Back in China, Song had to stay in the family compound but once she moved here to Canada, she's discovered the freedom of anonymity. She loves it. Tang, not so much.

"He told her flat out that she wasn't going to that club for New Year's Eve. She's been rebelling more of late, and he can't control her like he used to. He forbade her from leaving the compound, but she went anyway. Then, she didn't come home. He's some kinda pissed at me for being such a bad influence. For the two days he's been pacing and grumbling at me, so thanks for bringing her home. He *was* pretty worried, though. We all were. It's not like Song to be on her own, especially overnight, let alone two."

Mage bristled at anyone berating Song. He didn't

like this Tang fellow already, and by those looks in the Hummer's mirror, the feeling was mutual. "So, he's not Song's father, then?"

"No. But, Tang and Song's father were inseparable. The story goes that the two of them were on some covert mission for the Chinese Navy when they each saved the other's life. Details have always been sketchy, but since that time, Tang has been his bodyguard, manager, protector and friend. Don't sell him short. With Song's father now dead, Tang does all that and more for her. Don't be too hard on him. He loves her in his own way, and truly does have her best interests at heart. He's just having trouble adjusting to her freedom in Canada."

Mage nodded. "Soooo..., you say there's still more to this place?"

"Oh yeah. Lots more. There's even more to this music slash panic room. Over there's Tang's video surveillance room, so even in lockdown, he can see what's going on anywhere on the grounds. He's big on security. That hatch on the wall is an emergency access from the pool patio to the panic room."

Mage raised an eyebrow. "A pool you say?"

"With a swim-up bar, even. Great pool. Lately, Song and I have been suntanning topless back there just to fluster Tang. Cruel and unusual punishment."

"That's punishment I could go for," Mage said under his breath.

She guided him up a floor and to the rear of the house which looked over the back acreage. This place was extravagant, and huge, with fancy artwork and sculptures everywhere. "See down there is the pool, complete with its waterfalls and the swim-up bar I was telling you about. Behind that is the basketball court, and behind *that* are the tennis courts. See them? Now look to the right of them to see the batting cages, and finally way down at the very back is the golf course."

"You've got to be joking!"

"Do I? I don't think so. Look for yourself. It's only three holes. Rumour has it, you can actually take an underground zipline down to the pro shop, but Tang hasn't let us try it yet."

"An underground zipline? Man, this place is like Disneyland!"

Carrying on with the 10-cent tour, Jackie led Mage up a few flights of the wide, curving staircase. "On this level is the kitchen....., there," she pointed, "the dining hall there, and the theatre and the library there and there, and finally the grand ballroom way at the back."

"A Grand Ballroom? This I gotta see."

"Then this way, kind sir. This is the 4th level, but it's even with the entry gates you drove through." Jackie led him toward the front of the mansion where she threw open a big set of double doors leading into an enormous, ornate room sporting a three storey, sculpted ceiling.

The all-marble room was larger than a gymnasium with stately, thick marble columns rising up the three stories. Other than a few fancy divans near the centre, the room was empty. Jackie led Mage through the room, across the ballroom's dance floor to the mansion's main entry doors. Throwing them open wide, she declared, "These doors are 15 feet tall and 15 feet wide and when both are swung open like this, you can easily drive the Hummer through. I've seen it happen."

Mage looked up at an enormous, crystal chandelier hanging down a floor and a half in the centre of the room. *'Wow!'* Also up high, he spotted some odd looking doors near the top of either end, asking, "What the heck are those for? Anyone walking through them would fall a good twenty feet!"

"Those are our inside balconies, my dear. For the ladies of the manner, don't ya know. One from my bedroom and one from Song's. If we ever have a grand ball, we'll be able to look down on the unwashed masses and see the common folk dancing below," she giggled. 'C'mon. There's more."

*'How can there possibly be more?'* he wondered. Jackie wandered over to an elevator, asking "Going up, sir?" As they stepped out of the lift, Jackie steered him toward the rear again where there was a private theatre and what looked to Mage like a museum.

"This room here is for the sauna and hot tub. Why four floors above the pool, you ask? Because Song's father wanted it closer to his bedroom. But really, every floor has a waterslide to the pool, so it's a quick trip down from anywhere in the house. See? Over there is this floor's." Mage was seriously shaking his head at this point.

Jackie headed up another floor, stating that the next two stories were bedroom levels, along with a laundry. "There are 8 guest rooms, in addition to mine and Song's. Each has their own bathroom, complete with showers, baths and bidets – and toilets, of course. There are 20 bathrooms in all on the compound, including those for common areas like the sauna, pool and grand ballroom." Maze peeked in to see all golden plumbing fixtures, and gilded mirrors in the all-marble privies.

"You look overwhelmed," said Jackie. "How about a drink?"

` "I think I could use one." She led them back to the kitchen level and pulled out a couple of bottles.

"There is this lovely 16-year-old Lagavulin....... "

"Scotch? Eewww, no. How about just a cold beer?"

"We can do that," Jackie said, just as Song came up a staircase to join them.

"So, did you get a tour?" Song asked with a grin?

"Yeah, all 10-cents worth. This place is mind boggling. You've been holding out on me, Darlin'." She already loved him calling her Darlin'.

"Not what you expected?" Song teased.

"Not what anyone would expect. It's a wee bit nicer than my apartment. And Jackie told me you're both musicians. Is there anything else you haven't told me?"

"Lots."

"Will you play for me?"

"I guess so. Care to join me, Jacks?"

"Totally," she responded, handing her a Scotch.

Song led the trio back down to the panic room where the girls took their places. Jackie ran a scale or two, warming up her fingers, while Song slowly applied rosin to the hairs of her cello bow. Running it across the strings, she briefly tuned it, and that deep, vibrant sound alone was enough to impress Mage. Jackie was right. The acoustics really were amazing.

Song nodded to Jackie, who led into the opening strains of 'Hallelujah', by Leonard Cohen. She had a delicate, soulful touch on the ivories, and when Song joined the chorus, Mage was suitably impressed. Blown away would be more accurate. The full, richness of the cello and the crispness of the piano filled the room with sounds as beautiful as any he'd ever heard. Jackie's sang with her soul, and as the final strains diminished, the quiet enveloped them once again.

A few moments passed, before Mage leapt to his feet screaming like he was at a rock concert, jumping and waving his arms. Jackie joked to Song "Your boy cheers like Kermit the Frog."

"Wow, wow, WOW! You girls are totally amazing! The sound of live music in this room is so much better than the songs I've been using in my project. You have to let me record you! I *know* it will be cleaner, and more pristine. Less variables. Can I bring over some of my recording equipment? Song? Please!"

She loved to see him as excited as a kid at Christmas. "Sure, knock yourself out."

# *Chapter 4*

*"My heart, which is so full to overflowing has often been solaced and refreshed by music when sick and weary".*

**Martin Luther**

"Thanks for bringing your truck, Daniel," said Mage the following day. "I could never have crammed all of my recording equipment onto the motocross bike."

"Are you kidding? I give you a bit of help moving your equipment, and you're going to take me to Disneyland? If this place is as cool as you say, I can't wait. Besides, what are best friends for, eh buddy?"

"Appreciated none-the-less. This place is going to blow your mind."

"So, Mage the Magician's found himself a rich girl, eh? Lucky bastard. Am I going to have to start calling you Mr. Moon now?," Daniel chided.

"Ha, ha. You should be a comedian."

"That's what I always say! People are always telling me I'm funny."

"They don't mean you're hilarious, just that you're odd."

"Whatever. As long as they think about me at all. And speaking of thinking about me, that blonde girl from the club is going to be there, isn't she? She was so hot!"

"Yeah, Jackie will probably be there, seeing as she lives there."

"Did you tell her about me, old buddy, old pal? Your handsome, rugged and funny friend?"

"Uh, no. Jackie has no idea who you are."

"Not yet at least. But she will."

"Yeah, introductions work like that. Now, quit daydreaming and help me load the soundboard. The sooner we're loaded, the sooner you'll find out."

"I'm down with that! Hurry up, magic man!"

Twenty minutes later, the boys headed through Stanley Park over the Lion's Gate. The bulk of the snow in Vancouver had melted into a slushy mess, but the roads were now mostly clear. Gazing up from the bridge, Grouse and the other North Shore mountains were magnificent today. The thick snow glistened on their peaks, contrasted by deep blue sky. Vancouver was truly a beautiful city, but today she was glorious.

Mage soon directed Daniel to pull his truck into a short lane leading to the mansion's front gates. He tried to hand his buddy the pass codes for the gates, but

Daniel was lost already, his eyes scanning higher and higher. The tall, privacy walls and iron gates alone were intimidating, but the pagoda mansion was like nothing he'd ever seen.

"Holy crap! This is the place?"

"Yeah, Song texted me the pass codes for the gates. Here." As they pulled through the second gate, Mage watched Daniel's face as he drove down the driveway. *'That must be what I looked like – stunned,'* he mused. By the time they pulled down into the in-house garage, Daniel was laughing aloud.

"That's the Hummer limo I told you about. Pull in beside it."

"Is that a Ferrari? That's so cool!"

"Lamborghini, actually." Song replied, as she walked into the garage to greet her guests. "It was my Dad's toy, though Tang seldom allowed him to leave the compound unless chauffeured. Hello. I'm Song," she said to Daniel.

"Yeah, I know. I've heard of nothing else today. Hiya, I'm Daniel."

"And I'm Mage," he chuckled as Song leapt up, wrapped her legs around him, and kissed his face repeatedly.

"Hi baby," Song said softly. She'd never been in love before, and had to say, she was liking it a lot!

49

"Hi yourself. I see you brushed your hair today."

"Hey!" Song responded, punching his shoulder.

As Daniel looked on, he'd never seen Mage happier. Since the accident that killed his parents, his buddy's life had been downright morose, so it was great to see him smile.

Song climbed down from Mage, ignored Daniel's handshake and gave him a hug instead. "Nice to meet you, Daniel. Mage has told me all about you, too."

"That sounds ominous. Not everything, I hope. Nice shack you have here, by the way. I think my beat-up truck has already lowered your property value, though."

Song provided the obligatory laugh. "I'm not too concerned about that. Shall we go inside?"

"Hang on. Not so fast." He filled each of their arms with recording equipment. "These need to go down to the panic room."

"You mean the music room?"

"Okay Song, the music room."

Following her down the staircase, and trying to sound nonchalant, Daniel asked, "So, ummm, Song. I hear you have a roommate."

Song looked at him with amusement. She'd seen men get nervous around Jackie before. "Yes, I have a roommate, Daniel. Would you like to meet her?"

"Ummmm, I guess....., you know....., if she's around."

"C'mon, she's down in the music room already. This way."

Daniel's head began rotating in every direction, just like his friend's had. He'd heard about 'rich' before, but this was on a whole new level. They approached a heavy, metal door and as soon as Song spun the hand wheel open, soft piano music drifted to their ears. Jackie stopped playing and rose to meet their guests. Flashing her best 1,000-watt smile, she said, "Hi Mage. Nice to see you again. Who's your friend?"

"Jackie, ...... Daniel. Daniel, meet Jackie."

"So, this is your friend I've heard so much about."

Daniel attempted a response, but was utterly speechless for perhaps the first time in his life. Anchored to the floor, his entire body seemed as rigid as a statue, with a mouth equally inoperative. He tried desperately, but unsuccessfully, to form words. He wasn't sure whether he should just say hi, shake her hand, or hug her, so instead gave a lame wave, instantly regretting it. How embarrassing.

Jackie smiled even wider and came forward herself to welcome him with a hug.'"Oh, my God."

Daniel laughed nervously, looked at the floor, then back up at her face. He panicked, braced for her hug, and promptly dropped his load of the electronic equipment to the floor. He stooped to pick it up, then straightened, seeing Jackie was still waiting with her arms spread wide. *'Oh, God.'* he thought. *'She moving in.'* "Hi" was all he managed to croak. Chastising himself, he gave her an awkward hug for a little too long. He awkwardly released her, but his mouth still wasn't operational. He stuffed both hands into his front pockets. Wild-eyed, he stumbled, and mumbled, "I sh..., I should go get more." and fled the room.

Song joked. "Well, that went well."

"Awww, c'mon, he was so cute. Just a shy, little boy. It's endearing."

Mage caught up with Daniel and teased, "Smooth moves, Romeo."

"No. Yeah? You think so?" Mage loaded his pal's arms with more equipment, but only smiled in response. "Yeah. No, I guess not. But she liked me, right? Do you think she liked me?"

"Oh, sure. You impressed the hell out of her."

Daniel smiled. "You know who she reminds me of?"

"Who's that?"

"Betty Cooper. You know. From the Archie

comics. Especially with her hair up in a pony tail like that. Her hair was down at the club. Did you notice that?"

"Betty Cooper, eh? So, does that make Song Veronica Lodge?"

"Well, she *is* very rich."

"Yes, she is that. I guess makes you Jughead?"

"Ha ha. Very funny."

"And that Tang guy, he's grumpy Mr. Lodge."

Later, when the guys finished setting up the equipment, Mage suggested, "Shall we test it? You want to call the girls back down, Jughead?"

"I guess. But don't call me that in front of Jackie, okay?" Steeling himself, he marched out with purpose!

Soon, Song and Jackie took their places behind their instruments, awaiting their cue from Mage behind the sound board.

"Hey, Jackie," interrupted Daniel. "I play too, you know. Like, yeah, I've got a guitar. I play, you know, stuff."

"Well, I'm looking forward to playing with you sometime," she responded, winking at Song.

Daniel had a goofy grin that lasted all day.

From beneath his headphones, Mage flicked a few switches, turned a few knobs, and nodded. "All right ladies, whenever you're ready.........,"

Jackie began, carving through the quiet with a delicate intro with Disturbed's version of the Sound of Silence.

Daniel blurted, "Hey, I know this one!" Mage put a quieting finger to his lips, silently mouthing 'Recording'. Soon, Song caressing her cello's strings in harmony with the Steinway.

Urgent and forceful, the cello imposed on the quiet like a rumbling thunder. Head down, eyes closed, she took herself to another world. Working her bow, deep resonance flooded the room before fading and ceding to Jackie's haunting finish.

Daniel was still incapable of speech as Mage took off the headphones, looked up in wonder and said, "that was truly awesome ladies. Wow. Thanks for letting me record that. The purity of that sound can only help my project."

"That algorithm project that's way too complicated for little, old me?" Jackie teased.

"That'd be the one," Mage answered sheepishly.

# *Chapter 5*

*"Human subtlety will never devise an invention more beautiful, more simple or more direct than does nature because in her inventions nothing is lacking, and nothing is superfluous."*

**Leonardo da Vinci**

It was the first day of Spring as Jackie ambled across the grounds of U.B.C. feeling very upbeat and pleased with her marks on the recent midterms. Especially in her *Machine Learning and Data Mining course*. Not many students would have much interest in such a course, but Jackie loved it. Numbers were her thing.

The weather had sucked for the past few weeks, setting a few records for rainfall, which in Vancouver meant something. But today was finally a clear day, with sunshine massaging warmth into her weary bones. The songbirds were chirping, and Spring was on its way. She waved casually to a couple of classmates who were defiantly wearing shorts in an effort to hasten summer's arrival.

Up ahead, she saw Bryce talking to some pretty girl. *'Surprise, surprise. Men will be men'*. He absently was checking Jackie out too before he got up to the face and realized who she was. Startled, he bade the babe goodbye, and instead approached Jackie cockily with his winning smile, leaving her strangely unsettled.

"Hey, sexy. What's up?"

"Nothing much. Class just ended and I'm heading to see a guest speaker. Wanna join me?"

"You mean go to a lecture that I don't have to? Thanks, but I have to listen to too many intellectual has-beens as it is."

"C'mon. You should come. The guy's one of the top climate scientists in the world. It should be enlightening."

"Are you serious, Jacks? Another global warming quack? It's fake news, you know. Long term climate change has always cycled in and out over time."

"Well, I'm going and it starts in five minutes. So........see you later?"

"Yeah, later," Bryce muttered dismissively.


Climbing the steps to the auditorium, she was a little excited, and a little anxious. There had been so much grandstanding by both sides of the climate debate, she didn't know what to believe. What she did know was that weather was getting weird, and natural disasters were nightly staples on the evening news.

She found one of the last seats just as introductions were being made, happy she hadn't missed anything. It was not a required lecture for any course, but the auditorium was packed none-the-less.

"..........so, ladies and gentlemen, it is my distinct pleasure to welcome today, Dr. Andrew McKenzie. Dr. McKenzie is a senior advisor to NASA and the National Center for Environmental Information in the U.S., as well as an adjunct professor at the Canadian Meteorological Institute. He's one of the world's preeminent experts on Climatology, and we're fortunate to have him here with us today. Let's give him a warm Vancouver welcome. Dr. McKenzie?"

"Thank you, professor. And thanks to U.B.C. for having me. And thank you all for being here on a day as beautiful as today.

"I'd like to begin today with a simple question. What process do you think has advanced humanity to the top of the food chain? Is there a single reason? The invention of fire? The wheel? Opposable thumbs? In my mind, the answer is simple. Curiosity. To advance, humans have had to be curious. Curious about how things work. Curious about better ways to do things. Curious about God. Curious about the good-looking guy talking to you now." The audience snickered. "But, for curiosity to be rewarded, it must also be acted upon. Some brave soul had to wonder, 'what if.....?', in order to fail or find solutions. Someone who likely endured ridicule from his or her peers until the theories were proven. Many famous men and women throughout human history have asked questions and provided answers that have changed the trajectory of their era. Curiosity? Solution.

"Now, if we were to apply the same fundamentals to the world now, what should we most be curious about? What do we most need a solution for? Well, I say this.

"What in the heck is going on with the weather? It's been pretty crazy lately, eh? Will it really get worse, or is it just a blip in Earth's long history? People are curious. And curiosity begs a solution. I get asked all the time whether this global warming rhetoric is true, or just another fear factor for the evening news? I hope to answer that satisfactorily for you all here today.

"Many of us suffer from Apocalypse Fatigue. We tune out the scary things we don't fully understand. It's human nature. But, this solution is important so I am here today to help you understand.

"Yes, the rhetoric is true. Unfortunately, this is something that we cannot ignore and hope it goes away. Habitat is critically important, not just to humans, but to all life on Earth. We need to get it under control. A century from now, should humans survive that long, historians will be looking back wondering what on Earth we were thinking? We killed our only home, and poisoned our own habitat in favour of an arbitrary numerical theory we call money. We know it, yet little changes. What's it going to take for the curious to find solutions?

"This is not a political issue, folks. Anywhere. This is a survival issue. And to survive as a species, we need to treat the Earth with respect, for we know her wrath is catastrophic. Floods, forest fires, hurricanes, tornadoes, drought, warming oceans....... these are all symptoms of a larger problem. Melting glaciers, dying coral reefs, air pollution, ocean garbage, flooding cities, water acidity, species extinction – all warnings we've ignored. A two degree rise in sea temperatures? Too far in the future to worry about, right? But Mother Nature will deal with it for us, won't she? She always does, right? We just may not appreciate the way she goes about it.

"The common denominator of this crisis is us. Humans. There are simply too many of us for the planet to sustain. Earth is capable of sustaining 2-1/2 to 3 billion people, and we are already approaching triple that. We exert ever-increasing pressure on our world....... our only habitat. There are hard choices ahead, and the longer we wait, the harder they will be. We can no longer strip our lands of their precious resources. We can no longer treat the oceans as our garbage dump. Conviction is required on a global scale and we will need curious people to find solutions.

"People say, *'But, Andrew, these are all monumental problems. What effect can I have?'* "My answer to them is, *'be curious'*. Ask the important questions, and learn the important answers.

"Globally, we could give the environment legal rights. We could end fossil fuels. We could tend to our oceans instead of using them as our trash heap. We could reduce our personal expectations for the greater good. But on every level, in every corner of the world, we all need to be more curious and find solutions.

*'But, Andrew,'* some ask, *'it'll be so expensive. The government should pay. What about the corporations. Why don't they pony up for it?'* Governments and Corporations are funded by us. We are the ones these costs would be passed along to. Accept it. Accept it or pay the price that weather exacts on the world's infrastructures. Accept it, or accept the deaths in ever-increasing natural disasters.

"We, as humans, really do have options to assist, but don't be tricked into thinking your idea is too minuscule to make a difference. 'Reduce, reuse, and recycle' will help, but it is not a solution. Banning plastic straws will help but its not a solution. Reducing our energy consumption will help, but its not a solution. Using clotheslines instead of dryers will help, but it is not a solution. Planting trees will help, but it's not a solution. But when all of the small solutions are combined, progress gets made.

"On a larger scale, wind energy will help, but the blades are non-recyclable, and need to be buried for disposal. Electric vehicles will help, but the batteries have their own environmental cost. Solar panels will help, but are non-recyclable. So we all must remain curious to understand the solutions to come.

"Most people in this room will now be affected by some weather-related disaster in their lifetime. Let's just hope it's not the final day of your lifetime. Tough laws must be enacted and enforced. Grass roots organizations must drive for change. Governments and corporations must be held accountable.

"There are many issues we face, but there are none more important than repairing our habitat."

Dr. McKenzie tapped his laptop's power point presentation, displaying on the big screen behind him, atrocious photographic evidence of current global warming tragedies. "These are not all from some vague future. They are already here." The scenes silenced the entire auditorium.

Jackie vowed to be curious, and to find some solutions.

"..........and if there's one thing I'd like to leave you with here today, it's this. More than 99% of Earth's historical species are now extinct, and we are adding thousands more every year. It is folly to think humans could be exempt from such a fate, that we could not be the cause of our own extinction.

"Consider this. Two hundred and fifty million years ago, Earth suffered a crisis known as the Permian Extinction, or The Great Dying. Believed to be caused by massive chains of volcanic eruptions in Russia, which produced enough lava to cover the United States a kilometre deep. The result was a rise of ocean temperatures by 11 decrees Celsius. Marine oxygen levels fell by 76%, wiping out 96% of the ocean life on Earth, and 90% of land creatures.

"Applied to our global warming models, a rise of 4 degrees Celsius could come by 2060. Most of you here will only be in your 50s by then. If temperatures continue to rise and grow on a parabolic curve, levels comparable with The Great Dying could occur in little more than a century. Will your children or grandchildren suffer such a fate? I urge you all. Be curious and find the solutions. There is no issue more important than the preservation of our habitat.

"Thank you all for your time. I'll take personal questions at the front for those who want to stay."

Jackie's mind was troubled, and she didn't want to hear anymore right now. She chastised herself for wanting to get out of there, but that's the problem alright. Apocalyptic Fatigue. She'd always been a worrier. As she exited, the sunny spring day remained but she didn't hear the songbirds anymore.

The last few months had been the best of Song's life. Mage was a caring and attentive man, who spoiled her even more than her parents had, but with distinctly different rewards. This new year had brought her freedom back, and she was only now beginning to feel in control of her own fate.

Mage took her to her first live hockey game, and shared in in celebrating a Canucks goal. On Valentine's Day, he'd taken her up Grouse Mountain for dinner, where they gazed down the ski runs at the twinkling blanket of Vancouver's lights below. Song experienced the energy of her first rock concert at B.C. Place, and Mage, his first Vancouver Symphony Orchestra performance at the Orpheum. He was astounded and proud that Song had been featured among such a talented group of musicians.

At the mansion, Mage had practically moved in. Often found down in the music room, he now had his full computer and recording equipment spread all around him, where he tinkered away when he didn't have to work in Gramps's shop.

Daniel often called him Mage the Magician, but he really was a magician when it came to technical electronic systems. With several recordings of the girls to work with, he'd hunkered down beneath his headphones, attempting to incorporate new sound structures like he had witnessed at the Symphony. He was in his element, constantly adjusting remixes, algorithms, octave mirroring, and any number of sound experiments he could think of, with one hand on his soundboard, and the other on his computer keyboard.

When Jackie got home from the climate lecture, she headed to the music room for some much needed solace. She found Mage already at his post, though he didn't notice her until she began playing. With a smile and a wave, he was soon engrossed in his project once again.

It took three or four songs before Jackie began to relax again. That lecture had really shaken her. Her private high school may have taught how to conform the masses, but university was all about critical thinking, and the responsibilities inherent therein.

When she'd finally calmed herself with the power of music, curiosity got the better of her and she approached Mage at the sound board. He removed his headphones to greet her properly. 'Hey Jacks. How was school?"

"Well, good and bad, I guess. Got my midterm marks back for my 'Machine Learning and Data Mining' course, and I aced it. That's the good part. The bad part was, I went to see this guest lecturer talking about climate change this afternoon, and he totally freaked me out. I needed my beloved Steinway to heal my soul. Music always makes me feel better, don't you think?"

"I do."

"What are you working on anyways? You seem to always be down in this room, lately."

"Actually, I'm working on what you just said. Music has charms to soothe the savage beast, right? Well, I want to know why. So, I've been running the songs I recorded of you guys, and am trying to find out if that elusive healing quality can be magnified. It's just my silly little basement project."
"Curiosity needs solutions," said Jackie, under her breath.

"Huh?"

"Oh, nothing. Just something I heard today."

Sometimes it feels like the answer is right there, but I just can't get it to work. I've created programs to convert the songs' melodies into numbers and patterns. I'm trying to create an algorithm to convert it to a healing frequency. Maybe I can help some old folks by enhancing their favourite songs, to stimulate the feelings associated with health."

"That sounds so cool, Mage. Numbers, music and pattern recognition. It sounds like my kind of project. Show me what you've been up to. I want to learn."

Mage spent several hours showing Jackie what he'd accomplished so far, and what was trying to do. "It's definitely an interesting premise, Mage. How did you come up with it."

"It was actually at the hospital I.C.U. when the first inkling sprouted. I was so sad, waiting for my dad to wake up, which he never did, of course. I could see that pretty girl there being sad too, and I so badly wanted to make her pain go away. My pain, too. In fact, every person in the I.C.U. waiting room looked as though their world was crumbling. A fantasy blossomed. If only I could wave a magic wand and make everyone just a little bit healthier. Maybe even get to see that pretty Asian girl smile. And that would make me smile."

"Aw, that's so sweet Mage. What a kind heart you have."

"Yeah, I told Daniel, and he told me that if anybody could do it, Mage the Magician could wave his magic wand and cure the whole hospital. Since then, I've been trying to find the right spells."

"Daniel the trusty sidekick, loyal and true, eh?"

"Well, he is that, I guess."

She bent over the table, studying the technical aspects Mage had covered so far, and where he exactly was trying to get to.

"Now you can see what I mean about the numbers and music not quite jiving. It's like an optical illusion, where the answer is there, but if you try to focus on it directly, it disappears. I'm so frustrated."

"Well, I can see why. It's a pretty major goal, Mage. You shouldn't beat yourself up about it."

"But, that's the nature of an obsession, isn't it? Can't sleep because the mind keeps spinning. The only way out, is to solve it."

"Be curious, and find a solution," Jackie murmured again. I'll tell you what. How about if I take this data into my Machine Learning and Data Mining prof. tomorrow. Maybe he can help."

"I hope so, because I'm getting nowhere."

The following day, Jackie organized and collated all of her info before going to see Professor Brooks, and he was suitably impressed. "This Mage fellow must be quite something to have put all of this together."

"He is," she realized. Song had landed herself a smart one.

It was only about a week later that Jackie returned from school, flushed and excited. "Mage! Where ar..... , oh there you are. Mage! It just hit me driving to U.B.C. this morning. I bounced the idea off of my professor, and he was encouraged. In your math calculations, you're using base ten, right?"

"Well sure," responded Mage. "Almost all math is in base 10. The metric system runs on it. Why would that matter?"

"Music is a universal language, worldwide, agreed?"

"Pretty much."

"And so is math right? Both cross all language barriers."

"I guess. Never thought about it like that."

"So, if you're converting music mathematically, shouldn't you use base eight, not base ten? Eight notes to an octave. Can you integrate that into your calculations somehow?"

"Base eight, you say. That's thinking outside the box. I like it. Its beauty is its simplicity. Quite brilliant, actually."

"Oh, psshhaawww," she uttered, looking at her shoes, pretending to kick the dirt like a nervous kid. For the next few hours, they worked on it, side by side. Mage was good with the programming, and Jackie was good with the theoretical math. Both thought the other was smarter than themselves, which made for a very open-minded collaboration.

"Wait, what about the half notes, Jacks? Like the black keys on a piano?"

"I dunno. If they're half notes, couldn't they be half numbers? An f sharp would be, like 4.5?"

"Okay. That's plausible. So if we......"

It was another hour before Song wandered in to drag them both up for a late dinner.

"Come on, you two. An empty stomach waits for no man......, or woman. And you both have visitors."

Dinner that night was a raucous affair. Song, Mage, Jackie, Bryce, and Daniel listened as the normally quiet Mage was talking quickly, bubbling over.

"You guys all know I've been working on a project in the music room, right? Well, for the past couple of weeks, I've been converting the songs I taped of you guys to a numbered system, then tried to convert them mathematically, but have been stuck and seriously frustrated. I've come close, but now Jackie's helping me with the number work, and it looks like her ideas show real promise."

Daniel cries, "She's beautiful *and* intelligent! All

hail, Queen Jacqueline!" and he kisses the top of her head as he gets up for seconds. "Mwah!" Bryce glared at a blushing Jackie, but she just shrugged. She was as keyed up as Mage, and wasn't going to let Bryce ruin that.

But, being ignored definitely irked Bryce. "What are you trying to accomplish with this stupid project anyway?"

Mage explained, "It's all theoretical at this point, but here's my thinking." "Did you ever notice how music makes you feel better, taking your mind back to a happier time? You could be having a bad day, but when you hear an old song on the radio, it cheers you up, right? Or you're home sick from work, you throw on some old music, and the next thing you know, you're dancing around the house. Well, that's the opening premise of my project. I want to explore whether music can actually be manipulated scientifically to make people feel better on any measurable level. Healthier on demand, through music, so to speak. Happier, at least."

"That's the stupidest thing I've ever heard. How can you be interested this stuff, Jackie? You're smarter than that. What's next? A Ouija Board?"

"Because it's fun. I like music, I like numbers. And Mage asked me if I would help, so why not?"

"Because it's stupid, that's why."

Mage interjected to say, "Jackie may have just given us a chance to make it work. She had a revelation today that might make a big difference. You should be proud of her."

"Proud for what? Is she going to sing a song and cure cancer?"

"That would be an admirable goal, but helping anyone feel just a little bit better would be nice, would it not?" asked Mage.

"That's it. You guys are totally nuts." Bryce cried. "You mean you're just going to take some tunes, put them through some mumbo-jumbo algorithm and they're going to create some voodoo 'healing frequency'? Wait 'til I tell my Dad about *this* one! *'Hey Pops. You don't need to sell your pharmaceuticals anymore. Just play 'em a happy song!'* This is ridiculous. C'mon Jacks, let's go."

With a thin-lipped half-smile, Jackie said, "I'm good. See you later."

Song watched Bryce march off, secretly happy that her best friend was starting to see Bryce's pompous personality. *'The guy is all ego,'* she thought. *'Good for you!'* Song cried, "All Hail, Queen Jacqueline!"
"All hail!" Silence. He was gone.

"Okay now, why exactly is Jacks so brilliant?" Daniel asked. "I mean, I've known her for a few months now, and she's clearly brilliant." He gave her a wink. "But, what revelation did she bring to the table?"

"She suggested changing the numbers in my

calculations to a base eight formula, instead of base ten."

"Brilliant!" Daniel raved, though he didn't really understand. But it gave him an excuse to wink at Jackie again, for which he was awarded a smile."But what does that mean?"

"Do you know why cats purr?" Mage asked the others, seemingly out of left field.

"They purr when they're happy," Daniel answered, pleased to take part in an otherwise intellectual conversation.

"Yes, they purr when they are happy. But they also purr when they get injured, or have suffered a stressful event. Studies have shown that purring cats heal quicker than controls, and one accepted theory says they purr on a 'healing frequency'. I am trying to incorporate that theory into the project."

"I'm starting to wonder if Bryce is right," Daniel observed. "It does sound a bit out there, buddy."

"Totally. And I get that. But, it's just a pet project I'm trying to get to work, and Jackie may have provided a key piece of the puzzle. If I can make it all work, at least I'll be able to get some sleep again."

*"Be curious and find the solution,"* Jackie said again to herself.

The following morning, Jackie was up very early, unable to sleep. It happened sometimes when she drank too much. So, she trudged down to the panic room to play a song or two, like she did most mornings she had no early class. *'It's like Mage said'*, she thought. *'Playing music always cheers me up'*. It had its work cut out for it today, as her hangover crashed around her brain in a sleep-deprived fog. She pulled open the huge steel door to see Mage already there, head down with headphones on.

"You're up early", she greeted, with a yawn.

"Haven't been to bed yet."

"You've been down here all night?"

"Yup. I couldn't wait to try out your theory, and once I changed your numbers from base ten to base eight, certain things began falling into place. Jacks, it's been like like a domino effect. Once the first part of the algorithm established the pattern, the others fell in line, one after the other."

"Really? So you think my idea helps your project?"

"It appears so. Put on these spare headphones. Listen and have a look at this," he said, pulling up a couple of screens on his laptops. "This chart on the left shows the music of your latest recording, raw. That's how it looks before any manipulation at all. Now, watch when I do this. This right side screen shows the same music mirrored into different audio ranges. They are all represented by the same notes, but when I channelled them into high and low octaves humans can't normally hear, the pattern converted into stable sine wave, all by itself."

"So what does that mean?"

"I'm not sure, frankly. I've been trying to disprove my theory, like good research scientists do, but thus far, every time I run the algorithms, the sine wave appears. So far, can't find any holes. Then I tried other songs you've played for me, and they're all doing the same thing. It all just seems to work! The song itself is irrelevant. It's just a delivery device of some kind."

Jackie was pretty pleased with herself. She had grown to really like Song's boyfriend since he'd moved into the mansion, and helping him solve a big riddle made her feel good.

"The songs are all converging now at 65 hertz," he continued

"So?"

"Sixty five hertz is the middle of a cat's purring range. And if cats can heal themselves at that range, why can't we?"

"Very cool, Mage. But what now?"
"We test it, I guess. The theory has been panning out, but we need to see if we can *dis*prove it, and make it practical, somehow. I'm not really sure, but these results are encouraging."

"Can I take this in to my Machine Learning and Data Mining professor again? Maybe he has an idea as to what's next."

"That actually sounds good. I hope my brain will relax, knowing the ball's in someone else's court for awhile. Maybe I'll be able to sleep."

Removing her own headphones, Jackie gathered up Mage's research for her prof., and realized her headache had vanished.

It was a few days later before Jackie's professor asked her to stay after her class, and he was beside himself. "What the hell is happening with this research, Ms. Beausoleil?"

"Is there a problem?"

"It's the opposite of a problem! I took all of your data home with me, ran the algorithms, and played the songs over and over. It doesn't sound any different, but it is. In fact, the Machine Learning and Data Mining programs show it to be *very* different, indeed."

"Is that good or bad?"

"Most definitely good! I've been staying with my mother, because she's sick from her diabetes and long COVID. She complained of me playing the same song over and over while she was trying to rest, but the strangest thing happened. The following morning, I got up and she was sitting at the kitchen table with a hot coffee in hand."

"Okay, but how.........."

"Jackie, she hasn't been out if bed in over a year. And now, suddenly she's sitting at the table with coffee she made herself? She was sitting there reading the newspaper, complaining about some politician. It's like she time travelled back to her healthy years! She was cheery and looked great, and when I helped her check her morning blood sugar, it was perfect. And it's been perfect every day since. She actually signed up for an aqua fit class yesterday!"

"That sounds great, professor. Mage will be so happy."

"This is all bigger than 'happy', Ms. Beausoleil. Do you realize that you've grabbed a tiger by the tail? I took it to my friend in the medical research labs on campus, and nobody can explain it. It's like a miracle, Jackie. Very impressive work. We'd like to get this Mage person here to answer some of the questions that have arisen. Do you think he'd do that?"

"Gosh, I don't know. I can't see why not."

"Then get him here as fast as you can. We have some very curious researchers."

*'Be curious,'* Jackie said to herself. *'Find a solution.'*

"I couldn't believe it when I saw Mom sitting at the table reading. It's nothing short of a miracle.

Yesterday, I had coffee with a colleague who is a geneticist. He offered a novel, possible explanation."

"And what was that?" Jackie wondered.

"Remember a few years ago when they completely decoded the human genome."

"Yeah, I remember."

"The thinking at the time was, once decoded, we'd be able to demystify every genetic disease out there. It turned out that it didn't work that way. When they traced back a patient's DNA, results were mixed. In some cases, the same gene was causing two completely different diseases. What they eventually did learn, is that the genes can be essentially switched off or on. Different stimuli the patient experiences through their lifetime could flip a gene's switch on or off. It's a new field called epigenetics."

"Okay, but how does that apply here?"

"My friend suggested that maybe you've switched on a healing gene somehow. You know how some animals can grow back limbs? It could be something like that. He's quite interested in working with you and your friend to do some clinical trials. Would this interest you?"

"Totally! I'll have to run things by Mage, but I think he'd be down with that."

"Well, good. Talk to this Mage fellow and see

what he says. In the meantime, I gave a copy of your documentation to this research friend to study. Let me know if Mage has a problem with that."

"I don't see that as a problem. Mage was already saying we need to run tests, so having it documented in a clinical trial by professionals who do research for a living will be more than he hoped for."

"That's great, Jackie. Let me know. My professor friend is really excited. Usually, he's doing trials on new medicines, but is curious just how far this healing music, for lack of a better term, will take them. Healing ourselves could make the pharmaceutical industry less relevant. How big would that be?"

"That's really great news, professor. I've gotta go tell Mage."

"Well, don't take too long. Everyone here is talking about it. Word will spread fast."

That night at dinner, Jackie spoke excitedly about the day's events. Everyone was so happy for both Mage and her. But Bryce wasn't there to quash their enthusiasm. She remembered what he had said about the project, and thought she'd make him eat his words now.

But, when she called him, it turned out that he didn't eat his words. She told him excitedly about what the two professors had said about the project, and added, "The doctor who wants to run the trials thinks we could even make some medicines obsolete. Wouldn't that be cool?"

"Yeah, right." Bryce grunted, obtuse as ever. "The guy's a quack, Jackie. Wait until Dad hears about this one. He always likes a good laugh."

"Well, you could just be excited for me, you know. This is a big deal to me."

"Big deal? What's the big deal, I say? The only thing big about this is Mage's h........." It was then that Jackie hung up on him. *'He can be such an ass,'* she fumed. *'Just like his asshole father.'*

# *Chapter 6*

*"I hope we shall crush in its birth the aristocracy of our monied corporations which dare already to challenge our government to a trial by strength, and bid defiance to the laws of our country".*

**Thomas Jefferson**

A few days later, Mage rose, eager to work on his project. But it was Monday, and his Grandfather needed him at the shop. He'd spent all weekend poring over his tests and monitors, but had yet to disprove his theory thus far. Things still looked promising. He'd also been unable to reverse the process. When he tinkered with the sine wave, he could not split it back into the many octaves and algorithms required to create it in the first place.

Jackie had promised to see her professor, and ask how any preliminary testing was going. If the research prof was right, and it was an epigenetic event that switched on some healing gene, the body has 6.4 billion base pairs to analyze. Finding just one with a flipped switch would be a daunting process, and patience was not a trait that he had in abundance.

Perhaps the Machine Learning and Data Mining software at the university could provide some answers, or determine the best way forward. So, as itchy as Mage was to keep pushing his 'basement project' forward,

Jackie cautioned him that the process may be slower than he liked. But he didn't have the processing power to do it himself, and the university did. Patience, patience, patience. He hated that word.

For now, a day in the shop took precedence. His grandfather hadn't been well.

A stormy day had forced Mage to don his rain gear before commuting on his old motocross bike. He wondered if he should ask Tang about taking the Hummer to work on rainy days, but thought he already knew the answer to that one. *'I should ask Song instead. Better yet, I should ask her about taking the Lamborghini!'* he mused. *'Yeah!'* Tucking his chin down, he pulled out of the garage, and into the day's drab drizzle.

He exited the main gates and turned toward town, while trying to defog his helmet's face shield. Just missing a stoplight, he waited impatiently as his watch indicated he was running late. He'd been trying so hard to show Gramps his responsible side since the death of his parents, and he didn't want to be late again. So, when the light changed, he punched the bike's throttle, failing to notice a black sedan three cars back do the same. 'When he changed lanes again, his shadow followed. By the time he reached the shop, the rain had stopped. *'It figures,'* he grumbled to himself.

Entering the shop from the back lane, as always, he called out a greeting to his grandfather, only to find the counter unattended. For the past couple of days, his grandfather hadn't looked well, and all he wanted to do was sleep. Mage clambered up the stairs to check on him, and poked his head in the door of Gramps's apartment, but all was quiet there, too. He found him still snoozing, and after feeling his warm forehead, Mage left him to rest.

Downstairs, he powered up the computers and till, flicked on the lights, unlocked the front door and flipped over the 'Open' sign. His day flew by, and though business was brisk, he was able to keep up alone just fine. Constant thoughts of Song, and the success he was having with his project, had Mage whistling a happy tune.

Shortly before closing, two men came in who didn't resemble his grandfather's usual clientele. Both wore long, dark trench coats, sunglasses though it was raining, and black, pork pie hats. The bigger of the two drifted over to perfunctorily look at some merchandise that he wasn't really interested in. He glanced at Mage, then at his partner, who approached the counter with a swagger.

"Can I help you?"

"Well, I'm not sure if you can or not, son. You see, I'm looking for a brand new unit that can help make folks feel better. Sounds crazy, eh? There's gadgets for everything now, am I right? Well, I've been told that you are the man to see for one of these gadgets. Are you? The man to see? Understand?"

Mage looked at him nervously. "I actually don't know what you mean. It sounds to me like you're in the wrong store. Maybe try the medical supply place up the street."

The man paused, looked at his partner, and turned back to Mage slowly. "Well, that is a disappointing response, son, because my sources tell me that you are just the guy to help us." The man cracked his knuckles, continuing, "It's something my bosses want to see for themselves, and they are very persistent men. So, you're sure you don't have anything that'll do that for us? Upstairs maybe? That yours, too? Maybe in storage up there."

"Look........sir. I don't think we have what you're looking for. I'm sorry, but it's time to close up shop. So, if there is anything else I can get for you, great. If not, you have yourself a good day."

The other fellow removed his mirrored sunglasses, and ambled slowly over to join his partner at the counter. They both looked at Mage with intimidation on their brow. Silence. Mage waited them out, and eventually the two men turned to leave. "You be sure to tell us once you have what we want, won't you?"

Mage's eyes darted around the store nervously. "Sure. Maybe if you leave your number?"

"You won't need it. We'll be back,"

Once the men left, Mage ran to the front and bolted the door shut. *'What the hell was that?'*

He cashed out, then climbed the stairs to check

again on Gramps, who was now sitting up in his bed. Mage made him some seaweed soup and they chatted over a pot of green tea. Once his grandfather had eaten what he could, Mage offered to stay for awhile but was sent on his way. Gramps said he was just going back to bed, anyway.

Satisfied, Mage headed down to the back alley, pulled on his helmet, and mounted his crotch rocket. He pulled out, and steered for home........ well, for the mansion, anyway. Within seconds, the black sedan again appeared directly behind him. Mage noticed them this time. Through its tinted windows, Mage could make out his 'customers' in the front seat. Turning his bike down Main Street, he gunned it as he cut through Chinatown, before spinning a 180 at the end of the street. A simple move for his bike, for sure, but on the one lane, slick brick roads of Gastown, it would be far more challenging for his pursuers. Cutting west, Mage jumped a curb, and slipped through a walkway into Blood Alley, stained by butchers of old. He pulled out the other side street where his pursuers had very little chance of intercepting him again. Dodging in and out of rush hour traffic, he lost them for good.

When his adrenaline slowly ebbed to normal, he came to the realization that he was clearly famished. He hadn't eaten all day, except to test the temperature of Gramps's soup. So, he pulled off to pick up some Thai takeout for the whole crew on his way home. By the time he pulled onto Song's street, he once again saw the black sedan across the street from the mansion gates, idling quietly. *'The bastards beat me home. They're where I work, they're where I live. Not good!'*

Tang was in the garage as Mage pulled in, scowling as usual. He still hadn't warmed up to Song's paramour in the months since New Year's. Standing with him was a shortish, slim man Mage had spotted once or twice, but not yet met. *'Bobby....... something,'* he was told. Tang was a mountain, in comparison.

He pulled the bike right up to them, shut it down, and simply stood to disengage himself. His legs were far longer than the bike was tall. But as tall as he was, it was Tang that had always loomed larger, as intimidating as a vulture. But this was important. *'So what if he doesn't like me. He'll know what to do.'*

An awkward moment passed when the slim gentleman stepped forward, extended his hand. And said, "Hi, I'm Bobby. Great to finally meet you. Tang has talked so much about you."

"Well, that can't be a good thing. Hi, I'm Mage. And Tang hasn't told me about you at all. But then again, he doesn't usually talk to me anyway."

"Welcome to our little shack, Mage," Bobby said with a smile.

"Oh, so, you live here too?"

"I do now. Moved in full time a couple of months ago."

"How do we live in the same house for months, and not meet?"

"You've gotta admit. It's a pretty big house. Tang keeps me hidden away."

"Robert lives with me," Tang told Mage. "He is my... boyfriend." Bobby waved and smiled.

"Oh! Okay. Cool."

"Cool," Tang said, coolly. "Mr. Moon. Are you bothering us for a reason?"

"Oh, uh, yeah! Kinda important, actually. And I'm Mage, not Mr. Moon...... please."

"Spit it out, man!"

"Okay. Well, um, I guess I'm being followed."

"Followed? Followed by whom, Mr. Moon...... Mage?"

"I have no idea. That's why I've come to you. 'Cause you'd know what to do."

Tang nodded in acknowledgement. "Tell me everything."

And so Mage did. He told them about the thugs visiting the shop in the afternoon. Then about being followed by them after work, losing them, and finally finding them parked across the street when he got home.

"Why?" was all Tang said in response.

"I don't know, like I said. But it has to have something to do with our project. They were clearly aware of what we've been working on, but how would they even know? And why would they care?" Mage lamented.

"What project?"

"The kids have a music project," answered Bobby. "Remember, I told you about that. Music? Healing?"

Rolling his eyes, Tang grunted, "remind me."

"I swear, he doesn't hear a word I say," Bobby said.

"Okay, Mr. Tang."

"Just Tang, no Mr.," he was corrected.

"Alright. I've been working on a project..... I mean, Jackie and I have been working on a project, to essentially transform music to heal, basically. We've been using recordings the girls made in the music room, where the results are crystal clear. Then we ran those recordings through my program and Jackie's algorithm, and it appears that we've created a process which makes people feel better. The researchers at U.B.C. think it may turn on a human healing gene."

"I didn't know humans had a healing gene."

"We don't. At least, we didn't. We might now."

Tang was skeptical. "How?"

"You know how most people feel better when they're listening to music? We are trying to figure out how, and why, that is, and to exploit it." Mage then recounted the project from its inception, and that they were experimenting with music manipulation.

Needless to say, that Tang was skeptical. "How does that relate to you being followed?"

"The program could be game changer. If it works like we hope, there will be winners and losers. I think maybe these guys have heard about it, and are potentially on the losers' side?"

"I need more."

"Alright. There are two primary languages that are universal in this world, right? Music and mathematics. We are trying to combine the two to create a health app, if you will. We took the pure music recordings of the girls, and ran it through my computer program's algorithm. I was having problems until Jackie solved a math impasse, which appears to allow my algorithms to now fall into place. We transform the sound recordings to octaves above and below a human's capability to hear. We may have succeeded to some extent, but lots of testing still needs to happen. And I mean *lots!*"

Tang scratched his whiskers, and considered what they knew so far. "Why are these men interested in you now then? You say you've had some success. What success? And who knows about it?"

"As I said, the goons in the shop specifically mentioned wanting a 'new unit that heals people', but I don't know who could have even known about it. I mean, the people who live here know. And, Jacks is going to talk to her professors again, so maybe they'll be able to tell us more. I'm hoping they can give us a timeline, also."

"So, there are professors at the university who know of your project?"

"Yeah, I guess. A couple, anyway."

"Jackie's professors. What professors?"

"You'll have to ask Jacks about that. Her Machine Learning prof knows, for sure, and she said he'd shared it with one of the medical researchers on campus. but other than them, there's just Song, Daniel, Jackie and myself. And Bryce. And now Bobby and you."

"Nobody else? You're sure?"

"I think so. I don't know who else could know. I haven't even told my grandfather yet. You can check with Song and Daniel, but I don't think they've talked about it with anyone, either. Its only recently come to fruition."

"So, that's nine or ten people so far," Tang declared. "How bad do you have Song mixed up in this?"

88

"She's not, really. She's been my sounding board, but that's all. I get anxious sometimes, and she hopes to help me with that, but she doesn't know any details. She was the person who told me not to write off Jackie's intelligence, though, just because she was pretty. And without Jackie, there wouldn't be a project at all."

"Okay. The men in the shop know more than they should. To commit to having two men intimidate and follow you shows more than a casual interest. Someone is paying them. So, five of the nine or ten people who know, live here in the compound. That leaves Daniel and two professors."

"Well, I think we can rule out Daniel, too. He doesn't have a vested interest in anything........, except maybe Jackie." Bobby grinned.

"So Jackie told two professors. What about Bryce? What did she tell him?"

"Who knows? But he was pretty sarcastic about it. He could have told anyone. He did say he was going to mention it to his father to share a laugh."

"And who could he have told?"

"I can't say. Anybody, really. Work contacts, perhaps?"

"What does Bryce's father do for a living?"

"Jackie says he owns some mega pharmaceutical company."

"Interesting. We need to understand who may gain, and who may lose. For now, the university professors may gain, and the pharma guy may lose. I'll start with those. But, from now on, we must be tight-lipped. Jackie doesn't talk with her professors, and Bryce doesn't talk to his father."

"Yeah? Good luck with Bryce. He doesn't come with a mute button."

"Then be careful what you tell him. Information lock down, understood?" Tang contemplated the variables quietly before further advising, "the men at the shop are using intimidation tactics, and should not be discounted. However, if they wanted to be aggressive, they could have harmed you when you were alone at the shop, or approached you outside our gates. So, we will be prudent for now. Everyone stays within the compound."

Mage left the garage, headed down to the music room, and climbed into his computer chair. Something looked different than the way he usually left it. He had an anxious feeling. The screen also displayed a hacking alert, indicating someone had tried to access his computers remotely. Checking further, he determined that they'd gotten past the standard firewall, but his own, self-designed system reported the attack, and had securely closed off the hacker's options. Thank goodness he was Mage the Magician when it came to electronics.

He then noticed his monitor also displayed the project's file, still open, which was odd. If the hacker hadn't been able to get in remotely, there's no way he could have left the file open like this. And, since Mage always closed everything up before shut down, he wouldn't have left it this way. It was a habit. That meant only someone within the house able could have accessed it directly like this, but that couldn't be right. He chastised himself instead for forgetting this time, and he checked the 'recent' registers to be sure. They also indicated someone had been there, at his workstation, on his laptop.

To be safe, he shut everything down completely, unplugged the wi-fi, his computer, the sine wave generator, his sound board, and then disconnected all of their cables.

Satisfied he was now as secure as he could be for the moment, his mind drifted to a more pressing topic - food! He *still* hadn't eaten anything that day. Returning to the garage, he found the big load of Thai takeout still on the ground beside his bike. Since there was certainly plenty for everyone, he knocked on Tang and Bobby's door, inviting them up for vittles. Bobby thought it was a delightful idea, and even Tang couldn't think of an excuse in time.

"Just one sec.," said Bobby, dashing from the room on a quest. "There's something I need to bring."

Mage took the opportunity to inform Tang of the hack attempt. "I think someone's been into my computer system, and not just remotely. I found a remote hack attempt which my security programs blocked, as well as someone working direct from my laptop. Just now, I found the project's file open on my monitor, which I never do. The register indicates someone has been into the project files, and did it directly from my workstation here inside the mansion. It seems unlikely, but the register doesn't lie. Something's not right, and I thought you should know."

Tang grudgingly nodded to acknowledge the boy. "You did right."

When Bobby rejoined them, Mage led he and Tang up the staircase, where they were greeted like the kings of hunter gatherers, proud providers of a bounteous feast. The girls had clearly been into the wine already, so when Bobby pulled a couple of champagne bottles from behind his back, the cheers returned.

Sidling up to her beau, Song teased melodically, "There he is. My conquering hero!" She jumped into Mage's arms, wrapped her legs around him tight, and planted a soft, sensual kiss on his lips. "Hello, Lover."

"Well, hello to you too, whoever you are," Mage replied with a grin, earning another punch to his shoulder.

"Jackie tells me congratulations are in order with the project!" sang Song.

"Yeah, about that."

"Dinner first," demanded Jackie, absconding with the Thai takeout. "Wait, why is this cold?" she asked the hunter gatherers.

"My fault," admitted Mage. "I had a couple of things to deal with when I got home from work, and forgot it in the garage."

"No worries, this will just take a jiffy in the microwave."

When everyone was seated and dishing out their plates, Mage announced, "We need to talk to you guys about something."

To an increasingly attentive audience, Mage spelled out how his day went at the shop, and how he'd being grilled about the project. He told of being followed after work, his escape through Blood Alley, and how his pursuers were across from the mansion when he got home. He then had detailed a report to Tang, along with his suspicions about the hack attempts.

"Are you saying one of us is behind this?" Jackie asked, defensively.

"No," answered Tang, picking up the ball. "We're saying we need more information. Until then, you stay home and talk to no one about the project. Especially you, Jackie."

"Why me, especially?" she asked, more defensive than ever.

"You've added a few unknown variables. More people means more risk. Until we know *which* people, we lay low."

"But I have an appointment with my professors tomorrow. What do I tell them? Or Bryce?"

"You don't go. You say nothing."

"That's ridiculous. My professors are trying to help us?"

"No talking to Bryce, either. Perhaps his father's pharmaceutical companies are worried about losing sales. And as for the professors, research opportunities could develop into lucrative, new treatment options. It is also possible that Bryce's father's local company would have close contact with the university's medical researchers."

"That's unfair! What about Daniel? Or Bobby? No offence, Bobby." He waved it off. "They are all 'variables' too, aren't they?"

"We may be able to identify the men in Mage's store. I have contacts with access to traffic cams in the area, and we may identify them through their licence plates. If so, we should have actionable intel within days. And we will look at everyone, Jackie. But, until the threat is contained, you all stay home and quiet. Understood?"

"You're such a buzzkill," Bobby accused Tang. "Here these girls were, enjoying a nice bottle of wine, until you came along."

"I did not create the problem, Robert."

"You didn't have to scare them, either."

They were definitely shaken. Jackie felt accused, and Song felt fear for Mage. "What in the hell is going on?" Song asked, first rhetorically, and then literally.

"That's what I'm going to find out."

The next day, Jackie crossed the campus in a daze, with her head down, engrossed in her own thoughts. She heard no songbirds today.

Everything was getting so weird, so fast. She'd have skipped class as ordered by Tang, but she had an important term paper due in her Data Mining course. She knew Tang wouldn't be pleased, but she wasn't going to write off a whole term of work for the sake of one missed assignment. It was going to be tricky, though. Her plan was to hand it in and scoot right back out, but so much for that idea. The moment she entered the lecture hall, her professor pounced, herding her away, into a corner.

"Uh, hi doc. Here's my paper." She could see that he, too, was jittery. He kept looking over her shoulders, checking the doors. It didn't take a data mining expert to know something was wrong.

"Jackie, we need to talk about your project, right now."

*'Oh great!'* she thought. *'The one thing I'm not supposed to do.'*

"We're going to have to postpone it, I think. Things have gone crazy around here. That friend I have that's looking at your project? He's vanished since I gave it to him. He hasn't shown up for class and nobody can reach him on his cell. His wife has officially reported him as missing. What's going on, Jackie? Do you know? His neighbours said some men had forcibly loaded him into a black sedan. The police have been around asking questions, and the subject of your project was broached."

"I'm sorry, professor," Jackie said, nervously scanning the lecture hall herself. "I'm not really allowed to talk about it."

"You aren't allowed to talk about it?" he cried. Then, quieting to a whisper, spitting through his teeth. "What do you mean you can't talk about it? Jesus! What's going on? Do I have to worry? Am I next?"

"I'm sorry, professor. I've gotta go. I shouldn't be here." She forced her assignment into his hands before bolting for the door. Scooting across campus towards her car, she fumbled for her keys. Across the lot, she noticed a black sedan idling, with two men in front, just like Mage had described. They were looking straight at her. *'Oh, God. They're following me, too?'*

Jackie was petrified, and dropped her keys. She was a worrier by nature, and this threw her into a panic. She scooped them up, tried to slide her key into the door lock, and dropped them again. Finally inside, she started the car, jammed it into reverse too soon, causing her old car to lurch and stall. Saucer-eyed, she twisted the ignition again, and sped off campus. The sedan pulled in directly behind her. *'Oh, my God. Oh, my God! What should I do?'*

"Probably not panic," she said aloud. When Mage had lost them yesterday, they were just waiting at the mansion anyway, so what was the point of racing home? Instead, she fought back her nerves, allowing them to follow her all the way back to the compound. The sedan sat outside the gates, but kept its distance. *'They can't intimidate me!'* she vowed to herself, despite visibly shaking. *'I am not whitewater; I am a calm, flowing river. Breathe in through the nose and out through the mouth, Jackie.'*

She pulled through the mansion's gates a nervous wreck until safely through the second one. She sighed aloud, knowing Tang was would be there. But now, she had to go poke the bear. She'd briefly considered keeping it all to herself, so Tang wouldn't berate her for leaving the compound just to hand in a term paper. But, she knew he had to know, and though she knew he'd be mad, she sucked it up and went in search of him.

Tang was in the farthest back part of the property by the golf course, checking wall-top cameras. He could see she was visibly shaking, her beautiful face creased with concern. She relayed her brief story, and despite his eyes boring into her with his fearful stare, to his credit, he didn't berate her.

"Are you okay, Jackie?" was all he said.

She fell into his big arms, weeping, saying, "No I

don't think so. Not yet."

Tang held her for a time before escorting her back up to the music room. He knew her well enough now to understand that when she was this upset, she would need to play. Music was her solace. Maybe Mage was right. Perhaps music *did* have charms to tame the savage beast.

Surprisingly, the young 'magician' was not behind his soundboards and mixing equipment. He too went AWOL on Tang that morning, but the cat wasn't out of the bag on that count yet. He'd been worried about Gramps being alone, and needed to check on him, regardless of Tang's orders. And he especially wanted to take a copy of the healing songs to see if he could perk the old guy up. His grandfather hadn't looked good the last time Mage had seen him, and regardless of what else was going on in his life, he had to do right by his grandfather. He'd deal with Tang's wrath later.

Mage had headed to the shop early for another workday. Early enough to dodge Tang, and he'd have a chance to talk with his grandfather for awhile. He had a plan,

He kept an eye on his bike's rear mirror, but couldn't see anyone following him. He changed lanes and turned several corners, but saw nothing. *'They must have made their point,'* he thought to himself.

When he arrived, Gramps was sleeping soundly, but seemed frail. *'He looks a decade older,'* he thought sadly. He decided to wait until later for their chat, and let Gramps sleep. But before going downstairs, Mage hooked up the healing recording to play in a loop, over and over. It was worth a try, poor old guy. The shop was slow, and the day uneventful, but Mage perked up in the late morning when his phoned chimed with a text from Song.

"Picnic today." the phone read. "Meet u in shop @ closing time." Mage grinned as his boring day just got better. Song had been harassing him about a trip to Stanley Park, but he'd been shrugging it off. But today, the sun was back, and he thought, *'Why not?'* He punched "K" into his phone, and smiled at how seamlessly she had slipped into his life. Girlfriends of the past felt like work, but never Song.

At lunch, he went up to his grandfather's apartment above, and sitting there bright-eyed was Gramps, with some green tea he'd made himself. They chatted idly but happily about the shop and life at the mansion. Mage didn't bring up the goons from the day before, though. There was no point in causing unnecessary anxiety. But, he did succeed in making sure Gramps had some hot soup and toast for lunch.

Mage took the opportunity to broach what he thought would be a touchy subject, and asked his grandfather to come to live at the mansion. He had recently realized with astonishment that Gramps was approaching his 80th birthday. That was hard to reconcile, given the lifetime of strength and vitality taekwondo had provided him. But this past week Mage's last relative in the world had revealed an unfamiliar frailty. And if Tang wanted them in lock down, Gramps was going to be there with them at the mansion. At their picnic, he'd talk to Song about moving Gramps in, but already knew she'd love the idea.

He'd felt guilty, of course, being gone so much. And if Tang had his way, it would only get worse, so now was the time. He had expected resistance, since Gramps had lived at that location for so many decades, but the old guy actually sounded excited by the prospect. Mage had told many stories of the mansion, and the thought of living in the lap of luxury sounded quite nice for a change. He'd never been in a mansion before.

The shop could have closed long ago, but it had been something in common between Gramps and his son, and after the accident, between him and his grandson. So, he kept it going, despite his age. It had always been his wish that his son would take over the shop someday, and now hoped it to be Mage. It had taken longer for the boy to mature than he thought it would. It was a tragedy that it took a tragedy to accomplish that.

Those had been dark days, when Mage's parents died. Gramps felt sure he'd have to shut down without the help his son in the shop, but Mage had stepped up in a big way after the crash. The computer parts and repair service he'd implemented had put the shop back in the black, and Gramps knew he no longer need worry about the boy. Especially now that he'd found himself that pretty, little rich girl. She was a gem. A mansion? Yes, that was fine.

100

That aforementioned gem bounded into the shop at closing time carrying a classic, woven picnic basket, topped with a red and white checkered cloth. As soon as she walked in, her energy raised the light level of the room by a few lumens. They both said goodbye to Gramps and donned their helmets. They sped off with her gripping him fiercely with one arm, and the picnic basket with the other. It was rush hour, but Mage wove his motocross bike effortlessly through the traffic, exiting into Stanley Park within minutes.

Mage had always loved its thousand acre respite in the heart of the city, and the seawall that surrounded it. He drove Song around the shore before pulling up at a quiet, grassy spot behind Lost Lagoon. They lay back upon the red and white checkered cloth, holding hands and gazing up at the evening sky. Below them in the lagoon, regal swans gracefully floated by, their heads held high and haughty. Minutes ago, the young lovers had been inundated with the noise of the city, and now heard just the call of the loons.

"This is a really beautiful spot, baby."

"Thanks. I'm glad I could get a reservation on such short notice," Mage replied.

"You had to make a reservation, did you?"

"Sure did."

"Well done, my love. And, it's also supposed to be a beautiful sunset tonight."

101

"Yep. Ordered that too."

"Wow. You must really know people in this town."

"Oh yeah. Me and Lord Stanley go way back. He keeps telling me he's gonna bring his cup over, but it never seems to get here."

"Is that so? That must be hard for you."

"Yeah, it's been fifty years, and he still hasn't come through. It just might be time to take him off my Christmas card list."

"Oooohh, you really play hardball."

"Yep. Hockey's a tough sport, eh."

"Well, a big, tough man such as yourself must get hungry sometimes."

"I reckon. Whatcha got in that there pic-a-nic basket, Boo Boo?"

"Whaaaaaat?"

"Don't tell me you don't know Yogi Bear."

"Oh. No. I've heard of him, but he was banned when I was a kid in China."

"Now you're joking, right?"

"True story. My mom forced my dad to buy grey market versions, though. They weren't legal, but the laws weren't enforced much, either. So, you might say I'm smarter than the average........ panda."

"Okay, panda-monium, enough with the jokes. Where's that grub?"

"Hungry as a bear, are we?"

"As a grizzly. Now, feeeeeed, meeeeee!" and he roared the most fearsome of roars.

"Be good now, or I'll send you to your cave to hibernate."

"A months-long sleep sounds great right now."

"Then here. Eat this. It should bring your energy level up." She handed Mage a monstrous, triple-decker clubhouse-style sandwich, six inches tall, with turkey and bacon and cheese overflowing its boundaries.

"Whoa! That's a Yogi size sandwich, for sure!" and he roared again. "What's in that big thermos?"

"I'm not sure. Let's have a look."

"You don't know what's in your own thermos?"

Song poured some into a paper cup, announcing, "Wine. It's white wine."

"Let me guess. Bobby prepared the pic-a-nic

basket?"

"He insisted, once he heard of my plan."

"And just how did you both get this plan past Mage?"

"Subterfuge and trickery."

"Uh huh."

"And he was busy with Jackie, so she basically ran interference without me even asking."

After the big sandwiches and Bobby's Nanaimo bars for dessert, Song and Mage laid back again, pointing their overstuffed bellies toward the heavens.

"It's a beautiful sunset, baby. Thanks for ordering it."

"Yep. No problemo, little lady. Stick with me and you'll see sights you ain't never seen before. Yep. A beautiful spot for a beautiful lady," he said, pulling her in for a wet, noisy smooch. Neither of them had ever truly been in love before, and every day seemed better than the last. It really was like heaven on Earth, if Earth was made strictly of endorphins and hormones, that is. Everyone remembers their first true love, and this was that bliss for the both of them.

"It's so romantic, baby."

"Yep. Ordered that too." Song snuggled in but

was quickly rebuked. "Whoa there, pretty lady. That there wine is takin' its toll. I'm going to have to reconnoitre a little boys room."

"Nooooo, don't go," Song whined, groping for his arm as he stood.

"There's nothin' to be done for it, little lady. Stay here and guard the swans," he said, and off he went.

As he walked back from the loo, Mage thought again about his grandfather, and reminded himself to talk to Song about moving him to the mansion. She'd be okay with it. He was a lucky man, and wondered to himself whether he should marry this girl. Already, he'd become accustomed to seeing her every day, and now couldn't see a day without her. And with Song, they would have the financial freedom to live any life they chose.

Daydreaming of years to come together, he beamed a smile in Song's direction. But, the red and white checkered blanket was bare. He looked around, confused for a moment. The adrenaline kicked in when heard her scream. Across the field, he spotted her being carted away by the two men from the shop. They were too far away to catch on foot, so he mounted his motocross bike as he donned his helmet in one smooth motion. Ignoring the paths and roads, he tore straight across the field directly at Song's assailants, launching a flurry of seagulls into the air.

Mage raced up a berm, launching his bike right into the parking lot near the sedan. He spun toward the closest man, purposely skidding into him with the bike. The man fell, with the bike landing right on top of him, burning his face on its exhaust pipes. Without a conscious thought, all of his taekwondo lessons kicked in effortlessly. A single quick kick to the chin rocked the second man, who tripped over, and landed on his partner in crime. Song managed to break free while Mage took it to the two men, repeatedly. Speed, youth and dexterity were on his side, and each time one assailant came to their feet, he flattened them again, all without taking a single blow. Song lifted the bike upright, allowing Mage to scramble on as she leapt behind him.

"Wow, pretty impressive, baby. Can we go now?"

"Yep. I'll be your Uber driver for the evening."

Abandoning their blanket, picnic basket and helmets, they tore once again across the grass, avoiding the street and pathways. But the two men had quickly recovered and were once again in dogged pursuit. Their sedan floundered and bounced, tearing up large strips of sod from the field. Mage yelled for Song to "Hang on!" as he spun the bike around, back the way they came. He once again guided his bike up a steep berm and sailed right over the top of the sedan in the opposite direction. Now heading into the park traffic the wrong way, he wove his bike through the oncoming traffic like a slalom skier.

The men in the black sedan were nothing if not stubborn, and continued the chase. They took advantage of a break in the oncoming traffic and used it to gun the sedan and closed on their prey. The bike had the manoeuvring advantage but the sedan had more power. Mage took a quick swing into a field causing the pursuers to carom over a curb, flatten a tire and lose a hubcap which rolled lazily down the road.

Incredibly, the men managed to swerve close behind once again, and proved far too persistent for Mage's liking. Song gripped his waist like a vise as he turned the bike hard down a narrow path leading towards the water, and when the pursuers tried to follow, the flat tire's hub sprayed a shower of sparks into the bushes as it left the road. Song heard a loud crash and turned to see the men unable to exit the steaming vehicle, with both doors pinned closed by trees.

Once clear, Mage slowed right down and took as many back roads as possible en route to the mansion. There was no way that sedan was going to make it back this time. Once home, nothing looked amiss. They entered the gates and parked down in the garage without incident.

"Safe at home!" Song announced with relief.

"Maybe....... but then again, maybe not so much," Mage replied. "Not feeling very safe over here right now." An irate Tang was bearing down on him, and Mage recognized that the goons in the shop hadn't been nearly so intimidating. He went straight at Mage, who deftly side-stepped Tang's advance. The big man made another attempt, but Mage again eluded him cleanly. Tang was genuinely taken aback. He'd regularly subdued any man he chose, but this young punk had slipped away twice, untouched?

Enraged, he yelled instead. "What did I say about leaving the compound? 'Stay here to be safe', I said."

"Sorry, Tang. No disrespect. My grandfather needed me." Glancing at Song for support, Mage continued. "I'd been watching for the goons all day until the shop closed, all with no problems. And we had already been in the park relaxing for more than an hour. I guess I let my guard down."

Tang turned his wrath on Song, and demanded, "Who said you could go to a park?"

"I did," Song said coolly.

Recognizing she was probably the more formidable opponent, he turned back to Mage. "You let your guard down?" Tang demanded. "You let.......What the hell happened, boy?"

Song interrupted, raising her voice slowly from pianissimo to forte.

"It was my idea to go for a picnic today Tang, not Mage's. If you want to yell at somebody, yell at me! Ever since I was a child, nobody would let me leave the compound, I was like a prisoner in my home. 'For your own good,' you all said. Well, forgive me for trying to have a life!" she fumed. "It was just supposed to be a picnic, Tang!", and she fled inside, weeping and ragged from the evening's events.

The two men regarded each other quizzically, equally shocked. She'd hadn't erupted like that since

New Years. Who knew little Song had a tiger inside her?

After she was gone, Tang asked again, quietly, "What happened, boy?"

So Mage explained about his sick grandfather, and why he had to leave the compound. Then, how Song had led him astray on a picnic after work, and how she'd disappeared after dinner in the park.

"I took one of them out with my bike, and I drop kicked the other a few times. One of them burned their face on my exhaust pipe. While they were down, Song righted the bike, we both climbed on and bolted across the field. The goons tried to follow as I pulled onto the park road, so I 180'd the bike to head into oncoming traffic. Easier for us to maneuver through than them. We heard a crash, but they were still coming, so I pulled onto one of the paths leading down to the seawall. This time they couldn't follow. The path was too narrow. We escaped and I brought Song home. They're not getting that sedan unstuck for awhile, and the one guy is likely headed to the hospital anyway. It was hairy, but in the end, Song and I came out of it intact."

Tang's eyes widened in surprise. He really hadn't expected that from the kid. His face relaxed and softened a bit. Then he nodded in, what, begrudging respect?

"Thank you," he said to Mage, who was actually touched by the gesture. "I'll get my contacts to check hospitals in the area for anyone matching their description." Then the old Tang roared back.

"Tell everyone, they are to stay within the walls of the compound. No exceptions this time. Do not test me. Stay inside the mansion, or in the back by the pool, or the golf course, or wherever you like, as long as you remain inside the walls of the protected compound. Not outside the walls. Inside. No cars outside. Inside. Call Daniel and get him here now. Once he arrives, I'm locking the garage.

"Don't call Bryce." Tang added. One of Jackie's professors has gone missing, and I suspect Bryce's father knew the researcher from past dealings. If you are indeed successful with your project, the father's financial losses could be substantial. And money is almost always behind these private, covert operations."

# *Chapter 7*

*"See deep enough, and you see musically".*

**Thomas Carlyle**

"It was pretty scary at school today." Jackie lamented. "First, my professor demanded answers when I tried to hand in my term paper. The colleague he shared the project with has vanished. And then, when I was headed back to my car, I saw your friends in the black sedan in the parking lot. It totally freaked me out. I was so nervous, I dropped my keys twice before I finally sped out of the parking lot. Then I remembered you say they already knew where we lived, so I slowed down and tried to be cool. They tailed me the whole way, and I've never been so glad to see Tang's face. He was pissed at me for breaking his curfew, but he didn't say it. He was awesome. But now, I hear you and Song were tailed, as well?"

"Looks like it. That, or they put a tracker on my bike. No sign of them at the shop today, and I didn't see anyone following us after work. Song kidnapped me for a picnic in the park, and it was really great. But, when I was coming back from a pee, they were loading Song into the sedan. So, I took them out, we scrambled onto the bike, and took off across the grass."

"You 'took them out', did you?"

"Yeah, well, I guess I did," Mage responded, humbly. "You know, a motocross jump and some taekwondo. They followed us across the field, crashed in some traffic, then followed us down a narrow pathway to the ocean. It wasn't wide enough for them, and the sedan got boxed in by trees. We won't be seeing that sedan again. It's a write-off."

"Oh, my God! Is Song a mess?"

"Yeah, she's a bit shaken, but tougher than you'd think. But you should have seen her lambaste Tang when he was castigating me for not following his orders. I'm not sure who was more surprised, him or me; Tang, because she rarely loses it like that, or me because I'd never seen *him* so astonished. He couldn't have closed his mouth if he tried."

"Tang seems tough, but he's a teddy bear inside."

"If you say so. For me, still a wee bit intimidating. I'd just as soon avoid a confrontation with that bear. But, you can count us as his captives for the foreseeable future. He's never going to let us out of those gates again."

"After today, I can't say I *want* to be out there. I was petrified."

"I bet."

"I should go check on Song. What are you up to later?"

"Daniel's coming over to work on the project again. The app is performing really well, and we haven't poked a hole in the theory yet. Tonight, we are testing different song types to see what changes, if anything. And Tang says Daniel has to move in for awhile. I hope that's okay."

"I suppose I could live with that," she replied with a demure smile.

"He's bringing his guitar this time and says he has a perfect song for the project. While he is staying here, he wants to record it with you girls. He sounded like an excited little boy."

"Yeah, I love that," Jackie said, then blushed inexplicably.

"Yeah, Daniel's a great guy. He brings 'happy' with him everywhere. He can light up a room, just like you, Jacks. Just in a different way. You light it up with your beauty. He lights it up with his joy."

"Oh, pshaw." Jackie joked, a bit flustered at the compliment, but unconsciously nodding her head about Daniel. "He told me he was genuinely proud to be a friend of Mage the Magician, electronic genius extraordinaire."

"The feeling is mutual. He may look goofy with that perma-grin, but he has the heart of a lion."

"Yeah.......,' Jackie sighed, unsure whether she said it out loud, or not.

113

Daniel arrived post-haste and joined the others in the music room. His usual smile was pasted on his face, and when she saw Jackie, it got wider. "Hey Jacks. You're looking especially gorgeous tonight. Is that a new blouse? It looks new. Is it new? Well, it looks hot either way. You do, I mean." Jackie actually blushed. The blouse in question was a plain, white t-shirt.

"Hey Daniel," interrupted Mage. "You know that algorithm we've been working on? Look at this. Look at the way Jackie's adjustments affect it."

It had been a few days since Daniel had been around, and he hadn't been brought up-to-date lately. He studied the computer screen, asking, "Okay, what am I looking at? The same app as before? But...... Holy Crap! Is it working?"

"As far as I can tell."

"Like, completely?"

"As far as I can tell."

"That's awesome, dude! Totally!"

"Could never have done it without Jackie's insight. Her 'eureka moment' was remarkable in its simplicity. Inspired, actually."

"That's Jacks, alright," Daniel grinned. "Gorgeous *and* smart!" Jackie was blushing again!

"I've run it several times, and it appears stable.

And if Jackie's professor's comments about his sick mother's recovery is true, this needs testing. A lot of testing. We need patients of all kinds to discern the project's effectiveness. It needs to go to a proper lab setting next."

Jackie broke in, "that may not be easy to do if my professors are any indication. It seems likely to me that either the profs were behind the goons, or Bryce's dad was. Or both. But, scientists don't much like the idea of disappearing, and rumours of abduction would keep a lot of research labs out of the mix. And even if they do study it, a lot of pressure could be leveraged to skew the results"

"Abductions? What abductions?" asked Daniel.

"We've got a lot to catch you up on, bud."

"Bring it on!"

"Let me show you first what happens when I run it." The computer drive whirred away before displaying a page with eight musical staffs – four treble and four bass. "OK, so Jackie made the suggestion to go with a base 8 numbering system, it followed that 8 staffs were worth a try. These represented eight octaves, shown here as four treble clefs and four bass clefs. These are *not* continuous scales like on a piano, but are separated by ten octaves, which is how many octaves humans can hear. The four treble clefs here represent the first four octaves *above* human's ability to hear. The four bass clefs represent the first four scales *below* human hearing. Clear so far?

"Okay," he went on. "So now let's introduce an actual song into the program. I've been using this recording of you girls, but in theory, this program should work for any song, anywhere. Now, we direct the music file into the treble and bass clefs I just showed you. See how they all mirror the original recording's notes."

"Got it," confirmed Daniel, nodding at Jackie, ever the intellectual.

"Okay," Mage continued. "Now this is where the magic happens. I adapted my original algorithms from old base ten programs to Jackie's base eight theory. Now, when I press play for the song, you can see the program reading and playing the music note by note, but we can hear nothing, right? Anybody hear anything?" he asked, and they each shook their hears no.

"And the piece de resistance, voila! " His monitor showed all eight silent octaves melding down into one single wave on the oscillator. "You see how eight become one? That 'one' wave is at 65 Hz, the same frequency as purring cats, which is good."

He seemed very excited, but the others weren't really catching on. "I see you have trouble believing my theory. You can't hear it. I get that. Which is why we need to do testing. So, my guinea pigs, now that you've all 'heard' the song without hearing it, I want you all to report the slightest sign of illness. I don't care if its just a runny nose. We need to know of any failures with any illnesses, to see if we can duplicate them. We also need to see how many applications it takes to become effective, if at all."

Jackie asked, "How do we find enough patients? And how do we get it to different places in the world like Africa? The sick? The poor? The healthy and the wealthy?"

"Not sure yet. Maybe use the World Health Organization, if it shows any promise."

"You know you're brilliant, right?" Jackie asked Mage.

"Hey, I'm brilliant too!" Daniel whined.

"Yes, you are brilliant too," Jackie assured him as she would a small child.

"I knew it! Woohoo! Jacks thinks I'm brilliant, Song!"

"I say we celebrate everyone's brilliance!" Song cried. "Let's make some new music!" Daniel pulled out his guitar to join the girls for the first time. Mage set up to record while Song rosined up her bow, Jackie ran scales and Daniel tuned his guitar.

"So, what are we going to play?" asked Jackie.

"I've got one," Daniel told them. "This UHF song is perfect for the project. It's called 'When I Sing", and about about music makes you feel better."

"Cool theme," Mage joked. "I think I've heard that somewhere before."

"Ladies, it's in E major, 4/4 time. It starts slow for eight bars and changes to jaunty after that. After the first chorus, there's a 32 bars of scat. Harmonize with me."

"Jaunty?" Jackie teased.

"Yeah, jaunty. You'll see. You can pick it from there, alright? Here goes............"

With a slow strum of his guitar, Daniel began the lyrics on the song's very first note. Just four bars in, Jackie and Song regarded each other in disbelief. Daniel was good! Really good. Who knew?

***(Actual recording by U.H.F. here - https://www.youtube.com/watch?v=UrI6lSTvjFY)***

After he'd sung the final bass note, Jackie exclaimed, "Whoa, Daniel, That was so much fun. So awesome." A fake cheer went up from Song and Mage, with him doing his famous Kermit the Frog imitation.

"Thanks guys."

Mage added, "that's definitely the song were going to release the app with! Nice to see the project provided you with some inspiration. That's an awesome song."

"Thanks, bud." Daniel stole a look at Jackie, who was beaming at him with what only could be described as pride. It was the best feeling he'd ever had.

"Play it again. You girls can add harmonies this time."

And so it was. Within a few takes, they had nailed the song down, and were pleased with the results.

"That's so cool, Daniel," enthused Mage, removing his headphones. "Feeling better through music. What could be more appropriate? I applied the algorithm as you guys were laying down that final take, So, basically, the app is ready. We're done."

"So happy for you, baby. But, I'm done, too," Song declared. "It's been a heck of a day."

"Well, you're right about that," agreed Mage. "I could use some sleep, too."

"Not so fast, my handsome hero. As a reward for saving my life today, I'm going to show you a little humanitarian project of my own."

"Is that right?"

"It is. And, my project will also make you feel much better, without needing music at all."

"Is that right?"

"It is. Care to sample?" Song teased.

Mage raised one eyebrow, then stood, saying, "Look at the time! I guess we're heading to bed, folks."

He faked a melodramatic yawn which morphed into a real one at its apex. "I'm going to, you know, check out Song's..... samples. See you guys tomorrow." Arm in arm, the musician and the magician ascended the plush stairs to the master suite.

That left just Daniel and Jackie in the music room. Feeling a bit awkward, he looked away and coughed. Twice. She found his nervousness so completely endearing. Silence wasn't his strong suit, and he found himself blurting, "So, how's Bryce?" before he immediately chastised himself. *'Stupid! Stupid!'*

Jackie let him squirm for a moment, enjoying his comic discomfort. "Bryce won't be coming around anymore."

"Huh. Like, at all?"

"Like at all."

Daniel's face lit up for a moment, before he could reign it in. "Oh, uh, that's too bad, Jackie. Are you okay?"

"Yeah, I'm perfectly okay. He's known it's been coming for a long time. We haven't been intimate for months. And I'm pretty sure he or his father had something to do with the hack of Mage's computer. He almost boasted about it in our final call. He was spitting angry with me, but I found that I couldn't have cared less. Any feelings I had for him are long gone."

Daniel's smile betrayed his sombre response. "I'm

sorry to hear that, Jacks."

"Yeah, I can see that. You're all broken up about it. It's okay. I'm not broken up about it either. In fact, I've had my eye on a guy for awhile now."

Daniel was crestfallen. "Some guy on campus, I'm guessing."

"Nope. A little closer to home, actually."

"Oh. Okay. A neighbour?"

"Nope. He actually just moved into the mansion. Maybe you know him?" she asked, gracing him with her biggest, brightest smile. The sensuality of it nearly undid the poor guy. He stumbled twice, looking anywhere but at Jackie, like a lost little boy.

"Uhhhh....." was all he managed.

"Say, you just moved in today too, didn't you?"

"Yeah, I guess....."

"So, have you picked a room yet?"

"Uhhhh....., nuh uh."

"Well, I've got one we can share." Jackie whispered. She began walking toward the steel panic room door, winking at Daniel over her shoulder.

Dumbfounded, Jackie got to the third stair before Daniel was sure he wasn't misreading her. But the smoking sensuality she was exuding was impossible to deny. He leapt to his feet, let out a war whoop, and was off in hot pursuit. Very, very hot pursuit.

# *Chapter 8*

*"I have little shame, no dignity – all in the name of a better cause."*

**A.J. Jacobs**

Waking from her slumber, Song's nose could smell bacon and coffee. Her first thought was perhaps Mage got up early to spoil her, but one look at the opposite pillow showed him still softly, snoring away. Donning her robe, she followed her nose down to the kitchen, where she found Bobby cooking away.

"Mmmmm, coffee," she croaked. "Morning, Bobby."

"Greetings, fair maiden. You look radiant this morning."

"Not feeling radiant. Whatcha up to? And why are you cooking breakfast up here today?"

"Well, its not exactly breakfast, but Tang is still snoozing and I didn't want to wake him up."

"So, you came up here just to wake us up?"

"Yup, sure did. Bacon and coffee. I know how to get you out of bed." Indeed he did. "Plus, my oven is already baking stuff, so I came up here to use yours."

"What's the occasion? Surely, Tang is not allowing us visitors."

"Tang doesn't know about any of this yet. It's a surprise. I had a brainstorm last night. Ever since those goons showed up, Tang hasn't relaxed. None of you have. So, I've decided you all need a day of forced relaxation."

"You mean he relaxes?"

"You'd be surprised what you don't know about Tang."

"I hear that. I grew up with him around all my life, but didn't even know he was gay. And, I really couldn't tell you much about his past."

"Tang is a different man down in our little bungalow below. At least he usually is, but since there's been trouble, he's been unable to relax at all. Everyone else in the house has been a little uptight too, and I'm tired of the worried faces. So, I decided to do something about it."

"Uh huh. And you decided to cook us all breakfast?" Song asked while stealing a piece of bacon. Bobby quickly smacked her hand, admonishing, "That's not for breakfast. None of this cooking and baking is for breakfast."

"You mean to say you've woken me with coffee and bacon under false pretenses?"

124

"Yup. You can have some coffee, though."

"Well, it's good to know I can have coffee in my own kitchen," she teased. "But really, Bobby. Why?"

"Because today is...." he tooted a fanfare, "the First Inaugural Bobby-lympics, of course!"

"You're losing it, Bobby. But, I'll bite. What on Earth is the Bobby-lympics?"

Bobby looked thoughtful, pondering before answering, "It's more of a decathlon, really."

"A decathlon? I still think you're losing it."

"Am I? When Tang had this shack built for your parents, he was told to have lots of entertainment built in, right?" Song nodded. "Well, by my count, there are ten games available to us within the compound. So, today......." he tooted another fanfare, "we have the Bobby-lympics. Ten events. Winner take nothing. Yay!"

"I think I'm gonna need more coffee. But, maybe everyone could use a break. Mage had been asking about throwing a party, but since we're all sequestered, this may be just the thing."

"Everyone in the house will compete in all events," Bobby continued.

"Even Tang? You're going to get him to play games?"

"Hence the name. He can't exactly not compete in an event named after me, now can he?"

As the other inhabitants slowly followed the smell of caffeine, Bobby greeted each in the kitchen, pumped. Strewn across the ceiling now was a long piece of paper towel, emblazoned with 'BOBBY-LYMPICS' scrawled across its length. Mage was not awake enough to show any enthusiasm, but Jackie and Daniel were giddy, and game for anything. Daniel always had a smile on, but today, as he rested his hands on Jackie's thigh, it was permanent. And Jackie, why, she was no different. Her thousand watt smile had gained several thousand lumen overnight. Both looked perky, like they'd been awake for awhile.

Bobby greeted them, "Ladies and gentlemen, boys and girls, welcome to the inaugural Bobby-lym........."

He was interrupted by the arrival of Tang, looked tired and gruff. "What is all this, Robert?" he demanded. "Why are you up here bothering these people?"

"He's no bother," responded Song. " And he is welcome anytime."

"As I was saying before I was so rudely interrupted................. Welcome to the Bobby-lympics, everyone! Now that we are all here, I'll map out our day. Today's athletes will be competing in ten disciplines – Archery, Pistols, Bowling, Tennis, Basketball, Golf, Swimming, Batting, Weightlifting, and the Waterslide Challenge. I think that's all of them. Prizes will be awar........ "

"Well, you kids have fun," interrupted Tang. "I have my rounds to do."

"Not so fast, mister," ordered Bobby. "These are the BOBBY-lympics, did you catch that? You think you can skip a challenge with my name on it? No sir! You are the reason it's being held."

"Me? How is this my fault?" countered Tang.

"It's not your fault. It's in your honour! Okay, here are the rules," and he had actually prepared a sheet for everyone. As they all scanned down, he read them out........."

1) Pistol Accuracy – ten shots, targets are numbered

2) Archery Range – ten shots, same rules as with pistols

3) Bowling – one single game, total points

4) Tennis – single game knockout for championship

5) Basketball – ten shots each from the foul line, sudden death knockout if a tie

6) Golf – three holes, least strokes

7) Swimming – any stroke, one lap there and back, best time

8) Weightlifting – heaviest lift

9) Batting – ten pitches each, total hits

10) Waterslide Challenge – total time to slide down ALL waterslides

.

"Any questions?" Bobby asked.

"Who are the judges?" asked Song.

"I am," he responded. "Bobby-lympics, my rules."

"What about ladies vs. men?" Jackie wondered. "We can't be expected to compete with you guys in stuff like weightlifting."

"Okay. I can see that. Oh, I know! We'll compete as teams, how about that? Mage and Song will be one team, Tang and I will be another team, which leaves Daniel and Jackie. Are you guys okay competing as a couple?"

"Totally!" Daniel cried, perhaps a bit too loud. Then quieter, "totally." And Jackie actually blushed a bit. It had been quite a night!

"Okay then! Let the games begin!" announced

Bobby.

"One question." It was Daniel. "Can we drink while we compete?" Eyebrows raised, he looked to his friends for support.

"It is encouraged. And don't worry about breakfast. I've got plenty of munchies to last the whole day."

"Well, alright then. Let's play!" Daniel cried.

"You guys go ahead. I'll be with you after I take these goodies out of the oven. Why don't you lead everyone to the pistol range."

"Alright, everybody," Daniel cried. "You heard the man. 'Pistols at dawn!' Good idea to have the pistol shoot first, before we all get drunk."

Still in the kitchen, Tang was giving Bobby the evil eye. "What have you got me into, Robert?" he accused.

"Fun. It's called fun, honey. You should really try it once in a while. Now, c'mon!" Bobby marched out, and Tang shuffled sheepishly after him. A cheer rang out for Tang when he arrived at the range.

"Who's first, Bobby?"

"I guess you are, Daniel."

"Cool. I've never actually shot a gun before. Or

seen one myself for that matter."

"Welcome to Canada," teased Jacks.

Headphones were worn by most of them, and the others pushed the heal of their hands over their ear holes, hard. Tang stepped up and advised everyone on gun safety.

Safety glasses in place, Daniel stepped up first, ready to shoot. He looked a bit nervous before flipping the safety off, and ringing out ten shots in quick succession.

"Most people usually just take one shot at a time, for accuracy," Tang advised.

"Yeah, sorry. Got a little excited there."

Mage tapped his friend, whispering, "I hope you didn't shoot all of your bullets as fast last night."
"Which time?" Daniel whispered back.

The first shooter had only managed to hit the target once. But when the last competitor stepped up, Tang hit ten out of ten, all closely grouped. Daniel in particular was duly impressed.

"Good thinking, Bobby." Song said softly. "Putting the pistol range first, which I'm sure you realized he would win."

"Did I? That would have been good thinking, wouldn't it, " he responded with a wink. And indeed,

130

Tang rough exterior had melted away, and was already competing like a kid with the rest of the 'athletes'. "And the winner of the first discipline is....... us! Bobby and Tang."

"It's fixed!", complained Daniel.

After the weightlifting event, Bobby gave his beau a kiss of congratulations in front of everyone. It was Tang's turn to blush, to the astonishment of all. He'd never kissed a man in public before, but it had raised another cheer among his friends. Mage handed him a tequila shooter as a prize. The morning got off with a bang!

Later, several events in, the alcohol had been flowing steadily. The pall Bobby had felt, had disappeared into laughter and frivolity. The Bobby-Lympics was a resounding success, and everyone vowed to make it an annual event. Delivering another tray of canapes, Bobby was like a house mother, and in his glory. Few noticed all of the work Bobby had done, despite competing in all of the events. He brought people pitchers of margueritas, set up a shooter bar, wiped up, swept up, and made sure everyone had sunscreen. Not to mention the cooking he'd done before everyone got out of bed.

Competitors were gathered around the pool as the Swimming races wrapped up. Daniel was at the swim-up bar getting a couple of drinks for he and Jacks. He turned and looked at her across the pool, and couldn't ever remember being so happy. He still had to pinch himself to believe it happened at all, but oh boy, did it happen! People say being in love is like winning the lottery, but he couldn't imagine that mere money could make him feel this good.

"Calling all athletes. Calling all athletes for the final event......." bellowed Bobby. Carrying his clipboard in his hands, he slurred, "Gather around or the final event's rules, you drunken wharf rats."

"Who's winning so far, Bobby?" cried Mage.

"Oh hell, I don't know." he replied, and he threw his clipboard into the pool."Let's just say it's the last event and winner takes all. How about that?

"The final event today is the Waterslide Challenge," he continued. "As you know, there's a waterslide to the pool for each floor. Each couple must travel down each slide from every floor. You can take the elevator back up for all I care, and you can start down any slide you want, as long as you do them all. Total time determines the winner. Ready? Okay, on your marks, get set......" Bobby laughed maniacally as he raced ahead, "GO!"

He led going into the first corner, and made it to the doorway before the others all jammed together into a space too narrow. "I feel like those goons in the sedan, who got jammed inside," Song joked. She got a laugh, but this crowd was serious about this race. Drunken determination was etched on every face. Well, every face but Bobby's, who laughed his way out front.

Each couple darted to a different floor, taking two and three steps at a time. Hitting the first slide, Daniel called to Jackie, "Hey, I like chasing you!"

"Well, you'll never catch me......... Jughead," she teased in return.

"Jughead? Who told you that? Did Mage tell you that, Jacks? Huh, he must have."

"Who's Jacks?" she asked innocently. "Aren't I Betty?" She dove head first down the first tube and was gone. Jughead resumed the chase! As he exited the slide, he couldn't see Jackie anywhere. He tore back inside where he ran smack dab into Song and Mage, sending all three sprawling.

"You guys couldn't find a better place to stop and kiss? Not worried about your time, eh?" He scrambled back to his feet just in time to be struck by a giggling Tang coming in behind them. He reeled back, and fell over the amorous couple again.

Tang leapt over all three and scooted past. He was trying to catch Bobby, wherever the hell he went. Still chuckling madly, he had to admit, Bobby was right. It had been a long time since he'd actually laughed out loud like this. His reasoning took him to the top floor. He didn't want to climb to the top floor later, at the end, when he'd be most tired. There was strategy to consider! Rounding the final corner, right at the top of the pagoda, he sped towards the awaiting tube, before quickly stopping short.

As dusk stole the twilight sky, he saw a dark patch high above the compound. Tang squinted to reveal an all black helicopter hovering in silent mode. It began sinking lower, toward the tennis courts as half a dozen men armed rappelled down dangled ropes. Tang's giggle was gone. All gone. *'I knew it!'* he chastised himself. *'Fun?'*

Below he could see Bobby and Jackie both looking back to see how their partners were doing, oblivious to the threat behind them. Tang attempted to wave a warning, but both just returned a drunken wave back.

Tang's reaction was swift and cat-like, despite his considerable size. He jumped feet first into the waterslide, landed upright in the pool, and bounced out in a split-second. He flipped up one of the bench seats that lined the pool, lifting out a shoulder-mounted surface to air missile.

The helicopter pilot saw the weapon and immediately began evasive maneuvers. The men still dangled from ropes, and began spinning in wider and wider arcs as the helicopter tilted away.

Tang wasted no time. He hoisted the weapon into place, and took aim through the scope. The moment he locked on, he launched the rocket which hit the helicopter rotor's gearbox above the cab. The chopper rolled and dropped like a stone before rotors bit into the ground, cartwheeling the wreckage closer like an Bobby-lympics tumbling routine. He realized in horror it was headed straight for Jackie, who'd stared and frozen for the smallest of moments. Tang wasn't going to be able to get to her in time.

Out of nowhere came Daniel, sweeping her up, and throwing her over his shoulder, fireman style. The hulk of the helicopter barely missed them, but the same couldn't be said for the corporate mercenaries' leader, who took a blade right in the midsection. The lower half of his body landed right where Jackie had been, and the upper half arced into the pool, where the tail rotor spun in vain, churning up a deep crimson froth.

Tang reassessed the scene, noting a few of the dangling soldiers had managed to get their boots on the ground, and would be on them in seconds. With a hand gesture, Tang signalled Bobby, who then bolted the door shut, seeming to cut off their escape route. Daniel had taken some shrapnel, so Jackie jumped down to support him while Bobby came to prop up his other shoulder.

"This way," he told Jackie.

Tang was herding Mage and Song toward the same far corner of the mansion, where he triggered a long, steel plate on the wall to flop open. Jackie and Bobby lowered Daniel onto the plate, and rolled him through the hole, directly into the panic room. Jackie followed, as did the others, with Tang bringing up the rear. Automatic weapons fire was pinging off the steel plate, just as they secured it back into place.

They were safely within the panic room.

Tang dashed to his security room and flipped a

few switches on his control panel. Throughout the mansion, steel blinds rolled down over the doors and windows. On his monitor, he flipped through several camera feeds until he was confidant that the various anti-intruder systems installed throughout the compound would do their jobs. What was an idyllic setting just minutes ago, now belied the carnage of the attack. Large chunks of turf were torn up, and there was a helicopter and half of a dead man in the blood red pool.

"We've bought some time, but perhaps not long. Take care of Daniel first. There's a first aid station over there, Jackie. Mage, go load your project's computer equipment and anything you might need for your project." Looking down, he could see that Song was scared, and Daniel was wincing badly. "The compound's water cannons and blinds will only last so long. We have to have vanished by then. It's time to get to the boat!"

"Wait. What? We've got a boat?" asked Mage.

It was then that Bobby saw the blood on Tang's shirt. "Oh my God, they shot you! You're bleeding! Lemme see! Lemme see!"

"I'm fine, Robert. I'm fine."

"Fine? You don't look very fine! There's blood all over you, tough guy."

"It's just splattered from the guy in the pool."

"Yeah, right. Dark blood has soaked right

through. Look."

"I told you I'm fine!" Tang said, losing his temper. "We don't have time for this!"

Tang's temper was no match for Bobby.

"Don't talk to me like that. Uh, uh uh! You know better. You know you know better."

"Tang, why don't I know we own a boat?" asked Song, quite reasonably.

"I'll explain later. Right now, we have to get aboard."

"But what about my grandfather?" Mage wondered. "He's supposed to be moving into the mansion tomorrow."

Tang peered at Mage, nodded his acknowledgement, and promised, "tomorrow, son. We'll have to make arrangements to pick him up tomorrow. Right now, we need to get everyone to the boat."

"So, we *do* have a boat, then?" Daniel asked.

"Better." said Bobby. "And I sold it to him," he sang, displaying his best gay, glamour grin. He stepped to one corner and pulled aside a mat, which revealed a larger steel hatch similar to the one they'd just escaped through. He lifted the hatch's handle to reveal a ladder descending into the dark. He climbed down to power things up, and he called for Daniel to be helped down.

Wincing from his leg, he made his way down the steel rungs to see a tunnel sloping down into the distance, lit by many strings of LED lights. Bobby guided him to a thick rope with 2 loops attached, about four feet apart. "Put your feet in one loop, and hold this other one in your hands," he instructed. "Good. Yup. Just like that. When you get to there, help the others as they arrive. Ready? Happy trails."

"Get where.........?" Daniel cried as Bobby flipped a switch, sending him hurtling into the depths of the earth. *It's just like Star Wars!*" he mused, as the LED lights above him streaked past.

Back at the panic room, Bobby asked, "Who's next?"

"I am," volunteered Jackie. "Daniel just save my life, and is injured because of it, so I want to be there if he runs into any trouble down there." It was then she reflected on her own words. *"I can't believe he put himself at risk like that. He literally saved my life!'* she thought. Easing her way down the hatch ladder, she put her feet in one loop and gripped the other, as instructed. Nodding at Bobby, she too soon zipped down into the tunnel's streaking lights.

One by one, they made their escape, until only Bobby and Tang remained in the panic room. Tang insisted he go last, but Bobby was having none of it. "Sorry. You've been shot. I'm not leaving you up here alone." The stern face and set chin made Tang realize there was no winning this fight. He'd been down this road before. Bobby was the sweetest guy, but once he made up his mind, he was stone. *'I can command a Chinese warship, but I can't win an argument with this man,'* he mused to himself as he entered the hatch.

As Tang crawled down the ladder, Bobby got a good look at the shoulder wound. *'Not so bad after all',* he thought. He flipped a switch and soon Tang was gone, too. *'Last one out, turn off the lights,'* Bobby thought, closing the hatch above him, locking it securely in place. He then fit a foot into the lower loop, and one hand gripped the upper. Reaching back, he threw the switch one final time, and sped down into the abyss to join the others.

They'd escaped.

# *Chapter 9*

*"From birth, man carries the weight of gravity on his shoulders. He is bolted to the earth. But man has only to sink beneath the surface, and he is free."*

**Jacques Cousteau**

At the bottom of the zipline, Daniel sighed in relief. Above him, he unbolted another hatch like the one in the panic room, and climbed the ladder to wait for the others. It was pitch black, but he could smell the ocean, so he knew he was in the right place.

Jackie arrived within a minute, greeted by a big hug from Daniel. She was crying. The events of the day caught up with her while she'd been zipping down that tunnel. She'd just witnessed a helicopter crash that would have taken her out, if not for the man's arms she was shaking in. And another man was chopped in half right before her very eyes.

"Those soldiers were there because of our project," she sobbed. "That man died because of us. If we never did the project, he'd still be alive." Collapsing onto the floor, she wept quietly. Her throat was raw with grief, and no more words came.

Daniel felt absolutely useless. This beautiful creature was inconsolable, and he'd never seen her like that before. It was heart-wrenching. He felt so inadequate. Tears came to his own eyes, and though he held her, he could do nothing to calm her.

Behind him, he heard another quiet thump, and Mage had arrived intact. In the dim light from the tunnel, the glazed look on his buddy's face was scaring him. Daniel hobbled down the ladder, bent and helped Mage to an upright position.

"Let me take that equipment." Putting it above, he came back for Mage. "Climb up these stairs, buddy." Mage followed the instructions, albeit woodenly. The events of the day had caught up with him, as well. "Good job, bud. Sit here with Jackie." He propped Mage up against Jackie in a vain attempt to keep them warm. Daniel had no blanket to throw over them, not even a jacket. The only things they managed to bring were the electronics, and the swimsuits they wore. Twilight had passed, and a cold wind was whistling in the dark.

The zipline thumped again, so Daniel focused on that. Song scrambled quickly up the ladder, looking distressed, but otherwise fine. "What can I do?" she asked.

"Both of them could use your help. Mage is a bit vacant, and Jacks is a mess."

Another thump brought Tang, who now bled freely. But he was lucid and alert, and saw that Jackie and Mage were having some difficulty. He climbed up and quickly punched a number into a dark corner's keypad. A large steel door opened into a dimly lit hallway, and he ushered them all through. Daniel led a disconsolate Jackie, and Song led a dazed Mage. Bobby brought up the rear, shutting down the tunnel lights and bolting the hatch closed.

"Everybody inside. Robert, take Jackie and Mage to their cabins, then come back to help with our departure. Song, I'd like you to take care of your two friends until we get underway. Daniel, I'll need you to help Robert with our start-up and departure."

Song followed Bobby down some steel steps, then down a corridor, into a darkened room with bunks. She guided Jackie to a bed, which she crawled right into, and covered her head with the blanket. Mage was doing a bit better than her, but still looked shell-shocked. Song loaded him onto another bunk, where he turned toward the wall, on top of his blanket.

"I got this," Song assured Bobby and Daniel. "Go help Tang." Bobby nodded, and they left. Daniel didn't like the idea of leaving Jackie, or Mage for that matter, but knew Song had their backs.

They found Tang on the bridge of some sort of ship, but it was unlike any bridge he'd ever seen, TV or otherwise. Glass wrapped around most of it, with a large bubble window to one side, but at the moment, the view was obscured by the deep darkness. He wondered if they were in some kind of warehouse, or at least a monstrous boathouse. He'd noticed that Tang treated him with newfound respect after he saved Jackie, and Tang had simply said his help was needed, so Daniel stepped up.

"Daniel!" Tang admonished. "You can look

around later!"

Okay, well with a bit more respect, anyway.

"Right now I need you to help Robert down below." Bobby was already moving and soon had Daniel on his tail. They descended several sets of steel stairs down to another corridor which led them back to a room labelled, 'Control Room'. Inside, Bobby was all business. He flipped switches and turned dials, and quickly brought the room humming to life.

Daniel spun around, watching room light up. Several computer monitors power up, as Daniel looked on in amazement. Every wall was covered in miniature, multi-coloured LEDs, and it looked more like NASA than a boat. *'Wow!'* he thought to himself. He felt completely out of his element, whereas Bobby looked completely in his.

"Bobby. You say you sold this thing to Tang. Really?"

"Really. Now, don't just stand there," Bobby ordered. "Anywhere you see an 'ON' switch along that far wall, use it."

So, he did. Some panels were marked logically, with 'Batteries', 'Water Coolant', or 'Hydraulic Pressure', and others had a myriad of descriptions he didn't understand at all. But he flipped them on, as ordered. He'd worked his way down the wall, suddenly stopped dead.

143

"Bobby?"

"Yup?"

"Why do these two big switches have a nuclear warning stickers?"

"I'll explain later. Turn them both to the ON position."

As Daniel did so, a roaring cacophony of sound assaulted the quiet of the Control Room, but eminating from outside the ship. Deep rumbling caused the floor to vibrate beneath his feet. This room was freaking him out, thank you very much. Bobby was concentrating on the many dials, monitors and switches, and in no time, he looked confidant.

"Bobby. Uh..... don't you need me to just untie us from the dock, or something?" A mundane task would be welcome about now.

"Not necessary," he clipped. This was definitely not the Bobby that Daniel was used to seeing. This one was all business and with headset on, he spoke calmly into his microphone, "Unlocking docking clamps, Captain." And to Daniel, he said, "throw those big lever switches over there to 'disengage'." A loud, clank echoed from deep in the ship.

"Docking clamps disengaged. All systems online," he reported. "Go for launch, Captain."

The ship shuddered to life beneath them and

Daniel knew they were underway, but there was no window in the Control Room to verify that.

His anxiety was now showing, too. So much had happened since the same time yesterday, when Jackie had only been a dream. He'd been through a roller coaster in the last 24 hours. Last night was unbelievable and the day had begun so well, in Jackie's bed. Then the Bobby-lympics had been a hilarious romp. *'Boy, times sure change when a helicopter full of soldiers crashes in your pool.'* What had been a day of fun and games had turned into a nightmare. It was too bizarre to even fathom right now.

Bobby regarded him sympathetically, removed his headset and suggested, "Why don't you go back up to help Jackie. I can handle things from here, now that we're underway."

"Great!" he cried. He didn't even realize he'd been holding his breath. "I mean, sure, if you don't need me. So, you know..... call me if you do." This whole 'boat' episode was freaking him out too, but paled in comparison with the helicopter incident earlier. Holding Jackie seemed like a much better option.

He retraced his route, climbing the steel stairs back to where Tang stood on the bridge, peering into blackness.

*'A control room without windows and now a bridge window you can't see out of. What could possibly go wrong?'* thought Daniel. "I'm gonna go see how Jackie and Mage are doing. You know......, if you don't

145

need me."

"Permission granted," Tang said with a weak smile.

In the morning, Song was the first up. There was no coffee and bacon to stir her awake this time, but curiosity got the better of her and she wanted to look around her boat. Wiping the sleep crystals from the corners of her eyes, she made her way back down the same corridor, to where she'd seen Tang the night before. She found him still standing at the helm, but he looked exhausted. Sometime during the night, Bobby had bandaged his wounds and cleaned him up, but he still didn't look good. He looked grey. Gone was the giggling child of the Bobby-lympics.

The view out the front of the bridge was still black. She couldn't even see any stars. She watched Tang for a few minutes, then announced, "I've got to find some coffee."

"Bobby's still sleeping, so you'll have to get it yourself. I'm going to need him to relieve me when he gets up. I am very tired." He gave Song basic instructions on where to find the galley, so she made her own way down through the vast ship, exploring as she went.

The interior was lavish and well-appointed. It screamed luxury wherever she went, except for the lower utility decks. Everything looked brand new, which she supposed it was. She found the galley right where

146

Tang had said it was, and searched drawers and cupboards until she found some vacuum-sealed coffee in a fully stocked pantry. Checking the plumbing, she found that the fresh water supply not only worked, but was instantly hot, if desired. The only coffee urn was a large industrial one mounted on the counter. She made a full pot anyway, knowing her friends were going to need it. Finding the mugs, she chose two large ones, for herself and Tang.

Her caffeine fix sated for now, Song began to wander the ship. Her ship. It was simply amazing everywhere she looked. Going below, she came across many large industrial-looking tanks, and a whole bank labelled 'Batteries". This boat was bigger than she expected, and the lower deck resembled the inside of a factory. Questions were running through her mind, as she climbed back up to the Bridge to hand Tang his coffee.

There was a huge bubble window beside her but she couldn't discern much. It was clearly below the water line.

"Thank you," she said quietly. "You saved us all yesterday. If you hadn't been there then, we wouldn't be here now."

"I live to serve," he said with a smirk. But, she was right. If Tang hadn't had the mansion designed like a fortress, who knows where they'd be now. They were lucky to be alive.

"So, tell me about my new boat. What's the

story?"

"It's just a boat I bought from Robert," Tang replied with a bigger smirk. "It's actually how we met."

"But Bobby moved in awhile ago. Why didn't you tell me about it then?"

"Your father ordered me to arrange it when he was still alive. It was a custom order which took more than two years to build. When he died, it was too late for me to cancel the order, plus it was a way for me to keep seeing Robert. Apparently, his share of the commission was enough to retire on. It was his final sale before he moved into my place at the compound. "

"I'll bet it was a tidy little sum, by the looks of this place."

"We actually only got delivery of it last month. Robert and I managed to get it stocked, we hadn't put it through sea trials yet."

"Well, I don't know a lot about boats, but I know enough that this one is big enough to be called a ship, not just a 'boat'."

Tang's grey pallor brightened and a smile overtook his face. "It's actually not technically either." She waited for him to explain, before having to prod him with a finger to his bandage.

"Okay! Okay! Welcome aboard "The Nautilus", Song; your new luxury private yacht submarine - for the ultra-rich. I think you qualify."

"So, we're in a submarine, not on a ship?"

"We are."

*Go to*
*http://www.hisutton.com/Nautilus-2020_Luxury_Submarine.html*
*in order to zoom in.*

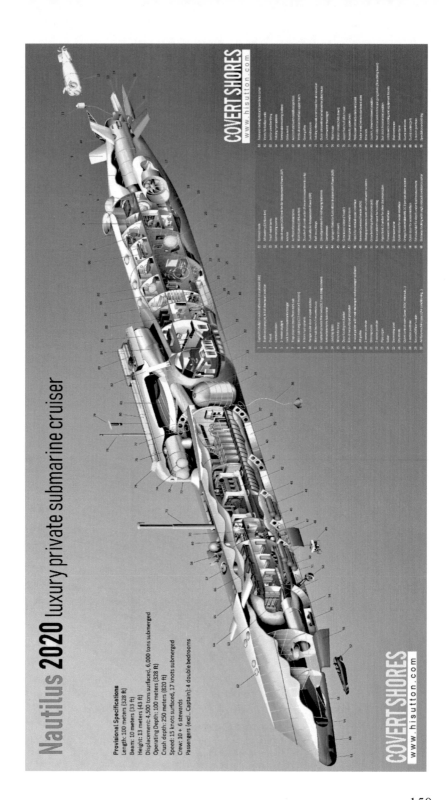

150

Song laughed aloud. "Is that why I can't see anything out those bubble windows?"

"Those bubble windows are called portholes, landlubber. And we're down about one hundred and fifty feet, so yes, that's why you can't see much."

"But the portholes are taller than I am. I saw one that's gotta be taller than even Mage."

Tang reached to a panel and flipped on a switch marked 'Floodlight'. Before them was the sub's upper hull stretching beyond the range of the floodlight. A whole undersea world opened up before them, eerie and quiet. It struck Song as odd, so she asked, "why is the submarine so quiet?"

"Because your sub is nuclear-powered, my dear. The engines are mounted on the sides of the vessel, away from the hull. They look like jet engines. Consequently, there is no engine room, allowing more space aboard the ship. And, as a bonus, we won't have to stop for petrol."

Song's mouth was slightly open, but no words came out. When she could speak, she exclaimed, "you're just full of surprises, aren't you Tang?" And then she danced excitedly, "Wow! I own a nuclear submarine? I gotta go tell the others!"

As she quietly entered the bunk cabin, she could see that Jackie was the only one awake. In the dim light, her face was already puffy and red. She'd already been crying that morning. Song sat beside her on the bed and held her friend close, which started another round of weeping.

"Come with me," she whispered, lifting Jackie from the bunk. "I need to show you something."

"First some coffee."

"I'll show you where."

Jackie followed Song like a zombie, dimly unaware of her surroundings.

Song handed her a mug of fresh java. They sat at a small table, but Jackie began to weep again, so her friend took the bull by the horns. "Okay, Jacks. You've got the coffee to wake you up. Now I'm going to cheer you up. Look out that window." It was dark as night, but there were indications that they were moving.

"Are we flying?" Jackie's brain wasn't thinking very clearly yet. "What is this place?"

"This is my new boat I didn't know I owned."

"Oh, right. The boat the boys were talking about after the helicopter crashed." Her face was briefly strained Her brain worked too hard yesterday. Eventually, she relaxed enough for curiosity to take over. "It looks like a pretty big boat, Song."

"It's not quite a boat, Jacks. It's a luxury, private, yacht submarine!!!" Song squealed.

Jackie's face quickly transformed from weeping to startled. "A what? What did you say? You're serious?"

"Totally!" she cried, jumping around the room. She walked Jackie over to the big porthole to have a better look.

Jackie slowly began to see the depths float by before her. "Have you explored yet?"

"Just what you've already seen between here and Tang. You want to have a look around?"

"Yeah, I want to have a look around! You're being totally serious?"

"Totally."

"Then let's go! Hanging with you is certainly never boring, my friend. Ironically, Song had always thought of herself as the ultimate bore.

The previous day was shuffled aside, while the two girls explored the entire vessel from stem to stern. It was like nothing either had ever seen before, but really, how many people had ever toured a luxury yacht submarine before?

They began at the lowest deck's bow, and the very first thing they came across was one of the coolest they'd find anywhere aboard.

"Whoa, what are these babies?" Jackie raved. "Check these out, Song."

"The signage identifies them as 'Ortega Submersible 3 Passenger Diver Scooters.' "Ha ha, yeah Jacks! I think they're underwater Harleys."

"They look more like underwater luges, like at the Olympics. Not the Bobby-lympics, the real ones." The sleds were long and sleek, with three seats for the passengers. There were full-body wet suits, and helmets with full face shields mounted on the wall.

"Look, they have their own oxygen supply!" Jackie pointed out. Both sleds looked about 12 feet long, and were dark blue with x-fins on both their bows and sterns. Resting on a sliding cradle, they led to a large, round pipe about five feet in diameter.

"That must be a launch tube or something. It looks like they'd shoot right out the front, like a torpedo."

"Ooooh, doesn't that sound fun? But, I think you mean the bow, not the 'front', Song. If you're going to own a 'boat' like this, you better learn the vernacular. Exploring further, Jackie found a diver's ready room and a a hyperbaric chamber for decompressing divers.

"Let's keep exploring, Jacks. If every room is like this one, I think I'm going to like my new boa........., I mean submarine!"

Not far away, they found a cabinet marked 'Remote Operated Vehicle (ROV)'. "Song. I've only ever seen these on TV before, but they use them for deeper water, where the sleds wouldn't be able to go. These

ROVs are built to take the pressure down on the ocean floor. There's even a remote camera mounted on top!"

The girls passed some huge tanks and battery banks, and many other items and names they'd never heard of before. The sheer scale of the place was awe inspiring. They passed the 'Control Room' Bobby had taken Daniel to the night before, but it was of little interest to them. Jackie bent to crawl through another hatch, moving further toward the stern.

"Whoa, Song. This is getting ridiculous. Look in here."

Song poked her head in and giggled, "A swimming pool? On a submarine? That's just crazy!"

By the time the girls had gone from one end of the ship to the other, they decided it was time to roust the boys. They found their way back to the upper decks, and entered the bunk room, loud and rowdy.

"Up and at 'em, rise and shine, you scurvy dogs," cried Jackie. "This ship isn't going to sail itself!"

Daniel opened one eye. Yup, it was the girl of his dreams, and it wasn't even a dream anymore. Shaking out the cobwebs, he observed, "You're pretty chipper today, Jacks."

"Yes, I am. And you will be too. Get up. Get up!"

Daniel was pretty pleased to see Jackie doing better. He'd been worried. But was Mage doing any better? Not so much. He rolled over, but Song was having none of it, waking him with a thousand small kisses until he capitulated. "Okay, okay, let me get dressed."

"Why? You've got nothing to change into." And it was true. They all were still in their swimsuits, some of which were grimy from the zipline escape, or bloody from shrapnel and splatter."

"Great," he mumbled. "What am I going to wear, then?"

"Well, you can wear your bathing suit, or your birthday suit. Those are your options. Now COME ON!"

"Sheesh!" Daniel complained. "It's usually Mage who's the impatient one." Climbing from his berth, he added, "You can wear your birthday suit, if you want, Jacks. It's very stylish. I think it looks very good on you. Nice snug fit." That comment earned him a roll of her eyes and a two handed push.

Soon after, both couples again entered the Pilot House's bridge. Mage was still rubbing his eyes and scratching his unruly bed head. Tang was gone, and at the helm now was Bobby, who greeted them smiling like a Cheshire cat. "Good morning, crew! Sleep well, I hope? I see you're all still alive, still kickin' and ready for a new adventure, eh?"

Adventure was not on Mage's to-do list today, but the others greeted Bobby cheerfully.

"Bobby, I think we need to wake the boys up," said Song. Would you reach up and switch on that Floodlight toggle above you, please?" He gave her a knowing wink, and the view before them burst to life.

"What the hell?" Daniel wondered.

"Welcome to The Nautilus, my new 'boat'!" Song exclaimed, using her fingers for quotation marks.

"The Nautilus?" asked Daniel. "Like the Jules Verne's 20,000 Leagues Under The Sea, Nautilus? Captain Nemo?"

"The very same! Except here, it's Captain Tang, not Captain Nemo."

"I'll have you know," interjected Bobby, "this is as realistic of a version of the Nautilus as we were able to make."

"You made this?" asked Mage, his attention now full.

"Well, not me exactly. The company I worked for made it. I just sold it to Tang. She's been customized to Song's father's specifications and I think you will find it a nice place to hide out until we can further assess our risk."

"You..... sold this....?" Mage wasn't sure whether to believe him or not.

"Yup." Bobby confirmed, once again flashing his toothy grin. "I did. And life with Tang has been one big adventure ever since."

"Where is Tang, anyway?" asked Mage.

"In the Captain's quarters, sleeping. He was up all night sneaking us through Georgia Strait and out to deeper water. I relieved him, but we'll have to figure out a training schedule soon. He and I can't do it all ourselves. Need to get you all ship shape! But, before any of that, get the lay of the land......or the sea, I guess. Have a wee look around."

"Right this way then, kind sirs," Jackie said with flourish. "Leave the helmsman to tend to his duties. Your future awaits."

The ladies led the way to the lower deck, retracing their earlier explorations, and began with the sea sleds in the bow.

"Whaaaaaaatttt?" Daniel did a close-up inspection.

"They're basically three-person underwater motorcycles!" Jackie cried. "I can't wait to try them out."

"Totally! And I can chase you around!"

"Gotta catch me to kiss me."

"Deal!"

"Oh, get a room, you two," Song moaned.

"Great idea," he answered, lifting his eyebrows at Jackie, repeatedly, before alternating them.

"Jeepers, not right now, you guys. Come on! There's so much more to see on my new boat."

"Your new *sub*?"

"You know what I mean."

Moving further astern, Daniel piped up as they reached the door marked, 'Control Room'. "Hey, I've been here before. Last night when Bobby and I readied for launch."

The girls had just skipped it on their first tour, but as the door swung open, Mage was in awe. The 'NASA' room, as Daniel came to call it, was an electronics Disneyland for Mage. He began inspecting every switch, every light, and every dial, squinting to read the labels.

"See that wall of switches? Yep, that was all me. Flipped every one of them. Yep. Sure did. Couldn't have started this baby without me last night."

"Come on, guys!" Song whined impatiently. "You can look at all that later. We've got something that I guarantee you're going to like even better! Come...... on!!!!!" She grabbed Mage's hand with both of hers, dragging him forcibly from the room.

159

She then led the quartet to the very stern of the sub, where they found a 2-metre, circular yellow door as tall as Mage. She spun open the hand wheel, but needed Jackie's help to swing the heavy door wide. Stepping aside, they bowed slightly, swept their arms low, inviting the boys to enter.

Not surprisingly, Daniel scampered in to explore first. To his right and just below his catwalk, he saw an open yellow hatch, so he jumped down, got on his knees, and peered down inside. It was dark, and it took a moment for his eyes to adjust. "No way," he said quietly, almost to himself, then "NO WAY!" He wasn't quiet this time. He gave a quick look over his shoulder at his friends, grinned, and dropped inside. "You guys have got to see this to believe it."

"Oh, we've seen it." replied Jackie. "Why do you think we brought you here?"

As the other three all dropped down, they found themselves in a room about twelve feet long, including a two-seat cockpit at one end. The 'windshield' was a two metre bubble, with one meter portholes to the side of each pilot's chair. Behind the cockpit was a passenger area with a row of bench seats lining either side wall. On the walls behind those benches were more one metre bubble portholes on each side, like those in the cockpit.

"Look, Mage! More switches and dials for you, bud," giving his pal a friendly swat on the back. Mage had seen them, alright. He settled into the Captain's chair, and ran his fingertips up and down the corner instrument panels, and gripped the  joystick mounted between the seats. Daniel climbed into the other seat and, looking at the labels, declared, "It's another sub, right?"

"Yes!" cried Song and Jackie, almost in unison.

"Italian by the looks of things," Mage observed. "See the i.d. plate? 'Triste GSE Mini Submarine, Made in Italy'. This cockpit's almost like a Ferrari, or Lear jet. It's so cool."

"Hell, yeah! A sub in a sub!" Daniel cried. "Can we take it for a spin?" A withering look from Mage answered that question. "Well, yeah, we should probably learn how first, eh? We can ask Bobby, though."

"I found a mini-bar!" Jackie cried out.

"And I found a bathroom." Song added.

"Song, I already told you. You've got to learn marine parlance. If it's on a ship, it's called a 'head'.

"Nobody's peeing on *my* head," Daniel joked. "In fact, since it' belongs to you, Song, all of us can only pee on *your* head. Right Jacks? Get it? It's a pun."

At the end of their explorations, they all returned to the bridge, where they found Tang had rejoined Bobby at the helm. "Alright gentlemen," led Song. "Spill."

"Alright," Tang agreed, scratching his stubble.

"The 'Nautilus', as you may remember, was the name of Captain Nemo's submarine in "20,000 Leagues Under the Sea', and our 'Nautilus' is a tribute to that."

"Yeah, yeah," Song said impatiently. "How is it that we have one? And why?"

"And does it have torpedoes?" Daniel added excitedly.

"No it does not have torpedoes. How is it we are aboard a submarine? Not to simplify, but your father just wanted one, Song. It's as simple as that. But, the Chinese Navy didn't want to lose your father when he announced he was going to follow your mother here to Canada. Nor did they want to lose me, added Tang. "So, a compromise was brokered between the Chinese military and the Canadian Forces. It was kept quiet due to potential political complications.

"*This* Nautilus is *nuclear*-powered. China's Atomic Energy Authority and the Canadian Nuclear Energy Commission agreed to a joint project. They wanted to study nuclear energy options, and the possible introduction of nuclear batteries to ships. It's been important that both sides kept it off the books. So, your father, Song, suggested a solution. He wanted this sub as soon as he knew they were an alternative to luxury yachts. He volunteered the Nautilus for the testing of those nuclear batteries. Therefore, the Chinese Navy could claim your father and I as still in the field, while allowing him to move to Canada with his wife. We were to create a joint report to both governments as to sea trials, and the success or failure of its nuclear power options.

With the death of your father, and a shake-up in the Chinese military, the whole program was mothballed. But Bobby came to me to say the nuclear power for the Nautilus had already been installed. Both governments believed the project to be dead, so I left things as they were. And by the time Bobby had fully trained me, we'd fallen in love, so I stayed in Canada.

"We took delivery of 'The Nautilus' a little over a month ago, but had yet to get her out on the water. There was a slight delay for Transport Canada's ship registration, but that has now been straightened away. So, here we are with the perfect escape vehicle. Only nations with their own submarine fleet can truly find us, but most are diesel powered, meaning they can only so far from shore before they need refueling. The Nautilus does not have that limitation.

"In fact," interrupted Bobby. "We can go thirty years without a fill-up."

"Our ship is 100 metres in length, by 10 metres in width", Tang continued. "Bobby and I are both capable of handling her, but we will need you all to be trained as crew. We may be at sea for awhile. This is your new home until things settle down, and we do not know how long that will take."

"We live on a submarine," Daniel exclaimed. "That's so cool!" All were completely captivated by their new home, and smiling like fools. Even Mage had perked up.

The conning tower broke the surface, unveiling an overcast day above the waterline. Looking toward the bow, the top of the submarine stretched far out in front of them.

"I will be your Captain," Tang informed them. "I have commanded a sub in the Chinese Navy so I will be in charge here, but Robert can answer any question too. He and I will take the Captain's quarters, and Song, you and Mage should take the 2$^{nd}$ Officer's cabin.

"As for you and Daniel," he said to Jackie, "There are six private crew cabins to choose from closer to the bow. Bobby will show you your quarters, and the location of the Crew Mess, which will be right above your cabins. You'll have some privacy there. When you are all settled in, you are free to rest, or have a look around. Find your bearings, and get to know your ship. There are sub schematics posted on several walls if you get lost. We will all meet together again at 18 hundred hours for dinner. That's 6:00 p.m. for you dirt dwellers," he said, looking straight at Daniel.

"I know that. I knew that. I did!"

"Any questions?"

"What about food? I'm kind of hungry, how about you guys? Guys?" Daniel again.

"Robert will show you the Crew Mess where we'll be meeting later for dinner. The Crew Galley is right beside it, and is stocked with non-perishables. Help

164

yourself."

"Anything else?" asked Tang.

"Just a thank you, Tang," said Song. "You too, Bobby. We owe you our lives."

"And we owe you *our* lives," Bobby added. "It's your ship that saved us."

"There were many heroes yesterday," Captain Tang declared, looking straight at Daniel, whose face glowed at the compliment. Jackie slipped her arm in his.

By dinnertime, the sub was cruising smoothly with Tang once again at the helm, and he was actually smiling! Back in his element, perhaps. Mage approached him shyly, asking "what about my grandfather, Captain? He was supposed to be moving into the mansion today. And he's been so sick, I'm really worried. I can't even call him because my phone was in my jeans."

"I'm sorry, son. We're probably too far out for cell service now, and when we're below the surface, forget it."

"Well, it has to happen," Mage persisted. "Has to." *'Poor old guy'* he thought.

Tang was quiet for a few moments, and made a decision. "I'll tell you what. We'll briefly risk going to the surface tomorrow. I should be able to get a link on my satellite phone. Then, you can call your grandfather, and we can order provisions. But, we're too visible on the surface to stay up there, so we dive as soon as we are done."

"Why?"

Bristling a bit, Tang said, "Because we don't want to be found right now. On the strait between the mainland and Vancouver Island, is a submarine range at Nanoose Bay, used by both Canadian and American subs. At the southern tip of the island is CFB Esquimalt, home of Canadian Maritime Forces Pacific. Did you ever hear of the movie, 'Run Silent, Run Deep?' That is what we are doing now. The nuclear propulsion helps greatly with the silent part. My goal is to get out into deeper water, but still within Canada's 200-mile marine border. We're too close to American waters for my liking."

"If this submarine is registered in Canada, why isn't that enough?" Mage wondered.

"Because we don't want to take that chances. Plus, I'd be a Chinese Navy man operating a nuclear submarine in American waters. Questions and delays would be inevitable, and the Nautilus could be seized."

Clearly, the boy was miserable......., again. Tang had been hard on him at first, but gave him a break because he made Song so happy. But, he'd also come to realize just how smart the boy really was. And the close relationship between he and his grandfather. That needed to be encouraged.

"I tell you what." Tang said. "We will need fresh provisions and clothes. So we'll sail north to Prince Rupert and get them there. Tonight, I want you to make a list of any and all gadgetry needed for both our project, and the Nautilus. Tomorrow, you can call your grandfather, while I can talk to the lawyers and order provisions. By the time we get to Prince Rupert in several days, we should be able to fly him up along with the provisions and your electronics, assuming he's healthy enough to fly. But, I think we've done everything we can, for now, son."

Tang put his arm around Mage's shoulder, declaring loudly, "Now, let's go for dinner. I'm starving!"

"Don't you have to steer?"

"We can drift down here for a bit. I'll leave the proximity sensors on. But we need to have a full meeting with everyone. And what better place than around the dinner table, eh?"

"You're starting to sound like a Canadian, skipper."

"It seems you are all a bad influence on me."

Swaggering into the galley, he asked Bobby what smelled so good, and of course, Bobby replied, "ME!", giving the big guy a hip bump.

Song was already seeing Tang in a newer, softer light. When her father had been alive, Tang was all business, all the time. But since his death, and Bobby moving in downstairs, Song actually saw him more like a friend now, a confidante. Bobby had brought out a whole new persona in him, and it wasn't until now that she saw such a wide gap between the old Tang and the new.

And Bobby? There was little doubt about Bobby's mother hen roll with the crew. People needed him, and he liked that. And he liked to cook. The aroma of dinner drifted through the air, to the noses of the entire crew, who were undeniably famished. They hadn't eaten since the Bobby-lympics.

It was a noisy, animated group they joined, and he let them gab all through dinner. But before long, Tang stood, and the room went quiet. "Ladies and gentlemen, boys and girls...... and Robert," he teased, earning a meat fork to his butt. "Welcome to the first dinner ever served aboard the Nautilus." Song and Jackie gave a quick clap. "It has been an anxious few days for everyone, and you are all likely wondering where we go from here. Is it safe to go home? No, I don't think so. Not for awhile. But, we don't need to. There's no safer place in the world for us than right here, than aboard this submarine. At the first sign of any trouble, we can simply slip below the surface to the security of the depths.

"However, as long as we are the sole caretakers of Mage's project, we are in danger. Any contact with the outside world should be avoided, for now. As it is, communications from this ship are limited to the surface anyway. Underwater, standard radio signals are ineffective. I have a satellite phone, offering a partial, but limited form of communication, but only when we are on the surface, which carries more risk.

"Mage is putting together a shopping list for electronics yo make us more capable in that regard. And, I want a list from all of you, as well. Clothes, provisions, needs. Anything we don't already have aboard. I'll order it to be picked it up in Prince Rupert a few days from now. And Bobby, a long-term grocery list for us all please, with an emphasis on fresh fruit."

"Gotcha. No scurvy."

"Plan for the long haul, everyone. There will be no popping out to WalMart in the months to come. Song and Jackie? I want you to tour the ship looking for anything incomplete. Check the fresh water tank levels, liquid Oxygen, diving gear, diesel levels, test the generator and anything else you find. We need to know if something is a problem, and not die because we didn't know it was."

"What about me, Skipper? What can I do?" asked Daniel.

"You? You will be the first to learn how to handle this vessel."

"Hell, yeah! I'm totally down for that! Did you hear that, Jacks? I'm going to be a submarine pilot!"

"The term you are looking for is 'helmsman'," teased Mage.

169

Turning to the others, Tang added, "You should all be made aware that this won't be a pleasure cruise. Normally, this yacht sub calls for 10 crew, and 6 stewards to spoil the passengers. We have five crew and Robert. Therefore, all of you will be taught every operation of the 'Nautilus'. Until everyone is up to speed, we are all compromised. Accordingly, this ship will run on a tight schedule. Breakfast will be served at 10 hundred hours."

"I know when that is," Daniel said confidently. Nodding repeatedly, he added, "I do, Jacks."

"We are all so proud," Tang deadpanned. "Training sessions will begin at 11 hundred hours, every day until you're all trained. Bobby and I will be switching off between guiding the ship, and training you crew members, so we'll be tired and grumpy. Be aware, and beware. Sub school will end at 15 hundred hours, and other than dinner, you can use the time however you like.

"Tomorrow, I will bring the Nautilus back to the surface long enough for the sat phone to link up the satellites, and I will order all of the items on your lists. At that time, you may go topside to catch some sun, weather permitting. When we get back underway, I suggest you porthole watch while we're still near the surface, This coast has some of the best diving in the world, and you'll be able to see it without getting wet. That's it for me," wrapped up Captain Tang. "Anything questions?"

"We should have a name," Daniel decided. "For us, you know, the crew of the Nautilus? Like the X-Men, or something. The Scurvy Dogs? We should have a moniker for our own single sub navy."

"We're not superheroes, Daniel."

"We kinda are, though. Right? We wanna save people, right? So, what do you ladies think?" he asked, turning toward Jackie and Song. "Should we have a name?"

"If you want a name, call us anything you want."

"Cool! How about the Humanity Manatees? Eh? Eh! What do you think Jacks?"

"Anything, except that. I love you, but we're not going to be known as the sea cows. Not gonna happen."

"How about the 'Fellowship of the Deep'?" Mage suggested. "It could be a tribute to my mother. She loved sorcery stories, especially the Lord of the Rings. She was such a fan, she actually wanted to name me Gandalf. My father said no, so she suggested Merlin next, also with no luck. My father finally relented when they agreed on Mage. But, 'Fellowship of the Deep" feels right to me."

"Well, all right then," said Daniel. "Cheers to Mage the Magician and the Fellowship of the Deep!"

"To the Fellowship of the Deep," they cried as one, hoisting their glasses high.

# *Chapter 10*

*"When I forget how talented God is, I look to the sea."*

***Whoopi Goldberg***

Cracking her eyes open the next morning, Song felt a bit hung over. After their first Fellowship of the Deep meeting, it was decided that a celebration was in order. Bobby likes celebrating. He'd found some champagne and she got a little tipsy. Shaking loose the cobwebs in her brain, she rubbed her eyes awake sleepily. As she replaced dreams with reality, she had that odd feeling of being watched. Peering in at her through her large, porthole window of the 2nd Officer's cabin was a single eye of a curious Orca. Convinced Song posed no risk, she swam on by lazily, followed by her calf. *'What a way to wake up!'*

Mage snored on quietly, so she slipped silently from her berth. In a closet, she found slippers and a robe. *'Yes!'* she whispered to herself. *'Finally get rid of these'*. Peeling off her bikini, she rubbed the tender, chafed spots and decided to go commando beneath her robe.

Tiptoeing from the cabin, she went in search of coffee. Stopping by at the pilot house, she found a very drowsy Tang, guiding their vessel through the depths. *'How tedious it must be to pilot into blackness for hours on end.,'* " Zǎoshang hǎo duìzhǎng," she said aloud.

Despite his weariness, Tang graced Song with a tired smile, "And good morning to you, too, Song."

"Where are we? And how are things going, Captain?"

"We are just northwest of Vancouver Island, heading north towards Prince Rupert. Seas above us are calm, and I haven't noticed anything unusual. How about yourself?"

"After the nightmare of yesterday, this morning seems like a surreal dream. I woke up to an Orca's eye voyeur in my porthole! That is definitely a first for me. She had a calf swimming alongside her."

Tang laughed. Out loud, even. "Well, that explains why the Nautilus's proximity sensors sounded before mysteriously going quiet again. We will be living underwater for awhile. You will witness many new things." Looking more serious for a moment, he said to Song, "We were lucky to have this ship to escape with. And since it officially belongs to you, I want to clarify a few things. First, are you agreeable to me acting as Captain while we are aboard?"

Surprised, Song answered, "Of course I am. Who else would be?"

"It is your ship, so you should decide who guides it. I felt it best to clarify."

With a melancholy look, she said, "I miss my father. He should be here for this."

"I miss him, as well. He was truly a great and noble man. And I miss your mother, too. She had character. Maybe her fiery, red hair brought it out. When I first began to come to your home in China, she forced me to learn English. Your father wanted me near, so I followed his lead. Inside the house, though, we could only speak English. Being Canadian, she wanted you, Song, to speak her native tongue fluently, as well as Mandarin. You were a young child, who picked it up easily. For me, it was not."

"And yet, here you are, speaking English fluently, with little sign of an accent. Any accent you do have sounds more Newfie than Mandarin."

Song's mother had hailed from Newfoundland on the east coast of Canada. She was always fiercely proud of her Newfie roots. 'Who knit ya?' she would ask when she met someone new, meaning 'Who are your parents? Where are you from?' If you were CFA or 'come from away', you were 'nae a native Newfie, b'y.' As a fresh, young 20-year-old, Song's mother had been bright-eyed and adventurous, travelling solo to China to teach English. In the Orient, her alabaster skin and brassy, red hair drew men's and women's eyes alike.

"My mother was teaching English before either you, or I, came on the scene," offered Song. "It didn't pay much, but she made some money on the side, singing in the local nightclub in our Wuhan neighbourhood. It was there that she met my father, who said he was forever smitten."

"Yes, he told me, and I saw Melody perform

many times in both languages," responded Tang. "Her hair and skin stood out like a spotlight was always shining on her, in the sea of Asians in the crowd. But, it was her ice, green eyes and their mischievous sparkle that undid your father. His life took an unexpected detour and he was never the same. You share your mother's extraordinary eyes, Song. After I came to live with your family, I came to recognize what a truly extraordinary woman your mother was. I was a bit smitten myself, and I am a gay man!"

"Mother liked to sing more than anything in the world. She told my father that songs could relieve all of life's troubles, and would sing to him when he came home beaten down by his day. I wonder what she would think of our little project, using music to make people feel better."

"She would probably say, 'See? Told ya, b'y,'" Tang chuckled.

"Do you know why my name is Song, Tang?" He shook his head. "It was a tradition in our family. Mother's name was Melody, and her Scottish mother's name was Piper. Song, Melody and Piper - three generations celebrate music."

"Interesting. I did not know about that one." Tang rubbed his eyes sleepily, and yawned.

"I need coffee. You? You look tired."

"Thank you, but Bobby already brought me one. I've not slept yet today. After our training drills, I will be going to the surface to order everyone's supplies. After that, while you frolic topside in the sun, I'll be asleep. Everyone will be on their own for dinner, because once we get underway again, Bobby will need to man the helm."

"All right. Well, I need some of Bobby's coffee." She wiggled her fingers as she left the bridge, following her nose down and toward the bow. She found Bobby with Jackie in the Crew Mess. "Good morning, Fellowship members! Or should I say fellow ship members?"

"Howdy, Song. Caffeine?" Bobby suggested, already pouring, knowing the answer.

"Oh my God, yes!" She sat and scrutinized Jackie, glad to see that the puffiness of sorrow from the previous morning had left her face. In fact, *'nobody deserves to look that good first thing in the morning,'* she mused. "How you doin', Jacks? You look better. Daniel still sleeping?"

"Thanks. Yeah, Daniel is still up in his berth. And I'm okay. Just feeling a little mortal. If he hadn't been there, I wouldn't be here. He literally saved my life."

"I saw."

Jackie shuddered, "That guy who got chopped in half in the pool. That would have been me,"

"Yeah, but it wasn't, Jacks. Daniel stepped up, and rather heroically, too."

"I know! He could have been that guy, too, but it didn't even occur to him. If he'd hesitated, I'd be toast."

"Consider it a happy byproduct of him never taking his eyes off you."

"Yeah, it's cute, isn't it? He's like having a happy, human puppy, always keen to join whatever I'm doing."

"Well, that puppy turned into a guard dog, yesterday."

"Make room, ladies," Bobby interrupted, "and brekky will appear before your very eyes!" The breakfast platters he placed before them were worthy of Sunday brunch at the Hilton. Reaching for a microphone, he announced ship-wide, "Calling all hands. Breakfast is now served in the Crew Mess. If you continue to snooze, you *will* continue to lose!"

Daniel soon arrived, with a scratch and a yawn, followed shortly thereafter by Mage. Both looking as crumpled as a Sharpei. and were hung over like Song. The moment they sat down, Bobby plunked down their platters, and a basket of fresh, hot muffins.

"Now that the rabble are fed, my work here is done," declared Bobby. "I'll be on the bridge relieving the Captain if anybody needs me. "Ta ta."

Soon, the captain joined them for breakfast, still rubbing his eyes, and scratching his stubble. But he was looking decidedly content, being back at sea. "I'm hungry enough to eat an Orca," Tang declared, winking at Song. "How is our fine Fellowship doing this morning?"

Most just nodded, their mouths busy savouring the flavouring. But a sombre Mage stood up, looking messed up. Clearing his dry throat, he announced, "I've made a decision. Since a man was killed because of project, I don't want that to happen again. However, there are so many months of testing still required to work out any kinks. That's too long to put anyone, let alone my best friends, in constant danger.

"We've already seen how university research facilities can get compromised. I can't abide anyone, anywhere, being at risk for months to come, just because of my project.... our project, he said, glancing at Jackie, If Bryce's father and his big pharma buddies were brazen enough to attack the compound itself, they'll come after us anywhere. Also, pharmaceutical companies fund a lot of other medical research, allowing them to exert pressure on university funding, and threaten the careers of serious researches.

"With the approval of the rest of you, I plan on releasing the project as soon as we can, free for anyone to use. Both Tang and I feel we're in great danger until we do, so I'm going to just give the code and algorithms away. But once it's uploaded to the world wide web, everyone will have access, not just us. That should cause the corporate combatants to back off. And then from there, we'll just see where the app takes us. If it's available everywhere, people will try it for things we haven't even thought of yet. But first, I'm asking if any of you have a problem with that."

"It's your project, Mage," said Daniel. "You can do whatever you want with it. But, why give it away? It could be very profitable."

"It's not just mine, though. Every one of you has a stake in this. And without Jackie, we wouldn't be where we are today."

"Oh sure," Jackie joked. "Blame it on me!"

"You guys know what I mean. You've all been a big part of its creation, so if anyone at all has concerns, speak now or forever hold your peace."

"We've talked, and I agree with Mage," offered Song. "We don't want anyone else to be hurt. We've seen the pharma guys try and fail to hack into Mage's firewall, and then they stormed the compound."

"What about the money?" asked Daniel again.

"Don't need it," answered Song. "And by not selling it, we limit our liability if things go sideways.

"It's the best way to combat a foe we don't know, rejoined Mage. I've given Tang a list of the components needed to upload the project via satellite to websites like WikiLeaks, and a few major news outlets around the world. Once it's out of our hands, anyone in the world will be able to contribute to testing. It will spread to too many servers for big pharma to combat. Every university, laboratory and think tank will have access to the program, and once the bad guys realize there is nothing they can do, they should stop hunting us. I started this project on a lark, just fooling around, but it's becoming a monster. We can't even return home until we know it is safe, and we don't know how long that will be.

"But, thanks to this submarine, we are protected from any corporate entities, and even internationally. There are not many submarine capable countries. Our chances of being found are greatly reduced. Song's got plenty of money, so let's just give the project away. Upload it to everywhere. Objections?"

A few eyebrows rose, but no-one spoke until Tang weighed in. "The people doing the hacking and attacking were likely after Mage's computers in an effort to destroy your project, and keep it from ever spreading. But they'd soon realize he could just recreate the app again, putting you all at unnecessary risk. Even if the mercenaries attacking the compound had succeeded in destroying Mage's computers, they'd still be after those who created it."

Song spoke up, "None of us were in it for the money. If anyone is concerned, I assure you that you'll never hurt for money. And if Humanity 2.0 works like we hope, there will probably be plenty of demand for our speaking services around the world. It's a story people will be drawn to."

"There is a precedent," observed Mage. "Have any of you ever heard of Linus Torvalds?"

"He's that Finnish guy that invented Linux, isn't he?" Jackie asked.

"Close enough. He released Linux software to everyone a couple of decades ago. While Bill Gates turned Microsoft into a world leader, and Steve Jobs did the same for Apple, Linus Torvalds just gave his code away, as a gift to the world. That's what we are going to do."

Jackie looked at Daniel, and he back at her. Each acknowledged a nod before Daniel spoke. "We're with you guys. We've always been with you."

"Then it is settled," Tang determined. "I will order the items on the lists you each gave me, but they'll have to be in stock. No back-orders. It will take a couple of days for everything to be shipped to Prince Rupert for pick-up, which is about how long it will take for us to get there. Once we have Mage's new electronics aboard, we upload before sinking beneath the surface again. Agreed?"

"Agreed," all responded.

"Then on that note," Tang continued, "submarine training commences in.....15 minutes."

"Hell, yeah!" Daniel cried. "I'm going to drive this puppy!"

Captain Tang led his new charge onto the bridge, wide-eyed and visibly pumped. Daniel knew this was going to be better than any Christmas, *ever!* Flashing lights reflected in his eyes as he scanned their numerous gauges and labels. "Trim? What does trim mean? And does everybody have to call me Captain when I'm driving? Steering? Oh, and is there a periscope? When can I drive? Where's the key?"

"First of all," interrupted Tang, "you are to be called helmsman, not Captain. There's only one Captain on a ship. Trim means the angle of the sub when rising to the surface or sinking below. And yes, there is a periscope."

"So cool. This is like being on Star Trek's bridge!"

"I assure you, it is not."

"Wait until Jackie sees me! She'll be so impressed."

Shaking his head slowly, Tang addressed his lover, currently manning the helm. "Robert, I leave this scalawag in your care. See what you can do about training him, will you? He makes me tired."

"Aye, Captain," Bobby responded, giving Tang a peck on the cheek. "Go get some sleep."

"At fifteen hundred hours, after training, bring us to the surface. I need to use the sat phone to call our man in Vancouver, and the crew has been promised some sunshine, topside."

"Aye," Bobby said again.

Turning to his new charge, Bobby advised Daniel, "You heard the Captain. We'll need to bring the Nautilus to the surface later. Would you like to practice that?"

"Totally! So, to go up, I need to pull on the wheel, like with a plane, right?"

"Definitely not right."

"Am I the first to learn this because you know I'll be good at it? Being helmsman, I mean?"

"You are first because the Captain thinks you'll take the longest to train."

"Oh. Well, I still get to be first."

"Now, no more questions unless I *ask* you if you have any questions. Got it?"

"Roger that. Um, Bobby that. 10-4. Copy."

"It's a ship, Daniel. Let's go with aye, aye."

"Aye, aye. Roger tha...... - yes, sir............ This is SO COOL!"

With his rare serious face on, Bobby lectured his student "Listen, Daniel. It may be 'cool', but the responsibility of this position is no laughing matter. Remember, you are driving a football stadium sized nuclear bomb."

"Whoa," Daniel whispered.

"There are bubble portholes here, here, and here," he went on, "and the switch for the underwater spotlight is mounted above us there, which you've already seen. The Pilot House, or bridge, is part of the conning tower, so once we reach the surface, we'll be above the water line."

"Aye aye, Captain."

"I'm not the Captain." Bobby corrected.

"So what do I call you when you're aboard? What's your title?"

"Hmmmmm, First Mate would be doubly appropriate, I suppose. But, you can just call me, Matey."

"Aye, Matey," Daniel responded, and saluted.

"As you would expect, this vessel is equipped with sonar up and down, meaning sky and sea. At the tip of the bow are side- and forward-facing sonars, to warn of anything nearby. Other sensors are spread around the hull. If you see *anything* on these monitors here, call me or Tang, pronto."

"I see the periscope there in front us, eh? That tall tube going up, right?"

"No, helmsman. That's actually what is called a 'folding telescopic snort mask'."

"I'll never remember that," Daniel joked.

"Yes....... you will. And a whole lot more if you're

going to guide this vessel."

"Errr........, okay. So what does a folded telescoping snort mask do?"

"It's for bringing in fresh air without fully surfacing. But, we do also have a periscope, which is behind us, near where we boarded.

"You've been told that this sub is nuclear powered," Bobby went on. "Your training will include details of how fusion works, and how it applies aboard the Nautilus. Are you ready to study some nuclear physics?"

"Are you serious?"

"As cancer."

"I'll manage. Jackie's super smart. She'll help me."

"Well, she's going to have to learn it too, so you can study together. Alright, then. One bonus of using nuclear batteries for propulsion, is that a large area normally needed for an engine room, keel and long propeller shaft, allows instead, a berth for our little, yellow mini-sub."

"It's so cool, Bobby! Have you been in it yet?"

"Yes, of course I've been in it. I was the one that sold this puppy to Tang in the first place, remember? May I continue?"

"Yes...... sir. I mean, aye matey. Aye, first

matey."

"Matey will be fine. Now, instead of standard propulsion, the Nautilus's thrust is provided by two Rim Drive Pump Jet Expulsors mounted on either side of the hull, near the stern. They look like jet engines, but can tilt in many directions for maneuvering unmatched by any in the submarine world. And being nuclear propelled, and not diesel, we need not stop at gas stations. That allows us range unavailable to most subs. Now, you can see by this gauge here.........."

Meanwhile, down on the lowest deck, the girls realized their chore was bigger than they'd first thought. Specialty equipment was everywhere, and though they tried to learn what they could along the way, many batteries, tanks and gadgets were simply unfamiliar to them. Deciding to split up, Song worked forward from the stern, and Jackie from the bow, back. Once they met, they'd compare notes. Anything confusing they'd take to Bobby.

As a result, Song began at the mini-sub. Once again, she spun the hand wheel and swung open the big, circular hatch outward. Climbing onto the catwalk, she noticed that everything in this room looked waterproof. *'Of course,'* she reasoned. *'To launch the mini-sub, this room would get flooded'.* Looking closer, she saw huge hinges at the very back, which would allow the outer, stern cone to swing up out of the way, leaving the aft wide open. Below was an extendable cradle which would then slide straight out the stern cone opening, for launch. It was an ingenious system. When the little sub returned, it simply drove right up the Nautilus's butt and dropped itself back onto the cradle.

She hopped down from the catwalk to the mini-sub's roof, then on down into the open hatch. This time, it was she that settled into the small cockpit. Control switches and gauges were plentiful, but she had no idea what most of them were. *'Focus, Song. Do what you can'*. So she tried a few of the more obvious choices, starting with 'Power'. Instantly, all of the dials and gauges lit up in front of her. She could see that the fuel tanks were full, battery power was good, air pressure was good. Flicking on each interior light, then the outside floodlight, all were burning bright. She stopped herself just in time from toggling the Open Cone switch. *'We definitely don't want to flood the chamber. I'd be swimming, drowning, or just drifting off as the Nautilus continued on her merry way.'*

*Powering* everything back off, she turned out the lights and pulled herself up through the ceiling hatch. She was soon back on the catwalk heading through the big, round yellow door. *'Huh. Yellow sub. Yellow door.'* She began humming an old Beatles tune to herself.

Swinging the door shut, she climbed a ladder beside it, which she found led directly into the Captain's cabin. This upper floor was mainly dedicated to his stateroom, study and chart room. Moving forward, she came across the server farm. *'This looks like a Mage room to me,'* she said to herself. *"I'll ask him whether it needs anything.'*

Next to the farm was a 'lobby' with several crew lockers. Inside the first locker was a row of a dozen pairs of overalls. She shed her robe on the spot, rendering her instantly naked. She donned the smallest pair of overalls she could find, but still had to roll up the arm and leg cuffs. But, compared to what she'd been wearing the past couple of days, she felt ready to hit the fashion runways of Milan.

Going down a floor, Song found both the fresh water and liquid oxygen tanks, confirming they were nearly at capacity. *'So far, nothing for my needs list.'* She found some batteries, fully charged, and fuel cells registered at max. She moved lazily into another cabin, and stopped in her tracks. *'Oh, I've got to tell Jackie about this! She'll pee herself.'*

Before her was a large and impressive pipe organ, likely modelled after a Jules Verne vision. Pipes ran up through the walls in an extravagantly colourful, artistic display. It's keyboard, though, was state of the art electronics. *'I think I found the new music room'.*

Room after room became more impressive. She even came across an indoor garden above the aft galley. There was a salon, a dining room, an art gallery and a pool. From the art gallery, she leaned out into a two metre bubble porthole to peer toward the stern, where side mounted expulsors churned away. *'They really do look like jet engines,'* she thought. Just then, the propulsion unit tipped down toward her, and she immediately felt the sub tipping up toward the surface. She decided her portion of the sub was 'ship shape'.

Near the bow, Jackie found her favourite toy. To her, it looked like a 3-man bobsled you'd see at the

Olympics, or maybe a luge. Either way, it had fun written all over it. Climbing in, she found the fuel gauge, which read full and batteries were completely charged. Donning a helmet, she tested enough to know the oxygen feed was working fine.

Tearing herself from her toy, she began exploring, moving aft. She confirmed the hyperbaric chamber had power and oxygen, and it was like that for the whole ship. Everything she checked was at max. She'd have to tell Bobby what a good job his company had done.

Song found Jackie just as she was kicking the diesel generator to life. "Well, that works too. Ooooohh, look at you, all fancy in your coveralls," Jackie teased.

"Here. I brought you a pair."

"What has the world come to that we're excited about wearing coveralls?" Jackie hadn't found the robes like Song had, so was still in her bikini. It stuck to her skin as she peeled it off and, laughing like a fool, pulled on the work duds.

"Why is it that I had to roll up my frumpy cuffs, but yours look like it was tailored just for you?"

"Everything fits me."

"No. Everything looks good on you. There's a difference. Anyways, follow me. I want to show you something." Stopping at the entry to the Salon, she shouted, "Ta da!" Jackie's face lit up at the sight of the pipe organ stretching up the far wall. She scooted inside and laughed as she tested a few keys. Looking up, she laughing again at the wall's resonance. More keys emulated various instruments.

"Ooooh! I love your Steinway, Song, but on this I'll be able to sound like any instrument."

Checking her watch, Song realized today's four hours of sub school was no longer in session. "Isn't Daniel at the helm right now? We're supposed to be surfacing soon. Wanna come get some sun? Jackie? Jacks?"

"Okay, see ya," Jackie said absently, already sitting on the organ's bench. Song waved her hand and slipped out of the room as Jacks breathed life into the organ.

Song went in search of Mage instead, finding him at the Server Farm. His face danced as he gushed to Song about the electronics onboard. She didn't, of course, understand any of it, but she did understand the elation behind it. His mood was improving. Kissing him deeply, she suggested, "Let's go to the Bridge and see how Daniel is doing. Tang says we'll be able to catch some rays topside soon."

When they joined their friends, the faces of the two men in the Pilot House was a study of opposites. Bobby could barely keep his eyes open. He rubbed his temples, fighting off a headache. Daniel's eyes, however, couldn't have been wider. "Hey, guys. I'm the helmsman! See?" he announced with pride.

"Okay, helmsman. Do you remember our lesson?" queried Bobby. "I want you to bring us down 50 feet, then up again, this time right to the surface. We are currently at 100 feet. Take us to 150 before surfacing. What will you do?"

"Ummmm......, ballast tanks, right? Add water to sink us lower, and fill them with air to go up? And tilt the engines, right? I'm right, aren't I?"

"Yes, Daniel. You're right. And watch your trim to keep us fairly level. The sub will use some of its air reserve to bring us to the surface, but we will fill them up again, how?"

"By that 'snort mask' periscope-looking thing you told me about?"

"Yes, right again." Once they reached the 150 foot mark, Bobby advised, "Ready? Now bring us up slowly." Daniel reached for the switches, watching Bobby, who nodded. "Good. Watch your trim. Okay. Looking fine, helmsman," which elicited Daniel's famous smile. "Slowly......see our depth changing on that gauge? It won't take long. Keep going."

Soon, the conning tower broke the surface sending water cascading from both sides of the decks. Bobby scanned the horizon. "All clear, Okay, helmsman. Shut us down," They heard the engines shut down, and the Bridge went quiet.

"Alright! Go Daniel!" exclaimed Song.

"And that ends school for today," said Bobby. "I've got to go wake up Tang. He wanted to know when we hit the surface so he could make his calls." He disappeared, leaving the two couples to shade their eyes from the sun. The sparkling view was a big upgrade from the darkness that had enveloped the Nautilus since their departure.

"Where'd you get the fancy clothes, ladies?" asked Mage. "I could use a change."

The girls posed, modelling their new coveralls look for the boys. "Play your cards right, and we'll hook you up with some." Song purred. "But first, since you guys are still in your bathing suits, let's go up on deck. It's sunny!"

And sunny it was. Clearly, they could see the submarine stretching far before them, with bright sunlight glistening off of the wet metal in an impressive, twinkling display.

"Your boat is a big one, Song" Daniel said with a touch of awe.

"Yes. And there's as much behind us as you can see in front of us," responded Song.

"Whoa."

Captain Tang swept into the Pilot House as a man on a mission. With several lists in one hand, and his sat phone in the other, "topside," is all he said.

Song squealed, "C'mon Jacks. We have to go find where you left your swimsuit. In the meantime, you boys get drinks and meet us up there."

"Yeah, baby! 'Party on the patio!'. Well, you know, top deck anyway."

For the size of the submarine, the top deck wasn't very large, even when extended. But, it was plenty big enough for four people. Mage and Daniel were stretched out in the sun, with a beer already beside them when the girls arrived holding cold ciders.

As the girls stretched out to tan, Song handed Daniel the tube of sunscreen. "Would you be a dear, and sunscreen me?" Gladly, he relished his assignment.

Though the sun was beating down upon them, the sea air kept them from overheating. The sub drifted quietly, bobbing on the tide, its crew lazily drowning in the sunshine. Time moved more slowly on the top deck, and that was just fine with them.

Captain Tang had made his calls to the lawyer, and at sundown resumed their northerly trek. As darkness stole the sky once more, he risked a few hours cruising on the surface so his crew could lie in their berths, stargazing through their cabins' ceiling portholes. Thousands of stars and constellations never witnessed in the city twinkled brightly over the Nautilus. The crew slept well, to be sure.

It was two more days before the Nautilus

approached Prince Rupert, a small town of about 12,000 inhabitants, up the British Columbia coast near the Alaskan Panhandle. The wettest city in Canada wasn't known for tourism. It rained an average of 240 days per year, for more than a hundred inches. But, she had a good, deep water port, and was beautiful when arriving by sea.

Captain Tang put down anchor near the Kinahan Islands, while the boys unstowed the launch and life jackets. Mage and Bobby were selected to go ashore, since their goods would need to be checked the most thoroughly. Suppliers had been told to fly everyone's supplies to Rupert with the stipulation that the goods would be ready to pick up this morning.

The skies were overcast, but winds were light. Once Bobby and Mage were ready, the Nautilus slowly bubbled its way down into the briny beneath them, leaving the launch floating free. Only a small buoy remained to mark the sub's location.

Prince Rupert was a small enough town to walk to collect their supplies. Mage checked his electronics order closely, and was pleased to see it was complete. He and Bobby headed for the store holding the girls' packages, and were making good time. As they crossed the street en route to the grocery store, Mage spotted something in the window of a pawn shop. "Go ahead, I'll catch up with you," he told Bobby.

In the window sat a viola in great condition. It's tone would be lower and deeper than a violin, but higher than Song's cello. Mage was almost laughing he was so happy. The viola is perfect! The shopkeeper was also happy, throwing in additional strings for free. He'd had the viola for years, and was happy to finally see it go.

Mage's elation did not last, however. The TV screen behind the counter was on.......

*In other news, the mysterious helicopter crash at a private mansion in West Vancouver is baffling investigators. Officials report an armed incursion took place, by unknown assailants, but have little to go on. Blood was evident on the scene, but no bodies were found. Incredibly, defenders brought down the helicopter with a shouldered surface to air missile. The helicopter itself had no markings to indicate who the attackers were, and the investigation is ongoing.*

*Officials have been unable to contact the property's owner since the incident. Records indicate that the Zhao family, immigrants from China, built the luxury home a few years ago. The property was equipped with advanced security deterrents, including water cannons, bullet-proof blinds, and a blinding mist inside the home, all of which had been deployed. Neighbours suggest the compound was owned by Chinese military strongman Jian Zhao until his death two years ago. His daughter, Song Zhao, is a person of interest in the investigation. Vancouver Police and the Transportation Safety Board continue to investigate the scene.*

*And in a dramatic twist, Song Zhao is rumoured to also have connections to the fire near Chinatown that we reported a few days ago. One man died, and another, his grandson and heir, Mage Moon, is still missing. Moon and Zhao, shown onscreen here, are said to be romantically involved, and if anyone has information regarding the whereabouts of either, please contact the R.C.M.P. or Vancouver City Police. Arson investigators are on the scene, and have deemed the shop fire suspicious.*

Mage froze as his eyes flitted around the room. Fortunately, the cashier hadn't been listening, nor had he seen the photos of Song and Mage onscreen. He paid quickly and bolted for the door, heartbroken. He felt as though he'd taken a fist to the gut. Elation to despair, all within seconds.

He was crying uncontrollably when he caught up with Bobby in the produce aisle, "We gotta go!" and scooted right back outside. Mage's face reflected his hopelessness and tragedy. Bobby temporarily abandoned his cart, and once outside, he held Mage by the shoulders, imploring him to say what was wrong. What had happened to upset him so?

Mage's words were almost unintelligible through his choked weeping. "They had Song and my pictures on the TV! The goons burned down my grandfather's shop and the news made it sound like I did it," he sobbed in anguish. "He's dead, Bobby! Gramps is dead! They killed my grandfather, all for my stupid project! He's dead and they think I did it, Bobby. And Song is a 'person of interest' for the helicopter crash," Mage choked. "What am I going to do without him, Bobby? He was my only family!" Gathering Mage into his arms, Bobby let him cry it out. He was nothing if not empathetic. But, it was truly gut-wrenching to see a friend hurting like this.

"Shit, shit, shit!" Mage's eyes darted left and right, then back over his shoulder. "Everybody is going to know who I am, aren't they? They had my picture! I gotta get out of here, Bobby. I'll meet you back at the launch."

"Hey, wait a minute! We still need other fresh food. I can't carry it all by myself."

"Find a cab. They didn't have a picture of you."

Clutching his electronics order and viola to his chest, Mage ran off in the direction of the beached launch.

By the time Bobby joined him, the wind was picking up and a storm threatened on the horizon. Another day of rain was no surprise to Prince Rupert's residents. With the worsening weather, Bobby knew he had to get Mage back to the Nautilus, and fast. Staying to wait out a storm wasn't an option.

Steering into the chop as much as he could, Bobby gunned the little outboard until they finally came to the marker buoy. The moment they arrived, the Nautilus bubbled up from the deep like a sleeping dragon, right on cue. They crew had been waiting, and watching through the periscope.

Tang was the first top-side, followed closely by Song.

"Are you alright, Bobby? I was worried about the sudden change in the weather," said Tang, under knitted brow.

Bobby looked Tang in the eye, then turned to Song, and said, "I'm okay, but Mage needs help."

"He needs help? What's wrong with him?" she cried.

"First things first," Bobby replied. "Song, you need to get Mage down to your cabin. Get Daniel to help if you need to."

"But what's wrong?" she implored.

"I think it best for him to tell you, Song. Get him to bed. I think he's in shock. He's going to need any help you can give. And Song?.......... Its bad."

"What's bad? Why won't you tell me?"

"Its best if he tells you. His news also affects you. You were both mentioned."

"Mentioned where? What the hell is going on, Bobby?"

"See if you can calm and stabilize him. He's the one who saw it. Console the boy. Get him to sleep."

Daniel and Jackie arrived, smiling to welcome the returnees home, but quickly realized it wasn't a happy reunion. "What's up, bud?" he asked Mage, but got no response. Just dead eyes.

"He's in shock, Daniel. For now, help Song take him to their cabin." Bobby directed. "And don't pester him with questions. I'll tell you all at dinner."

"At least I made dinner," Jackie said meekly. "I wanted it to be a surprise, seeing you were out doing errands for me."

"Thank you, Jackie. Your timing is impeccable. I don't think I could cook now. Daniel and Song have Mage covered. Can you and Tang help me unload the launch and stow it?"

"Of course."

When the goods were unloaded, and the launch returned to its its berth, Jackie spotted the viola case and smiled at Mage's consideration. She took it to the salon, and placed it beside the pipe organ. *'Song will be so happy to have this. Good for Mage.'*

Outside, the sea began to heave and crash against the hull. The storm was arriving in force. With the decks cleared and hatches secured, Captain Tang once again sunk the Nautilus below the gale, into the quiet peace of the deep.

# *Chapter 11*

*"Men always want to be a woman's first love. That is their clumsy vanity. Women have a more subtle instinct about things: What they like is to be a man's last romance."*

***Oscar Wilde***

The crew met that night in the Dining Room, alarmed and full of questions. The only member of the Fellowship not in attendance was Mage. Song had finally gotten him to sleep.

Dinner was a quiet affair, with everyone unwilling to break the silence until Song was ready. During dessert, she stood and tinkled her glass for attention. She needn't have bothered. The crew was already looking at her, with anticipation and dread. "Everybody, listen up. By now, you've all heard that the boys learned of tragic news when they went to town. Mage saw a truly disturbing newscast, and is understandably heartbroken.

"A few nights ago, his grandfather's shop was burned to the ground with Gramps in it." Jackie gasped, holding one hand to her mouth, as the other grabbed Daniel's wrist. "Mage thinks the pharma goons were likely trying to destroy any and all research he may have kept inside his old apartment. Tang thinks they may also have been making a statement. Considering their attempt to hack Mage's computer, as well as the helicopter attack at the compound, it's reasonable to believe the bad guys are serious about completely destroying the project files."

"That would leave us all as loose ends," Tang added, ominously.

"Mage is inconsolable," Song continued."He has no appetite, so I thought his absence here at supper would give us an opportunity to discuss the situation freely, without upsetting him further. We are a Fellowship, after all. We discuss things as a group, and make decisions as a group, right?"

"Right," Bobby agreed. "I'll start. So, after beaching the launch near town, I headed for groceries while Mage went to a pawn shop after picking up his electronics. He'd spotted a pawn shop with an item he thought Song would like."

"A gift? What gift?" Song asked.

"I'll show you later," Jackie told her with a grim smile. "It's down below."

Bobby continued. "While Mage was buying said gift, a TV behind the counter displayed pictures of Mage, and you, Song. The story talked about the helicopter crash back at home, and your father's ties with the Chinese military. They know you are now the owner now, so they want to talk to you."

"Don't say anything to the press until I have talked to the family lawyer," Tang advised.

"One thing Mage was able to make clear on our boat ride back to the sub, was that his grandfather had died in the fire that levelled the shop. They suspect arson, and since Mage is the heir, they want to talk to him as another 'person of interest'."

"What the hell?" Daniel demanded, indignantly.

"At this point, they just want to talk to the boy. But, the photos of him and Song were displayed together, so they've made the connection between the two stories."

Jackie turned to Bobby. "The photos on the newscast. Did they show just Song and Mage, or all of us?"

"Just them, I think. Before he went into shock, Mage only mentioned his own and Song's. Both as 'persons of interest'. And that Mage felt they were hinting at implicating him in the fire."

Daniel blurted, "That's crazy. It's offensive! Mage loved the old guy. I did too."

"It seems to me," observed Tang, "that those pharma fellows may be spinning the narrative here. By making Mage a suspect, more eyes will be looking for him. They may be just trying to flush him out."

"Sensationalist journalism," scoffed Song. "The juicier they can make it sound, the more viewers they get. Wealth, arson, murder – it's a trifecta for TV. They'll milk the story for weeks."

Jackie was anxious. "If anyone *did* recognize Mage in Rupert, the Mounties may be looking for us up here already. How long will it be before all of our photos get shown? And what about my professors. Are they at risk, too?"

"We must be careful here," warned Tang. "Until we know more, its counter-productive to speculate. The newscast did not say anything about your project, which means were have a bit of time to strategize. If big pharma *is* pulling strings, they're capable of bribing just about anyone. So, Song? I will contact our family lawyer. He can act as a middle-man for us until we understand the risks. He has copies of the mansion contracts too, and consulted on the building of the compound. If we have to submit affidavits, he can help with that. I'll also ask him to put a team on the legal status of Mage's grandfather's electronics shop. You don't want the authorities seizing it. The same goes for the compound."

"Have him make arrangements for Mage's grandfather's ashes to be released to his custody, for now," requested Song. "With all of the press coverage, Mage won't even be able to arrange Gramps's funeral. That's going to crush him."

Solemnly and with respect, Tang nodded. "I'll have his ashes delivered to the compound.

"It is still my thinking," he continued, "that the Nautilus is the safest place on Earth for this crew right now. Let's let the sea be our cocoon. The situation is volatile for us all right now, and when Mage uploads the project to the world, it could get worse. For now, we stay aboard this ocean palace."

"But Captain, what about you? Are *you* good?" Bobby asked with concern. "Big responsibilities you didn't sign up for."

"I signed up to protect Song, and by extension, all members of this Fellowship. As soon as Mage is able, he'll upload to the world. That should let some air out of pharma's tires. We do not know how, or even if, it will impact things. Until we do, there's safety in the sea."

First thing the following morning, the Nautilus was already floating on the surface. Captain Tang had spoken at length to the lawyer from his satellite phone again. Reception was good, aided by the cloudless skies of early Summer. Though the seas were still a bit choppy from yesterday, the Nautilus was mostly unaffected. Water rolled off the behemoth sub like surf from a boulder. But the sound of the waves crashing against the hull did make listening difficult, so he took his time to ensure he was understood, and that they were both on the same page.

In the meantime, the two young couples were in the crew galley eating breakfast. Everyone waited sympathetically for Mage to speak, but speak he did not.

So Bobby took it upon himself to perk things up. In an overly loud voice, he called "Who wants more waffles? Get 'em while they're hot. Or coffee? We've got lotsa coffee. Or, how about more loud, imposing questions?" he yelled, poking Mage to no response.

"Waffles," Daniel said, scarfing down his third helping. Jackie gave him a nudge. "Whaaaatt? Who doesn't like waffles?"

Mage just indicated more coffee, and cleared his throat. "I'm ready to upload to the internet. Last chance, folks. It's a big step, and it can't be taken back."

"Make it so," Daniel mumbled through a mouthful of waffles.

"Okay, I'll be on the top deck if anybody needs me," and he stood to go.

The girls briefly regarded one another, before Song said, "We want to be there, too...... with you."

"Okay," said Mage. "Let's go then." Bobby excitedly joined them.

"What! Now?" sputtered Daniel. "I'm not finished my waffles yet. Jackie? Jacks?" Muttering to himself, he left his breakfast and hurried to catch up.

Up on deck, the surf continued to crash against the hull, sending up myriads of misty rainbows. Tang was just finishing his call. He spoke quietly with Mage, and placed a comforting hand of assurance on his shoulder.

Mage had his equipment set up in minutes, confirming a strong link with the satellite. "Ready?"

"Ready," called the others. Daniel screamed it.

Checking his laptop's monitor one more time, Mage pressed a single key. "Done."

"What? That's it?" Daniel whined, over the crash of the salty surf. "Just....... done?"

"Done. We have just given birth to Humanity 2.0".

"Well, that was a bit anti-climactic, wasn't it? I left a perfectly good plate of waffles, for this?"

The sea was getting turbulent again by the time Mage's file fully uploaded to the satellite. It was as if Mother Nature had specifically waited for him to finish. A dark front of ominous looking clouds crowded above the Nautilus and within minutes they were all scrambling for the hatch. The strong wind had become a gale, and the expanse of blue sky was swallowed by the oncoming thunderheads.

The foul weather lasted for two more days, but all had been calm below the surface. Sub school continued, studying ropes and knots, maps and star maps, navigation and piloting. There was much to teach, but Tang was pleased with how they had all thrown themselves into becoming competent sailors. From operating the ship's generators, to refilling air tanks by the 'snort mask', to proper use of the retractable thrusters, the new crew members all performed well.

On the first sunny day, at 3:00 p.m., when sub school ended, the students all raced for the toys in the schoolyard. Now that they were trained, Jackie was keen to try the diver's bobsled, and Song was all about the mini-sub. What they assumed would be complicated lessons had actually proven to be quite simple. They couldn't wait! But, wait they would, when Tang wouldn't authorize use of either.

"It may be sunny, but it's too rough on the surface for the sleds. And you're not using the mini-sub or sleds while we are cruising. Understood?"

"What's the point of owning it when I can't use it," Song sulked.

"And what's the point of having a bodyguard if he's just going to let you die? We should keep moving."

"Come on, Song. Captain Party Pooper has spoken," Jackie said. "Let's get the boys and check out the swimming pool instead. We can still try out the new bikinis the boys picked up for us in Rupert."

Song entered the $2^{nd}$ Officer's cabin to change, where she found Mage curled up under the covers. He was awake but not interested in frolicking in the pool with the others.

"Are you sure?" questioned Song. I've got a new bikini I think you might like."

"Another time. I'm kinda grumpy." He rolled over to face the wall.

"Alright, but you'll be sorry."

Song wandered into the pool room to find Jackie already in the pool. "Where's Daniel?"

"He's gone to change. I'm already dressed."

"Dressed in your new bikini, I see."

"Yes, ma'am," she answered, with mischief in her eye.

"Me too," Song announced with a bit of mischief of her own. And with a flourish, she spun while she removed her robe, to Jackie's applause and delight.

"Oh, yeah! That's hot!" Jackie teased. "Mage is going to like that one!"

"Not today, he's not. Says he's too grumpy for shenanigans today."

"Such a shame," Jackie responded with a giggle.

Song dove into the water, rising up beside her friend at the side of the pool. Comparing how their new bikinis fit, they decided they both fit *very* well.

"Yo and hello!" Daniel arrived, waving to the girls. "Ready for a bit of pool time, ladies?"

"We're ready. Are you?" Jackie asked, as both her and Song pushed away from the side wall, floating on their backs. "Come on in. The water's fine!"

Daniel did a double-take. "Topless? Are you

serious?"

"Oh, does it make you uncomfortable?" Song asked innocently. "We're sorry. Perhaps we should turn over so you don't have to look."

"Please, don........!"

The ladies ignored him, flipped over, and floated bums up. Bums only covered by a thong of dental floss, that is.

"I'm starting to really like hanging out with you girls. Uh, but where's Mage? He'd be liking this too."

"Mage couldn't make it today. It's just me. I hope that's okay," teased Song. "But, maybe we should just go, if we make you uncomfortable." Kicking their feet to escape him, he gave chase, diving in and tackling first Jackie, then Song. The only thing available to grab was skin, and Daniel was okay with that. Both soon turned on him, attacking and pushing him under. Jackie pushed down on his shoulders, causing her breasts to squeeze together, mashing them up against his ear. So Song repeated the move, pushed one of her own against his other ear.

"Nice headphones," teased Jackie.

"What? I can't hear you." Daniel responded. "They must be those noise cancelling headphones I've heard about."

It was unquestionable. Daniel was having a great

day.

The girls tired of drowning him, so when Song found a volleyball in a storage locker, they were soon playing keep away. But his concentration on the ball was woeful, distracted by the bobbing, naked lady flesh. At last, though, he managed to deflect the ball out of the pool, and hopped out, beating the girls to the ball. He stooped to pick it up while Jackie scissor locked him from behind, knocking the ball free again. She clung to him, etching her bare nipples into his back. He captured it again, but held it high above his head where his lover couldn't reach.

From the pool, Song laughed and pointed at poor Daniel. With the ball held high to avoid Jackie's lunges, he was unable to conceal a considerable lump straining against the confines of his trunks. Jackie hopped from his back, knocking the ball loose a second time. Daniel beat her to it again. and as he stooped over for it this time, Jackie goosed him from behind, right between the legs, and right on target. "Goose the gander!" she called out. He bolted upright in surprise, as Song's tears of laughter mixed with the pool water. Jackie pushed one foot against his butt to propel Daniel back into the pool, and leapt on top him. Wrapping her long legs around him, she kissed him passionately and ground herself ever so slightly against his lump. Song stood awkwardly alone, while the two young lovers became lost in each other. So she hopped out, threw her robe over her shoulder, winked at Jackie, and left the pool room to the young lovers.

Making her way back to her cabin, she wandered

past Tang at the helm on the bridge. She thought he was going to have a coronary on the spot when he saw she, still wearing nothing but her thong, with the robe thrown over one shoulder.

Left alone back in his 2nd Officer's Cabin, Mage had been reflecting on the past year. The highs had been very high, but the lows, very low. His parents and grandfather were alive just a year ago. The electronics shop, which he'd immersed himself into as the vehicle to straighten out his life, was now gone. He was without a home, without a family, and without a job. But even with all of that, Song's luminous, green eyes always beamed colour back into his life. Together, they could have the luxury of following whatever path they chose in life. Without her, he would have nothing right now, but with her, he had everything.

She sauntered into the cabin, tossing aside her robe and scratching her wet head. "I see you feel better."

"Yeah, a bit I guess."

"Well, you certainly look better."

"Whenever I feel bad, I just think of your angelic face and I'm healed."

"Awwww. So sweet. And so sappy. But, it isn't me making you feel better. It's you."

"How so?" he asked, with a kiss.

"I was sneaky. Before I left for the pool, I switched on your app, and had it playing Humanity 2.0 for you the whole time I was gone."

"What ?"

"Humanity. I played it in a loop."

The penny dropped. "Ahhh. The silent version?"

She snapped her fingers, pointed at him and winked. "That's right. You created a silent version that only played the notes beyond human hearing. You see? You think I'm not always listening, but I am."

"So tricky!" Mage cried, tickling her and pulling her onto his lap, face to face.

"I am *very* tricky." she said softly, as she let her robe fall from her shoulder.

"So, is this how you went to the pool?" Mage joked.

"Uh huh."

"What, you were dressed like this when Daniel was there?"

"Uh huh. Don't worry. Besides, I did tell you that Jackie and I were going to wear the new bikinis we had Tang order. They just happen to be topless," she whispered, innocently. "Just a thong, really."

"So, Daniel really saw your breasts?"

"Yup. I stuck one in his ear, actually. Together, Jackie and I made him headphones."

"I'm not sure how I feel about that."

"You should feel good. Jacks and I have decided this will be the year of our sexual awakening. The new swimsuits are all we'll be wearing for swimming and tanning from now on."

"Okay, I'm warming to the idea."

"I'm sure you are. I'll be sure to tell Jackie you were sorry you couldn't make it this time. I'm sure she'd be happy to make it up to you. She's a bit of an exhibitionist, you know."

"I think you both are, if you walked by Tang like that."

"I'm learning. Does it turn you on, lover?" She looked down at the gap between them, and rocked her hips against him. "It turns me on."

"So it seems."

"Ever since you introduced me to sex, I'm excited all the time!"

As he stood, he lifted her with him until they were face to face. Her feet dangled more than a foot off the floor as she kicked off her thong. Using first her hand, then her legs, she managed to get Mage naked, as well. She wrapped her legs around him, and kissed him passionately. Slowly and exquisitely, he lowered her, leaving a moist streak trailing down his belly. Mage was a tall boy, and she was feeling it all as he lowered her further. He allowed her time to settle in with a few deep breaths, before rocking his hips slowly. After months of torrid sex, they were learning the ecstasy of the slow burn. When the gasps, shudders and spasms were complete, Mage rolled off to find that Song had actually lost consciousness.

He chuckled to himself, thinking, *'I think I'm really going to like this sexual awakening thing.'*

# *Chapter 12*

*"Sex is like money. Only too much is enough."*

**John Updike**

The following morning, the bright, blue skies were back, which contrasted nicely with the dark, ocean blue. Blue on blue. It had been less than a week since the carnage back in Vancouver, but with Humanity 2.0 now officially out there, the Fellowship of the Deep were settling into their new home. Captain Tang recognized all of the stresses of the week, and designated the day as one of rest and relaxation. No cruising, no sub school, and no outside world. And frankly, he and Bobby could use a break from their 24/7 marathon of piloting the sub and training the crew.

Up on the top deck, the quiet lapping of waves against the hull was the only sound in the still vastness of the open ocean. *'Too quiet'*, Mage decided. Windowing his laptop to his music files, he plugged in his auxiliary speakers, clicked on his favourite jam, and cranked it. Pulling the sundeck to its extended position, he telescoped out the diving board for everyone's use. It was time for the entire crew to blow off some steam. Warm sunshine and the top deck awaited the crew.

First out of the hatch came Bobby, running and dodging away from Tang, laughing like a kid. He felt Tang's arm tug on his shoulder just before launching himself from the diving board, screeching with glee. The poor captain had stretched too far, lost his balance, and couldn't stop himself in time before he slipped, bumped his butt, and caromed off the side of the diving board.

Mage cheered madly, yelling "Five point six, Tang. Sorry, but you failed to meet Olympic standards!" Bobby swam to Tang, pushed him underwater, and climbed onto his back. The two were cackling like the loons they were, as they raced back up the ladder. This time, Tang ran straight to the diving board himself, before Bobby could catch him. Springing high, he touched his toes and pulled off a perfect swan dive.

"Better!" cried Mage. "Eight point five."

Daniel arrived holding a beer in each hand . "Here, bud," he offered. Squinting up at the sun, they counted themselves lucky. Somehow, a couple of poor boys from an inner city school had ended up here, bobbing around the Pacific aboard a billionaire's submarine! No beer had ever tasted as good. "You know, you're lucky to have me out here in the middle of nowhere with you, bud."

"Yeah, and how's that, Daniel?"

"Well, for starters, I brought you a cold beer."

"An accomplishment, to be sure. But, I don't see any more."

"Well, technically the girls said they'd bring up a

cooler, but I snagged us a couple first."

"So, I should be thankful for them, not for you?"

"Well, it was my idea, at least."

Soon, the girls dragged a cooler up the ladder, giggling away. As promised, each was wearing only their topless, thong bathing suit again. When Bobby saw the girls' garb, he stole a look at Tang for a reaction, who just smiled and shrugged. *'My man is certainly mellowing!'* Bobby thought, happily. And, rather than join the kids, he winked and pulled Tang down the entry hatch behind him. Tang recognized that wink.

As the ladies put down their small cooler, Song lamented sadly, "Mage was distraught he'd missed out at the pool, so back by popular demand...................... is us!" Both spread their arms and thrust forward their chests out at the boys, "Ta da!"

"See what you missed at the pool, buddy?" Daniel teased.

"Yeah, I can definitely see........ those." The two girls were about as different as two girls could be, but both were smart, gorgeous, embracing their womanhood, and testing their sexual awoken boundaries.

Jackie approached Mage, bent over him and said, "I hear you missed me at the pool"

Mage looked up at her, shading his eyes from the sun. He needn't have worried, as Jackie's dangling breasts shaded him just fine. "That I did, gorgeous."

"That's too bad," she replied with a fake pout. "Let me make it up to you." She dropped the sunscreen in his lap, while sharing with him her sexiest, smouldering look. "Would you be a dear and sunscreen me?" Song just looked on with a smirk.

"I can definitely take care of that for you!" It was no small task, as her upper, white patches needed extra attention today.

Jackie stretched out, face down, on a towel, and donned her new dark sunglasses. As Mage looked down at her back, she may as well have been naked. The thong's dental floss between her cheeks was her only apparel. Mage took his task very seriously. He squirted a generous dollop of sunscreen onto Jackie's back and went to work. She shivered at the touch as he massaged her entire back firmly. Next, he worked from her toes, upward to her knees, and then her perfect buttocks. It was a long and dedicated process, as he made sure to protect her everywhere. Jackie flinched, but let him go about his work.

Unprompted, she rolled over, and as she did, he couldn't tell if her eyes were open or closed through her dark sunglasses. No matter. He worked up from her toes again, up the front of her shins and thighs before protecting those dastardly exposed creases just outside the front portion of her thong.. She was literally quaking at his every touch, now. Song watched intently as Jackie's breath became ragged. She stole a look for Daniel's reaction, and caught him checking out her own breasts.

Mage squirted another dollop of sunscreen onto her belly, working into her flesh until he was tucking his hand slightly beneath her waistband. You can never be too careful.

"We better *really* protect this white, untanned area," he said with concern. He began rubbing sunblock into her considerable breasts, and when finished his final upstroke, he squeezed their bulk, tugged once on her nipples and rolled them over with his thumb and released her. Mage smiled at Song and mouthed, "thanks, baby."

He could see that Song was getting worked up just from watching so, with his job complete, he tossed the sunscreen to Daniel, and nodded toward Song. Jumping to his feet, Daniel approached Song. She nodded her head, so he squirted some sunscreen on her back. But Song had been watching Mage and Jackie, and was already shuddering with each stroke of Daniel's strong hands. He followed Mage's lead, and did her back side before the front. He also dedicated himself to her creases, as Mage had with Jackie.

"I caught you checking these out a few minutes ago," Song said to Daniel. "Hall pass. Get to work!" Ever industrious, he first touched them with reverence, before rubbing in the tanning oil in diminishing circular patterns. And when the circle was smallest, he too gave her nipples a rough tug and twirl, following Mage's lead, as a shudder ran up her spine.

Smiling at Mage, Daniel tossed the sunscreen to

Jackie.

"Your turn, Jacks." She didn't need to be asked twice. Both women were smouldering by now. Mage laid on a towel, and Jackie was on him like a hungry lioness. Using the template employed by the boys, Jackie worked up the back of Mage's legs, then straddled him to do his back. Her face was the epitome of sensuous seduction, working the sunscreen into his torso and just inside his waistband. When she had him flip over, he was stone. She began on the front of his legs, working the sunscreen right up, just under the hem of his shorts causing an involuntary buck of his hips. He was sweating profusely as she covered his chest still straddling and rocking with each upstroke. She looked devilishly at a smiling Song and Daniel, before quickly tugging on the tip of him, and rolling her fingers.

"Fair's fair," she said to Mage, and tossed the sunscreen to Song. She who jumped up and pushed Daniel to the deck. She gave him a perfunctory covering on his back before forcibly flipping him over. With every stroke on sunscreen to the chest, she also rocked. Song needed relief, and everyone could see it. She gave Daniel a quick tip grip, and launched herself onto Mage. She didn't care that her friends would see. She glanced over at her best friend to see Jackie removing her own thong completely. Even Song thought she was quite a sight.

Watching the other couple while making love themselves kept the heat on. The intensity of the day was something none would ever forget. The sun blazed down on their spent, naked bodies as they lazed on the top deck for hours. They were fortunate to have been so thorough with the sunscreen.

Mage was stirred awake by a sudden noise. He looked over to see Song still passed out, but Daniel and Jackie were gone.

He looked back up in time to see Jackie shoot ten feet into the air on one of the submersible scooters, getting serious airtime. Slapping back to the surface, she looked over her shoulder to see Daniel in hot pursuit. Jackie took evasive action, diving quickly back into the sea. For several minutes the world was quiet again until Daniel came blasting out first this time, with Jackie right on his tail. Watching them was like watching otters play. After a couple of laps around the Nautilus, they went deep again, for good this time.

But that wasn't the noise that woke him. It was up in the sky. Mage cracked an eye to see a plane passing directly overhead. It banked and dropped in altitude, clearly descending towards the Nautilus.

"Let's get inside," he told Song. "That plane is too interested in us. Tang should be told. Let's head in."

Captain Tang barely noticed when Song and Mage came down the ladder naked. They pointed to the aircraft through the ceiling porthole, and within seconds was flipping switches and pressing buttons, powering up the Nautilus.

Daniel and Jackie came up the stairs, and asked, "What's up?"

"It's a reconnaissance plane taking pictures. I

think it's time we disappeared again. Recess is over, people. We need to div, NOW. Are the hatches all closed?"

"Aye, Captain," responded Mage. "But the upper deck extension and diving board aren't stowed."

"We can't wait." Tang filled the ballast tanks with water, while swivelling the engines on either side of the sub. The Nautilus's stern rose up right out of the sea as the bow dipped sharply at an angle steep enough to force the crew to lean back for balance.

Tang took her down to two hundred feet before relaxing. "Are we safe?" Song asked the Captain.

"Yes, for now. But, whoever took those photos will be trying to track us. They could have been Canadian out of CFB Comox, or American, out of Anchorage. Either way, we are not wanting to be found quite yet. If we stay submerged, we should be safe for awhile. But we need to put some distance between us. "

Bobby added, "The diving board has to come in, and the deck extension re-stowed before we can go full speed. So tonight, as long as Mage's comm rooms show no sonar or radar activity, and the periscope is clear, we can surface just long enough to re-stow them and be gone."

"The good news," continued Tang, "is that Canada doesn't have any operable submarines at the moment, and the U.S. has no naval bases in Alaska. But we are deep enough now that planes will not be able to find us, so we should be okay."

"But, what's next?" Jackie wondered. "Where do we go now? And what if we're followed?"

Fear and anxiety were back on the faces of his crew. He didn't like it. So much for their day of rest and relaxation. Hoping to calm them, he answered, "As far as the reconnaissance planes are concerned, it's a big ocean and we could go in any direction. We should be too deep to find so we just need to get going. Even though the Americans don't have an Alaskan naval base, they do patrol with their own nuclear subs. And the Russians have a submarine base in Vladivostok, so we don't want to go that way, either, as they have nuclear subs too."

"So where do we go?" she asked.

"Anywhere you want," Tang responded, even managing a smile. "Is there somewhere in the world you've wanted to go?" He thought for a moment before declaring, "my suggestion would be to head for the Philippines. It's away from the U.S. and Russia, and has more than 7,000 islands, many of which are unsettled. I know the area well."

"That sounds good," offered Song.

"Any objections? No? Okay then. Daniel, to the helm. Take us on a bearing of 250 degrees."

"Aye, aye, Captain." Daniel snapped off a salute. "Two, five, zero."

"And Song," said Tang. "You should get dressed." Looking down, she blushed as she realized they were still nude.

"Don't be embarrassed. You're not the first couple today to come down that ladder naked today."

And so, the Fellowship of the Deep headed southwest to an uncertain future. A week ago, they were carefree and living in a mansion. Today, they were fugitives of their own making. But, at least they were still living in a mansion of a sort.

What will the future bring for these six, intrepid souls?

# *Chapter 13*

*"Medicine is the restoration of discordant elements;
Sickness is the discord of the elements infused into the
living body".*

**Leonardo Da Vinci**

$$t = H + 1$$
**time = Humanity + 1 year**

A year had now passed since the release of Humanity 2.0 to the world, and the crew were getting cabin fever. All but Daniel, that is. While the Nautilus was a luxury, it was still not the same as home. Song, Mage, and Jackie were determined to convince Captain Tang to finally return to Vancouver. They were young, and missed parties, live sports and concerts. Jackie's studies at UBC had also been on hold, and she wanted that back. It was time for some degree of normality in their lives.

A year ago, they'd claimed an uninhabited Philippine island as their own. The Fellowship had erected a lean-to/shack, lining the roof with mango and palm leaves. It was a bucolic spot beside a waterfall which drained directly into the blue lagoon. Palm trees provided bananas and coconuts, papayas and jack fruit, all on a predator free island. Predator-free if you don't count the snakes, that is.

They had only been on the island about a week, when Jackie awoke to spot a cobra only about 15 feet away, standing and facing right at her. Neither took their eyes off of each other. In her peripheral vision, she suddenly saw a blur as Daniel ran up behind the snake with his trusty hatchet in hand. The cobra's head flew off clean, while the rest of the body wriggled about for a few moments. Darned if he hadn't saved her again!

That night, she had borrowed Mage's satellite equipment, and researched snakes on the internet. On Bobby's next shopping run, she had him pick up lots of lye and vinegar. Digging a trench around the encampment, she spread the two ingredients liberally, and it was the last snake she saw in their camp. But just in case, she always spread a fresh layer before sleeping on the beach.

On this particular morning, the kids were aboard the Nautilus. Bobby and Tang had gone to a neighbouring island for supplies, allowing the two young couples to plot how best to approach the Captain with their request.

Jackie began, "We need to be a united front."

"Totally," Song agreed.

"I vote for mutiny," Daniel cried aloud, pumping a fist into the air. "That was Captain Nemo, right?"

"No, you're thinking of Captain Bligh, bud," said Mage. "And we're definitely not going to mutiny."

226

"Too bad," Jackie teased. "You might look good with an eye patch, baby. So manly,"

"Arrrrgh, avast me darlin'. Shiver me timbers!"

"I vote for the direct approach," proposed Song. "We just tell him we want to go home, and if he says no, I'll pull rank on him."

"So our plan is to mutiny or pull rank?" Mage laughed. "Tang deserves better for keeping us safe. I have a much simpler idea, We just tell Bobby, and he'll talk Tang into it. Our skipper can be a tad pig-headed, but Bobby always gets his way."

"Perfect!" she responded. "A simple plan is usually the best plan. And it can't get much simpler than having someone else do it. I'll talk to Bobby when he gets back. I'm going to stay aboard today anyway, but you guys should head to the beach."

Jackie asked, "You okay? Do you want my help?"

"Nah. Don't worry about me."

"I'll stay with you, darlin'," Mage pledged.

"Then accompany me, fair maiden." Daniel bowed to kiss her hand. "Arrrrgh," wink, wink. "Tis not the time to hang the jib. We be bound for our own private, treasure isle."

"Well, I'll be bound for the poop deck first, matey. I hate having to go onshore," Jackie said.

After her brief stop, they were off to the bow on the orlop deck, where the the diver sleds were stored. They helped each other into their gear, and Jackie tested the comms. "Check one two, check one two". Daniel gave her a thumbs up.

Once ashore, there wasn't much to do but loll around in the sun. Even paradise could get boring.

"Let's take a hike today," she suggested. "I feel like working up a sweat."

Daniel grinned and said, "I know a good way to work up a sweat."

"We can do both. Work up a sweat climbing, then rinse by jumping each other's bones under the waterfall. How does that sound?"

"I love the last part, but not so much the first."

"Well, you're not going to get either unless you keep up with me. Come on. Vamanos!"

Daniel groaned and trudged after her, but at least the view was good. They climbed and climbed, then they climbed some more. "Geez, Jacks. How high are we going?"

"I want to find the source of the waterfall. The island isn't that big. It can't be much further."

"This better be worth it," he mumbled, under his breath.

"When has it never been worth it?" Jackie teased. She had a point there.

At last they reached what was once the corona of a volcano, but Jackie was a bit disappointed. She'd expected to find the water bubbling out of the ground, but alas, there was just a large pond in the depression within the rim from which the creek flowed. Daniel was just glad it was over. He had definitely worked up a sweat.

"Look at that view," Jackie raved. There were islands as far as the eye could see. Most looked perfectly pristine. In the distance she could see smoke rising from one, with the town that Tang and Bobby had gone to.

"Hell, yeah. That's some view."

Jackie punched him in the shoulder. "I meant out there."

"Yeah, its nice.... too." And it was. The blue of the sea contrasted the blue of the sky, with island in the foreground. Daniel spotted a small boat cruising their way from the smokey island in the distance. "I think I see Tang and Bobby."

"And I think you're right. We'd better go meet them. Come on."

"Meet them? What about our waterfall?"

"You'll have to take a rain check, my love."

229

"Oh, maaaaaan!"

"Come on. Let's go home."

"Huh. You called the sub *home, Jacks.*"

"Yeah, I guess I did."

They boarded the sea sleds without helmets for a surface rendezvous with the launch.

"Ahoy!" Jackie called, as the men pulled up.

"Ahoy!" Bobby called back. "Get to the sub. We've got news."

News? That would certainly be welcome about now. They'd been out of touch for far too long.

"We need to have a meeting," the Captain announced, sporting a smile as big as Bobby's for a change.

"Okay," she responded. "What's up?"

Neither spoke. "You'll just have to wait and see," teased Bobby.

"Well, okay then. We'll meet you aboard the sub."

Donning their helmets, Jackie and Daniel sped towards the Nautilus's buoy and promptly dove under. Once the sleds were stowed and the diving gear hung to dry, they hurried up to learn the big news.

Finding no one on the bridge, Daniel raised anchor and initiated surfacing procedures. The Nautilus responded, floating gently upward to to break the sea's ceiling. Song and Mage had been in their cabin, and feeling the Nautilus stir, they joined their friends on the bridge.

It was still a beautiful sight to Tang, watching his silver dragon emerge. He and Bobby pulled up alongside, to be met by all four kids standing on the top deck. The girls helped Bobby with the groceries, Tang carried some vinegar and lye, while Mage and Daniel re-stowed the launch.

Once the work was done, so was Mage's patience. It was never his virtue. "Okay. Spill. C'mon!"

"As Captain, I hereby call for a meeting of the Fellowship of the Deep. All hands to the Dining Salon. Now!"

Tang seemed excited, which was rare, so the crew scrambled down the steel stairs to settle into their usual spots. Song asked Bobby for some snacks and drinks, but he was shaking his head. "Oh, noooo, I'm not missing this!"

"Lords and Ladies of the Fellowship, I greet you gladly," Tang began in grandiose style, his arms held wide like a pope addressing the masses. He pulled out a copy of the Manila Times, and said, "I would like to introduce you all to the winner of this year's Nobel Prize for Medicine.......... Our very own Mr. Mage Moon!" Tang tossed a copy onto the table for all to see. Each of their six faces was adorning the front page under the caption, 'Who Cured The World?'

"I bought six copies. This newspaper, the Manila Times," advised the Captain, "is the oldest English language newspaper in the Philippines. They have dedicated the entire first section to Humanity 2.0 on the one year anniversary date of its release. I have only read part of it, but your little project has changed things, folks. We, and specifically Mage, are the most famous unknown people on the planet right now. Everybody has been looking for us, everywhere.

"Conspiracy theories abound. How could anyone be so altruistic as to not profit from the greatest discovery of all time? Where are we? Perhaps we are dead at the hands of the helicopter and fire mercenaries.

"You will see that the paper has bios for all of us, and I think we can safely say, we each have Wikipedia pages by now." Tang laughed and added, "You can check out your copies back in your cabins, but let me read this article to you......."

### *Humanity 2.0 - What a Difference a Year Makes*

*It's been one year since the app Humanity 2.0 was released upon the world, and while it is arguably the biggest discovery in the history of mankind, credit still goes unclaimed. The impact has been dramatic and quick, changing the dynamics of our world immeasurably. Its value monetarily is incalculable.*

*The Secretary-General addressed the U.N. General Assembly as follows:*

*One year ago, our planet was given a gift. A gift that has affected every citizen on Earth. Based on the universal languages of mathematics and music, the global app caused a sensation within weeks of its release.*

*Initially, social media spread the news, making outrageous claims about a new music app sweeping the globe. By simply listening to algorithmic adapted music, people around the world began heal through the magic in the music. I, and many others, were skeptical. When the claims proved to be true, it changed not only my attitude, but the entire balance of power on our planet. The World Health Organization is on the brink of being rendered obsolete due to the eradication of the most serious human diseases within a single year. The blind can now see. The deaf can now hear. The bedridden are now active and the infertile are now fertile. A healing gene has been switched on.*

*This gift brought about a period of great cooperation and goodwill between the many civilizations of the world. War, like many of the planet's diseases, is in remission, and many of the downtrodden now thrive. Our African friends have probably benefited the most, transitioning areas of illness and sorrow into growing economies. In western countries, surgery wait lists are no more. As a result, love for our fellow man has never been greater.*

*However, as with all major discoveries,*

233

*there are winners and losers. The people worldwide are winners with health they can count on. Employers are winners with sick days abolished. The arts are winners with enormous, new endowments formerly bequeathed to health care. And the world is a winner, with unprecedented vitality and goodwill between nations.*

*But, dramatic shifts within such a short period of time have also created challenges. Hospitals and health care systems are now essentially inactive, rendering the infrastructure and expertise of their staff irrelevant. Pensions plans have faltered, as insurance companies face an uncertain future. Pharmaceutical corporations have collapsed, and mortuaries have closed. Financial markets everywhere continue to be in turmoil, a year later.*

*We at the U.N. understand that virtually every entity and individual on Earth has benefited in new and unexpected ways. And, there are many uncertainties and challenges in our future. So, here at the United Nations, we are creating a new entity to be known as the Humanity Initiative, dedicated to helping all the world adapt. It will be an enormous challenge to help so many member countries at once, so let us continue to support each other as we all transition our economies.*

"Wow," Daniel said quietly. "That's unbelievable. I've always known that you're a magician with electronics, but a Nobel Prize? Didn't see that one coming. Nope, nope. How do you feel, bud?"

"Astonished? Stunned? Gobsmacked? Shocked is

too mild of a term. I can't believe that it worked at all, let alone like this. I thought perhaps it would benefit a few illnesses, but........ The article suggests we have turned on a healing gene, so Jackie's professor's theory was right. That is pretty cool."

"I'm so proud of you, honey," gushed Song. "I've always known you were brilliant, and now I get to sleep with a Nobel Prize winner! Go me!"

"I think the Nobel is for all of us, not just me. So, we all get to sleep with Nobel prize winners. I'd never accept it just on my own. We did this as a group, and continue to be a group – a fellowship, you'll recall. We've all paid a heavy price. All of our lives were completely upended."

"I can certainly live with being a Nobel laureate," Daniel decided. He stood and introduced himself to each of the Fellowship in turn. "Hi, Daniel Dyck, Nobel Prize winner. Hello, Daniel Dyck, Nobel Prize winner. Hi, Daniel Dyck, Nobel. Greetings, Daniel Dyck, winner of the Nobel Prize for Medicine. Hi. Daniel Dyck, Good to meet ya."

"Sit down," Tang ordered, raising a hand to quiet his crew. "Before you all get too excited, here's another article," he said, and began reading again.....

### *The Science of Humanity*

*The success of Humanity 2.0 has astounded the world, but how exactly does it work? While it all may sound too simple, there is actually some solid science behind it. Dr. Akbar Singh from Johns Hopkins University's Center for Epigenetics explains, as follows:*

*When scientists completed the mapping of the genome back in 2003, it was thought that we'd learn which defective genes were responsible for which diseases and conditions. However, it didn't quite work out that way. In fact, researchers found that a single gene was, in some cases, responsible for two completely different maladies, and they were confused. At that point in time, genes were thought to be hardwired into us, and just bad luck for the inheritor at birth. Since then, however, we have discovered the possibilities of an entirely new field called Epigenetics.*

*Consider this. In computer parlance, genetics would be the hardware, and epigenetics, the software. As such, we are not bound from birth to be a certain way, as we once thought. We can now change the coding. Zeros and ones..Offs and ons. Epigenetics is ostensibly the switching of genes off or on, based upon environmental factors we experience around us. Pollutants, smoking, medications, stress and diet are examples of environmental factors that change us. By turning genes on and off, mechanisms couldn't reversibly alter cellular and physiological phenotypic characteristics without altering the genetic sequence.*

*In this case, Humanity 2.0's augmented music program provides the environmental factor which changes our epigenetic code. The app has essentially been successful in switching on a self-repair gene. Have you ever noticed how music often makes you feel a bit better? Humanity 2.0 expands on that. Essentially, the program mirrors the song into octaves beyond human hearing, then applies a complicated mathematical algorithm, which results in changing a single gene of the 3 billion base pairs in human DNA.*

*This is not a new phenomenon in nature. On land, iguanas, newts, and even a spiders can regrow limbs. A cockroach can lose it's head and grow another. In the aquatic world, the octopus, the starfish, and the sea cucumber can all regrow limbs. A salamander in Mexico named the axolotl, can regrow spinal cords, hearts and other organs. There is even a jellyfish which can potentially live forever. As their bodies decay, they regenerate into polyps, skipping the usual larvae stage. Those polyps can then burst into new jellyfish. So scientifically, the effects of Humanity 2.0 are not anatomically unique.*

*Thus far, we've found no disease or illness it hasn't helped. Astonishingly, it even heals the deaf, as the octaves are out of our hearing range anyway. In fact, one needn't hear a sound at all with the music in silent mode. Most of the world's retailers now play H2O as Muzak.*

*Since the release of Humanity 2.0 last year, we have seen cases where amputees have grown their limbs back, and the blind are regaining eyesight. Rest homes are closing, but travel companies are booming. People are learning how to be healthy again. The world has been celebrating for months, showing little constraint. With no hangovers, healed livers, and no STDs, people are letting loose.*

*The Humanity 2.0 process was designed for humans, but initial tests have shown some effectiveness with many mammals. Zoos now play the muzak to endangered species, citing increased reproduction rates. Owners now play it to their pets. Ranchers are playing it to their livestock. Chinese live street markets are playing it for their customers and animals alike..Pandemics may be a thing of the past, but scientists are still trying to understand the algorithm.*

*"The designers of Humanity 2.0 are superheroes to this writer. They've literally saved the entire world."*

"You see?" crowed Daniel. "I *told* you we were superheroes! I want a cape!"

"Serving with this Fellowship of the Deep," Tang declared, "has been the pleasure and pride of my life. It has been an honour. The paper has several other articles, but I'll leave them for you to discover." He turned to Mage, snapped him a quick salute, turned back on his heel, and marched out.

Nobody was more surprised than Mage. "I guess he doesn't hate me anymore."

"He never hated you," Bobby responded. "He just didn't trust you."

"Well, either way, he's coming around," Jackie stated. "Say, Bobby? How about those snacks and beverages now. And might you have any more of that Dom?"

"I'm sorry, Miss Beausoleil. I'm a Nobel Prize winner. I cannot be seen doing menial tasks." Once he got a reaction, he added, "Except for you guys!", and skipped away to the galley.

As he left, Jackie said, "Hey guys. Listen to this one," and she read.........

## *Worship in the Age of Humanity 2.0*

*There are currently more than 4,300 religions practiced around the world today. Each is convinced that only their god could be responsible for a blessing like Humanity 2.0. Mainstream faiths such as Christianity, Islam, Hinduism, Buddhism, Sikhism, Taoism, and Judaism have all added Humanity 2.0 into their teachings through interpretations of their texts.*

*Perhaps the greatest beauty of Humanity 2.0 has proven to be its ability to bring people together. We are healing as a world, we are celebrating as a world, and we are worshipping as a world. Never in Earth's history has there been so much goodwill between faiths. But there is also a downside to the religious fervor. After an initial boom in the growth of congregations, religious attendance has been dwindling badly as people lose their fear of death.*

*Now, there is a new worldwide religious movement called, as you might expect, the Humanity Church, and it's worshippers, Humanitarians. While the standard religions have difficulty holding onto their flocks, the Humanitarian religion is exploding. Their figurehead is simply known as 'The Magician', based on the perceived creator of the app being named Mage Moon, nicknamed 'the Magician'. When this person or persons surfaces, they will instantly be worshipped as a deity......"*

"Oh, great." whined Mage. "That's just what I need."

"Hah!" Daniel laughed. "You'll be just like Brian in that old Monty Python movie. Remember? The Life of Brian?"

"Yeah, I remember. The reluctant deity who just wished people would stop following him around."

"Totally!"

Song held up a hand, saying, "here's another one, guys. Check it out........"

## *The Losers of H2*

*As with every paradigm shift, there are those who benefit, and those who lose.*

*Thus far, health care has been the biggest loser worldwide. Sitting empty now are countless hospitals, with the doctors, nurses, technicians and specialists suddenly having their hard-won medical degrees deemed useless. Surgeons are having to become Emergency room doctors or plastic surgeons in order to survive. Plastic surgeons are thriving. doing a booming business. People feel young, and want to look young.*

But, emergency rooms are essentially empty, playing 'Huzak' through the speakers of their deserted hallways. Medical schools are shutting down, with much of their traditional funding transitioning to the arts, and more specifically to the musical arts.

Midwifery is making a comeback at the expense of neo-natal services. Humanity 2.0 is a sharp new tool in their arsenal. Most mothers have made the choice of birthing at home, playing H2O, after more than a century of hospital births.

Another early loser has been big pharma. Demand for their products has plummeted, with more than one C.E.O. committing suicide due to falling stock prices. Even Viagra and Cialis couldn't survive, as sales diminished in direct contrast to hair dye sales, which have skyrocketed.

Wall Street is not sure what to think. With the health care sector crumbling, many medical stocks have stopped trading while adjusting to the world's new financial realities. This is particularly true in the U.S. with their user pays medical system no longer needed. Countries with universal health care are celebrating, redirecting money saved toward the needy and vulnerable. Many cities around the world have turned their hospitals into homeless shelters, and old folks homes into apartments.

How the future of H2O will play out in the long run is unknowable, but it's safe to say, even the losers will benefit on a personal level, enjoying perfect health."

*Alcoholics are complaining though, saying they can't get properly drunk before the alcohol is neutralized by the body. Not so with drug addicts, however. Because the length of the high shortened, addicts have been taking bigger doses and overdosing before the H2O can work.*

Song looked up at the others. Their initial excitement about the Nobel Prize was now bolstered by their realization of the effect it was having on the world. It was too big to fathom.

Were they excited or overwhelmed? It was tough to tell, but their restlessness to return home to Vancouver was now questionable. Were they ready to be in the centre of a firestorm? Were they ready to be worshipped as deities? Uhhhh......*no!* Home might have to wait.

The following morning, Song asked Bobby to make up a special picnic basket for her day's adventure. Even after a long, sleepless night, she was supercharged with excitement.

Mage, however, was not. He'd been sulky and mute since reading the paper. He realized his life would never, ever be the same, and he was pretty sure that wasn't a good thing. It broke his heart to know that if he'd created Humanity a year earlier, his parents would still be alive. So would Song's mother. But, if that was the case, he would never have met Song at the hospital. Tragedy brought people together. His brain just felt full.

When everyone split up, down in the galley, Song

was literally skipping with excitement.

"Well, you seem in good spirits today," Bobby commented, as he finished loading Song's basket, "What's the occasion?" But really, he knew the occasion. He was the only one aboard who could guess the answer.

Gathering up the basket, Song replied with only a mischievous grin and a wink as she skipped out of the room. Making her way astern, she climbed down the ladder and turned the hatch's hand wheel, swinging the big round, yellow door open. She hopped down from the gangway and placed the picnic basket by the ceiling hatch of the mini-sub. Satisfied, she went to find Mage. He'd been quietly introverted and a bit surly since the news Bobby and Tang had brought home. Undoubtedly, becoming a living god would seriously mess with anyone's day.

But today world seemed new again. And Song was determined to take Mage's mind away from all of that. Rather than shaking him awake, she laid feather-soft kisses on his cheek until he stirred. She kept smooching his face repeatedly as he stretched, but his brief smile turned sad again as his mind awoke. She couldn't possibly understand what he must be feeling, but if she put herself in Mage's shoes, it would completely freak her out. Fortunately, she had just the thing to distract him.

"Come," Song said, dragging him in tow. Mage stumbled along behind her until he finally recognized the big, yellow, circular hatch was their destination.

They had been aboard Nautilus for a year, but he'd only been inside the mini-sub a few times. Song and Jackie had shown him the previous year, and he'd done his sub school training, but he'd never taken it out for a spin.

"What are you up to?" he needled Song as she directed him to follow her through the ceiling hatch.

"Just never you mind. Seal the hatch and join me," she ordered. Song was already settled into the pilot's cockpit powering up the diesel engine. She toggled open the rear cone of the Nautilus's stern, flooding the chamber around them. Satisfied with the gauges, she punched the button labelled 'Cradle'. Mage soon felt the sub stir beneath them. As the cradle extended out the stern, it carried the mini-sub with it. Once she was sure she was clear of the Nautilus, she maneuvered the little, yellow craft up and clear before descending down into the dark. Mage belied his nervousness as their craft travelled deeper than the Nautilus had ever been.

"Worry not, darlin'." assured Song. "This little sub can go more than twice the crushing depth of the Nautilus to, like, 500 feet. The Nautilus is only good down to two hundred or so."

As they sunk, the sea around them was black and silent. It was like driving with their eyes closed. Mage crawled into the co-pilot's seat beside Song, who smiled with a mischievous grin. Watching her gauges, she slowed their descent until they bumped gently against the sandy, ocean floor. She powered down everything and set anchor. Few people, save a spacewalking astronaut, had ever experienced such a profound depth of silence. It was like a sensory deprivation tank.

"Did you know that almost all sea life glows?" she asked.

"Glows?"

Yeah, glows. We can't see it because of the spectrums we see. When a ray of sunlight enters the ocean, different colours of the spectrum are visible to different depths. But the sea life themselves can see it because their eyes evolved that way. The scientists blocked certain spectrums, and found that about 90% of life in the oceans glow. They even took it to the local aquarium, and saw the same results. So, while we humans are in the dark this deep, to the fish, it looks more like this......."

She switched on the floodlight and all manner of strange creatures lit up around them, eliciting giggles from Song. "They'd make great sci-fi aliens, don't you think?" Through the ceiling bubble porthole, they saw an enormous jellyfish pulsing right above them, followed by an giant squid, whose suction cups spread haphazard on their windshield. Out one of the side portholes, Mage pointed at a particularly ugly fish straight out of a nightmare. A few moments later, a curious medium-sized shark swam by looking particularly menacing, but decided the sub was not food, and moved on. They even saw a transparent fish you could see right through. It was all so magical.

"Follow me," Song said as she climbed out of the

cockpit. She embraced him, and the quiet enveloped the again. It was Song who broke the spell. "Hungry?" she asked in a whisper. Rooting through their picnic basket, she pulled out some fruit picked from their own, private island, along with pastries and sandwiches Bobby had added. The sound of their chewing and swallowing were strangely amplified by the quiet around them.

Both were hesitant to speak, lest it burst the ambience, but thirst finally got the better of Mage. "Got any beer in there?"

"Just this," she replied as she lifted a bottle of pop from the basket, handing it to him.

"Ginger ale? No champagne or anything?"

"Well, it *is* Canada Dry, the champagne of ginger ales, don'tcha know. But no, Bobby didn't pack us any alcohol."

"That's not like Bobby. He's always up for a drink or six."

"Well, I had him pick up the ginger ale while he was in town. And" she said, gingerly handed him a pen-like object, "Bobby knows pregnant women aren't supposed to drink champagne."

Then, briefly the silence was back. Boy, was it back! Mage stared at the cross marking on the pen, alternately looking from her to the test pen and back. He couldn't speak. He'd gone mute! His face transformed from normal to confused to elated, all within seconds.

His eyebrows were fully raised and he looked mutely at Song with childlike wonder.

Looking innocently at Mage, she asked, "is ginger ale okay after all?............. Daddy?"

"Yeah? *Yeah?* Yeah, baby! Hoowah! That is fantastic!" He picked up Song and twirled her above his head, bumping hers repeatedly against the sub's ceiling. "I'm going to be an 'Appa'? For real?" Song nodded excitedly. Tears began to flow down Mage's cheeks. It had been such an emotional time of late, he wasn't sure what to do with *good* news. "I'm going to have a family again?"

"I'll always be your family."

"Always?"

"Always. And I'll have a family again, too. Just like you."

He kissed her deeply and completely while he struggled with her buttons. They made love hundreds of feet below the surface of the sea, before dropping off to sleep, spent and content.

Mage woke with a start, and shook Song awake. "We better get going. The floodlight was on while we slept, and we don't want to take any chances. After all, we have a family to take care of now."

Once back in their clothes, she prepared to clamber down into the cockpit when Mage touched her arm, asking, "May I?"

"Of course, Daddy." Reaching for the switches, he powered up the sub's engine, its noise cacophonous in their once silent boudoir. He weighed anchor, and began their ascent back to the Nautilus far above.

Soon, the baby sub pulled up behind the mama sub, and Mage lined up his approach directly into its stern. He took it slow, and settled it gently onto the cradle. He shut down all power, and activated the cradle switch, which pulled it into the Nautilus docking bay. After dropping the stern cone back in place, he flushed out the seawater, and climbed out of the cockpit.

Looking up, he asked her, "you gonna get that?" pointing at the ceiling hatch.

"Yeah, right. I couldn't reach it if I jumped, and for you, it's right there." So, Mage lifted her high enough to open the hatch herself, after all. She climbed through, took the picnic basket from Mage, and helped pull him out. After securing the hatch back into place, she climbed to the gangway where Mage waited impatiently. "C'mon!" he said excitedly. "Let's tell everyone our news!"

The following afternoon was sunny and calm, so the crew took advantage by surfacing the Nautilus for the ceremony. Gathered on deck was the entire crew, all gussied up in their Sunday finest, such as it was. Jackie and Song were adorned with halos which Bobby made from flowers on their island. Song's was white; Jackie's was multi-coloured.

Bobby led Song up the deck toward Tang, weeping uncontrollably. The honour of giving the bride away had left him a soggy mess. Mage stepped in to lead Song the rest of the way, up to a makeshift altar. If either of them were nervous, it didn't show.

Captain Tang began, "Ladies and Lords of the Fellowship, we are gathered here today to join the lives of Song Tsung Zhao and Mage Moon in holy matrimony. They have asked me to keep this short, for which I thank them. In all of my years commanding Chinese warships, I was never asked to perform a wedding ceremony." That got a chuckle. "So, I'll go with the parts I know. Skipping ahead, I'll just say, if any present know of any reason that this couple should not be joined in holy matrimony, speak now or forever hold your piece." Daniel raised his arm in jest before Jackie smacked it down.

Tang addressed Daniel, "Best man, do you have the ring?"

"Your honour, the groom does not yet have a diamond ring for the bride, so we offer this floral ring in its place." The ring was a miniature version of Song's halo. "And until such time as he can purchase said diamond ring, he presents the bride with all of the diamonds of the sea." Daniel swept his arm to demonstrate. Indeed, there were millions of glittering diamonds twinkling and stretching to the horizons, carpeting the sea like sparkling gemstones."

"Very well," said Tang. "Mage, repeat after me. I, Mage Moon, take thee, Song Zhao, to be my lawful, wedded wife"

"I, Mage Moon, take thee, Song Zhao, to be my lawful, wedded wife"

"To have and hold from this day forward, for richer, for poorer, in sickness and in health"

"To have and hold from this day forward, for richer, for poorer, in sickness and in health"

"To love and cherish, in good times and in bad, until death do you part."

"To love and cherish, in good times and in bad, until death do us part."

Tang winked at Song, and repeated the vows for her, which she returned.

"Then, as Captain of the Nautilus, I hereby pronounce you man and wife. You may kiss the bride."

And kiss her he did, until all the others left them alone on the top deck, surrounded by their diamond ocean carpet.

# *Chapter 14*

"No man is entitled to the blessings of freedom unless he be vigilant in its preservation."

**Douglas MacArthur**

$$t = H + 5$$
*time = Humanity + 5 years*

Tune squealed with delight at the dolphins jumping and dove at top speed, flanking the Nautilus. From her perch at the helm with Uncle Daniel, she could watch through the 2-metre bubble portholes on both sides. Each time a dolphin jumped, Tune jumped too.

*'There is nothing quite like sharing the new eyes of a four-year-old'*, he thought to himself. He'd always wanted to try something at the helm, and this was his chance. The two side-mounted engines near the stern of the Nautilus had the capability to point in almost an direction. So, he alternated between filling and emptying the ballast tanks, while rotating the stern engines. The sub pitched up, then down, up, down, up, down, jumping and diving across the surface, alongside the dolphins. Tune squealed with delight.

Predictably, Captain Tang stormed onto the bridge to chastise Daniel but, seeing Tune giggling uncontrollably, his face transformed from anger to smitten in a heartbeat. Song and Mage's daughter had poor Tang smitten since the day the Captain delivered her 3-1/2 years ago. Tune had a fondness for the helm and often sat with whoever was there. Consequently, Tang spent many hours with the tyke, philosophizing together on any subject Tune wondered about. The hardened old Chinese bodyguard was never the same. If Tune was in the same room as him, the Captain was incapable of anything but a smile.

Daniel turned for a moment, and spotted the Captain for the first time. He quickly reached for the controls, but Tang stopped him with a shake of his head.

Swooping her up in his arms, Tang made Tune dip and jump, just like the dolphins. What happy days these were.

It had been 5 years since the release of Humanity 2.0, and while the world was changing around them, the lives of the crew were not. With their time in sub school long complete, they were left with the grinding schedule of being lazy and content, day after day. It was brutal, but they struggled the best they could. Jackie was the exception. Whenever the Nautilus was on the surface, she took online courses in marine biology to keep her academics sharp. And if they were below the surface but motionless, like when the sub at rest at their island, she'd take young Tune out in the yellow mini-sub for a 'field trip'. They both loved to find exotic creatures of the deep.

Gone were the cries to return home to Vancouver,

as the Nautilus had become home to the Fellowship in every way. Mostly, they stayed near their private island in the Philippines, but when the troops got restless, the Nautilus explored more exotic shores.

Today, they were returning from a trip to Indonesia's glowing beaches, on a northwesterly heading. They considered Indonesia to be relatively safe to visit, with more than 17,000 islands to hide among. But the Indonesians and neighbouring Australians deployed submarines, so it was never good to stay too long in one spot. In addition to standard sonar scans, many countries now employed underwater buoys, which measured the sound of sub propellers, or the displacement of water. For this reason, Captain Tang had decided to go north, above New Guinea, before diverting west toward Tuvalu. Bobby, the Nautilus's designated tree-hugger, had requested the side trip to see the country before global warming relegated it to the sea.

Tuvalu would be the nation most affected by climate change and the subsequent rising tide levels. As the Nautilus slowed on approach, the dolphins bid them adieu and continued their race to nowhere. Daniel brought the vessel back to the surface where a warm wind was blowing softly in the tropical, blue sky.

"Oh, my God! It's so tiny!" exclaimed Song, as she spotted the island. She lifted her daughter for a better view and bounced her playfully in her arms. "Like you, my tiny Tune Moon. Mwah!"

"I've been reading up on this place, " Bobby

offered. "That's why I asked Tang to bring us here. There are only about 10,000 people in the whole country, with an average elevation of only 2 metres."

"That's about the same altitude as you, bud," Daniel told Mage.

"But, it's so tiny!" observed Jackie.

Bobby replied, "There's actually 3 islands, plus six atolls. The total land area is only ten square miles, and shrinking. But because the islands are so spread out, they claim 300,000 square nautical miles."

"That's crazy!" Daniel exclaimed. Tune mimicked him.

"What's crazy is the poverty. Most workers earn less than a buck an hour, surviving by subsistence living. And as the sea level rises, the salty soil becomes less arable."

"That's so sad," observed Jackie. "They'll have to leave their beautiful homeland."

"That's questionable. They're too poor to go anywhere. Ninety-five percent of the people don't even have plumbing. And if they did somehow scrape up enough to leave, they'd have to learn to speak something other than their native language of Tuvaluan. It's all a tragedy waiting to happen."

The gorgeous site before them made much more impact than any 30-second mention on the evening news. It was sobering. Paradise lost. Breaking the awkward silence, Tang suggested they keep moving, Everyone simply nodded.

The Moons went to take a nap with Tune, and the Captain went to his quarters. Soon it was just Daniel and Jackie left on the bridge.

Studying the marine charts, Daniel announced, "Hey, look! We're on the International Dateline, Jacks. Right where it meets the equator. That's *gotta* be lucky, eh? Centre, centre."

"No Daniel, that doesn't mean you're gonna get lucky," Jackie sang, poking him in the belly.

"You know me too well, oh love of my loins."

"Sorry loins," she said, and purposefully turned a cold shoulder.

"Hey, Jacks. How about this? If you jump me now, I'll take you time travelling!"

"You are such a goof." But Daniel was clearly waiting for an answer, so she told him, "Okay, fine. If you make me time travel, I'll let you jump me. You do realize I already sleep with you, right?"

"Yeah, but this is on *my* timetable!"

"You're still a goof, Jughead."

"Hey!"

Daniel, true to his word did indeed take Jackie time travelling, zig-zagging the Nautilus back and forth over the International Date Line, and Daniel's schedule was *now*. They made love right there on the bridge. Yesterday, today. Yesterday, today....

Sated, they beheld a sunset like no other. Red sky blazed on the horizon, its reflection off the water painted everything red, both above and below. But, a Pacific sunset at the equator is brief, and darkness soon regained its nightly dominance over the sky. Interior lights would be needed, so Jackie initiated dive procedures. There was no point in announcing their presence on the surface. She filled the bow ballast tanks and the Nautilus responded, pushing the behemoth under. From the oncoming darkness of night, they dove into the eerie depths.

It was two days later, with Bobby was at the helm, that proximity alarms sounded for the sub's side scanning sonar. Tang and Mage both had raced to join him, when the Captain took charge. "Robert, bring us to the surface. Mage, check the comms room for both sonar and radar." Bobby brought the Nautilus to a halt as soon as they broke the plane of the sea.

The girls rushed in with Tune, anxious. "It's probably just a big whale. It's happened before," Bobby reassured them.

"That's no whale," Tang murmured.

*'So much for reassuring them.'* Bobby threw a testy look at Tang, and Tang threw a *'What?'* right back.

Mage confirmed that the port sonar was indeed registering something very large, but it wasn't within view yet. "There's also a surface ship approaching our six, and a surveillance plane high in the sky, directly overhead."

"That's just great," muttered Tang. Within a minute, from the inky depths rose an imposing, black bulk, bulldozing its way through the sea.

"We've been found. That, my friends, is a U.S. Hunter Killer submarine. Robert, hold steady, but do not shut down." Tang looked uncharacteristically nervous, with too much of the whites of his eyes showing. Song noticed his discomfort, assuming it had something to do with that 'Chinese military man piloting a nuclear sub' thing.

Manning the periscope, Daniel called, "a helicopter is coming too, and a U.S. Navy cruiser is closing fast on our stern. Three against one is just not fair!"

"Four, if you include the surveillance plane way up there. But, who's counting?" observed Bobby.

"Prepare to be boarded!" squawked a bullhorn from outside.

Song had already decided her course of action. Planting wee Tune on her hip, she made her way to the hatch, and assured Tang, "I got this."

The Captain was both stunned and relieved. *'She's*

*got stones.'* he marvelled. *'More than many of the soldiers I trained.'*

"Don't let anyone but me back through this hatch, If they grab me, dive. That's an order."

Climbing the ladder, she opened the hatch leading up onto the top deck, Song held Tune close and tight to keep her warm. As she sealed the hatch behind her, she whispered to her daughter, "This is how you handle bullies."

A dinghy of Navy Seals approached, armed to the teeth and ready for bear. The zodiak pulled up right alongside, and their leader soon clambered aboard. Song stood firm and resolute, a tiny Asian Canadian woman and child versus the mightiest fighting force in the history of mankind.

"Good evening, Ma'am. My name is Commander Joseph Morse of the United States Navy. Can I ask you what you are doing here?"

"No, I don't think so. You're trespassing on my ship. Go away."

"I'd like to speak to your leader, if I may, ma'am."

"You are," replied Song. "What do you want?"

The Commander paused and went on to say, "A boarding party will be coming aboard for inspection."

"An inspection of what, exactly?"

"Er, the whole ship, ma'am."

"Again, I don't think so."

"Ma'am, this is not optional. May I ask what you are using to power this submarine?"

"You may not," she replied with a polite smile. "What is not optional, Commander, is your men boarding my vessel. You are not welcome here."

He was beginning to look bad in front of his crew, and made a decision "Step aside, Ma'am." He motioned to his team in the zodiak to come aboard.

"Nope. I'm not stepping aside, and your men are not coming aboard, either. This is an unarmed, private vessel in international waters. I am a private citizen of another nation than yours. You do not have my permission to go inside, and I'd like you to leave my sub."

Commander Morse could hear his crew openly snickering. One of them called his Commander over, speaking too softly for Song to hear. Upon his return, Morse asked, "Is your name Song Zhao?"

She smirked and said, "No sir." It *was* true, after all. She was no longer Song Zhao, but Song Moon!

"My men report that you are a woman responsible for Humanity 2.0. Is that right?" Song stayed quiet, didn't even nod. "We'd like you to come with us, Ma'am."

"How many times do I have to say, I don't think so. On what grounds?"

"You are to report to the U.S. Senate for hearings."

"But Commander, I am not an American. And I do not wish to go with you," she said, turning away. The Commander gripped her arm before instantly realizing it was a mistake. "Unhand me, sir!" Song bellowed.

"Then come with me........ma'am."

"Do I need to repeat myself yet again, Captain? I am a private citizen of another country, on a private ship, in international waters. You have no jurisdiction here." The moment the Commander grabbed Song's arm again, the Nautilus dive klaxon sounded. The Commander released her and the alarm ceased.

"Do you have a warrant from Interpol? A warrant from anywhere? I swear, if you try to abduct me, I will stay on this deck with my baby while submarine dives. Then, you can explain to the U.S Senate why you drowned a foreign, unarmed woman and her baby, out of your jurisdiction. Think of the media frenzy. You can also explain it to my country's government, and then to my lawyers. If I am who you think I am, you know I'd be perfectly capable of having lawyers keep it in the headlines for decades."

The Seals back in the zodiak were openly teasing their Commander now, and he'd had enough. "Ma'am, one way or another, you are coming with us."

260

Song raised her eyebrows. "Oh? Are you going to forcibly take me aboard your U.S. Naval vessel with no grounds? Is that really your plan? What about my baby? Are you going to snatch her from my arms? She could easily fall overboard, and you're back to explaining things to your superiors. We are not at war, nor are we a threat. This submarine is unarmed. But, you should know that if you attempt to either board my ship, or take me forcibly, I've ordered my crew to dive. You heard the alarm. You, me and my baby would be in the drink. That would be quite the story for your sailors there. And even if you were to take me, you'd still have to deal with my submarine. What would you do then? Torpedo her? More 'splainin'......., sir."

Red faced, he gripped Song's arm again, only to hear the dive klaxon sound once more. He released her, but Song recognized his frustration would soon lead to a calamity, she offered an olive branch. "I'll tell you what, Commander. I will be returning back inside my home now, but will *allow* you to *escort* our submarine, not tow it, to Canadian waters. Not American waters. At that time, the Canadian Navy may continue to escort us to their naval base at Esquimalt."

As he considered his options, Song asked, "you do know where that is, right? South end of Vancouver Island?"

"Yes, I know where the damn base is!............. Ma'am."

"Now, is there anything else I can do for you?" she queried melodically. "Its cold and I'd like to get my toddler back inside."

Commander Morse looked back at his Navy Seals, frustrated, but returned his attention to Song. "For the time being, we will agree. Circumstances may change when I discuss this with my superiors, but for now, you may come with us."

"May? Just keep in mind that we'll be back doing the same song and dance if terms change. We will be contacting our own government immediately, and if the U.S. Navy tries to block our communications, you can explain that to them, as well. Now will there be anything else, Commander? I have some calls to make." After an awkward silence, she said, "No?.... Ta ta, then."

Song turned on her heel, and headed for the hatch. As soon as it was unsealed, she heard the Fellowship's laughter and cheering spill out. Even the Seal team was smiling. This would be a good story for the canteen, regardless of what happens next.

It took their little armada nearly three weeks to return across the Pacific to Canadian maritime border where a Royal Canadian Navy vessel was waiting to take command. Once the transfer was complete, Song met with the Canadian crew, introducing herself as if they were at a cocktail party. Initially, this commanding officer treated her with respectful dignity, but once they were alone, he actually gushed. Word of the standoff had spread in the weeks since the incident, and the entire Nautilus crew were treated like rock stars. Not to mention, they were already the most infamous people on the planet.

The Canadian ship was escorted from Canada's marine boundary to C.F.B. Esquimalt, and docked in the naval yard. It had been a long time since they had plied these waters, but it still felt like home. Officials asked to meet with them right away, but Song stopped the brass cold. It was late, they were tired, and none of them had been home for 5 years. They just wanted to sleep in their own beds. So, she debriefed them on the U.S. Navy and U.S. Senate requests, making an agreement that a Navy Admiral and a government official could meet them at the mansion in two days time for a complete debriefing. Arrangements were also made to return the Nautilus to the base the following week, to refill fresh water tanks and restock her provisions.

Upon their arrival at the dockyard, Tang made a call to the lawyer to ensure the mansion was safe. He was informed that any repairs needed were complete.

So, within two hours, the Nautilus was again shipping out. *'Two hours'*, thought Song. *'I wonder how long we would have been detained if we'd agreed to submitting to the U.S.'?* Soon the lights of Vancouver sprang to life off their port bow, welcoming the Fellowship of the Deep home. Such a beautiful city. Captain Tang guided the ship on the surface, lights on, for the final leg, and soon were docking under the huge covered dock that had been home to the Nautilus five long years ago. Tang bubbled her up into her berth while the now seasoned crew fastened the locking clamps in place.

Mage carried Tune and helped Song off the ship. Jackie looked to Daniel for a similar gesture, but he was busy kissing the dock. But, as soon as she hit the dock, he was kissing her, so she thought it acceptable after all. "Terra firma, Jacks. You know what that means, right?" He'd earned himself another punch on the shoulder.

"Whaaaat?"

The Captain was the last one off of the ship after shutting down all systems for the first time in half a decade. Stepping down, he whispered back to the Nautilus.......'Good job.'

"Uh, Captain? How do we get back up to the house? Does the zipline go up? I can see the house waaaaay up there, but we don't have to hike, do we?" Mage complained.

"No. And I'm not captain here, so Tang will do. We'll unload everything else tomorrow." He grinned, and lifted the access hatch. There was their underground tunnel used in their flight from the helicopter attack.

"The lawyer assured me the zipline is now operational in both directions. "Mage, you first with the baby. Then you, Song so you can take Tune while your husband helps unload us."

Mage climbed down into pit, put his foot in the loop, one arm into the other loop, and an arm cradling Tune in his lap. When Bobby engaged the clutch, they were whisked up the Star Wars tunnel with Tune screaming with glee until they were out of sight. Jackie and Daniel took the ride, leaving Bobby and Tang alone.

"Good job, Captain," Bobby said proudly.

Tang surprised him with a full dip movie kiss, and replied, "Thank you, Robert. I had a lot of help."

# *Chapter 15*

*"As I see it the world is undoubtedly in need of a new religion, and that religion must be founded on humanist principles. I mean an organized system of ideas and emotions which relate man to his destiny, beyond and above the practical affairs of every day, transcending the present and the existing systems of law and social structure. The prerequisite today is that any such religion shall appeal potentially to all mankind; and that its intellectual and rational sides shall not be incompatible with scientific knowledge but on the contrary based on it."*

**Julian Huxley**

$$t = H + 5$$
**time = Humanity + 5 years**

Home. On land. The concept seemed surreal. When they left Vancouver, most had just been scared kids, but on their return, they were world-wise adults.

Each member of the Fellowship climbed back on the zipline and up into the panic room, exhausted, but happy to be home. The lights were still on, five years later, and the room looked just as it had back when they'd made their escape. Song gave her cello a hug, while Jackie ran her finger along the Steinway, checking for dust.

Tang slipped into the security room to check the security video screens, which were also still powered up. It all looked surprising normal. Disengaging the interior security features, the steel roll windows and doors could be heard receding throughout the mansion. The view of the back fourty was dark and rainy, but at least the helicopter in the pool was gone, as was the blood.

Too exhausted to chit-chat, the younger couples were already getting into the elevator. Stairs would have been too much work, and Tune had already fallen asleep in Mage's arms.

Tang gave a quick check of all rooms of the mansion, but nothing looked out of place. The family lawyer had assured him that any repairs needed, had been done, and that did appear to be the case. Tang took a short tour of the grounds before joining Bobby, who was already fast asleep in their bed.

Morning came early for Song, but Tune was already wide awake, squirming but quiet laying between her and Mage. "Don't wake Daddy," she whispered, stealing her away. The smell of coffee lured her into the kitchen, where Bobby was already trying to find a way to feed everyone.

"All of this food is too old to eat," he reported. The flours and oatmeal are rancid. The meats have freezer burn. And don't even think of opening that fridge! So, it looks like canned peaches for breakfast, Song. Thank goodness that the coffee was still sealed, so hopefully it's okay." Pouring a cup, she nodded and grinned her approval, blowing gently on the steam.

"What is this weird place, Mommy? And where did my dolphins go?" Song realized her daughter had not set foot in any building before, and expected the window view to show underwater. The closest she had come was the lean-to on their private island. This mansion was a wee bit different from the jungle retreat.

"This is our home for awhile, baby. We all used to live here, and now we're back."

Tune's reply was a simple, accepting shrug. "Okay. Can I esplore?"

"Sure, baby. Mommy will show you around." Tune shed her mother's hand, and raced from the room on a new adventure. "Thanks for the coffee, Bobby. Looks like motherhood's begun for another day," she grimaced.

"Okay. Welcome home, by the way."

"Thanks, You too. Oh, and since children were not a factor last time we were here, the place isn't kid-proofed. So, please keep an eye out? For now, maybe you could use elastics on the handles to keep cupboards safe.

Bobby snapped a palm over his heart, vowing, "I solemnly swear........."

Giving him a quick wave, Song went in search of

268

her daughter who'd already been exploring her fascinating new world. Her mind drifted way back, to a memory of a similar moment with her own mother, when the family had just moved into their fortress in China. She'd been only five years old, and not much bigger than Tune was now, racing around their home with wide-eyed glee.

Song's memories drifted to their family's first arrival here at this mansion. Her father had kept details to himself in order to best surprise his wife, and most definitely succeeded. Mother and daughter had explored the pagoda mansion together, darting from one room to another, each's green eyes sparkling with anticipation.

*'You've got a granddaughter now Mom,'* Song whispered up to the ceiling. *'She's beautiful, kind, and smart as a whip. You would love her and I'm so sad you'll never meet. But we did continue your family tradition of musical babies. Her name is Tune. Now, little Tune has a mother named Song, a grandmother named Melody, and a great-grandmother named Piper. I miss you so much, Mǔqīn.'*

Her thoughts were interrupted by Tune rounding a corner at full-speed, straight into her mom's legs, spilling her coffee. Tune pulled Song from room to room, animated and amazed, pointing out nearly everything she saw. She explained what each room was for. Which ones had princesses living in them, where the unicorns slept, and whether there were any bad ogres.

"Speaking of ogres," Song said, "should we go wake Daddy up? He was snoring like an ogre when we left."

"Yeah, yeah, yeah! But, he's a good ogre," Tune admonished with a furrowed brow, pointing to emphasize the point.

"Follow me. We have to be very careful when hunting ogres. Do you hear anything?"

Tune paused and listened in earnest, before announcing, "I hear him snoring! Ssshhh, be quiet," she cautioned, tip-toeing ahead carefully. "There he is," she whispered. "See?"

Whispering back, Song asked, "What's the best way to wake up an ogre?"

"Like this," Tune instructed, again pointing for emphasis. She turned, squealed loudly, and launched herself onto her father, landing with her knee right in his crotch. Mage awoke, bolt upright and groaning. Though unintended, he'd done a good job of sounding like an ogre.

"D'ohhhh, what the h...... ?" He stopped himself when he saw Tune clambering up for a morning kiss.

He said up to Song, "that's gotta be the best and worst way to wake up, all in one. G'morning, my lovelies."

"Good morning, ogre Daddy," Song teased, climbing in beside him for her own morning kiss.

"Have you seen this place, Daddy? It's amazing!"

It wasn't long before the whole household rose and followed their noses toward Bobby's coffee. Tang came in from outside soon after, visibly morphing from security mode back to grandfather mode. Tune velcroed herself to his legs, as he accepted hugs from Bobby, Song, and Jackie, in order.

"Don't look at me, big guy," Daniel joked. "I'm not hugging you."

*'This is nice,'* Tang thought. *'Family. Even Daniel the brave.'* Since Tune had been born, he had mellowed considerably. The soldier was leaking out of him, replaced by a jolly, family patriarch. Of the six crew members aboard the Nautilus, Tang was by far the softest touch when it came to Tune. He scooped her up and gave her a big raspberry to her belly button.

"Stop! Stop, Zǔfù!" Tune's giggling was contagious, brightening the room like the ray of sunshine she was. Zǔfù was actually the first word Tune had learned, before Mama or Dada. It was Chinese for grandfather, and if the shoe fit...... Bobby thereby dubbed himself, Zǔmǔ, or grandmother.

But after their muted, breakfast smorgasbord of canned peaches and fruit cocktail, Tang asked, "May I call a meeting of the Fellowship of the Deep when we are on dry land?"

"Sure," said Mage, nodding along with the others.

"We have some logistics to work out, and some safeguards to put in place," he began. "Some simple things we did when we were here before are now problematic. For instance, this wonderful breakfast Zŭmŭ put together for us is a problem. This is not a remote island in the Philippines anymore. We are from here, and people will recognize us now. In that regard, we are more vulnerable. Mage, this applies to you especially, but we have all been in the press lately, so we need to decide some things, going forward.

"Rumours of our submarine return will soon leak out to the media, if it hasn't already. We're a juicy bit of gossip for the spouses and friends of the Royal Canadian Navy officials we met last night. For five years, we have been a mystery to journalists and governments alike. As a result, things are not the same as when we last gathered around this kitchen. Once the populous and press know we are back, it could get crazy. The entire world has changed in our absence, and most believe that we are the reason. As six of the biggest celebrities on the planet, we cannot do things like before.

"Take, for instance, the food we are eating. Bobby wanted to pick up some things to make proper meals, but that simple task is no longer workable. The people at the store who know Bobby would spread the word of our return like wildfire. And I know none of you want the added early notoriety."

"Hey, I've always wanted to be famous!" was Daniel's attempt at levity.

"You already are. And not just with me, baby,"

Jackie added with a wink.

"Laugh all you want, but once *anyone* knows we are here, bedlam will ensue." warned Tang. "It will be on a scale none of us are used to. Already some will have noticed the compound's lights switching on and off, after not doing so for five years. And, tomorrow we meet with the Navy, and authorities like Customs, the R.C.M.P. and Vancouver City Police. We can ask them to keep it to themselves, but it's unlikely they will. They will all want to be the first to tell the world. We're going to wish we were back on the boat.

"Now, as you know, I spoke with our lawyer from aboard the Nautilus just the other day. He is coming here at noon tomorrow. We meet the other officials here at 1400 hours. Mage, the lawyer specifically wants to talk to you about inheriting your grandfather's shop's property."

"I hadn't even thought of that."

"Well, luckily, our lawyer has. He has copies of the autopsy, death registration, fire investigation and several other legalities. He's been holding investigators off for five years, but now you'll need to deal with it. Mage and Song, if you want to update your will to include Tune, start the process tomorrow."

"I will update the will to include all of you," interjected Song. "You are all my family now."

"So, after tomorrow, we will also need to do some media interviews. If we don't, every hack in the world is going to want to get the exclusive. We want to be as elusive as possible for as long as possible. For now, everyone needs to stay within the compound."

"Not this again," whined Daniel.

"*Any* outside communication should be done through the lawyer's office. Bobby, you're going to have to start ordering your groceries online. I know you like to be picky with produce, but that is no longer an option. Even arranging delivery and payment for the food will trigger unwanted scrutiny. If anyone needs anything, it is through the lawyer or bought online. We will need to hire a designated shopper to buffer our anonymity, a shopper who signs a non-disclosure agreement.

"Today is our one day of normalcy. The weather report calls for a beautiful day, and the lawyer just had the pool filled, so soak it up. I had a look at the golf course, tennis courts and other diversions are also ready to use. So, enjoy your day. Relax and recharge. Your bodies *and* minds could *both* use it.

"Robert wants the food we left aboard the Nautilus, so maybe Mage and Daniel can help bring up whatever we might need up here. Tune's stuff, as well. But I'd recommend leaving anything aboard you might need if another quick departure is called for. Okay, that's about it, for now. Any questions, comments or complaints?"

"Is the wifi working?"

"Yes, Mage. The lawyer has everything paid and

up-to-date. Anything else?..... Well, if questions come up, I'll be somewhere in the compound all day. Find me."

"Is the swim-up bar stocked?" Daniel wanted to know.

"Yes, but I wouldn't trust the beer. It may have gone skunky by now."

"It looks like we'll be in the compound for a *lot* of days." mumbled Song. She hadn't thought about anything beyond getting home, and now that she was there, it was going to be as restrictive as the sub was. "I want to get away! I want to take Tune to the park, or to fly a kite. Or to the mall to buy her some toys," she whined.

"Those days are over babe," Mage observed quietly. "So over." Redirecting his attention to his buddy, he asked, "So, Daniel, do you want to help me get that stuff from the sub?"

"Yes! Jackie's thong bathing suit is down there. And it's a pool day!"

"Sorry, Jughead," Jackie responded. "Song and I decided that, with Tune getting older, it's back to regular swimsuits for us."

"What?!? I don't get a say? Mage, back me up here, bud." No response.

"You're such a goof!" Jackie said.

"Oh yes, but, I'm your goof."

"C'mon, Daniel," Mage ordered. "Let's go."

"Right. The stuff from the submarine. Good idea. There's *definitely* non-skunky beer there."

Tune was soon restless with no toys in the whole mansion yet, but Zŭmŭ saved the day by bringing out every piece of plastic ware, and a few noisy pots and pans for her to play with. "I found this out in the garage too," Bobby added, lugging in a huge, cardboard box bigger than a freezer. Deftly using a kitchen knife, he cut a quick door and window into the box along with a few turrets, announcing to Tune, "your castle awaits, princess." It was a squealing success.

"Thanks Bobby," said Song. "I'm not up to adulting yet."

It was too cold for the girls to hit the pool just yet, so they just turned on the TV to vegetate. It'd been years since they'd watched regular TV, and were actually looking forward to it. Until they turned up the sound, that is......

"...........*is not the problem. The problem is us! Humans! Since that Humanity 2.0 app was released, the Earth's population has increased by nearly 50% already! The people that were in the retirement homes back then are on the golf course today, and women dying of cancer are instead sharing in the greatest baby boom in history! Nobody's dying anymore, unless they get hit by a truck. Wars have stalled, initially due to goodwill between countries after H2O, but as the population rises, there are increasing border skirmishes around the globe. A drastic increase in climate refugees has put undue pressure on national governments. Infrastructures were not ready for such a population explosion. Many cities are struggling just to provide water for their citizens."*

*"But Senator," interjected the show's host, "you can't deny that Humanity 2.0 has been a boom for the economy and a boon for mankind."*

*"For the economy, perhaps. The rising population has greatly increased the number of consumers. There are simply a lot more people alive, everywhere in the world. What company wouldn't like a 50% increase in customer base? But there is a dark side to all of this. The numbers are not sustainable. Many of those added customers are unemployed because there simply aren't enough jobs to go around anymore, so crime is also rising.*

*"There is enormous pressure on existing housing, on the water supplies and on the energy required to keep everyone warm. Countries like China have been forced to re-open coal-fired power plants that had been closed to ease climate change. And it's not just China. Only 13% of signatory nations still hope to reach their Paris Climate Accord commitments. As a result, Mother Earth doesn't much like what we are doing to her. As pressure grows, more and more bizarre weather catastrophes are already being unleashed. Expanding deserts? Earthquakes? Tornadoes? Drought?*

*Volcanoes?' Hurricanes? Polar ice? Mass extinctions? What will be the extent of the costs? Costs that we consumers will pay one way or the other, employed or not."*

*"Senator, your negativity is at odds with our booming economies, and global growth. Don't you think you're acting a bit like Chicken Little. The sky is not falling, sir. The world is thriving!"*

*"I challenge all of you watching to look deeper than the fancy frosting covering the feces beneath," advised the Senator. Jobs have fallen well short of population growth. And everyone has to eat, which has led to food shortages around the world. By the laws of supply and demand, prices climb higher and higher, paid for, once again, by us consumers. It's only going to get worse as the planet's population continues to soar unabated, costs for services like welfare, policing and other social ills are rising exponentially, and there is no indication that trend is going to change. While we struggle, ranchers are now forced to clone their animals just to keep up but that, once again, drives prices higher.*

*What happens to the people left without jobs completely? They are being forced to commit previously unthinkable acts just to feed their families. Theft is on the rise. Formerly stable civilians have been forced to become refugees. But countries of the world already have enormous population problems of their own, and are blockading their borders. Right-wing extremists are gaining power throughout the world, on the backs of the poor. This endless cycle of profits over people is going to be the death of our world.*

*"Senator," the moderator argued, "this goes against all of the good news stories out there."*

*"Some, but what's beneath the frosting? In the U.S., analysts crow about the precipitous drop in personal health bankruptcies, but that all comes at the expense of big pharma who have been rendered irrelevant. One sector's gain is another's loss. Now, I recognize there isn't a lot of sympathy for the pharmaceutical industry, but their bankruptcies still have a cost to the average taxpayer. Do you know which countries benefited the most by the paradigm shift in the health care industry? Those with universal healthcare. An enormous cost has been deleted from their national budgets. What used to be paid in places like Canada, the U.K., Australia and Sweden are now surpluses, either being returned to the taxpayer, or redirected to fund the arts. Admittedly, Humanity 2.0 has brought a lot of goodwill to fund the arts.*

*"But again, Senator, there are............."*

"Song?"

"Yeah, Jackie?"

"Cartoons?"

"Yeah, Jackie." Click. Cartoons were a good choice, judging by Tune's dancing.

"So....., Song?"

"Yeah, Jackie?"

"What's it like being the wife of the new Jesus?"
The pillow fight that followed was Tune's first. Seeing feathers float for the first time was so fun!

In the afternoon, everyone went out to laze beside the pool as planned, but there was some lingering unease, considering their last moments there. Bobby made it his mission for everyone to feel right at home again, so he set himself up as the swim-up bar's bartender. Soon they were all as loose as a goose.

"At least the tequila didn't spoil while we were gone!"

There were still scars from helicopter blades etched into the concrete, but any signs of death had been scrubbed clean or painted over. In the pool. Mage was floating Tune on the surface, encouraging her to kick. kick, kick. Every half hour or so, Bobby would bring out some new creation from his newly-arrived groceries. Barely anyone spoke, except Daniel, who was never at a loss for words. That is, until he noticed Jackie looking anxious and freaked out.

"What's up, baby?" he asked.

"Being here again has brought that day back. That man was chopped in half right there, and I keep thinking it could have been me."

"Well, it's a good thing you had me to save that

pretty, little butt of yours."

She took a deep breath, and hugged Daniel close. "You really did, didn't you?" she whispered in his ear. Sorry. Sometimes I forget that.

"No worries. I won't ever let you forget."

"As you wish," Jackie answered, as she bumped Daniel backward, into the pool. But, he was quick to grab her ankle and pull her in beside him.

"Auntie Jackie and Uncle Daniel are kissing," Tune shrieked with delight. And they were. Jackie's anxiousness was already fading into the background.

"Burgers!" Bobby announced. "Who wants fresh barbequed hamburgers?"

"Me, me, me, Zǔmǔ."

"Okay, little Sūnnǚ. What do you want on your bun?"

After a day of drinking in the sun, the two young couples veg'd to quiet, movie night with Tune passed out cold in Mage's lap. After the pool, Tang had taken her on a voyage of discovery, showing her every little thing in the back fourty. The day had just had too much excitement.

The following morning, Bobby was busy at work in the main kitchen putting his fresh groceries to good use. The aromas drifted throughout the mansion, leading the Moon family into the kitchen early. Orange juice was provided for Tune, and 'coffee of life' for her parents.

Jackie and Daniel arrived about a half hour later, red-faced, but happy. "We were just re-establishing our morning routine," Daniel crowed. "Damn, it's good to be home!"

Jackie blushed.

All were pumped for breakfast, though, or what Bobby called 'Bobby Brunch'. It was amazing. A five star restaurant would have paled in comparison.

The girls brought everyone up-to-date on the previous night's TV program. "So many unexpected consequences. Who would have thought our little project would affect the world so profoundly?" observed Song.

"It's been a disaster from the beginning," Mage grumbled.

"Don't you dare say that!" Song said with uncharacteristic anger and intensity. Everyone looked at her, surprised. "You've given the world the greatest gift it's ever had. Do you realize how happy you've made millions of families around the world? Yes, you lost your grandfather and it's tragic, but literally millions got theirs back. People disabled by chronic or terminal illnesses are now out on the golf course or in the maternity ward. Spouses have got their sick partners back. You single-handedly eradicated the world of illness. Where's Ebola? Yellow fever? Dengue fever? AIDS? Done! Gone! Trillions of dollars of medical funding has been saved. You've saved the entire continent of Africa. So, no, don't you *ever* say say giving the world the greatest gift it has ever seen was a 'disaster'."

Song marched out, red-faced and enraged.

*'Wow!'* thought Mage. *'I haven't seen her that mad since Tang picked us up that first New Year's'.* Mommy's unexpected outburst had Tune about to cry before Mage swooped down to kiss her cheek. "Don't worry, Tuney. Mama's mad at Daddy, not you." Apparently, that was a reasonable excuse, so Tune went back to bouncing happily on Jackie's knee, as carefree as ever. *'Such a great age."*

When the lawyer arrived at noon, Tang introduced him to everyone before cutting Mage from the herd to meet one on one. When they finally emerged, his eyes were swollen and red. He headed straight up to the bedroom, legal papers in hand. Tang and the lawyer talked until their visitors arrived at the front gate at 2:00.

Bobby ushered them into the front Grand Hall's divans, leaving them to admire the 20-foot chandelier dominating the huge, marble room. The grandeur and elegance was intimidating.

The lawyer and Tang did most of the talking with the others chipping in details only when asked. But, it was 'Captain' Tang back today, relating the unbelievable tale from beginning to end. Their guest's mouths stood agape as detail after detail came to light. It was fortunate that the different authorities and police all came at the same time, as the story alone took Tang more than an hour to tell.

The tale spoke of wealth few in the world could relate to, but a luxury submarine must be possible, right? The navy guys had seen it themselves. Regardless, the Mounties, the lawyer, the customs officials, the Navy Admiral, and the men from the government all insisted on 'inspecting' the Nautilus.

Tang led them down to the panic room, identifying items from the story, and as they went, added a few more. He pulled back the carpet, accessed the hatch, and climbed down the ladder into the pit. The visitors recognized the underground zipline from the story, but using it themselves? That, they had not expected. Their eyes flitted about before the senior officer proved brave enough to go first. Tang pulled the cord and the man zipped out of sight. Tang went last. On arrival at the bottom, he found the men talking excitedly, but reverting to professionalism once they saw him.

By the time they had all finished the tour of the sub an hour later, they were back to chattering like chipmunks, whether Tang was there or not. It was clear that these guys were not going to be able to keep the returning Fellowship of the Deep a secret. In fact, they were already itching to get home to tell their spouses. Tang pulled the senior Mountie aside and requested additional security details for outside the compound, short-term. It was an easy ask.

After bidding the visitors adieu, Tang inspected the grounds again, before checking the garage. The lawyer had the cars serviced and insured, as well as Mage's motocross bike, so they were all licenced and ready to go to all of the places they couldn't go anymore. *'Ironic',* he thought.

As he opened the side entry door, aromas assailed his senses. "What's the occasion, Robert?"

"Thanksgiving. Roast turkey and pumpkin pie. I am giving thanks."

"But, it's not Thanksgiving."

"It is to me. Thanks that we are all home safe and sound, and that's because of you, big guy. And we even had a stowaway!" He hugged his partner before tying a towel around Tune's neck as an apron.

# Chapter 16

*"I never approach my heroes in public and leave all my
illusions about them intact."*

**Stewart Stafford**

$$t = H + 5$$
**time = Humanity + 5 years**

Now that the Fellowship was home after years of being confined aboard the Nautilus, they found the restrictions here on land to be similar, or worse. Anyone hoping to leave the safety of the compound found that the freedoms of the past were distant memories.

It only took a couple of days before the curious came calling. Tang had hired a private security company to man the front gate, and the police unit patrolled the outer walls of the compound. Neither was an encroachment inside the walls, so the occupants of the mansion were not directly affected. But, anyone hoping to leave the compound was advised to take along at least one bodyguard, and only if Tang authorized it. The simplest trips had to be planned in detail.

Mage in particular was having the most difficult time with the restrictions, accustomed to hopping on his motorcycle and cruising wherever he wanted to be. Now, there was nowhere in the world where he could get away from it all. His patience with his friends and family dwindled as his frustrations grew. On this night, he had snapped at Song, and sniped at Tang, but it was when he lost patience with Tune that he felt he really had to get out of there. He went to the garage, slid into the anonymity of his helmet, hopped on his motocross bike, and left before anyone was even aware he'd gone.

Outside the gate, he saw a small gathering of tents in the park across the street. They were the devotees that were ruining Mage's life. One alerted the others, crying, "There he is! I think it's the Magician!" but Mage was out of sight before any could react.

His escape gave him the solitude and freedom he'd missed for too long. His clothes flapped briskly in the wind and soon he was laughing aloud, free. Taking the on ramp to the Lion's Gate Bridge he marvelled at downtown, all aglitter. It had been too long since he had driven through Vancouver's beautiful nightscape. At the other end of the bridge, he took the exit to Stanley Park and took a lap of its shores, ending where he and Song had had their picnic. But tonight, it was silent and dark, with no madmen in sight. The built up tension in his muscles slowly unclenched.

Chinatown was close by, so he headed up to Main Street and his grandfather's shop. All signs of the fire were gone, with just an empty lot in place of what had been home for his entire life. There were absolutely no indication of more than sixty years of laughter and loss. It was heartbreaking.

At the corner traffic light, he slipped off his

helmet to wipe his steamed up visor. As he ran his hands through his hair, he turned absently toward the car beside him, where a female passenger was hitting the arm of the driver repeatedly, frantically pointing toward Mage. *'Great!'* Re-donning his helmet, he was off like a shot the moment the light turned green. Unfortunately, the trailing car switched lanes and followed. At the next light, the woman exited their car, trying to get to Mage, even in the traffic. When a few cars honked in anger, she shared her knowledge, again pointing ahead at Mage.

He didn't wait for the light this time. Taking a right turn instead, his mirror showed three vehicles jumping the curb to follow. They filled both lanes behind him now, and were closing. Mage repeatedly checked over his shoulder, but couldn't shake them. If it were daytime, he could weave through cars to lose them, but the roads were clear, with no cars available to weave through. His best bet would be back roads, so he turned hard onto a narrow side street, his knee nearly scraping the ground. His headlight reflected the eyes of a very surprised cat causing him to veer. That was the last thing he remembered before waking in a hospital bed the next day.

It was a long night for Song when Mage hadn't return home. Early in the morning, with his side of the bed still not slept in, she sought out Tang. Bobby welcomed her in, and made her sit. She didn't look good. "What's wrong, honey?" he asked.

"Mage left and didn't come home last night."

"What?!?" Tang roared as he entered from the bedroom.

"He's been edgy lately. Cabin fever and guilt. After he yelled at Tune last night, he disappeared. And now I see his bike is still gone." She put up a brave face, but a single tear ran down her cheek.

"What was he thinking?"

"That's the problem, I don't think he was. He was reacting. He was angry at the world, and when he snapped at Tune, he was angry at himself. He left."

Unconsciously, Tang stared at a concrete wall without seeing it, twisting a fist into his other palm, repeatedly. Song put one of her own hands over his, breaking the trance.

"And how are you, little one?" he asked.

"Worried. Just worried."

"Okay. So, you say he just left? Did he say where he was going?"

"No idea. I didn't know he was going until after he'd gone."

"Can we track his phone?"

"It's on the dresser upstairs. We've been at sea for five years, and he hasn't looked at it since we got back."

Back at the hospital, Mage was still unconscious when the morning shift arrived. Carrying no identification at all, he'd been declared a John Doe. But, though his face was obscured somewhat by bandages, one of the nurses coming on shift recognized 'the Magician guy from that Humanity app.'

Once they put a name to his face, they located records listing his grandfather as his emergency contact. But the nurse who i.d.'d him remembered that the grandfather had died in that fire on the news years earlier.

Soon, a few E.R nurses and doctors alike were gossiping excitedly at their station. Despite their oath of anonymity, they quickly called their friends and families, and some actually posed for selfies, with him out cold in bed. The head nurse and attending physician arrived, cleared out the rabble, and decided to contact the Royal Canadian Mounted Police.

By the time the cops arrived, a small crowd was gathered outside Mage's room, so an officer was tasked with door security. Confirming the identity of the John Doe, the Officer-in-Charge called headquarters, eventually reaching the detective who had debriefed the Fellowship at the mansion.

Tang got the call, and within minutes, everyone was loaded into the Hummer, Tune included. They recognized Tang's concern, and though they were all worried for Mage, it was also a chance for them all to get out of the mansion. When Bobby asked his beau for details, Tang tore his head off. Bobby immediately closed the privacy window to the back, and the Hummer veered left and right a few times, but Tang must have maintained control, because they continued on their way.

"I don't know the details," Song told the others. "He was upset and feeling trapped in his new martyr role. He was grumpy and we had a fight. Tune started crying, and he snapped at her too. Next thing I knew, he was gone."

"So, why is he in the hospital?" asked Jackie.

"I don't know. All Tang told me was that he'd been in a motorcycle accident. He's got to be okay, right? I never should have argued with him."

"C'mon, Song," Daniel offered. "Couples argue. I've argued with him myself tons of times. It's not your fault. Don't sweat things we don't know yet."

By the time they reached their destination, a dozen people were milling around the hallway outside Mage's room. Seeing the 'Fellowship five' arrive en masse, the place erupted. But, Tang bull-dogged his way through like a blocker leading a running back. He was not to be denied. Ushering each into the room, he thanked the officer at the door, snarled at the crowd, then slammed the door shut and locked it.

Their collective hearts dropped from their chests when they saw Mage's face and hands now almost completely wrapped in gauze. One leg was in traction, suspended in the air. Song sobbed helplessly into Jackie's shoulder, and Jackie wept back, clutching her tight. Once she felt strong enough, Song turned and went to Mage, leaned down, and kissing him on the eyes, the only facial area bandage-free. A few teardrops fell into the gauze. She spoke to him softly, like an angel. Softly enough the others couldn't hear. The friends gave her a wide berth until she looked their way, inviting them in.

Each reached out and touched him somewhere, as if to ensure he was real under there. Words were sparse and awkward, so when the attending physician knocked, they were happy to make room.

"Mr. Moon," said the doctor to Song, "is looking at some significant rehab time, I'm afraid. The first few days after traction can be difficult. The muscles get weak from the additional time in bed. Moving around and walking may be challenging and will easily tire him. However, it's important to stick with a rehabilitation program so that he can improve his chances of a complete recovery. The bandages on his hands look worse than they are, but he used his face for a brake, so it is badly scraped. The attending EMTs said his helmet had come off, so I guess it wasn't fastened under his chin. There are no actual facial fractures, but he may end up with some scarring. We can recommend some plastic surgeons for that. His hands are in a similar situation, raw but unbroken, though his left wrist is sprained. As for his leg, it's broken in three places, and he'll need months of rehab. Less with his app."

"Does he need to stay here the whole time? What

about surgery?"

"The E.R. physicians reset his leg and gave him some stitches. He needs no further surgery. His brain is inflamed from the head trauma, so we want to keep an eye on that for the next few days. The traction is also important for the first week, but if he responds to treatment, he should be back on his feet in a month or two. As to whether he will be here long, it depends how his body heals. But, as soon as possible, it may be prudent to look into home care. In most cases, we would keep him here until he's well on his way to recovery. However, as you've already noticed, there are security concerns with such a high profile patient, and we're on a skeleton staff. Once word gets out that Mage is here, mayhem may follow. As soon as his traction is stable enough for him to be moved, it may be wise to have him convalesce at home."

"Thank you, doctor. I will hire security guards while he is here. Please let us know when he will be able to travel."

"Can we stay with him?" asked Daniel.

" He's not in a coma; he's just sleeping. Are you family?"

Song replied, "Yes. We are all family."

The doc smiled. "You are a very multi-cultural family. Well, don't tire him out."

"Thank you, doctor."

"You are fortunate this hospital is still running, albeit just for trauma. Most in town have shut down completely. You guys are putting us out of work, ha ha. It's a good thing I like golfing. But seriously, congratulations on your remarkable achievement. An old sawbones like me has been toiling my entire life to make a small dent. You folks solved it all in one fell swoop. You deserve that Nobel Prize for Medicine. It's truly been my pleasure to meet you all."

Once he'd left, Daniel asked Tang, "so what about that Nobel Prize? Now that we've been outed, can we just go get it? I know I could sure use one."

"Let's wait for your boy to come home first, before taking him to the other side of the world, eh?"

"Eh? You're becoming more Canadian every day, Tang....., eh?" Daniel went to play punch the big guy in the arm, but Tang's dead eyes stopped his fist cold. Tang then laughed, put Daniel in a headlock, and gave the top of his head a noogie.

Eventually, it was clear that Song wasn't leaving, so Bobby, Jackie and Daniel elected to take Tune home. The child's patience had expired. She'd had enough drama for one day. That pile of bandages sure didn't look like her Daddy. But if Song wasn't leaving, neither was Tang.

While Mage slept, Tang began working his phone to arrange for additional security personnel. His fingers felt fat and clumsy on the numbers. He hadn't used it in awhile. Out the window, a TV news van pulled up out front, so he implored the folks at the other end of his phone line to hurry. Then, pointing at the window, he indicated to Song he was going down to deal with the press.

The TV newsgirl recognized Tang and was soon pushing a microphone in his face. "Mr. Tang. Mr. *Tang!* Is it true that Mage Moon is receiving treatment at this hospital? If so, what is his condition?"

Tang gently pushed the microphone away from his face, stating "There will be no comment of any kind today, so I urge you all to go home."

"There will be no comment of any kind today. It's too early for the doctors, so please do not interfere with those who are here to save others. Let them do their jobs. We will be available to the press tomorrow, right here at 11:00 a.m. That is all."

"Is it true Mage Moon was involved in the release of Humanity 2.0, Mr. Tang? Mr. Tang. One last question. Do you find it ironic that you're closing downs hospitals, yet here is Mr. Moon, in need of one?"

"No." And with that, he did a military turn and strode back into the hospital.

Once he crossed the threshold, a man in a blue, hospital security uniform stepped into the doorway, blocking anyone trying to follow Tang. He smiled at the growing crowd and said, real friendly-like, "Which of you folks would like to tour our detainment facility today?"

The next morning, Song was feeding Mage through a straw when Tang and Bobby arrived to check in on the patient. Bobby, of course, made Tang stop for flowers on the way. Mage gave a weak smile to his friends, but winced slightly at the effort. He shouldn't have bothered. They couldn't see his face anyway. But even so, it was encouraging to see him awake and lucid, eyes bright and alert. He had no recollection of the accident, but the M.R.I. had come out okay. There was some inflammation, of course, but he'd dodged the bullet on brain damage.

Tang and Bobby soon begged off to hold the 11:00 press conference. Mage rasped through the gauze, "What press conference?"

"Your press conference," Bobby offered. "You, sir, are big news."

The hospital had a table set up, where they were joined by the attending physician, and the senior R.C.M.P. member from the mansion. Officers from both the R.C.M.P. and Vancouver City Police were dispersed among the crowd, some in plain clothes, talking to their wrists. Bobby and Tang alternated answering the questions, but to their credit, stayed until every journalist had asked every question they could come up with. Mage's health was first and foremost, so they allowed the doctor to field all medical questions before he headed back inside the hospital.

Bobby closed out the proceedings with a promise to host the press at the mansion in a month's time. They could interview the entire Fellowship at once, after Mage was home and healing. He also made it clear that there would be no other press conferences until then, and asked that the man who healed the world be permitted to heal himself. Any news agencies which violated their rule by harassing either the hospital or mansion would be excluded from next month's group press conference. Each agency was to be permitted only one reporter due to the world press interest, and were to submit the name and photograph of their reporter to ensure the validity of their press passes.

The senior R.C.M.P. member closed out the day, warning the public of their intolerance with anyone interfering in the process. It was because of such interference that Mr. Moon was in the hospital in the first place.

In the following weeks, the crowds in front of the hospital, as well as across the street from the mansion, grew exponentially. Both locations kept the police and private security personnel busier than a one-armed wallpaper hangar.

The after-effects of the initial interview caused an unforeseen problem. When Mage's religious Humanitarian followers heard the manner in which their Magician had been injured, they took it upon themselves to become his standing army, in defence of their holy deity. Tempers flared and fights broke out between factions of the tent cities; one that wanted to blame him, and the other to protect him.

The growth of the encampments themselves was exponential, with zealots of many religions and activists arriving from locales the world over. Government and police tried to arrest their way out of the problem, but others simply snapped up the newly-available camping space. The more divisive the factions became, the larger they grew. And every time a vehicle left the mansion, an 'honour guard' would follow, as would a variety of news vans.

With the help of Song playing the H2O tracks, Mage was healing well ahead of schedule. When he was well enough to be discharged, he was stunned by the crowds. *'Where on Earth were they all coming from? Everywhere on Earth',* he supposed. The newest twist was the Humanity Church camp's addition of 'magicians', dressed to entertain the crowds, conjuring this, and exploding that. Humanity muzak blared over the speakers day and night, all within a carnival atmosphere. Anti-Humanitarians would occasionally storm the Muzak tent, but the devout would just smile and play it silent mode from another tent.

When the time came for the full interview a month after his release, Mage was the front page story again, on *every* front page in the world. The mansion sessions proved to be relatively easy for everyone. Bobby and Tang had done such a thorough job in the previous interviews that there wasn't much new to tell except the patient's medical progress. And when they tried to corner Mage on the subject, he merely said, "I feel fine." Not much of a quote, there. Desperate reporters expecting to bring back a scoop for their bosses were sorely disappointed. But they were just happy to be in the same room as the most famous man on the planet. They'd be able to tell their kids and grandkids about this day.

Though the press became less intrusive, the general public became more-so. Some tried climbing the mansion's gates and walls, but if they got past the water cannons, Tang was there. A fireplace poker was his weapon of choice these days. For the most-part, they were individual teenagers or young adults. Time after time, one would try climbing the walls only to be blown clear by the water cannons. It had all become so routine, that Tang put together a blooper tape from the security footage showing devotees being taken out by the water cannons. Bobby overdubbed it with the Maple Leaf Rag, giving it the feel of an old Keystone Kops clip.

Bobby became the boredom whisperer, and took on the responsibility of the mood of the Fellowship. One day, when everyone seemed on edge, he brought home to the mansion an old friend with a special talent. Everyone was lazing by the pool when he led a middle-aged woman out back and introduced her to the others.

"Everyone, listen up," he called. "This is my old friend, Sally. I have known her forever, and she can be trusted to be discreet. Sally, meet the Fellowship of the Deep!" She was a bit flustered, fidgeting nervously, but nobody could act the gracious host like Bobby could.

"Don't be shy, Sally. You've met famous people before." She was surprised at the warm greeting of the famous residents, but in truth, they'd been starved for *any* new social contact.

"Well, I've never met a God before." She was joking, but it fell flat. Polite smiles, but flat.

Bobby rescued the awkward moment. "Sally works in movies as a make-up artist for the stars. She *also* does is costume make-up for the sci-fi flicks, and such." Everyone smiled politely, waiting to learn whatever it was that Bobby was up to. "Sally has brought her supplies, and today is transformation day for you all!"

Clearly, they were still missing the point, so he elaborated. "Sally can make you look like anything you want. Most importantly, she's able to give you anonymity." He raised his eyebrows twice.

The penny finally dropped, and Daniel yelled, "Hell, yeah! Can you make me look like Spiderman?"

"Um, sure, if that's what you want." Sally responded.

"That's not what he wants," said Jackie.

Bobby continued, "Daniel, you may wish to pick an identity that's more subtle. Attention is what we're trying to avoid here. So today, we can experiment. You can be anything you want. Who do you want to be? Who wants to go first?"

"Hell, yeah, I will!" offered Daniel. "Make me, ummm....,Jacks, what should I be? Who do you want to be in love with today?"

"How about, make him look old and wise, Sally. I want to see what my future will look like."

"Not what I was expecting, but okay, I guess." said Daniel. "Making me look old will be a challenge for her, but the wise look shouldn't be much of a stretch." He threw Jackie a wink. She just rolled her eyes.

"Can you make him old, wise and mute, Sally?"

"Sorry. Exteriors only."

It was a fascinating process to watch, and she'd never had a group more interested than this one. Sally added latex to his nose and cheeks, and sculpted wrinkles into his face. She added the thickest of white eyebrows and an equally bushy, white walrus moustache.

"You look like an old jazz musician," Jackie teased.

Sally topped him off with a scattered, white wig.

"I recognize him! That's ummmm...., not Albert Einstein," struggled Song.

"Mark Twain!" Mage blurted out.

"Very good!" said Sally. "I know you won't be able to leave this place looking like that, but I wanted to give you an idea of what we could do."

In his best southern drawl, and a surprisingly good imitation of Mark Twain, Daniel observed, "Why, Samuel Clemens once said, *'Wrinkles should merely indicate where the smiles have been.'*"

"Quoting Twain? You surprise me more and more each day, baby,"

"What?" said Daniel defensively. "I read......., you know, stuff."

"Who's next?" asked Sally.

"Me!" Jackie cried.

"A beautiful girl like you is tough to hide," Sally said. "How about I make you ugly?"

"Yes!" Ever since she was about 16 years old, she'd received a lot of attention. It might be nice to be invisible. Supermodel good looks gave way to deep saggy wrinkles and droopy eyes. Sally tucked Jackie's long hair under a ratty, brown wig, and added a wart here, and a scar there. In no time, she was completely unrecognizable. Sally handed Jackie a cane, then wrapped a thin, black shawl around her shoulders. The finished product looked like a witch from a Disney movie, and Jacks absolutely loved it. "Would you like a bite of my apple, Mr. Twain? Or should I call you Mr. Clemens?" she croaked at Daniel.

"No! Yuck. Get away from me you old hag! This isn't fair, you know."

"How's that?"

"You got to pick who you got to sleep with tonight, but I end up with a crone." He paused for effect, then swept her into his arms, kissing her right on her nose wart.

"Next?" called Sally.

"Me! Me next!" cried Song, jumping a little. Dress-up was a new concept to her. As a child in China, there was no trick-or-treating and the only dress-up she'd ever done was when Jackie dragged her to the Halloween Ball at their private school. They'd rented sexy witch outfits, conjuring spells with a toss of glitter. Everyone but the custodian thought they looked great.

Song was stone still, as Sally went back to work, this time morphing her into a small, white teenage girl. Once a red wig was added, the transformation was remarkable. In the mirror, staring back at her, was her mother as she'd looked in childhood. Song had seen photographs of that era. They could have been twins. Same big smile. Same green eyes. And now, the same flaming red hair. This wasn't Raggedy Ann wool hair. It was the real thing, long with thick red curls down to her chest. *'Wow!'* she thought. *I look hot!'* Apparently Mage thought so, too. It was the most they'd seen him smile since the return from the hospital.

Tune had laughed and laughed as she watched her mother transformed into her grandmother. What could be more fun for a small child than a day playing dress-up? She reached out to gently touch her mama's make-up, saw it on her fingertip, and squealed like a piglet.

"Oh, you like that don't you? Yes, I think you you do," said Sally. "Are you next? Do you want me to do your face too?"

Tune;s eyes grew large, as she sought permission from her mom. Once she got the nod, she clambered up into the chair beside Sally like she'd been in movies her whole life. All 3-1/2 years of it.

"Who is your favourite cartoon, dear?" Sally asked her.

"Elsa! Elsa! Elsa!"

"Elsa from 'Frozen'?"

"Yeah! Yeah! Yeah." The Nautilus's TV didn't usually get reception below the waterline, so Tune had watched the Frozen DVD a million times.

"Well, let me have a look in my bag. Oh, yes, this will be perfect!"

Tune had never sat so still for so long, ever. She closed her eyes and loved the attention. Rouge was added to her cheeks, lipstick for her lips, and mascara that made her eyes look twice the size. Sally tied a pale blue shawl around her to look like a ballroom gown. Finally, she topped it all off with a long, thickly braided blonde wig.

"Do I look like Elsa, Mama?"

"Oh yes,,,,,,. Elsa! Go have a look." Tune raced to the door, in search of a full length mirror. Another squeal was heard deep inside the house. A steady squeal that lasted all through her entire run back out to the pool. Her face glowed, and only partly due to the rouge. "Oh, you look so regal, baby!" her mom gushed.

Tune ran to her daddy, leaping up without warning, as she often did. "See Daddy? See me?" He was happy she'd missed his crotch this time, but he winced badly when she landed on his injured leg. He hid it well.

"Now who is that talking to me?" he asked. Looking above her head, and around her tummy, he asked, "Where's my little Tunie gone?"

"Here, Daddy! I'm right here!"

"No, that can't be so. I can't see my Tunie. There's only this princess! Wait a minute." He looked at her face closely, then opened his eyes wide in mock surprise. "Elsa, did you kidnap my Tunie?"

"No, Daddy. It's me!" Thoroughly convinced she'd straightened things out, she cried, "You. Your turn, Appa."

Mage was more difficult to transform, but Sally was up to the task. At first she considered using his height to make a NBA star lookalike, but anonymity was the goal. Song suddenly brightened, then said, "Just a sec." She returned with a large portrait of Mage's grandfather. "Him," she said. "Bring Gramps back to life, even if just for the day."

Sally worked on Mage right in his wheelchair. The finished product, however, had young Tune a bit confused. She pointed at the portrait, then at Mage, and back at the photo. You could almost watch her young mind's gears at work. Then, problem solved!

Jumping and clapping, Tune ordered, "Now you, Zŭfù!"

Tang chuckled at the little imp, and tried to weasel his way out of it. "I don't think so, little one. Sally must be getting tired."

She checked her watch and did indeed have to go. "I'll just leave all of the props and make-up stuff here. I'll bring more next time, too, now that I see exactly what I'm working with."

Once Sally took her leave, Bobby spoke up. He'd been making good use of the shooter bar, as he was prone to do, and was already pleasantly pickled. "One more announcement, people. People? Listen up. Listen, listen. Tang and I have another surprise, too. For you. We've been busy procuring another deception. Yup. *Hic.* A couple of RVs. Yup. Big ones. They slide. They have slide-outs. We bought two exactly the same, in case one needs to be a decoy. And.... and...., we've booked two campsites in the Rocky Mountains for next month! Mage should be mobile by then."

"Hell, yeah!"

"Sally has agreed to travel with Tang and I in one unit, and you four will have the other. If you need her, she'll make you up however you want. We'll be able to mix freely with other humans!"

"Hell, yeah!"

"The RVs are at a secure parkade in Surrey," Tang interrupted. "We will leave this compound at night to dissuade followers. We'll transport everyone to the parkade in the Hummer. We've been provided with an entry code to dissuade anyone who may still follow us. We will then take the elevator to another level where the Rvs are waiting, and depart out a secondary exit on the other side. Anyone trying to follow will not be able to get into the parkade, and when we depart, we'll be in the new RVs. Sally will need to return home at some point for a new movie shoot, but she has promised us lessons. We start near Banff, a full day's drive away. Once we're confidently clear of any followers, we'll set up camp."

"And make smores around the campfire!" added Jackie. She'd mentioned the smores specifically for Tune's benefit, but the wee one had no idea what Auntie Jackie was on about.

Song didn't miss the reference, though. "Thank you, Bobby. And Tang. I've never been camping. Ever!" She gave them each a big hug and beamed at her friends. "Where are we going to go after Banff, guys?"

"We'd better stay up here in Canada. We can't trick anyone at a border crossing," Mage decided.

"Anywhere in B.C. is good with me. I've lived here all of my life, but our family never went camping, either. I've barely seen British Columbia. I wouldn't have a clue how to get ready or where to go."

"Well, it looks like you city slickers are going to need me for this. I can teach all you guys." Daniel said, pointing to each in turn. "'Cause I'm a lumberjack and I'm okay......,"

A few days earlier, Jackie had pined about getting out of the city for awhile. Between being on the Nautilus, and the necessary security on land, she needed a few days of pure freedom. Bobby had overheard her, and hatched the idea for the RVs. "The Okanagan," offered Jackie. "I say summer in the Okanagan is the place to be,"

"And the Kootenays!" chipped in Daniel. "And the Shuswap! They are all nice during the summer."

"I've heard good thingsh about renting houseboats up on Shuswap Lake," Bobby slurred.

"Ugh," muttered Jackie. "I've heard the same thing, but after 5 years aboard the Nautilus, I could do without another boat for awhile."

"Mama?" asked Tune. What are arvies and crampings?"

"An RV is like a cabin on wheels we can drive around. Remember that day that we saw some cars? Like that, but bigger. And camping is a bit like when

308

we're on our island. Campfires and stuff."

"Okay," she answered with a shrug. The adults were far more excited by the idea than her. But playing dress-up would be fun.

# Chapter 17

*"Discovery is always the rape of the natural world. Always."*

**Michael Crichton**

$$t = H + 10$$
**time = Humanity + 10 years**

A decade after Humanity 2.0 was released to the world, mankind was facing some inhumane realities. Unless folks committed suicide or perished in an accident, people simply were not dying. Any injury would heal, and missing limbs or digits would grow back. Centenarians were becoming common, and women were capable of giving birth far later in life. The population stats confirmed the problem. In ten short years, the world's population had doubled and continued to grow on an exponential scale, completely unsustainable.

The leaders of several countries dared to suggest population culls, or moratoriums on babies, but as often happens with complicated challenges, nobody could agree on solutions. Water had become the new oil – scarce, expensive and worth warring over. Goodwill among nations was disappearing as resources were exhausted. Continents like Africa, which had initially been the big winner of Humanity 2.0, were reverting to third world status, unable to provide water and food to their people.

City fresh water reserves dried up all over the world, be they in rich or poor countries. Sao Paulo, Capetown, Beijing, Cairo, Bangalore, Jakarta, Moscow, Istanbul, Mexico City, Tokyo, and London were all dry, causing a widespread refugee crisis like the world had never seen. Extreme shortages of food were common, and costs skyrocketed. Traditional food belts like California now exported very little because they couldn't water their crops, putting pressure on local farmers and ranchers elsewhere. But with most of the glaciers melting down, many regions of the world now had no water source at all now.

In California, for example, controversy over whether water should be used for drinking or watering crops became heated at times. L.A.'s primary sources of water were the Colorado River, and Lake Mead, which no longer had enough water to go over Hoover Dam. Los Angeles wasn't alone. Nearly three quarters of the cities around the world were fresh water challenged, and their potential solutions prohibitively expensive. Cities still fortunate to have water access found themselves swamped with refugees who did not contribute to their tax base, so even in areas of plenty, tensions were high. Without plumbing, they were fouling the very water keeping them and the city dwellers alive. Protectionism spread throughout the world, and borders were closing everywhere.

While fresh drinking water supplies dwindled, seawater levels rose. The churches of Venice were now knee deep in water, and the downtowns of many cities were flooded and unusable. Underground parking garages became underwater parking garages, and subway routes were now underwater tunnels. On the streets above, water was often ankle deep, forcing snakes and spiders to take refuge in the trees. Humans weren't so lucky.

Infrastructure for electricity and plumbing was being tested in a time of massive population growth. Demand caused power blackouts, while overwhelmed sewer systems vexed city planners. Areas that had delayed in preparing for climate change were now faced with the logistics of either working underwater, or erecting conduits above ground. And since the population explosion was a worldwide problem, suppliers could not keep up with projects, causing shortages of building materials which drove prices even higher. Many resources were becoming scarce far earlier than expected.

Every sector of the economic world was struggling. Police and immigration services the world over exceeded their capacities, in an era where social programs were more essential than ever, but no longer sustainable. People who could no longer feed their families either became refugees, or suicide victims. Humanity 2.0 was great, but couldn't save people who were determined to take their own lives. Many others starved or died of thirst, other issues H2O couldn't help, and frankly, keeping more people of the world alive was unpopular fiscally. Yet global populations overall continued to skyrocket.

Abandoned coal generation plants were forced back online, bringing back their inevitable pollution with it. But people cared little about air quality when they were struggling for food and water. Most climate accords had been abandoned, as countries battled the logistics of explosive population growth and unpredictable demographics. Sea water temperatures rose as more old gas cars choked out more carbon pollution into the sky.

Humans were not the only ones affected. Earth's species extinction rate was growing as remaining fresh water supplies were diverted to cities. Many habitats began to die off, forcing animal migration to urban lands increasingly claimed by people. Available food for both the human and the animal migrants became scarce, leading carnivores of some continents to hunt small, human refugees.

The goodwill gained from the release of Humanity 2.0 was already a thing of the past. Turf wars increased, from local neighbourhoods right up to the largest countries of the world. At the pinnacle were India and China, both of which now held in excess of 3 billion people, separated only by the Himalaya mountains. China openly prized India's cattle supply, which outraged their southern neighbours to whom the cow is sacred. India prized China's land, sorely needed farmland for their rising population. Each were nuclear nations, with crumbling infrastructures and hungry citizens. It was a powder keg.

In contrast, life back at Song's mansion in West Vancouver continued seamlessly, buffered by wealth.

313

Water there was not an issue, as Canada held 880,000 lakes, the most in the world. Tune had blossomed into a precocious nine-year-old, bright-eyed gem, quick as a whip. She'd never known a world without Humanity 2.0., so had never been sick, not even with a childhood cold. For her entire life, she had lived among the same six adults, and few others. The complexities facing the rest of the world simply were not a factor to Tune.

The same could not be said for the adults of the mansion. Although great wealth had allowed them to live in luxury during the global catastrophe, it was their minds that were overburdened. Every day, they were inundated with images and stories of strife beyond the walls of the compound, strife they felt they'd caused. It was depressing. But ten years after its release, Mage himself was increasingly determined to leave the guilt in the past and concentrate on the present.

One bonus for the mansion residents was the shrinking crowds outside their gates. Only a few die-hard followers still camped in the park across the road. Most of the departed now had more pressing issues to deal with at home. The upside was, it was now possible to leave the compound without being followed. And thanks to Sally's guidance while camping, they had all learned to alter their appearance enough to not be recognized. It was wonderful. They were able to take part in a few of the basic activities other people took for granted.

For Jackie and Daniel, it was a chance to go on dates, something they'd never been able to do. He worried that now that Jackie had access to other men, she'd forget him, but Jacks was more loyal than ever to the man who had twice saved her life. They went to movies, dinners in restaurants, and outdoor adventures, as long as the sweat didn't ruin the make-up. Oddly, the opportunity of spending more time apart individually, resulted in them becoming closer than ever as a group.

For Bobby, there were two rules he was insistent on. Breakfasts together and Sunday dinners as a family. No excuses. No exceptions. One such Sunday, he had Tune working in the kitchen with him, time they often enjoyed together. He was as smitten as Tang with the little imp.

When Mage walked into the kitchen, they turned as one, each with flour on the tips of their noses.

"Hi Daddy. How's it goin'?" she asked. "Still a god?"

"A billion devotees in 94 countries," he replied casually.

"Well, honey," said Song as she walked in, "you'll always be a God to me." She gave Mage a morning kiss before sidling over to Tune for another.

"Me too, Daddy. Whenever I say, 'oh *my* god', I mean you now." Tune turned to receive her mother's kiss, dabbing flour on her nose, as well.

Jackie entered and, tickling Tune, asked, "why is your Dad the only one who's a god, anyway? He gets all the credit!"

That got under Mage's skin a bit. "Credit? You can have it! I just read an article about protein shortages. Ranchers have been hacking off body parts off their livestock, then crank up the Hu-zak for them to heal, before doing it all again. Do you want credit for that?"

"Eeeewww!" Tune opined.

"It went on to mention a whole new tragedy in *human* trafficking. People are being staked to the ground, and treated like the cattle. Then its like, 'Hack off another leg for dinner, Ma! Don't worry. It'll grow back!'"

"Okay, I think that's enough of this conversation," said Jackie. "You're going to give the kids nightmares."

"It's giving *me* nightmares."

Song ruffled the hair of the Jackie's son. "Hiya Nemo."

"Hi, Auntie Song." Nemo answered sleepily.

Sneaking up behind him was his father. "Gotcha!" Daniel exclaimed.

Nemo squirmed away, more interested in what Bobby and Tune were up to.

Song observed, "he's growing again. Look, he's as tall as Tune now, and she is almost six years older than him."

"I know, right? And speaking of Tune, home school starts as soon as you and Bobby are finished, little Missy."

"Yay!" she cried. Tune liked getting one on one time with Aunt Jackie, who had passed her interest in learning to her wee student.

At times, Tune would complain about having to play with young Nemo because of the age difference, but really, they were best buds and had been since either could remember. They were the only play pals each had ever known. Sometimes they argued, but just as kids do. And living in the mansion, there was adventure everywhere for them. If it was sunny, they'd be out by the pool, shooting hoops, or trying to play a bit of golf.

And if it rained, they'd go bowling. Tang wouldn't let them use the pistol or archery range yet.

But, their favourite thing by far was going camping with their parents, and for them all to play dress-up. The kids didn't need to hide, as Song and Jackie had been fiercely protective of their pictures getting out to the press. But, they weren't going to be left out of dressing up, that was for sure.

Nemo had heard the story a hundred times about how he was 'conceived' on a camping trip, whatever that meant. One day when they were alone, he'd asked Tune what 'conthiefed' meant, to which she;d replied, *thought up'*. Still confused, one night he'd asked, "Mommy? Did you and Daddy just think me up?" She'd told him *'no, we loved you up'*, leaving him more confused than ever.

But, when the families *did* go camping, it was a celebration of freedom. Tune had turned into a pretty good little make-up artist, and on the nights leading up to their camping trips, would hide under her covers at night, sketching out plans for each adult's face and costume.

It was decided long ago that there were two rules in this endeavour. First, the adults insisted that whatever the design, they still had to fit in unnoticed and not stand out like they had Mickey Mouse faces. And second, if the kids satisfied the first, the parents couldn't complain or back out, no matter what.

When Tune had her sketches finished, she'd sneak conspiratorially with Nemo under the piano in the music room, where they whispered and giggled over their plans. Then, with said plan finalized, they visited Bobby and Tang on the bottom floor. As always, Bobby offered them cups of tea, laced with excessive sugar and cream, and seemed to always have cookies baking for them. Little did they know, Bobby used the smell of the cookies to lure them in whenever he wanted gossip. He was like the witch in Hansel & Gretel, but nice.

Nemo whispered to him the secret plan. Another camping trip was coming and they needed Bobby's help. Tune leaned over, looked left and right, and whispered, "Uncle Bobby, can you get us some wigs and stuff?"

Bobby's interest was instantly piqued. Theatre? He whispered back, "Absolutely, I can. What's the plan?" Nemo earnestly nodded at Tune his approval for her to tell Uncle Bobby.

"We need some wigs. Real wigs. Long." Another furtive glance left and right. Then, satisfied their parents were out of earshot, she whispered, "And two big, red beards for our Daddies. And kilts." Bobby semi-stifled a laugh, not altogether successfully. "And we need shirts. You know, those bright, flowery shirts like in Hawaii. Oh, and mirrored sunglasses. And rainbow flip-flops!"

She was on a roll now, and Bobby liked what he was hearing. He whispered for both kids to follow him, creeping stealthily over to his laptop. The quiet didn't last, as soon they were hooting and shouting their way through the online websites. When everything was decided, Tune gave Bobby the 'shush' sign of secrecy, which Nemo copied. Bobby put a finger to his lips as he too tip-toed away. They'd made Bobby's day, as usual. Kids were a joy he'd thought out of reach. But here he was, the self-professed matriarch of his multicultural family of eight, playing his role of grandmother with panache.

When camp day came, Tune and Nemo were ready. Bobby called them aside to lead them down to his and Tang's place. Bobby gave them Hawaiian shirts, sunglasses and flip-flops he'd bought for them to match their parents'. They looked snazzy, ready for the beach. So, as Bobby ushered in the parents one by one, Tune went to work. Jackie was first, looking not at all out of place. Her naturally fair skin looked authentic with the long, straight red hair and wig, and she strutted out like she was on a fashion show catwalk. She did a quick pirouette, set her sunglasses atop her head, and strutted back, to the delight of the kids.

"Thanks, kiddos. I love it."

With one last look in the mirror to check the wig, Jackie got as far as the door before Tune ran between her and the door. "You can't go! They can't see you! Bobby will go get them............ BOBBY!"

Tune was the epitome of concentration with her mother in the chair. She lightened her face, adding a few beauty marks, and topped Song off with a red, pixie cut wig. The red hair made those green eyes pop.

Bobby brought Daniel in next. Each time he tried to crack a joke, Tune rapped him with her make-up brush, eliciting a wagging finger by Nemo. Once complete, Daniel stroked his red beard, winked at Jackie, and with a thick, Scottish brogue, inquired, "Oy lassie, would you like to see what a Scot's got 'neath his kilt?"
"Wink all you want, laddie," countered Jackie, also in accent, "I've seen 'neath your tartan, and it's not that grand, lad."

At last, Mage was dragged in to join the others. This particular tradition was not his favourite. Dangling the red beard, Song scolded, "Come on, baby. You know the rules."

He'd already seen Daniel in costume, so he knew what was coming. "This is a borderline infringement of the 'not standing out' rule," Mage whined.

When Tune had woven her *magic* on the *magician,* Song couldn't stop a chuckle or two from escaping her lips. She tried, but just couldn't do it. As hard as Tune had tried, Mage still looked ridiculous. Transforming a six and a half foot Korean Canadian into a bushy-bearded, curly-haired Scot was no easy feat at the best of times, let alone one in rainbow flip-flops and a Hawaiian shirt.

"Worry not, my love." teased Song. Nobody is going to think you are the most famous man on Earth looking like that."

# *Chapter 18*

*"The Earth will not continue to offer its harvest, except with faithful stewardship. We cannot say we love the land and then take steps to destroy it for use by future generations."*

**Pope John Paul II**

$$t = H + 15$$

**time = Humanity + 15 years**

It had been 5 years since they had all returned to the pagoda mansion, and the world's problems were becoming more and more extreme.

"People just don't understand why global warming is so dangerous to us all," complained Bobby, already hot under the collar about his pet peeve. "By killing our oceans, we're killing ourselves! It's criminal! Ocean problems are what's causing most of the weather disasters." The subject was the only thing that ever made him angry, but he was simply unable to stay calm. Every morning of late, Bobby used his mandatory breakfasts to detail yet another atrocity to the environment.

"Last year, we put more than 15 million tons of plastic alone into the oceans. That's thirty *billion* pounds of plastic. In one year! And you know that stuff doesn't break down, so each year we just keep piling more and more on top. Someday, future sentient archaeologists will look back at our civilization as just a thick layer of plastic embedded in the earth.

"Okay. I'll bite," Daniel said. "Why are the oceans more important than, say, the Amazon, or the arctic?" The subject wasn't an important one to Daniel, but he knew Bobby was going to ramble on for awhile, so he might as well ask about something that interested him.

"Because 70% of the oxygen on Earth comes from the ocean, that's why. It covers nearly 3/4 of the globe, yet is still treated as a garbage dump by many countries. Every year, more and more plastic is choking our sea life. Everyone frets about the rape of the Amazon rain forests, but nobody seems to be concerned about the oxygen in our oceans. Besides, the Amazon has been logged and burned so much, it's an oxygen-negative zone now, anyway. The oceans are something you should all care about, after our time aboard the Nautilus."

"Not this again," whined Nemo. "It's all you ever talk about in Ecology class." Members of the Fellowship each taught a course to the youngsters now. Nemo was coming up on his 10th birthday soon, and Tune was now a teenager. "Global warming, weird weather, acidic water, and all that junk. It's so boring."

It was rare for Bobby to lose his cool with the kids, but his eyes were bugging out. "You think this isn't important? Do you have any idea what the world will look like when you're my age? You may not even make it to my age, the way it's going."

"Stop scaring him," interjected Nemo's mother. "He's just a kid,"

"He should be scared, Jackie. You're a smart girl. It will be the defining issue of his lifetime. Our world is dying and it's our fault, as humans. Global populations now exceed 20 billion people on a planet only capable of sustaining 2-1/2 billion."

"This is too *boring*. Can I leave the table, Mom?" Nemo whined. "Can Tune and I go play?"

But Tune, now a teenager was more in tune with ecology and Earth sciences. "I want to stay and listen."

Nemo's shoulders sagged. "Okay. I'll be down in the music room practicing."

"I'll come with you," said his mom. That brightened his step. Jackie felt the same way sometimes. She'd quit watching the news entirely.

"So, Bobby," Daniel prodded him, "you've always followed this stuff. They've been talking about global warning for decades, and we've all tuned it out for years. What's the big deal all of a sudden?"

"Because we are perilously close to causing our own extinction, that's why. It's becoming irreversible. Every moment we ignore it, the problem gets worse. Earth's big dying event 250 million years ago was because of global warming. Sound familiar? The oceans heated up mostly due to a chain of erupting volcanoes in Russia. The water got warmer causing the seas to acidify. That's what killed off 96% of Earth's ocean life and 70% of the animals on land. Global warming. Ocean plants and bacteria were 100 times more efficient creating oxygen than land plants. They died. Oxygen levels dropped and most life forms on the planet suffocated."

"I read," added Mage, "that there's more than a thousand oxygen dead zones in our oceans already. Deep sea oxygen reserves are disappearing. That means they can't breathe."

"Add to that our proficiency at destroying the reefs," ranted Bobby, "and we're well on our way to a similar fate as 250 million years ago. Reefs are the marine equivalent of losing all of the bees on land. Both are mass extinction events."

That night, Daniel and Mage were up late watching the news but wondered why they bothered. Every single day had doom and gloom somewhere. News programmers knew that people watched for longer if scared or angry, so now, that's all they aired anymore. Police forces around the world were collapsing. Border wars over fresh water were now commonplace. Water was the new oil, trading on the world's stock markets. Canada was in a good position with 10 times the water per capita as Americans, but the Yanks coveted it, and were making no bones about it.

And, quite frankly, Mother Nature was not happy.

News story after news story involved her buckling under the weight of the population explosion. The oil and gas industry was near capacity, toiling in vain to keep the extra people warm. The downside was, burning those extra hydrocarbons accelerated the Earth's increasing temperatures, and perpetuating the cycle.

Worst case scenarios existed in nearly every sector – politics, economics, starvation, dehydration...... The 1.5 degree temperature rise decreed by governments at the Paris Accord was already in Earth's rear view mirror. Environmental concerns were swept aside by the more immediate concerns. Doomsday apathy skyrocketed. People's consciences could only accept what their brains could manage.

Such apathy even existed at the mansion.

"I'm so sick of all the doom and gloom," whined Daniel. Geez, Mage. Can't we have just one newscast not about global warming?"

"You sound like your son. But that's the problem, my friend. Nobody wants to hear the dire warnings anymore, so they've tuned it out. As a result, what we could have fixed, we now can't."

"Try another channel. There's got to be other news in the world somewhere."

"..........*as the oil and gas industry has struggled to keep up with demand, deep drilling and fracking are on the rise. Farmers claim water tables are lowering to fill the void spaces, resulting in stunted crops, in an era* when food and water supplies are already under considerable pressure. Scientists warn, such void spaces are susceptible to increased volcanic and earthquake activity, releasing methane pockets from the earth below.

"And, on the political front, representatives from the U.S. and Canada met in Ottawa today to discuss the resurrection of pipeline talks. A few short years ago, American cancelled the Keystone XL pipeline project which would have sent oil bitumen from the oil sands of Alberta to the refineries in Texas. At that time, the pipeline became a political football, and was dropped, at considerable cost. But with America's increasing population requirements, they would now like it fast-tracked. Traditional opponents of the project would allow the pipeline go ahead, but only to bring water, not oil."

"You can't drink oil," said their spokesman.

"The two nations have been locked in a stalemate, with America's relationship with its northern neighbour becoming increasingly strained."

"Prime Minister Chrystal Freeman had this to say in regards to a military build-up along the longest undefended border in the world".

"We remind our American neighbours that Canada is a sovereign country, and not subject to their demands. As America's largest trading partner, we are happy to negotiate, but let me be clear, Canada's land and resources are our own. The World Court in The

*Hague, and our 30 NATO partners would agree. Having said that, we are confidant that level heads will prevail, with continued cooperation between our two, great nations."*

*"At the Vatican today, the new pope welcomed thousands back into the fold. Global uncertainty has raised the number of faithful to well beyond pre-Humanity levels."*

*"None save God should have power over life and death," he said in regards to H2O.........*

Mage stood, declaring, "That's all I can take for now."

"Yeah, it must be tiring losing your disciples, eh?"

"Not a god. Just a 'magician' making himself disappear. G'night."

# Chapter 19

*"Even with all our technology & the inventions that make modern life so much easier than it once was, it takes just one big natural disaster to wipe all that away & remind us that here on Earth, we're still at the mercy of nature."*

### *Neil deGrasse Tyson*

### $t = H + 20$
### time = Humanity + 20 years

Two decades after Humanity 2.0s release came the day the world changed forever.

"G'mornin' Mage," said Jackie. "You're looking positively radiant, today!"

Mage rubbed his sagging eyes, complaining, "I couldn't sleep. I wish that my nightmares would leave me alone. There's already enough death and destruction in the real world."

"Tell your dreams that you're no more responsible than the rest of us, will ya? We're a fellowship, remember? We ruin this planet as a team!"

"If we could just take Humanity back, it'd be great, but it's out there forever now. A simple app hoping to make people healthier has screwed up 70,000 years of human evolution."

"That's why you're the deity, and we're just worshippers," Song teased.

"Speak for yourself," Daniel said. "Buddy? Sure. Magician? Okay. But god? Nuh-uh. I draw the line."

Daniel was smiling, but Mage wasn't seeing the humour this morning. The latest reports detailed millions and millions of refugees now dying of starvation or dehydration, but still not nearly enough to offset the ever skyrocketing birth rate. Sure, he'd enabled so many more people overcome illness and live a happier, healthier life. But ironically, it has caused far more grief worldwide than it's relieved. People had already become accustomed to the good health and longer lifespans, so the positives of the app had lost their lustre. All that remained were the new, daily disasters, as the anti-Humanitarian sects were only too happy to point out.

Geneticists the world over sought ways to switch the Humanity gene off, but to no avail. Once the switch was flipped, it couldn't be reversed. Authorities in many regions restricted the downloading of Humanity 2.0 now, but the black market simply filled the void. There was no stopping it. Given the choice between keeping loved ones healthy for life, or making personal sacrifices for the planet, people chose their families every time. And those families were getting bigger. A dozen children in a family was no longer unusual, with many siblings born decades apart. Good health and longer fertile periods led to more than two million additional people being born every single day, each inhaling more oxygen and expelling more carbon dioxide.

Scientists that tried to warn everyone for years, had been deemed sensationalist, over-reacting and attention-seeking. But now, time had caught up with the inevitable. Denial was no longer an option. The oceans really were dying, and taking down the oxygen-breathers with them. Uninhabitable zones once teeming with life were now devoid of it, both in the oceans and on land. Humans had failed.

As each problem arose, the world became more and more polarized - politically, religiously and personally. TV news segments were now two hours in length in order to report all of the disasters and conflicts around the planet.

On the home front, religious factions had once again created a tent city in the park across from the mansion, but now attracted the most radical of individuals. One side blamed Mage for all of Earth's problems, while the other was the 'standing army' of Humanitarians sworn to protect *Mage the Magician* and the *Holy Fellowship*.

"Don't listen to Daniel, honey. He might draw the line, but I still worship you."

"More people think I'm the devil than think I'm a god, these days. Did you see the riots across the street last night?"

"How could I miss them, bud?" asked Daniel rhetorically. "It was like a war out there between the fanatics and the zealots. Both sides are a little loco if you ask me."

"I saw people setting tents on fire," Song added. "And I heard gunfire, and explosions."

"I know, right? All night long there were cop cars flashing red and blue lights in our bedroom window."

Tang joined them in the kitchen for breakfast, looking more dour than usual. "I overheard you about the riots. There are not as many people as before, but they have a dangerous mob mentality. The anti-humanitarians were burning Mage if effigy last night."

"Yeah, it was scary," Song agreed. "They're so close."

Tang thought she looked a bit shaken up. After a few years of declining participation, those without homes nor anywhere else to go had gravitated to the tent city across the street. Each day, it got a bit bigger and a bit worse. They had to do something. "I can't see anything getting better soon." announced Tang. "This compound is becoming too dangerous again. We should consider alternative accommodations soon."

"Camping with the RVs?" suggested Daniel. "We haven't taken the kids out for awhile."

"No, I think not. We'll just come back to the same problems. It's time to make a move. We should return to life on the Nautilus for awhile, at least until things calm down. I suggest we all get together our things. I've already spoken to Bobby about provisions."

"Ooooohh, Nemo is going to like the sound of this," said his dad. "He's only heard about the sub from Tune. So, is it back to our Filipino island then, Captain?"

"I think so, yes."

"And speaking of Nemo," said Daniel, "here he comes now with his lovely mother in tow. Good morning my little family." Daniel didn't get the smile he was hoping for.

"Turn on the news!" was all Jackie said, clearly alarmed.

"You want to watch the news? You never watch the news anymore."

"This is different. I heard it on the radio upstairs." Impatient, Jackie grabbed the remote and jolted the T.V. to life. "Ssshhh. Ssshhh! I want to hear this."

"........... *the President has called a national state of emergency, requesting assistance from any and all allies. Reports from the United States Geological Survey warn, the Yellowstone eruption will undoubtedly have global consequences, with fatalities expected to be in the millions.*

*"As you can see by this incredible feed from the International Space Station, the primary zone already encompasses parts of 9 states and three Canadian provinces. Near the volcano itself, ash depths are estimated to be more than four feet thick. The secondary zone covers more than half of North America, with every state and province expecting some degree of debris. Residents are asked to remain indoors until the full extent of the danger is known."*

"Holy crap," whispered Daniel absently, before getting *SHUSH'd* again by Jackie.

*"Thus far, officials have failed in attempts to contact the primary disaster zone, which is buried under several feet of volcanic ash and an unknown amount of magma. Logistics are daunting. Volcanic glass particles have grounded air traffic over the entire North American continent until further notice. Automobile traffic is not recommended. Ash and glass will clog engines within minutes and leave motorists stranded. Remember that in many areas, emergency crews are also stranded. Residents are warned to stay indoors in order to protect their lungs.*

*"The debris is spreading high into the atmosphere, and it is becoming apparent that it will soon encircle the entire Northern Hemisphere. Scientists suggest it is too early to predict whether a volcanic winter wherein sunlight reflects off of the sulphuric gas and back into space. Temperatures could drop by as much as 10 degrees Celcius.*

*"All of North America is in crisis. Crops are*

expected to struggle for decades, in an era when the population explosion from Humanity 2.0 has already placed enormous pressure on limited food supplies. These are dark days.

"The United Nations has called an emergency session of the General Assembly to be held in South Africa, hoping the Southern Hemisphere will allow travel. Flights in the entire Northern Hemisphere are expected to be grounded until further notice.

"FEMA has released the following recommendations............"

Close all windows, doors, and dampers in your home, and where your animals are housed.

Turn off all machinery. Protect it inside a garage or barn, if possible.

Bring animals into closed shelters.

Stay indoors.

If caught outside, wear an effective face mask to reduce inhalation of ash particles.

Cover your eyes and keep your skin covered to avoid irritation or burns. Do the same for animals where possible and practical.

Do not attempt to drive in heavy ash fall; it will stir up the ash, stalling your vehicle. A one-inch layer of volcanic ash weighs 10 pounds per square foot. Ash can clog waterways, reservoirs, and machinery and its weight can cause roofs to collapse. If you have to work in *an environment where there is volcanic ash, be sure to take the following actions:*

*Wear an approved respirator.*

*Clear roofs of ash fall as soon as possible to avoid collapse.*

*Remove ash from any areas where animals will be confined. With ash covering the ground, livestock cannot graze.*

*Throw away any contaminated food or water. The ash will be contaminated with heavy metals toxic to humans and animals. In addition, pyroclastic material contains glass-like particles that can cut or irritate lungs and intestines. Secondary eruptions and lava flows are expected to continue in the days, weeks, or months ahead. Officials warn that such an event has no timetable, and no precedent. Ash may be carried by winds for thousands of miles and affect distant areas long after the eruption. What they can say is, that for the next few days, heavy ash fall will darken the sky as if it were nightfall. The increased demand for lighting could result in power failures, as the power grid in the buried areas no longer contributes to that grid. Globally, all stock exchanges throughout the world have halted trading until further notice. The pope is expected to address....................."*

Jackie used her remote to mute the TV. Nemo had clearly become upset, and looking around at her friends, it was mutual. No one spoke. No one moved. The adults were petrified for the future, but afraid to put a voice to it. Some wondered if there would be a future at all. Tune was not so shy, caught between childhood and adulthood. "What does it all mean, Mama? It kinda scares me."

Song held her close, replying "it means that Zǔfù is right. It's time for another trip on the Nautilus, honey. I want you to go pack a bag for a long trip. We could be aboard for a long time. Nemo, you go pack too."

"Yes!" Nemo exclaimed. "Finally, a sub trip!" He'd visited the inside of the Nautilus but had yet seen it in action. "Come on, Tune. Help me pack."

"I need to pack for myself, Neem. But, bring your video games. It gets boring on the submarine." That just didn't seem possible in Nemo's mind.

Back downstairs, Tang was already in Captain mode, going through checklists in his mind. "Pack for a long trip, everybody. Bring your instruments, laptops, and anything you might want. And, don't forget the things you forgot last time. We won't be stopping for supplies. Robert, load as much fresh food from the compound as you can. And ladies? Make sure the kids pack baggy clothes to grow into. Mage, bring all of your communication electronics. And Daniel, help by ferrying loads to the sub by the zipline. Alright crew, what are you waiting for?"

"Aye, aye, Captain!" Daniel said, snapping off a

smile and a salute.

"Aye, aye, my eye! Get moving."

Daniel was loading provisions into the zipline's hatch, when Bobby came in with with another load of food. "What do you think is going to happen here, Bobby? The world was going to hell in a hand basket before the eruption, but now?"

"A lot of people are going to die, Daniel. Millions, maybe billions. So, let's not let that include us."

"That shot from the Space Station on TV was pretty wild, though, eh? There are states that just got buried by tens of feet of molten ash."

"Yeah, well have you looked outside?" Bobby asked him.

Daniel went to the window, seeing blackened clouds depositing a hard, grey rain that wasn't rain.

"Whoa! Way up here?"

"Vancouver was on the projection map."

"Well, at least we don't have to go outside to get the sub loaded," he joked weakly. But he was right. From the mansion to the boathouse would keep them all indoors.

"We're lucky for a lot of things, Danny, my boy," Bobby observed. Even if we had a sub that was diesel, we couldn't use it. Basically, any vehicle or building with an air intake would get clogged and seize. But once again, it's the fearless Captain Tang and the nuclear Nautilus to our rescue."

"You really do love that guy, don't you?"

"What's not to love. He's a real man's man."

"I always wondered about that expression," said Daniel. "If a guy's a man's man, wouldn't that inherently mean he's gay? You know, a man's man?"

"This man's man," Bobby agreed.

The Fellowship of the Deep were seasoned sailors now, and were ready on the dock in less than an hour. For the kids, this was at last an adventure away from the mansion. Off to the high seas! Nemo was so excited he'd finally get to live aboard the Nautilus. Under the water! On his face, he wore the same infectious grin that his father usually did, but he was the only one in the group who was smiling today.

Once all of the supplies and crew were stowed, Captain Tang sunk the Nautilus down from her berth, and slowly eased away from its enclosure. After the upsetting news of the morning, Tang felt good to be doing something about it, especially when so many others couldn't. Young Nemo climbed onto a stool beside him at the helm, vibrating with excitement as he watched the sea through the Nautilus's wraparound windshield. Tang smiled at the lad, ruffled his hair and placed his captain's cap crookedly atop the boy's head.

339

He had a flashback of an excited Tune on that very stool.

"Zǔfù? Am I going to be able to steer the submarine?"

"Sure, Nemo. As long as an adult's with you. It would only be right that you man the helm. After all, the original Nautilus *was* led by *Captain* Nemo."

"Zǔfù? Who was this Captain Nemo guy, anyway? I was named after him, but I don't really know much about him."

"Captain Nemo was a character from the book *'Twenty Thousand Leagues Under the Sea'* written by a man named Jules Verne more than a century ago. It's a story aboard a submarine written many years before subs were even invented. The book detailed life beneath the surface with remarkable accuracy. There's a copy of it in the ship's library. You should consider reading it to be your first sub school project."

Nemo lost his smile. "Sub school? You mean I still have to go to school here, too?"

"Aye lad," replied Tang. "Even your Mom & Dad had to have sub school lessons when they first came aboard. It'll be like school at home, with the adults each tutoring you in the regular subjects. But on the Nautilus, you'll also learn to be a sailor, learning everything from knots to navigation."

"Regular school *plus* sub school? That sucks!" Nemo complained. "Does Tune know about sub school?"

"I'm not sure." *'With Tune's love of learning, she'll probably love the idea,'* mused the Captain.

Unimpressed, the boy trudged off in search of Tune to break the tragic news. Little did he know of the wonders he would soon see beneath the waves. His mom's latest online course in marine biology would prove very useful on the voyages to come. Young Nemo's subsequent undersea schooling would prove to be magical, but for now, he was unimpressed.

As for Tang, he sat at the helm for hours that day, feeling guilty for his happiness. The eruption had instantly devastated and ended millions of lives and would end millions more, yet here he was, leading his adopted family to safety in the lap of luxury. But, he was back at sea, so how could he help but be happy? He spent many solitary hours at the helm that day, lost in thought. History henceforth would now forever regard world events as pre-Yellowstone and post-Yellowstone.

Uncharacteristically anxious, his mind kept rolling through a million scenarios. There were simply too many possibilities, most of them hopeless. But still, the silence of his sea relaxed him, as it always did. As the fixer for Song's father, he'd always been able to affect a solution, but now there was no barometer to measure this new reality. Nobody anywhere on Earth had been through anything remotely close to such uncertainty before. So many other patriarchs and matriarchs would be helpless, with zero options.

North America had become a Shakespearean tragedy, still being written.

Song entered the bridge, breaking Tang's chain of thought. "Where to now, Captain? Do we have a plan?" He looked tense and relaxed at the same time, so she massaged his shoulders and back regardless.

"We shall return to our little island in the Philippines first, at least for awhile. It's much further south, almost at the equator. It will take the Nautilus a few weeks to get there, but we'd have a secure land base again, assuming it is still inhabitable. By then, we should have a better idea as to the extent of Yellowstone's effect on the rest of the planet. If the island is in the contaminated zone, we just keep heading south."

She began shaking slightly, fighting back tears. Song was usually strong, but not today. It was Jackie that was the worrier, but this all had such serious ramifications, she doubted anyone on the planet wasn't affected somehow. "What's going to happen, Tang? I'm pretty freaked out."

"I wish I had good news for you, Sūnnǔ, but the truth is, I don't know. I doubt that anyone does. There are millions of people buried under the volcanic ash already, but the long-term effects of it all could kill billions, if not the whole planet." The strain on Song's face was plain to see. She was barely keeping it together, and Tang had little wisdom to comfort her.

Thankfully, Bobby had arrived, offering to take the helm. He jumped into the discussion, and his assessment was dire. "More than likely, North Americans will need to evacuate. Maybe Europe and Asia, too." He gave Song a reassuring hug, but a hug was so inadequate today.

"All of North America?" she asked.

Tang flashed his boyfriend a *'You're not helping!'* look, which Bobby summarily ignored.

"Most of it, at least. A foot of ash can cave in a roof because it's full of glass and heavy metals. And, since it's covering many states and provinces, its inhabitants are all probably already dead. The ash turns to concrete in the lungs. Water supplies are tainted, making crops impossible to grow and livestock impossible to water. Machinery won't work, and..............."

"Robert!"

"Sorry, but this is a *'plan for the worst, hope for the best'* scenario. Ash will almost surely carry right over Europe, too."

"Yeah?" asked Song.

"Yeah. But the real problems will be caused by the sulphuric gas in the atmosphere. It'll reflect the sun, and its gonna get colder. This could be an extinction level event, you know."

"Okay, okay, that's enough of that, Robert," interrupted Tang. "Let's worry about facts that unfold, not ifs and buts. We'll know more by the time we get to our island. Until then, we stay deep. That should protect us from any ash particulate, and we already have our own supply of water. The biggest concerns to almost everyone else in the world won't be an issue aboard the Nautilus. For now, we are all safe again, thanks to you, Song."

"He's right, you know," Bobby agreed. "Even if we stayed back at the mansion, survival may have been dicey. But with the Nautilus, we are safer than almost anyone on the planet. If things are okay at our island, we're back in a tropical paradise. If not, we head further south until we find clear skies."

"A tropical paradise sounds pretty good to me," Song said.

"We are all grateful, Song. You did save us...... again."

Weeks later, Tang was manning the helm's night shift alone, the Nautilus bluntly intruding its way through the dark depths. Everyone aboard was fast asleep. Their island in the Philippines was only about a day away now, and Tang wanted to understand how things were going on at the surface before he approached the members of the Fellowship. He guided the sub up until it was twenty feet below the surface. Setting his controls to 'all stop', he raised the periscope for a look above the waves.

With no moonlight or stars, the ebony night

revealed few secrets. One thing that *was* apparent, though, was an enormous storm, with huge whitecaps racing like bleached stallions on a carousel, undulating up and down. Though the Nautilus was three hundred feet long, it was still being rocked by the big storm above. Captain Tang entered the Comms Room, and raised its radio antenna above the surface. Scanning bandwidths, he struggled to find a clear radio broadcast. The strongest signal was Filipino, a language he didn't speak. Others were too weak or hissing.

There was one option he hesitated to use, but there was little choice. He tapped into a satellite super-signal he'd used in the Chinese Navy, and received a weak but steady feed. He did what he could to minimize the static until he could hear a Mandarin broadcast repeating itself. Rather than the usual coded chatter he'd heard in the past, the station was simply looping a recorded message, over and over. He listened three times until he was satisfied he'd learned all he could. And it wasn't good.

Responsibility once again lay heavy on his shoulders. How was he going to break it to the crew? Should he let them continue in blissful ignorance, or scare the hell out of them? He retracted the periscope and radio antenna, before opening his ballast tanks for sea water, to send the sub back into the inky depths.

Bobby entered the bridge rubbing his eyes. "What's going on?" he asked. "I heard you filling the ballast tanks. Are you taking us up?"

"Not anymore. We're not going up, we're going

back down."

"So, you were already up on top?"

"Almost. Just close enough to raise the periscope and radio antenna."

"And.............?" Bobby asked, impatiently.

"It was too rough to take the Nautilus up to the surface completely. Surging wind and waves made visibility near nil. The periscope didn't help at all. But I did manage to get the radio antenna up and found an operational signal. It's bad, Robert."

Bobby reached out with a reassuring hug, before telling Tang, unequivocally, "Okay, spill."

"Yellowstone and its surrounding states were obliterated by the eruption."

"Okay, well we knew that already."

"The molten lava is nearly ten feet thick near the eruption, and they said more than a trillion tons of volcanic ash spread too quickly for anyone to act. More than half of the cities in the continental United States have declared a state of emergency, and those are the lucky ones. Other states have been buried entirely, along with everyone in them."

"Well, you have to tell the crew." He'd never, in all the time they'd been together, seen Tang look so beleaguered.

He snapped, "Don't you think I know that, Robert?"

Bobby released his hug, warning Tang with his devastating *'Don't you get snippy with me'* look.

"That's why I went up in the middle of the night." Tang continued quietly. "I wanted to get my own head around it before alarming the crew."

"They deserve to know."

"But, how do I tell our family that the world is dying?"

"You just tell them what you know. They're intelligent people."

"Even Daniel?" Tang asked, with a smirk.

"Yes, my love. Even Daniel. There's more to that boy than you think."

"Okay, let's have a Fellowship meeting. Can you start making breakfast?"

"I can. It's almost dawn. Give me an hour."

Daniel rubbed his eyes groggily. No more sleep would come. He turned on his side to watch his very own sleeping beauty. Before he knew Jackie, he had always been the last person out of bed, but now he almost always woke first just to watch her sleep. It had become his favourite way to start a day. She was truly the prettiest woman he had ever known, and a heck of a lot smarter than him, to boot. But, most of all, she was just plain nice.

His morning ritual progressed as it always did. He watched her for as long as he could bear before lifting the covers a bit, and sliding behind her naked form. Spooning up to her, he lodged his morning lumber against her cheeks and reached over her to cradle her breast in his hands.

"Well, good morning, Jughead. I see you're '*up'*." Some wives would be irritated at being woken that way every day, but Jackie loved it. Her first waking moment was always being loved. She reached her hand behind his head as he nuzzled her neck.

Their ardor was soon interrupted by Bobby's voice squawking over the intercom, "breakfast is served. All hands report for an emergency meeting of The Fellowship of the Deep."

"Oh, too bad, Juggy." Jackie teased, slipping out of his clutches. "Gotta go."

"What?!? Hell no!" He reached out to grasp one hip, tipping her balance back into the bed.

"It's an *emergency* meeting, after all."

"One emergency at a time. I have one of my own here," he cried.

"I can see that! Impressive!"
"Two minutes?"

"Okay, fine. Two minutes. Now get over here. Time's a wastin'."

Looking a bit flushed, they were the last to arrive at breakfast, where Captain Tang was already addressing his crew.

"............ the blast created it's own winds. Therefore, the initial cloud coverage was like an umbrella, going as far west as it did east. U.S. federal aid from FEMA has been slow out of the gate. Most have been left to fend for themselves. Even the president's Secret Service detail denied him a flyover. All air travel in the country is grounded, cars are still inoperable, and train routes are blocked all over the continent."

Jackie thanked Bobby for her coffee, then asked, "What about Vancouver?"

"I listened to the broadcast three times," Tang continued. "I made some notes," He unfolded the paper and, out of old habit, reached for his missing eyeglasses case before remembering he no longer needed them thanks to Humanity 2.0.

"In areas just outside the magma flow itself, there's 4 feet of ash on the ground. The entirety of Yellowstone Park was destroyed, along with all of its geysers, wildlife and tourists. Wyoming is completely buried, along with most of Montana and Idaho. In cities further away, like Los Angeles, San Francisco, Portland, Seattle, Calgary, Winnipeg, and Chicago, ash is about a foot deep. But at least to some degree, ash covers all of North America."

"All of it? Vancouver?" Jackie asked again.

"Yes, all of it," confirmed Tang. "Except Alaska and Hawaii. The U.S. Congress is making a contingency plan to temporarily move the federal capital from Washington to Honolulu. But, the broadcast did not mention Vancouver, specifically."

"Well, moving the capital seems stupid," Mage observed. "How would anybody get to the islands if the planes are all grounded?"

"How's anybody going to get anywhere?" Song asked, rhetorically. "Planes, trains and automobiles are all inoperable, as are many ships at sea, most likely."

"Well, at least folks can get to Hawaii by sailboat, right?" said Daniel, hoping for a touch of levity.

"I doubt that even that isn't possible right now," Bobby said. "People might not be able to leave the cabin. Adjusting the sails could be life-threatening, and it's probably a tad too breezy for sailing, anyway."

Tang took back control of the meeting. "Listen! From what I could tell last night, the seas are dangerous to any marine conveyance, except ours, of course. Air space in the entire northern hemisphere has shut down indefinitely, even Europe and Asia. According to the broadcast, China has also been hit hard. Particles that slowly settle aren't like normal dust. They'd be hard, with jagged edges, irritating eyes, noses and lungs. "

"So, other than land, sea and air, we're good? As long as we don't breathe?" Daniel joked, again to a deaf audience.

Tang continued from his notes. "Many are dying of starvation in their own homes. Citizens are advised not to go outside, and to keep forced air furnaces and air conditioners turned off. Almost all U.S. businesses have shut down, unable to even get their employees to their jobsites. Looting of said businesses is reported as mild. Those risking the curfew are being found dead by asphyxiation, booty still in hand. The volcano still erupts sporadically, which is complicating relief efforts. European and Asian flights are still shut down too, as are their stock exchanges.

"That's about all I have from the radio broadcast. We will be at our island tomorrow, where we'll surface, if it's safe. When I took the Nautilus up last night, a hellacious storm was blowing, so the surface may still be too dangerous. And if China is as badly affected as their broadcast says it is, I'm not confident. In any case, Mage, I'm hoping you can briefly see if your satellite dish system can get through the debris cloud. See what else you can learn."

"Satellites could be unreachable now," observed Mage.

"That's true. But let's find out what does work, and what doesn't. We should be close enough to the equator to perhaps reach some southern hemispheric satellites. So far, the debris cloud is only over the top half of the planet."

Tune raised her hand before asking, "Zǔfù, will I be able to talk to my online friends?"

"I don't know, sweetheart. Services in most of North America are shut down, and may be for a long time. But your Dad can let you know tomorrow after testing his equipment."

"I'm with Tune," vowed Nemo. "When can we go back to just having fun? The sub is great and all, but I just want other things to go back to normal."

"Sorry, little man. We'll never be getting back to the same normal. This is the *new* normal."

Jackie added, "Charles Darwin said it's not the strong that survive, it's those who best adapt. We adapt or we die."

"So boring," Nemo pouted.

"Well, my boy," Tang observed, "these are probably the least boring times in human history. You'd better get aboard."

Mage added, "the logistics of this must be mind-boggling. If no survivors can leave their home, all trade stops. Even if it didn't, there's no delivery system to get the goods to the populace. People can't even go outside for fear of stirring up the ash, or getting shards in their lungs."

"Food and water are the immediate problems." added Bobby. "If this does evolve into a nuclear winter, the entire Northern Hemisphere globe won't be able to grow crops or raise livestock for decades. And even if they could, there would be no way to get supplies. People will be trapped in their homes, choosing between suicide and starvation."

A shudder ran up Jackie's spine. "With four feet of ash across entire states, what are they going to do with it? It certainly wouldn't be safe to push it around with bulldozers."

"For every question, the answer is bleak," Tang observed. "And there are still far too many questions."

Bobby was nodding. "You mean like boiling lava and ash covering America's nuclear arsenal, or nuclear power plants? There's one question that can't be good. Or what about the infectious disease storage centres? Magma vs. the pathogen freezers? Hmmm....."

"It's the human factor that gets me," Song thought out loud. "So many are already dead, but also, so many dead men walking. Even if people in America survived the blast, and survived the ash, and survived the gas, many will still starve to death, or asphyxiate. And even if they had the financial means to escape to the southern hemisphere, how would they get there? We'd all be in the same boat if it weren't for the Nautilus."

"It's ironic, don't you think?" asked Mage. "The Nautilus saved us when the world was becoming immensely overpopulated, and now it's saving us from the opposite."

"Totally!" Daniel cried. "But here's the big question. Should we feel bad about H2O over-populating the world, or feel good about it now giving mankind a better chance for survival?"

Tang looked at Daniel with mild irritation. "We shouldn't feel good about any of this."

# Chapter 20

*"When disaster strikes, it tears the curtain away from the festering problems that we have beneath."*

**Barack Obama**

$$t = H + 20$$
**time = Humanity + 20 years**

Self-annihilation was on the mind of Sam Purvis, a New Zealand delegate and climate czar for the United Nations. He and his staff had been scrambling for days, ensuring all delegates had accommodations, translators and technical assistance for an emergency session in Cape Town, South Africa. Though most of the Southern Hemisphere now allowed flights, there were still a few that went down. Airlines faced enormous pressure to return to *normal*, but how many crashes were too many?

Out of the 195 countries of the world, only 32 were located in the Southern Hemisphere. Of those 32, most were considered third world, and less than a handful could be considered first world democracies. Australia and New Zealand were ruled out as hosts because they were island nations, too difficult to get to, so South Africa was a practical choice. If the delegate was unable to physically attend, a regional ambassador was accepted in their stead. This was an important session.

All five of the permanent member nations of the U.N. Security Council – China, France, Russia, the U.S., and the U.K. - hail from the northern hemisphere, which had actually helped Sam bring them to a consensus. He was mildly surprised to obtain it, but the each country had significant obstacles at home simply trying to provide the most basic needs of their citizens.

In the end, it had become abundantly clear to them all that the status quo internationally was inadequate and dangerous, hence the radical resolution. The planet was one disaster short of an extinction event, if that threshold hadn't indeed been passed already. Bold measures were called for, and Sam was to lead the charge.

The Yellowstone eruption was now a month past, though she continued to emit her toxic ash and gases on a schedule unbeknownst to any but her. North American casualties had officially topped the 200,000,000 dead mark, but their were many millions more still buried alive or missing. Starvation and lung contamination took most, while suicide and weather anomalies took many of the rest. Those that were still hanging on by a thread had the dismal choice of dying either from of dehydration and starvation at home, or asphyxiation as refugees on foot.

Infrastructure in the ash zone was still non-existent, and aid, ineffective. Flights continued to be grounded, and cars were still of no use. Any attempt to drive simply stirred up the ash, choked their engines and stranded the motorist in a hostile environment. Those needing medical assistance were largely out of luck, since many hospitals shuttered after Humanity 2.0's release. People were hungry, and people were thirsty. And, desperate people committed desperate atrocities.

Numbers in Europe had skyrocketed almost as quickly as America, but ash was not the biggest challenge there; sulphuric gas in the atmosphere was. The suns rays simply bounced off, back into space, so, with little light getting through, crops became non-viable and livestock untenable in a darker, colder world. Though most Europeans and Asians bow had access to potable water, it was small comfort for those still starving in the cold. Anyone with the means was attempting to move south, overwhelming areas already marginalized.

Sam was as nervous as he'd ever been about his upcoming speech. How would it reverberate around the world? It would certainly be the most radical assembly that the U.N. had ever held. But, the needs of the planet had been ignored for far too long. How had it ever been allowed to get so bad?

What had begun as a casual stroll through the lobby of his hotel became a purposeful march through the driving rain and wind. He was sweating anyway, even though temperatures in South Africa were unseasonably cool. It was a country mostly spared by the volcano's airborne contaminants, but even so far away, weather had gone completely zany since the eruption. Cape Town had been a city without water for more than a decade now due to Humanity 2.0's population explosion, especially in Soweto and the slums. Many had died of thirst, relying on aid from first world countries that didn't materialize. But in the weeks following the eruption, torrential rains had raised reservoir levels substantially, and they were not expected to abate anytime soon. Ironically, here they were, hosting and helping first world countries, many of which had failed to come to South Africa's aid back in their time of need.

After confirming for the third time that his speech was still in his jacket's inner pocket, Sam Purvis, delegate for New Zealand, strode confidently up the steps of the South African Houses of Parliament. Officials had graciously offered its use to the U.N. but Sam wondered if they'd be such gracious hosts *after* his speech.

"Good morning, Mr. Purvis. Would you step through the security scanner, please?"

"Good Morning," Sam replied. "Everything ready to go?"

"It is, sir."

Sam made his way backstage, nodding to delegates, some of whom he knew, but most he did not. Already up on the stage sat representatives of the five permanent member countries of the U.N. Security Council. It had been imperative to get them all on board with a plan so radical. Just a year ago, such a decision would have been laughable, but these days, all five member countries were literally fighting for the lives of their residents. None were happy with the resolution, but they recognized the necessity of it. Sam greeted them each warmly, and thanked them for their crucial support. He looked out over the other national representatives, and though he knew the numbers would be low, the crowd was dwarfed by the room. Only about one in four countries could get a representative to the location.

The U.N. Inspector General, Paul le Monde, greeted Sam and shook his hand warmly. Each searched the other's face anxiously for support. "Good morning, Mr. Purvis."

"Good morning, sir. Are you ready for all of this?"

"I am," responded le Monde confidently. At least he hoped he sounded confident.

"I wish I could say the same."

"Don't be nervous, Purvis. You have my full support, and that of the Security Council. Personally, after feeling helpless for so many years, I am actually looking forward to doing something about it."

"Is the South Asia incident still contained?"

"Yes, surprisingly. For the greater good, they say."

At 9:00 a.m. on the dot, the lights dimmed and Inspector General le Monde stepped up to the lectern. Attendees settled into their seats, donning their translator headsets.

*"Good morning, excellencies, guests, ladies and gentlemen, and welcome to this emergency sitting of the United Nations General Assembly. And thank you to our gracious hosts here in South Africa for the diligence required to have us here. For those who may not know me, my name is Paul le Monde, and I am Secretary-General of the United Nations.*

*"Most in attendance today are now aware of this morning's nuclear incident in South Asia. At 5:20 a.m. local time, India confirmed the accidental launch a nuclear missile targeting a military base in China's Chengdu Province. India managed to trigger a self-destruct mechanism at the missile's apex over Nepal, but effects of the airborne radiation are not yet fully known. But, this incident serves to remind us that discord between the two most populous nations on Earth would be perilous to us all. For now, both have agreed to stand down in favour of ongoing talks. A tragedy affecting the Southern Hemisphere is too dangerous to contemplate. On behalf of the entire United Nations family, we say thank you to them both."*

The murmuring audience gave quiet applause. Secretary-General le Monde continued.....

*"And though this nuclear incident was indeed significant, today we discuss even bigger issues. For the past half century, we've known that humans were killing our planet, yet little was done. As opportunities for change came and went, we sat on the sidelines, shaking our heads about why others didn't act. Yet, as the*

*planet's population grew, our resolve to care for it sunk further, under the task's enormous weight.*

*"Extensive regions of our planet are no longer habitable, and our oceans are dying. This is no longer debatable. This is no longer acceptable. And, as of today, this is no longer tolerable.*

*"I am not referencing some vague, future date. Environmental atrocities have already occurred. The good intentions for the Paris Accord on Climate, and every agreement since, went unmet as we all dealt with the exploding populations of the Humanity 2.0 era. And though we may all eschew good intentions, we cannot allow the human race the idiocy of perishing by our own hand. Doomsday fatigue is not an excuse to ignore our challenges any longer.*

*"Our world is on life support. It has been for decades, yet we acquiesced, in favour of profit. We've raped our planet's resources, polluted our air, and clogged our oceans. Earth is in peril like never before. In the past 50 years, 3/4 of all life on Earth has been wiped out. Three quarters, people! It is folly to think we could not add ourselves to that list.*

*"We chose to ignore scientists who dedicated their lives to understand it, because it wasn't convenient. They warned us for years, yet we sat on our hands. As a result, each of our nations has been forced to deal with the consequences of inaction. Problems in America have exacerbated it, but as weather becomes more untenable globally, our infrastructures are literally washing away. Countries are losing their rule of law, and governments are collapsing. Pollution is harming us all. Disasters*

*are no longer affordable, figuratively or morally.*

*"The challenges of these past decades have been daunting, but denial is no longer an option. The Dead Sea is indeed dead nowadays, its water now red. Harbours have floating debris to the point that the water itself is no longer visible. The oceans are the life blood of our world by providing most of our oxygen, but they're 35% more acidic than 200 years ago. Coral bleaching is killing the food supply of countless aquatic species in the food chain. Carbon dioxide levels are their highest in 66 million years. Mass species' extinctions are commonplace. But, we've still got the Amazon, you say? Once known as the lungs of the world, it now creates more CO2 than oxygen.*

*"On our critically important poles, melting permafrost has released 60 billion tons of methane into the atmosphere. Vanishing glaciers have left millions without an annual water supply, a supply that is never coming back. Farmers claim that oil fracking has lowered the water tables of their fields. The churches of Venice have water pouring in. Island nations are slipping below the sea, forever. How furious does Mother Nature have to get for us to see the possibility of our own extinction? When is enough too much?*

*"Well, delegates of the world, today is that day. Today, the Earth's land, sea and air will hereby gain inalienable, legal rights in the international arena. The United Nations Security Council has determined that climate has become a global security risk. As such, we are initiating U.N. control over global warming issues for the safety of all mankind.*

*"At this time, I'd like to stand aside and ask Mr. Samuel Purvis, representative of the great country of New Zealand, and the U.N. Secretary of Climate Action, to give you details. Don't shoot the messenger,"* he joked lamely as he ceded the stage.

Nervous Purvis's hands were trembling, and his forehead was pebbled with sweat. Quiet eyes followed him forward, as he himself squinted through the stage lights, his heart racing. *'This is it'.* he thought to himself. *'Do or die for us all'.* His resolve set, Sam stepped up to the microphone to deliver the biggest speech of his life.

*"Delegates of the world, ladies and gentlemen. Thank you for making the effort to be here today. Some of you are new, asked to represent your country today for practical reasons. Many leaders are unable to attend themselves, dealing with tragedy in their own lands. So, I'd like to acknowledge the efforts of the ambassadors and consular officials who are with us for the first time. Welcome.*

*"You know, when I was a boy, I saw a photo of the Earth taken from space."* He put the photo on the big screen behind him. *"I believe it was the first. My father had pointed out the thin, blue line around the edges.* 'That's the atmosphere, son. It's all that keeps us on this planet, so take care of it', *he told me. And so began my life of service to this planet.*

*"Thus far, we have been a world with no global chain of command, each country acting in their own self-interest. It is a model that has been unsuccessful worldwide, regardless of political persuasion. And it is*

*an obsolete model, as of today.*

*"The United Nations and its Security Council hereby declare global martial law......., please calm down, everyone...... From this day forth, our world does not exist as nearly 200 disparate countries acting in self-interest. From this day forth, we are one entity, with many departments working together to accomplish a feat unmatched in human history. Our survival. We urge member nations to be united on this issue that affects every one of us, and every one of our families.*

*"Today, we press restart on our planet, to enter a cleaner, healthier era of Earth's history. There will be many hardships ahead as we reset the Industrial Age. It will come at a price. Many will die, but we cannot succeed as a species unless we come to terms with what is best for Planet Earth is more important. So we ascribe to a bold, new direction. The reset required will be a hard road to follow, with many disagreements between our 'departments', but waging war between ourselves must stop. Let us all hope that we are not already too late. It is our hope that the ten other* non-*permanent members of the Security Council will join our 'World Warriors', tasked with policing member nations on climate issues.*

*"Effective today, production of hydrocarbons worldwide is now forbidden."*

Delegates exploded first in disbelief, then in outrage. Sam waited a few moments, continuing.......

*"We simply have no alternative. Our world is on*

*the brink of collapse, and the rights of humans as a whole trump those of the few. Refineries are to be closed permanently, effective immediately.*

For there only being about fifty people in the audience, the roar was loud and sustained. He went on, *"Consequently, the world will need to begin living without oil, and all plastics, which are also derived from hydrocarbons. Further, any substance requiring ignition to provide energy is also hereby outlawed globally. Carbon dioxide levels must be brought under control.*

Predictably, the outrage swelled in volume, with some delegates throwing items at the stage. Sam banged the gavel before continuing, but once he began speaking, everyone went quiet, hanging on every word.

*"The United Nations hereby claims the authority for all climate restrictions around the globe under the existing U.N. Control and Trans-Boundary Movements of Hazardous Waste Act. Oil and plastics are a hazardous waste threatening us all.*

*"Climate change is the world's biggest threat at the moment, both in the short-term and far into the future. It has become a security issue threatening billions on our planet. The five permanent Security Council members represented up on this stage today are committed to climate enforcement as 'World Warriors'. Any countries disregarding this edict will find themselves in direct military combat against one of these five member nations represented on this stage; the United States, China, Russia, France and the United Kingdom. Though geo-politically diverse, all have*

*agreed to work as one global military force to save our planet. Nations resisting this initiative shall have their U.N. membership suspended, thereby losing any protection gained through said membership. Gaining 195 new foes is not something any nation could survive, economically, politically, or militarily. The United Nations Security Council will hereby be the supreme authority in all matters affecting the weather and the health of our planet.*

*"No doubt, many of you delegates are surprised and even outraged at the measures taking place here today, but delay and discussion is no longer viable. Climate scientists claim it may already be too late to save humanity so we must take the initiative here today to rescue us all. Together, we shall be Earth's new, guiding hand on climate law.*

*"Corporations and politicians will no longer hold sway over member governments. Lobbyists for the oil and gas industry will no longer have influence, and are to be dissolved. Cabals will no longer determine international energy policy.*

*"How is this possible, you may ask? How will we ever expect countries to play by the rules? Not all will. How will we get Security Council foes to work together? Because they have to. All five member nations are located in the Northern Hemisphere and have already sustained enormous losses since the eruption in Yellowstone Park. We feel that, as a species, we are just one disaster away from global annihilation. For that reason, we are grateful today to India and China for their nuclear restraint.*

*"We recognize that such a policy will result in untold deaths, but some must be sacrificed for the species to survive. The world's population has been exploding exponentially, quickening our demise. By initiating the measures here today, we are allowing Mother Nature and natural selection to right the planet. Further, we........*

The small crowd roared in revolt, raising their fists and throwing the translation headsets at the stage. Many stormed out, indignant, while others had to be escorted by security.

Sam called out after them, *"Delegates may pick up a package of guidelines on the way out. You may direct any media inquiries to us............"*

# Chapter 21

*"We are called to assist the Earth to heal her wounds and in the process heal our own."*

**William Shakespeare**

$$t = H + 20$$
**time = Humanity + 20 years**

Aboard the Nautilus, Captain Tang tried to make himself busy. After weeks beneath the sea, boredom, worry and frustration had been eating away at him and his crew. Monsoon season had come to the Philippines, making the weather on the surface even more atrocious. Morale was down, even though they all knew most of the planet was in far worse shape than them. But, it was hard to see the positives in the world, of late. The allure of their tropical paradise had sustained their hopes for weeks, but the Fellowship of the Deep were unable to get to the surface, let alone onto their island. Their huts were probably flattened, allowing little shelter from the driving deluge.

Tang had anchored the sub just offshore at a depth of twenty feet, but with little to be done, he puttered about, looking for anything to occupy his mind. He checked the functionality of the periscope, but his vision was impaired by the whitecaps stacked up against themselves under the opaque sky. He raised the radio antenna to full height. Searching the bandwidths in hopes of finding music to calm his savage beasts, he was only able to find a single English language station, dispensing news. *'Better than nothing',* he thought to himself. He switched on the intercom, broadcasting ship-wide. The feed was scratchy, but intelligible.

*"......... speech yesterday rocked the world. Do you really believe such a radical step will be able to make a difference, Mr. Purvis? "* asked the interviewer.

*"I really do. It has to. The Gulf Stream is in danger of collapse, and Earth's magnetic north pole is on the move. These are dire days."*

*"But hydrocarbons have shaped the modern world. They've been crucial for power worldwide, and given our appetite for plastics, your goal to dissolve the oil and gas industry seems exceedingly unattainable. How will you convince those aligned against you to buy in."*

*"They don't need to buy in. The decision has been made, and we at the United Nations recognize that the security of our race is at stake, hence the Security Council resolution. Measures should have been taken long ago, but as you know, the petroleum industry has lobbied long and hard to keep polluting. Those most opposed to our measures are the same people who have been profiting at Earth's expense for decades."*

Bobby was in the galley preparing dinner, listening to the intercom. Jackie burst in, smiling and looking anything but bored. "This is the day you've been waiting for, my friend!"

"Are they saying no more oil? Like... completely?"

Nodding, Jackie replied, "seems that way. Come on. Let's find the others and listen together."

When they arrived at the Fellowship table, Daniel's face lit up. "Did you hear, Jacks?"

"It's being broadcast ship-wide, baby. There's no way I couldn't have heard. Now, shush!"

*"... realize there will be lives lost while the world adjusts. Many lives but not all,"*

*Sam said. "That is key."*

*"You will be upsetting some very important people. What do you say to get them on board?"*

*"They don't need to be on board. The decision has been made."*

*"And if they refuse to halt production?"*

*"There are several guidelines in place for the transition. Security Council members shall enforce the new statutes if production is not halted. Breaking the new climate laws will be considered a direct assault on the health and well-being of every human on this planet and carry consequences, in kind."*

*"When you say 'enforce', what exactly do you mean?"*

*"Missile strikes, primarily."*

"Holy crap!" Daniel cried. "They're going to bomb them? Anywhere?"

"Shuuuush!" Jackie admonished again.

*"You must be joking, Mr. Purvis."*

*"I assure you, I am not. This decision was not taken lightly. But the five Security Council member nations have endured some of the greatest hardships of late, and are committed to change on a global scale."*

*"What constitutes a breach?"*

*"The production, transport, or sale of hydrocarbons."*

*"Or you bomb them? Will your Security Council be allowed to use fuel?"*

*"Yes, but they also must stop production, so when their supply runs out, that's it. All Council nations now have at least some nuclear vessels, and innovation will advance quickly to fill the void. Drones and HIMARS may also be employed. But consider their commitment. Five nations that seldom agree, agree on this. Our world is in jeopardy and a unified approach will be required to save us all."*

*"What about the other armies of the world. Are they just expected to stand down?"*

*"They are. Climate Law will be prosecuted at the World Court in The Hague. Earth must now exist as one entity, not 200 nations. But those armies resisting will not just be taking the five Security Council nations, but nearly 200 enemies, with shrinking fuel inventories. War does not run on soldiers' stomachs, it runs on petrol. Without it, war is far less of an option."*

*"What gives you the authority to subject millions to such hardship, or even death?"*

*"All new laws come under the auspices of the existing U.N. Control and Trans-Boundary Movements of Hazardous Waste provisions. Petroleum products threaten the life of everyone, and are hereby deemed hazardous."*

*"Has OPEC+ agreed to this?"*

*"They were not consulted."*

*"Their economies depend on oil. Are the Arabs just expected to return to being bedouins?"*

*"Africa and the Middle East will be lands of opportunity again, capable of harnessing immense solar energy. Undoubtedly, millions of climate refugees will be displaced on every continent. Many Europeans will relocate to Africa to stay warm. We urge all countries to open their borders and welcome those in need. Many will move into zones between the Tropic of Cancer and*

the Tropic of Capricorn to keep warm. Help them. Cities with hydro-electric, solar, wind, tidal and other green forms of energy must expand their capacities. As a civilization, we will need to develop energy options on smaller scales than the old electricity grids. Economies and resources will need to become more localized."

"There are many refineries in the world. Are you just going to bomb them all?"

"Just the ones that don't comply. And we expect to have help. Individuals or environmental groups destroying oil's infrastructure will be considered 'World Warriors', and heroes, not terrorists. Hackers will be sanctioned to shut down such facilities. And any country selling hydrocarbons will be entering into an illegal contract. Payment would not be binding. At the very least, oil and gas will become prohibitively expensive to use. Once a refinery is destroyed, it's not an easy thing to rebuild."

"Ooooohhh, I like this guy!" Bobby cried. "I thought today would never come. Today is a champagne day! Anyone?"

"Beer for me," called Daniel, as Bobby headed to the kitchen.

"Is coal included in your ban, Mr Purvis? Firewood?"

"Coal is a hydrocarbon, and burning wood is technically a hydrocarbon, as well. As a rule, if a product must burn to release energy, it is now illegal.

*Production of wood products for building will be permitted. Burning it for heat will not."*

*"Let's talk about plastics, then. Their use is ubiquitous around the world. That completely stops too?"*

*"It does. For decades, plastic waste has piled up in our landfills and oceans. A water bottle doesn't break down for 400 years, for example. So, if countries need plastic, they can mine it from their own spoils. There's plenty. And I would suggest the planting of rubber trees, and trees in general. Re-purpose your obsolete asphalt. Prioritize your use of existing plastics, especially if they're required to create new, green energy."*

*"And how are we to get overseas with no ships or planes? How will we get goods across the pond?"*

*"A century and a half ago, there was no oil or plastic, yet our ancestors thrived. If the airline industry were a country, it would be the sixth worst polluting nation. That doesn't even include automobiles or ships. Within a few years, the planet's innovators will inevitably provide options to fill the void. We as a species have invented countless other technologies when such a void existed. But, until then, we urge all peoples to embrace a new age of sail. Build solar farms and wind farms. Re-engineer them to be made of light metals like aluminum rather than plastic. For every loser, there will be a winner."*

*"You're going to kill millions! Maybe billions!"* the interviewer cried, outraged.

*"Yes, many will die. But billions will have a chance to live. There will be geographic winners and losers, and major shifts in world politics. It will be a time of great upheaval, the likes of which Earth has never seen. But, the only way to move forward with such a dramatic step is through natural selection. Allow Earth to re-balance itself. We implore you all to look out for each other during this transition period, as well as the stewardship of our planet."*

*"These are radical solutions, but we'd like to thank you, Mr. Purvis for sharing your views here today. Not all will agree with your methods, but we appear destined for troubled times."*

*"Indeed we......"* he replied.

They were Sam Purvis's final words. Three gunshots rang out before the broadcast went silent, to dead air.

The Fellowship were in shocked disbelief. When Bobby arrived holding the champagne, he asked, "What was that noise?" He stopped, seeing the long faces. "What did I miss? You were all happy a minute ago."

"They shot him, my love," Tang said. "Three shots and the microphone went dead."

Hours later, Bobby was well past boarding the tipsy train. "The world finally woke up, so they shot the guy," he mumbled. "If humans had listened to the hippies of the '60s, we wouldn't be in this mess."

Bobby's partner and mate was not so sure. "There will be too much division in the world for this to be successful," Tang stated. "The western world will not accept unilateral decisions, nor allow the communist countries to gain new powers of control in the world."

Jackie suggested that the Security Council taking control was the best way to move forward. "In one of my courses, a study showed that groups exceeding 7 members will typically seldom reach a full, unanimous consensus. Getting 193 countries to agree will never happen. But, with the Security Council, there are only 5 permanent members. With just five, they had the chance and took it."

"I agree with my gorgeous and wise wife......... this time" said Daniel, throwing Jackie a wink. "I like the idea that corporations and lobbyists are cut out of the deal now."

"But," added Song, "China has been the biggest manufacturer of plastics in the world. To unilaterally end oil, gas and plastics will crush them economically. They'll be tempted. Russia's economy runs on oil."

"Not anymore it doesn't," chimed in Mage. "Since Yellowstone, Russia has lost as badly as America. And China."

Tang looked up when Song mentioned China, and added his two cents worth. "It is surprising to me that even the five members could come to an agreement.

There must be something in it for them. My guess is that they alone will be allowed to continue with oil and gas production."

"That Purvis guy said they could only use up what reserves they already have."

"I will believe that when I see it. If they are to be the enforcers of such a policy, they will need jet fuel for their air forces, bunker oil for their ships, and gas for their tanks. And bombing each other would be counter-productive."

"Well, that's not fair," said Song.

"Thatsh right," slurred Bobby, deep into the Dom by now. "Peeps' self-interest's always trumped society's. Shend 'em all to the World Court in da Hague. Toss 'em in the brig, the lot of 'em, I say," he declared, laughing and swinging an arm wildly for emphasis. And having spoken his peace, Bobby promptly passed out, right at the table.

"Remember, darlin'," Mage said to Song, "They are all in trouble as it is. Yellowstone's eruption has all five countries on life support. This is one way they'll still feel some control. America is trying to survive. China and Russia will be hugely affected. The U.K. and France will be happy to be at the table, and perhaps have an upper hand in crafting new policy. Plus, they are all in the Northern Hemisphere. If their crops don't grow, they are going to need support, big time."

"Hopefully," added Daniel, "the hackers will keep

them in check, too. They practically rule the world now, anyways."

"Well," Tune began, "I for one, am all for the changes. The Humanitarians have forced me from my home to live at sea, and from what I've seen out here, the sea is very sick."

Mage spoke up. "Lots of people talk about the top of the food chain, but the coral reefs are at the bottom of that chain. That's the critical area. Dying reefs will lead to a complete collapse of all of the species reliant on them. The small feed the bigger. Even the blue whale, the biggest creature on Earth, feeds on krill, one of the smallest."

"This is going to affect many nations badly," intoned Captain Tang. "Island nations are, as of today, completely isolated until sailing ship production gets back up to speed. They are fortunate to be mostly in warm regions."

"Saint Peter is going to be very busy," Jackie uttered, under her breath.

"It's not just humans we need to worry about, my sweet," Daniel added. "There are already 20,000 species extinctions per year. Several types of bees too, and without them, none of our food gets pollinated."

"With plants potentially dead in the north," grumbled Tang, "half of the world's bees will already be dead."

"We could all move to Mars," suggested Daniel, with his trademark grin.

Mage spoke up. "You joke, but people have always considered that a backup plan, which is ridiculous. There are huge roadblocks first. We are nowhere near ready. Besides, Earth is such a beautiful planet. Why move to an ugly one? Face it. The tree-huggers are right, there's no planet B."

"Earth is just a tiny speck in space," declared Song, now a little tipsy herself. "We humans need to drop our 'best species' ego and realize we've been the 'worst species'. Humans suck."

Jackie lamented, "I am feeling pretty helpless here. I want to help, but I'm not sure how."

"Well, I've been thinking about a little project since we heard the news about hydrocarbons," offered Mage.

"Oh, oh," muttered Daniel. "You know what happened last time you had a 'little project'. What's this one about, oh great Magician?"

"Saving the world."

"Again?"

"Yeah. The planet is going to need a new form of clean energy, right? And we've been the beneficiaries of one such solution aboard the Nautilus, for years. We've been using our test nuclear battery to run the sub, and have some experience now to draw on. While Jackie has been schooling herself again on marine biology, I've been researching nuclear power. Some of it is a bit crazy, and I don't have the math skills or deeper knowledge to supplement what I *do* know."

"Maybe I can help," offered Jackie. "Our last project together had some merit."

"I was hoping you'd offer, Jacks. I was thinking that when the Nautilus was built, the nuclear batteries were experimental, and only in the testing stage. But, in the past couple of decades, it has served us well."

"You make a good point, Mage," said Tang, brightening. "The Nautilus was fitted with the nuclear batteries in a joint project between the Canadian and Chinese nuclear agencies. When Song's father died, the project died. But, they *have* worked flawlessly."

"Right! So, I'm suggesting we work as a group, in an attempt to adapt similar nuclear batteries for standard power on land. The U.N guy said electrical grids should be smaller scale. Towns could use them on a small scale, instead of building nuclear power plants or even hydro-electric dams."

"Or even hold folks over until they have time to build the plants and dams. I like it," enthused Jackie. "Something to challenge the brain again, at last."

"So, I was thinking we could create a 4-man team to see what we can come up with. I was hoping Jacks would volunteer like she did, but we'll likely need some practical help and knowledge. Captain Tang, I'd like you to be part of the team. Whatever knowledge you can bring to the table would be welcome. You may have learned some things when you were buying the sub."

"I would be honoured to serve on your project, Mr. Moon."

*'Wow!'* thought Mage. *'I guess he's finally actually likes me.'*

"But who we should really include in this working group is Robert. Anything I know about the nukes, I learned from him."

"Excellent!" exclaimed Mage. "I suggest we start tomorrow. The world needs solutions. Maybe we can help."

"I'm so excited!" Jackie added, eyes shining. "I've been wanting to use this brain again, and the idea of creating something with you three gentlemen pumps me full of energy. I can't wait to start!"

"Hey!" said Daniel. "What about me? What do I get to do?"

"Baby, you get the most important job of all. You take care of the kids!"

Daniel couldn't help but feel he'd been played.

Captain Tang stood, which was the standard signal that discussion among the Fellowship meeting had come to a close. "As the U.N. fellow mentioned, we are like anyone else, and need to take stock of *our* current situation. Tonight, reflect on this new reality. Anticipate any avoidable problems aboard. Make note of any critical components that contain plastic. Consider solutions or work-arounds aboard the Nautilus."

Song advised, "I can think of one. The mini-sub will need a new power source. No more diesel."

"Correct. Okay, the first meeting of Nautilus Nuclear will be here, at 1100 hours tomorrow. Dismissed."

As Tang carried Bobby back to the Captain's quarters, he reflected on his day. The crushing boredom of the morning seemed like eons ago. He couldn't help but wonder how this new reality would play out. After decades of Earth's population skyrocketing from Humanity 2.0, would the natural selection process really bring it back under control? Culling the herd was critical, that was indisputable. They'd already lost billions to the Yellowstone tragedy. A few less humans to go, he supposed. Maybe the knowledge of his brilliant crew could help someone, somewhere. One thing for certain, there was too much suffering in the world these days.

As he laid Bobby on his bed, Tang was not confident in the masses' ability to save themselves. But, at last the planet had won a round at the U.N. The question remained, would such a drastic plan be enough, and in time, to save humanity?

With the world spinning out of control, at least the Fellowship of the Deep had a plan and purpose moving forward in this strange new world.

# <u>*Epilogue*</u>

*"Humanity faces many threats but none is greater than climate change. In damaging our climate, we are becoming the architects of our own destruction."*

**King Charles III of England**

**$t = H + 25$**
**time = Humanity + 25 years**

It was New Year's Eve again, twenty-five years after that fateful night Song and Mage had met, and nostalgia filled her senses. She remembered how Mage had been forced to carry her sorry ass home, and tucked her into his bed above his grandfather's old electronics store. She'd been so embarrassed, but he took care of her then, and had taken care of her ever since. A quarter century, How could that be?

Back then, she was a shy, quiet immigrant kid, just trying to fit into a new life in Canada. Now, 2-1/2 decades later, she was a wise and confident global figure in a world swirling with turmoil; a turmoil she and her friends inadvertently had a hand in. Little did they know then that their pet basement project would help anyone at all, let alone unleash the maelstrom it had. So much had happened in the world she and Mage now shared.

It was ironic that they had caused the world to flip

on its head, while remaining relatively untouched and safe themselves. She thought of her father, instructing Tang to find a luxury yacht for his family. The Nautilus had kept them all safe, long after his death. It was the last big decision her father had ever made, and it had served their new generation well.

It served Captain Tang well, also. Buying the Nautilus was how he'd met Bobby, and the point when true happiness began to blossom in his life. During his time in the Chinese Navy, he would never have believed his life would take the jagged path it had.

Circumstances for Song's friend, Jackie, had also altered that same year. Consequently, she and Daniel would be celebrating 25 years as well, come May long weekend. *'What a great choice she made.'* Jackie had been dating that Bryce guy, oh, so long ago. She'd dodged a bullet there. And now, Jackie and Daniel had the strongest relationships ever. Always in good humour, still with many lingering looks, they were fiercely loyal to each other. Song was a bit jealous of the ease of her friend's relationship, but others likely made the same observations about her and Mage. Things were not always as they seemed, but contentment was a common theme among them all.

The Nautilus had become home to the ragtag family again, with two people added to the Fellowship of the Deep's ranks since – Tune and Nemo. The two kids had grown into fine adults, despite the restrictions of growing up so isolated on the sub. One thing was self-evident to Song, that isolation built bonds unmatched in many people's lives. Three happy marriages and recently, a fourth.

The previous year's wedding of Tune and Nemo was due to result in the first grandchild any day now. Song cherished the fact that they'd grown up best friends, destined to be lovers almost by default. They'd shared every moment of each other's lives, so to share the rest of them seemed only natural. And, as with both sets of their parents, Captain Tang had married the kids on the top deck of the Nautilus. They'd honeymooned alone on the rebuilt family island in the Philippines; two weeks of chasing each other naked through the jungle. They built a new hut across the lagoon, separated from the parents. When they'd finished, Nemo carried a giggling Tune across the threshold, to do what newlyweds do.

The five years since the United Nations edict had witnessed global upheaval on a scale never before seen, which, after Humanity 2.0 was really saying something. As expected, outrage and indignation had proliferated, especially at the beginning. Resistance had been widespread, with many countries defying the big five's perceived oppression. The U.N. Climate Force of World Warriors gave fair warning with a week's grace period to remove all personnel working at refineries worldwide. Middle Eastern countries were the first to react, mobilizing their forces to defend their lifeblood. For a time, they were successful. But, 'The Fist' as the big five became known, spread their five fingers over the region and squeezed. Once they controlled the airspace, night after night, they pounded Middle Eastern refineries mercilessly.

The Fist knew the region would give the strongest resistance, so dominance needed to be established for other jurisdictions to fall in line. Refineries, tankers, storage tanks and pipelines were targeted by drone strikes from the air, while World Warrior eco-terrorists on the ground blew up pipelines and hacked their computer systems. The Chinese and French navies blockaded the Persian Gulf and Arabian Sea, as U.S. and U.K. ships attacked from the Eastern Mediterranean, and Russians from the Caspian and Black Seas.

Both the Arabs and The Fist took heavy losses in the first few months, but as the petroleum infrastructure began to crumble, so did the resistance. Supply lines became vulnerable, and there were very few options for the Arabs to replace their downed aircraft. In the past, most military goods were procured from their friends in the big five, but they were now the enemy. Other potential suppliers were unwilling to deal in any hydrocarbon powered weapons for fear of retaliation by The Fist. The black market filled some of the void, but those jets were dated, and seldom survived, easily shot down by vastly superior armaments.

The Fist thrived. By the end of that first year, the war in the Middle East was won. The Arabian countries capitulated. In a negotiated ceasefire, they didn't have oil production anymore, but they brokered a deal which allowed them to still have wealth. A reconciliation agreement worked out with China would provide a million solar panels, to repair the Arab energy infrastructure destroyed by The Fist, and guide their economy in the transition to green energy.

When the Middle East fell, other rogue countries were quick to follow. Their chances of success were limited, and diminishing. They had enough issues to deal with already and with petroleum becoming rarer and rarer, war became too expensive to wage on any significant scale.

Nowhere in the world had emerged unscathed by either the plethora, or scarcity, of humans. Most Canadians moved laterally to a safe place, with several options for hydro power and clean water communities. Canada was fortunate to have one thing everyone else wanted, fresh water and lots of it. Unfortunately, it was almost impossible to get it to anyone else. Oil rail cars and tankers weren't able to be repurposed for water, since there wasn't fuel to move them. And many pipelines to the U.S. were buried in magma.

The southern prairie provinces were Canada's hardest hit by the Yellowstone eruption. Most northern cities were spared the worst of it, except Regina, which had been covered in five feet of ash. Hazmat teams moved in to move a few survivors out. A year-long deluge of prairie rains, on a scale comparable only to Noah's, flushed the heavy ash until it was no longer a hazard to be stirred up. Some people were returning, but Regina itself was a prairie town, dependant on farming. That wasn't going to happen until the gas clouds dispersed and let the sun back in, assuming the soil itself could recover.

American cities were not so lucky. It was shocking just how quickly they'd gone from a 'have' country, to a 'have not'. The eruption had left many with no means of escape. The lucky ones were able to gravitate to the coasts, where Washington, Oregon, California and New York States all had decent hydro-electric power. But, homes needing to convert from gas furnaces to electric baseboards were out of luck. Global demand was unavoidable. And increased demand led to increased prices. Colder climes like New York City had shrunk considerably, while places like Los Angeles continued to balloon well past their ability to deliver drinking water and infrastructure.

In the event that America's climate refugees were forced to migrate, they were provided with very little guidance. Most media outlets were manned with skeleton staffs, trying not to become skeletons themselves. Cell phones and internet were still unable to access satellites, and with print media being increasingly rare, radios became a coveted lifeline. In the refugee camps, rumours proliferated, and fear became the currency of the day. Gangs understood that controlling the narrative granted them more power. Radios threatened that power, forcing its owners to listen silently through ear buds in their tents after dark.

Without food, water or power, most American refugees were forced to keep trudging south where they were stopped at the Mexican border. The Mexican government had imposed restrictions similar to those the U.S. had used on them in decades past, to the great indignation of the desperate refugees. Though they had little left, some of the formerly rich still reeked of entitlement. The huge walls erected by the U.S. were now, ironically, keeping Americans out of Mexico rather than the other way around. Coyotes smugglers moved refugees from north to south now, not south to north. Bodies lay strewn along the trails. Babies, kids, women – starvation and dehydration showed no favouritism. Despite the U.N,'s assurances about being one country with 200 departments, humanity just didn't work that way.

Those who'd travelled through Arizona and New Mexico soon learned just how cold it could get at night. Being wet made it all the more worse, and a desert storm was almost nightly occurrence since the eruption. The waters had yet to be cleansed like they had in Canada, so the grey drizzle still dirtied, rather than cleansed.

In the absence of policing, vigilante groups had asserted themselves as the law, and took it upon themselves to quash any use of hydrocarbons with an almost religious fervor. Self proclaimed World Warriors patrolled at night for random campfires. Easy prey were those who needed fires for warmth, plain to spot at night. Tormented fathers were simply cut down if they resisted their fire being doused. Mothers who plead on behalf of their coughing, wheezing children watched in horror as their children were slaughtered before their very eyes. One less body using up the limited resources. Similar stories could be heard on every street corner of the globe. Life had lost its meaning.

Hypocritically, when the gangs were chasing down people for burning wood, their own trucks were burning hoarded petrol. They didn't care about the environmental itself. Their true motivation was the terror they could inflict on others, when they felt so powerless themselves. It was addictive, projecting power where there was none. All it took was a redneck deeming someone as undesirable, and thereby not worthy of the oxygen. Some farmers hid their families around campfires in the barns, thinking it safer, but the gangs would then burn it down around them. It was U.N. sponsored anarchy, and the only business thriving was the mortician's. But it didn't take long for the farmers to band together in solidarity. Staging traps, they lured the World Warriors by lighting campfires in barns rife with rifles.

The volcanic winter had indeed dropped North American temperatures by a full nine degrees Celsius, as scientists had suggested it might. Only the heartiest of plants survived the 'semi-sun', as locals came to call it. Ranchers had it no better than their farmer friends. No crops meant no livestock feed, starving out millions of animals. As ranches were abandoned, they opened the gates wide, releasing the beasts to the wild. For the moving refugees, it was a boon to find a cow or pig recently deceased or frozen, but a live one was a reason for celebration. Unfortunately, those beasts only survived for the first few months.

In Europe, sentiments mirrored those in America. First World western Europeans were now, ironically, at the mercy of their African neighbours to the south. Italy, Spain and Greece were overrun by exhausted, drenched and desperate foreigners who camped for months before a ship or zodiak would ferry them south across the Mediterranean Sea to Africa. Once across, they hauled the zodiaks up on the beach, cutting them into wide swaths for their plastic and rubber value. Gold and diamonds were of no use to them, but these waterproof strips were easy to roll up, light enough to carry, and a valuable commodity in the refugee camps. Little consideration was wasted on those left behind, waiting for those zodiaks to return for them.

In Europe, the reflecting gas cloud had caused more grief than the ash's air particulate, but some sunshine was beginning to shine through in areas that had only dropped about four degrees Celsius. The lesser variation did not, however, translate into more crops. The lack of sunshine saw to that. The stubborn few who'd refused to leave their homes by winter were found in the spring, frozen or starved.

In Asia, the Russians faced more challenges than many areas of Europe or America, despite being furthest away from the volcano. The majority of the Soviet power had been generated by thermal power plants, requiring the burning of a fuel to heat water into steam. That was no longer a permitted option. There were a few hydro-electric dams and nuclear power plants in use, but most were confined to the southwestern region of the country. When stories filtered out that some Russian nuclear power plants were failing, most chose to trek directly south through China, rather than west in their own homeland. A third potential route took the climate refugees down through the Middle East to Africa, but with Russia recently bombing their refineries, the Middle Eastern countries were not particularly gracious hosts.

The trek of more than five thousand kilometres

from Russia to southern China took travellers nearly a year of traipsing through whatever fury Mother Nature could throw at them. Those that survived reached their destination only to find themselves crowded into a region already completely overwhelmed by more than a billion other desperate climate refugees. The Chinese people had been under the same gas cloud as Russia, so both populaces had gravitated to southeastern Guangdong Province, the only area in China south of the Tropic of Capricorn. They found themselves among masses from Russia, Mongolia, Ukraine, the Eastern Bloc, Scandinavia, and the -stan countries, as well as the Chinese themselves, creating a cesspool of humanity, both literally and figuratively.

Their options were limited. Either they could push further south yet, down the Malay Peninsula from Guangdong, or go west to cross the Himalayan Mountains into India. Since India was as populous as China, and the Himalayas were formidable, most refugees chose the Malay route. Lured by the prospect of 500 uninhabited Malaysian islands, and 17,000 Indonesian ones, solitude was a very appealing notion. No one knew whether they were viable, or even had fresh water, yet the crowds pushed on. Anywhere was better. As the filed south, they created a convoy more than two hundred miles long.

After the first year of the U.N. hydrocarbon ban, economies were still in turmoil, causing the collapse of several stock exchanges and legal systems. Every industry faced overwhelming challenges and entire cities had been abandoned. Western countries' economies devolved into third world ones when consumerism died.

It was a time when all of humanity's best and worst was on stark display. Early on, many nations bucked back against U.N. climate rules that crippled their countries. But, those mostly consisted of countries who had long resisted green power supplies in favour of the old, polluting ones. True to their word, though, the U.N. Security Council countries were only too happy to destroy the refineries that had not already shut down. The few countries to briefly put up a resistance had found themselves isolated in a world where they had no fuel to power their military. Attempting to mount a military campaign versus 200 countries, without the use of fuel, was now logistically impossible. Everyone knew The Fist member nations had refineries not yet held accountable, but the consensus was, they'd worry about each other when everyone else had been taken care of. But each of them had hackers working diligently to shut down their allies' oil.

As more refineries shuttered their doors, the value of oil climbed ever-higher. There were rumours of big five countries selling oil and gas through the black market, but they found that the buyers were not paying, and did not expect to. The U.N. had declared it illegal, therefore not binding. And there was always the messy business of how to get that oil to distant customers. Unprotected tankers that *did* try to sail were reduced to spectacular fireballs by The Fist.

U.N. climate laws outlawed the manufacturing, purchase and distribution of hydrocarbons between countries, but didn't address what they already had in storage. Every jurisdiction on Earth was forced to make policy on how their limited supplies of oil and gas would be best utilized. The smart ones used it to create parts and pieces for building clean energy.

Now five years since the great post-Yellowstone reset, the world was just beginning to make a partial recovery. Scientists in China had announced the development of a nuclear battery capable of providing long-term power on a localized basis. Testing them in smaller towns, they found each could power about 30,000 homes if usage was limited. Unlike most other conventional batteries, the nuclear versions were not affected by cold weather, as they created their own heat from within. Towns and villages from the Yukon to the Gulag benefited equally.

Unfortunately, the one concern about these nuke-batts was disposal. How to get rid of that volume of nuclear waste? So, in the spirit of the Great Reset, two former adversaries, Russia and America, developed a program to rid the world of nuclear waste once and for all. In the five years together working as The Fist, relations between the two former adversaries had become cordial and common. Together, they re-fit reusable rockets with nuke-bats capable of launching into space. Once the ships left Earth's gravity, they'd eject a heat-seeking payload canister of spent nukes, slingshot it around the moon and directly into the sun. The launch rocket would then re-enter orbit before returning to its landing pad, ready for another load.

In the skies, the sulphuric clouds shrouding the Northern Hemisphere were finally beginning to break down. Occasional patches of blue began to shine through, like music returning to a deaf world as it's listeners danced in the streets. Somehow, they had all survived the worst the world could hurl at them, and come out the other side. Not unscathed, of course, but it was now clear, humanity as a whole would likely survive.

Perhaps the most gratifying result to come from the Great Reset was the benefit to the environment. Mother Nature showed amazing resilience in bouncing back, giving people hope after period of unprecedented ugliness and turmoil. For the first time, large areas that had become devoid of oxygen were slowing increasing their levels, and smog over cities was largely a thing of the past. The air in Beijing and Los Angeles was as clean as Anchorage's. Young children in the Northern Hemisphere could now point at stars in the night sky, a sight they'd never seen.

For the masses, the Great Reset had been a period of unbelievable hardship and sorrow, and the world resolved to never let it happen again. Around the globe, good people were dedicated to environmental preservation, be it through new careers, or as volunteers. The Great Barrier Reef was colourful again due to the effort of many scientists and volunteer divers. Some were still pessimistic, but a few successes provided hope for the oceans.

People did their part by planting millions of new saplings in their yards. The U.N, had requested that each citizen of the world plant a tree in honour of the Reset. Within a year, billions of new trees sprouted in their parks, on their rooftops, and in their forests. Huge groves of rubber trees had already taken hold in the Southern Hemisphere. Horticulture had replaced medicine as the most popular university course.

The physical power plants formerly used for oil and coal were destroyed, often as a community celebration. And, in the five years since the U.N, lowered the boom, there had been many border skirmishes, but few official wars between nations. The logistics just couldn't support it anymore. The big oil consortiums had developed their own air force, of sorts, and briefly tried to battle back, but the world had moved on. The scarcity of petroleum products made it too expensive anyway. Revenues shrunk to zero, and the industry became irrelevant. Green energy was now the focus of every nation, with innovation leading the way. Coal, oil and gas were gone, replaced by solar, wind, and hydro-electric, where available.

Paul le Monde, the United Nations Secretary-General who'd finalized the end of oil, had been assassinated the day after poor Sam Purvis. In Cape Town, a large statue now stood outside the South African Parliament, depicting the two men reaching out to each other. Between them, they held a single piece of deep green jade, about three feet around, carved as planet Earth. The two men were now martyr's the world over, and credited by many with saving the human race. Would it have come to that? Who knows, for sure?

But, it was clear to most that Earth had been one disaster away from humanity's demise during the week of the Great Reset. The world's two most populous countries had come within a hair's breadth of nuclear war, and historians credited their level headed leaders for averting a disaster that threatened the planet's Southern Hemisphere. As a token of apology, India commissioned a statue identical to the one in Cape Town and gifted it to their Chinese allies. Standing proudly in Tiananmen Square, it had one key difference. In this case, instead of le Monde and Purvis, the two men holding up the jade Earth were the leaders of India and China on that dangerous day, five years past.

The planet was still a mess in many parts of the world, but there were others with increased hope. The United Nations standing up for Earth that day had opened some eyes to the possibility of a quest for global unity. A central authority within the U.N. was established for issues affecting all nations.

Without combustion, cities everywhere became greener. Downtowns had no cars with internal combustion engines, allowing cities to close many streets in favour of planting trees. Roadways formerly noisy and hectic, were now quiet and relaxed. Freeway asphalt was torn up for its oil, creating parks and bicycle grids in their place. Green energy became the focus in every land, with shared innovation leading the way.

The development of nuclear batteries had brought entire cities back to life, with the hope they'd return to their bustling former selves. Breakthroughs were realized for both vibration energy, and noise energy, and soon became a standard for manufacturers the world over. Vibration and noise were parts of just about any factory.

The U.N.'s ban on oil products was mostly successful, but many grumbled about the lack of plastics. It had become an inexpensive option, commonplace in almost every industry and home, and its loss was a hammer blow to those slow to adapt. But those countries who did, became very good at mining plastics from their trash heaps and oceans. Recyclers found new ways to increase the number of times they could be reused, often requiring little heat for the transformations, using compression in its place.

Plastics became one of the most valuable resources, and as such, was a magnet for crime. Towns that were abandoned due to a lack of an energy source had been hit hardest when inhabitants began to return. They found existing buildings were stripped of everything from plastic plumbing to wiring, and the cost of retrofitting everything was prohibitive and time-consuming, not to mention the building supplies back-ordered everywhere. Thieves in these abandoned towns had been able to work with little oversight by abandoned police departments. As a result, they even dug up the plastic piping used for the city's water and sewage lines. But logistics were a problem, even for criminals. How would they load and move their booty? Ironically, crime was the first industry to truly buy into the complete conversion to electric vehicles and trucks.

The new role of the U.N. Peacekeeping force, established by Canadian Prime Minister Lester B. Pearson in 1956, was the first resolution the new General Assembly adopted. In addition to climate law, they were now responsible for global peace, as most disputes now involved weather. The blue berets were offered to any country requesting their presence. A second key resolution was enacted, requiring any member nation spending money on their military to contribute equal funds to the U.N. peacekeeping force, subject to a U.N. audit. The hope was that the peacekeeping force could always afford to out man any individual nation, should war threaten humanity again. A decade earlier, such a resolution wouldn't have had a chance, but The Fist powerhouses were all still reeling from the triple-whammy of Humanity 2.0, Yellowstone, and the Great Reset. They would need decades to recover full services and infrastructure. War was no longer affordable or tolerable, and unless armies wanted to return to using horses, was no longer practical. Skirmishes, yes. Wars, no.

Of course, there were many that blamed the United Nations for killing so many friends or relatives, and trust was fleeting. So, the U.N. actively promoted discussions between the aggrieved party and an ally already within the U.N. membership. In this way, grievances were always dealt with by friends rather than enemies. Anything was preferable to war.

Probably the most important development after the Great Reset was the dip in the world's population. Natural selection had indeed culled the humans on Earth, to below pre-Humanity 2.0 levels. But, the app had not gone away. The planet could still be overrun by future humans. Some countries outlawed birthing multiple children in a family, by only allowing two natural-born kids. If folks wanted more, they had to adopt, as there were still millions of refugee orphans. Some other countries enacted maximum age levels of

100, but it was a problematic policy. Most people were perfectly healthy at that age now, and had no intention of being culled. Adventure touring for the aged was booming, with many people trying high risk activities, like skydiving or climbing Mount Everest at age 99.

Survivors the world over differed in their interpretations of H2Os place in history. Had the app caused the overpopulation of Earth, necessitating the Great Reset? Or had it's increased population given civilization the bump needed to survive as a species? Every person in every pub of the world debated fiercely on that question.

Back in the Philippines, the Fellowship of the Deep were smiling and in good spirits. Bobby, as was often the case, was into those spirits a bit more than others, but despite a slight slur, he created a masterpiece for dinner on the beach.

Sunshine had returned to their private island for the first time in half a decade, and the mood was infectious. The few clouds in the sky were puffy and white, rather than the gunmetal grey they'd been suffering through since Yellowstone. Their own paradise was now challenged for foliage, but new green sprouts were everywhere. For the crew of the Nautilus, it couldn't have been more beautiful.

Bobby planted a sloppy, wet kiss on Tang's forehead, before tinkling a champagne glass to get everyone's attention. "Everybody listen up!" he began. Holding a bottle above his head, he declared, "this is the last bottle of Dom Perignon aboard the Nautilus, and that's just not okay, okay? As such, we need to do some serious restocking, so Tang and I have talked it over, and.......... tomorrow we sail for Vancouver."

Nemo shrieked with excitement, swooping Tune up into his arms. And that was no easy feat. She was eight months pregnant with their first child. Daniel jumped out of his chair, lifting Jackie right alongside. Song and Mage were content to pass their special smile to each other, loaded with feeling, but muted.

That night, they all slept on the beach one last time, staring up at a partially clear sky littered with an impossible number of stars. The Milky Way shone as bright as they'd ever seen it, and it seemed that Mother Nature was finally back in a good mood. The Fellowship of the Deep was in a good mood too.

In the morning, Daniel was the first awake. He snuggled up behind Jackie as he did every morning, but to his chagrin, she launched herself out of their island cot, calling the others to "Wake up! Wake up! We're going home!" By the time the prospective parents, Nemo and Tune joined the others across the lagoon, Jackie had already packed the launch and was jumping with impatience. Daniel had not yet risen from the mat. "C'mon! C'mon! C'mon! We sail in ten minutes!" Tang was smiling, so she added sheepishly, "if that's okay with you, Captain."

"It's definitely okay with me, pretty lady. I'm looking forward to it as much as you are. Bobby and I checked yesterday to make sure Vancouver had recovered, and I called our lawyer to make sure the compound was secure, and ready to go. He told me that all of the crazies camped across the street had left, and were no longer a factor. I suppose everyone has new opportunities elsewhere." He turned, looking at each member of his crew with pride, then snarled in his best pirate voice, "Alright ye scalliwags! Back aboard the ship! Batten down the hatches! Shiver me timbers and show a leg! We sail within the hour!" Everyone loaded into the launch, and were shipshape to sail in ten minutes, as Jackie dictated.

They would soon escape their elegant prison. Song had to remind everyone of the other people who'd been forced to live in caves, and wondered to herself what their life would have been like if she'd been poor in such times. It was a daunting thought. She had a burning need to help some of those people now, after feeling helpless for years. *'Time to dig out my chequebook'*, she vowed.

In the weeks it took to return to Vancouver, the sky stayed mostly blue and clear. It was as if Mother Nature was rewarding everyone for saving her. Tang had the sub cruising along on the surface, no longer needing
the safety of the depths, and Song took full advantage. The sea was flat as she tanned herself on the top deck, alone.

Suddenly, Mage burst the hatch with wild eyes, shouting, 'It's time! You gotta come!'

"Take a breath, honey. Calm down, okay? Now,

It's time for what? Come where?"

"It's TIME"

"Oh, it's TIME? Oh, God. Oh, my God. Where?"

"The Captain's quarters," answered Mage, already pulling her along. "Hurry up! I don't want to miss this." He lifted her down the ladder and pushed her toward the stern. Mage gave a hesitant knock at the door, but Song just pushed past him. She found her daughter on her back, knees up, in the Captain's bed. Tune was screaming and cursing daddy Nemo, who was completely overwhelmed by the moment. He looked about to laugh or cry, but couldn't decide which. Screaming time and again, Tune bore down on her big, pregnant belly and began evicting its tenant.

Between Tune's legs, Tang was focused directly on her private parts. She knew he'd done it before, for both her birth and Nemo's, and trusted him implicitly. But, she still wasn't comfortable with him looking at her there. So, if this baby would just hurry up............. !

Tang was certainly calmer than Daddy at the moment. Nemo had watched all of the lamaze seminars with Tune online, but now, when faced with the reality, his mind went blank. He remembered something about breathing with her, but now couldn't remember the sequence for the life of him. So he faked it. "Puff puff in, puff puff out," he guided Tune, while Jackie watched her son with a knowing grin. The breathing was nothing like it was supposed to be, but Jackie just gave an overwhelmed Nemo a wink.

"Wait a minute," said Jackie. "Where's Daniel? The fool's going to miss the birth of his own grandchild!"

"I'm not waiting!" screamed Tune.

Bobby walked in with towels and boiling water, informing her that Daniel was just finishing up at the helm.

"I'm still not waiting!"

Rushing in, Daniel assured her, "I'm here, I'm here, What have I missed?" He looked down at his daughter-in-law before recognizing what he was seeing, and blushed accordingly. Maybe it was better that he missed it. He was still in better shape than his son, though, so he focused on Nemo instead. Daniel remembered that feeling of helplessness, as the love of his life had cursed him fully and completely. He put a reassuring arm around Nemo, and Jackie held him from the other side.

"Okay," Tang announced. "She's crowning. It won't be long now. Come on, Tune," he encouraged. "You're almost there! Give a big push now."

Tune likely never heard him, though, through her own screeching.

"One more push, Sūnnǚ. Make me a Zēngzǔfù!" Tune's screaming became louder, more sustained, and was soon joined by a small voice, also screaming loudly.

"Well done, little one! Congratulations beautiful, you have a baby girl." Tune graced him with a sweaty, exhausted smile, mouthing the words, 'thank you'.

The room erupted in celebration, except for Nemo who was gobsmacked, unable to speak. Responsibility suddenly weighed heavy on his shoulders. He'd never had to be responsible before.

"Way to go, Daddy." Jackie whispered in his ear. "She's beautiful." And she really was. Bobby wiped her clean and knotted the umbilical cord before laying her on Tune's belly. "Now go introduce yourself to your daughter." Nemo crept closer like he was an intruder, peering at Tune, at the baby, and back again.

He placed a hand on Tune's sweaty forehead, and kissed both of her eyes gently. "You did real good, Momma. Real good!" Feeling a bit bewildered, he nodded at Tang with quiet respect. "Can I hold her?"

"Sure, Neem. Remember to cradle his head."

She passed the baby girl to her Daddy and she immediately stopped screaming. "You're a Daddy's girl already, aren't you?" The baby began wailing again. "Maybe not," he added, handing her to her Mommy for her first meal.

That was all the time he was allotted with his two girls. Mage and Song pushed in on one side, and Daniel and Jackie on the other. For grampa Daniel, it was a rare time in his life that he was truly speechless. Literally. He opened his mouth, but nothing croaked out. When

Jackie winked at him, he became so emotional, he lost it, weeping openly, choking on his sobs. "She's beautiful, Jacks, just like you," he blubbered shamelessly.

"Well, I'm glad she doesn't look like Jughead," Jackie teased. She reached up, rested her hand gently on his cheek, and kissed him gently, with gravitas. "Congratulations, Grandpa." That did it. Daniel went back to weeping like......well, like his granddaughter.

"Have you thought of a name yet?" Song asked.

"Harmony," Tune and Nemo answered in unison.

Song smiled a melancholy smile. "It's perfect. The ladies of song persist – from Piper, to Melody, to Song, to Tune, and now to Harmony. It's beautiful honey. And you know Piper and Melody are breaking out the lyres in heaven right now to celebrate her birth with you. The world could use more Harmony right now."

A loud 'pop' interrupted their private moment, as Bobby cried, "who wants champagne?"

"Hey, I thought you said we were out of champagne," Mage needled.

"We were. Well, except Tune's bottle. I saved it for her. The poor girl hasn't had a drink for months!" He poured a glass and handed it to her, admonishing, "just one for you, young lady. But it will help the baby sleep." Bobby clapped Nemo on the back, adding, "Well done, lad. Well done. Here. Save this as a keepsake to mark the occasion." He handed Nemo the champagne cork, adding, "or you can use it as a baby soother."

"Thanks," Nemo joked. "I'm the one who's going to need a soother."

Mage asked the men, "so, what do we put on the birth certificate for the place of birth?"

Daniel finally choked back his tears, and found his voice. "Canada," he said proudly. "That's what took me so long to get down here. I had to make sure we were in Canadian waters before I shut things down."

"Well done, Grandpa," Jackie said, snuggling into his shoulder.

Daniel looked at his oldest friend, slapping Mage on the shoulder, and declaring, "I've got a granddaughter, bud! You see that? Me. Who'da thunk it?"

"I would have. And yeah, I saw that, Daniel. I've actually got a granddaughter now too, you know," slapping his shoulder in return.

"Oh. Yeah. I guess you do, eh?" Daniel's smile was larger than ever, and impossible to quell.

"We all do," said Mage.

"I think Tang and I now qualify as great-grandparents," Bobby said, poking his lover in the belly. "In fact," he continued, "I think we should have a baby of our own............ baby." He gave Tang his best triple

408

eyebrow lift.

It was Tang's turn to be gobsmacked, his eyes panicked. "I'm 66 years old now, Bobby. I'm old enough to retire!"

"And thanks to the Humanity app, you're going to live twice that long. So, I want a baby of our own."

"Nobody is going to give a baby to a retired gay couple," Tang said, a bit hopefully.

"It's a whole new world out there. I'm sure there are plenty of orphan babies who need a daddy and a daddy."

Tang looked like a cornered cat, wary, tense and ready to bolt. He looked around the room for support, but all he got from his friends were shrugs and grins. Tune saved him.

"Hey, there's a baby over here!" she called. All eyes turned back to the little pink bundle lying on her mother's belly, munching away.

There are times in life with perfect clarity. Song's mind drifted back to when she'd first met Mage on that infamous New Year's Eve 25 years past. Before leaving the mansion that night, she'd told her reflection she was no longer a child. She'd wanted to take hold of her life, and truly make it hers. What a remarkable life it turned out to be, filled with conflict and joy, despair and elation. And now, her best friends were officially her family. She definitely was no longer that child in the reflection of so long ago. Song lifted Harmony from

Tune's lap, whispering to her........

*'Well, I nailed the hell out of that!'*

## *The End *

*"In our obscurity – in all this vastness – there is no hint that help will come from elsewhere to save us from ourselves. The Earth is the only world known, so far, to harbour life. There is nowhere else, at least in the near future, to which our species could migrate."*

### *Carl Sagan*

**If you liked this story, please give it a review.**